VENDETTA ROAD

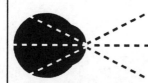

This Large Print Book carries the
Seal of Approval of N.A.V.H.

VENDETTA ROAD

CHRISTINE FEEHAN

THORNDIKE PRESS
A part of Gale, a Cengage Company

Copyright © 2020 by Christine Feehan.
A Torpedo Ink Novel.
Thorndike Press, a part of Gale, a Cengage Company.

Thorndike Press® Large Print Romance
The text of this Large Print edition is unabridged.
Other aspects of the book may vary from the original edition.
Set in 16 pt. Plantin.

**LIBRARY OF CONGRESS CIP DATA ON FILE.
CATALOGUING IN PUBLICATION FOR THIS BOOK
IS AVAILABLE FROM THE LIBRARY OF CONGRESS**

ISBN-13: 978-1-4328-7397-4 (hardcover alk. paper)

Published in 2020 by arrangement with Berkley, an imprint of Penguin Publishing Group, a division of Penguin Random House, LLC

Printed in Mexico
Print Number: 01   Print Year: 2020

For Anne Elizabeth, my very loved friend.
Thank you for a friendship that
goes beyond the norm.
You've always made me stronger.

FOR MY READERS

Be sure to go to christinefeehan.com/ members/ to sign up for my private book announcement list and download the free ebook of *Dark Desserts.* Join my community and get firsthand news, enter the book discussions, ask your questions and chat with me. Please feel free to email me at Christine @christinefeehan.com. I would love to hear from you.

ACKNOWLEDGMENTS

As with any book, there are so many people to thank: Ed, my go-to man, who answers my questions when needed. Brian, for competing with me during power hours for top word count. Domini, for always editing, no matter how many times I ask her to go over the same book before we send it for additional editing.

TORPEDO INK MEMBERS

Viktor Prakenskii aka *Czar* — President
Lyov Russak aka *Steele* — Vice President
Savva Pajari aka *Reaper* — Sergeant at Arms
Savin Pajari aka *Savage* — Sergeant at Arms
Isaak Koval aka *Ice* — Secretary
Dmitry Koval aka *Storm*
Alena Koval aka *Torch*
Luca Litvin aka *Code* — Treasurer
Maksimos Korsak aka *Ink*
Kasimir Popov aka *Preacher*
Lana Popov aka *Widow*
Nikolaos Bolotan aka *Mechanic*
Pytor Bolotan aka *Transporter*
Andrii Federoff aka *Maestro*
Gedeon Lazaroff aka *Player*
Kir Vasiliev aka *Master*
Lazar Alexeev aka *Keys*
Aleksei Solokov aka *Absinthe*

11

NEWER PATCHED MEMBERS

Gavriil Prakenskii
Casimir Prakenskii

PROSPECTS

Fatei
Glitch
Hyde

ONE

Isaak Koval, known to his brothers in Torpedo Ink as Ice, moved with the crowd of tourists down the Las Vegas strip. He could fit in anywhere. It was a gift, and one he worked on as often as possible. He'd learned early in life that if he chose, he could be invisible, or nearly so, fading like a chameleon into whatever background surrounded him. That gift had saved his life on more than one occasion.

He was very careful to keep several people between himself and the two men he followed. He wove his way through the tourists but was always careful his reflection wasn't caught in the glass as he passed windows and doors. That was simply a matter of matching steps for a moment. He kept his head down but his eyes up, scanning the crowd, the buildings and even the rooftops.

Heat waves bounced on the sidewalk, hitting him squarely in the chest. At times it felt as if he couldn't breathe, but then he'd been feeling that way for some time, even at home on the coast.

His quarry stopped for a moment just inside one of the doors leading to a casino, forcing him to stop as well. He couldn't get in front of them or take a chance they'd pick him out of a crowd if they spotted him more than once. There was a brick pillar just on the other side of the doors of the casino, and he paused there to pull out his cell and look at text messages, just the way dozens of others were doing. He glanced across the street to where his twin brother, Storm, mirrored his actions. Ice was able to keep the two men in sight while studying his phone, and then moving at a snail's pace with a group of tourists from India.

The two men they followed argued for a moment over something they read on their phones and began walking the strip again. They appeared to be looking for a good time, stopping briefly at the strip joints, as if debating whether they'd go in or not. They never did, and Ice didn't expect them to. His club knew just about everything there was to know about the men they were tracking down the strip. They knew for certain that neither man was looking for a night of fun with strippers, prostitutes or women

14

they picked up.

They were coming up to a red light. That was always a danger zone. The two men, Russ Jarvis and Billy Kent, were in the habit of taking the opportunity to look around them when they got to a crosswalk. The crowd pushed together at the stoplights, and both men would casually turn and survey those beside and behind them. They often looked across the street to study everyone waiting to cross to their side.

Still, Ice could come up right on them, do them both just as the light changed and walk across the street with the crowd before the bodies fell. He wiped the sweat from his face and kept sauntering. His club needed the two alive long enough to lead them to the asshole they were hunting. He forced himself to put one boot in front of the other.

He was dressed in blue jeans and motor-cycle boots. It wasn't like he had a lot of clothes to choose from. The tight tee stretched across his chest, damp now with sweat from the unrelenting heat. He fucking hated this place almost as much as he detested the two men he followed. Worse, he couldn't wear his distinctive colors. That felt like walking down the street naked, which would have actually been better than being without his colors.

Sometimes, like now, he thought he might go insane from the chaos in his head. He listened sometimes when Czar, the president of Torpedo Ink, their motorcycle club, and his wife, Blythe, said some things needed talking about no matter how difficult. That was such bullshit. Who did someone like him spill his guts to? And what fucking therapist would understand what he'd been through? What any of his brothers and sisters had been through?

He could just hear that conversation. How many men did you say you killed? How did you say you killed them? How do you feel about that? How did they fucking think he felt about that? It would be prison or a padded cell, and he'd been locked up most of his life and wasn't ever going there again. Not ever.

Ice swept off the silly ball cap he was wearing, the one covering his distinctive hair. He wasn't just blond; his hair blazed in the sun — platinum, gold, silver, it was all there. He wore it longish, but not as long as some of the brothers. He wiped at the sweat again and replaced the ball cap. As he came up to the light, he dipped into the brightly colored open tote a woman dangled so invitingly on her arm, lifted a small package and dropped it on the sidewalk just in front of him.

16

"Ma'am." He bent down. "You dropped something."

The older woman turned and her eyes went wide. "Oh no. Thank you. I bought that for my granddaughter."

He took his time rising with it, angling away from the light and keeping most of the crowd between him and his prey. He flashed a charming smile at her. "How old is your granddaughter, if you don't mind me asking? Because you sure as hell don't look old enough to be a grandmother." He meant it too, he didn't have to pour bullshit sincerity into his tone.

She beamed at him. "That's such a sweet thing to say. I'm definitely old enough. She's eight." She took the little package and dropped it into her tote, pulling her bag more securely to her. "I really like your tattoo. It's unusual."

He had a wealth of tattoos on his arms, chest and back, but she was referring to the three teardrops dripping down his face from the corner of his left eye. Those tears reminded him, every time he looked into a mirror, that he wasn't human anymore. Everything had been taken from him, leaving a shell. An empty shell. The tightness in his chest made it difficult to breathe again. He touched one of the tears as if just remembering he had them.

"Had them for years. You know the kind of thing you do when you're a kid."

She smiled at him again. "You still look like a kid to me."

Now he'd run out of things to say. She was nice. He didn't live in a nice world. He didn't know how to make conversation with nice people. He could beat the holy hell out of someone for her. He could kill someone for her if she asked him to. Shit, he might do both, but polite conversation was beyond him.

Of course there was always the alternative. He could pull out his gun and shoot the bastards right there in front of everyone. The cops would come and there would be a hell of a shoot-out, but in the end, he might have some peace. Might. There was probably a special place in hell for a man like him.

He didn't have the luxury of offing himself via cop because if he killed the two he'd been following for four fucking days in the hottest place in the world, then he would be condemning some little boy to a lifetime of hell. He knew what that was like. Shit.

The woman was talking to him, but he couldn't hear a thing she said. The crowd moved and he risked a glance over his shoulder. The two assholes were already in the street. He turned back to the street and moved with the woman, angling his head down and toward her as if fully engaged in everything she had to say.

He had a lot he could tell her. Specifically, that he was so fucked up that if he was in a roomful of hot babes stripping for him, he couldn't get it up unless he commanded it. That was getting damned tiresome. What was the use in having chicks blow him when he had to force his body to cooperate? Yeah, that would make a great conversation. He could ask her advice.

Maybe he should ask Blythe and shock the holy hell out of her, not that much shocked her. She'd taken Czar back and taken the entire club in as if she were a mother hen. He had to admit he actually felt affection and admiration for her when he thought he was long past real emotion. Blythe and her troubled children. He could relate to them — unfortunately for them.

He walked with the older woman for another block, listening to her chatter on about her adorable granddaughter. When she paused and he had no choice but to fill the silence with words, he talked about his darling "nieces" and "nephews." He supposed it wasn't a lie. They didn't have to be related by birth. All members of Torpedo Ink were his brethren. That meant their children were part of his life, right? That was how it worked in his world whether it did or not in the "normal" world.

Movement caught his eye as he turned the corner with a little wave at the woman, who went straight. A white dress with flowers all over it. Not just any dress. A fuckin' sundress like women wore in old movies. She was across the street, standing in the sunlight, and she might as well have been wearing a halo. She looked so beautiful she took his breath away. He actually stopped walking right there on the sidewalk to stare at her — which was fucking nuts because he was on a job.

The top of the dress was fitted, and its wearer had amazing tits. They filled out the material of the sundress to perfection, pushing against the bodice as if seeking freedom. The front of the dress was tight but gathered around the cleavage line. His palms itched to tug down that fitted camisole and free those mouthwatering tits. His mouth actually salivated. He would stand behind her and slowly pull the material free until the bodice was under those soft curves and her tits spilled into his hands.

She had a face most men would fight and

die for — at least him. High cheekbones. Large eyes. A mouth made for kissing. Lips to wrap around a man's cock. Just like that his fucking dick reacted. On the street. Looking at a fully clothed woman. The proverbial girl next door. What the hell?

He dropped his hand over the front of his jeans, just to make sure he wasn't having some kind of a hallucination. He was shocked when nothing ever shocked him anymore. He didn't have natural erections. That had been beat out of him a long time ago. There was nothing whatsoever normal about him and sex. Nothing.

He forced his hand away from his jeans and took another long look at the woman. Her rib cage and waist were narrow, accentuated by the tight bodice. The skirt flared out, drawing attention to her legs. She had gorgeous legs. He could almost feel them wrapped around him. Hell if his erection was going away anytime soon, not when he was having fantasies like that about her.

She hesitated at the crosswalk but then turned to walk back toward a man who seemed to be calling out to her. He thought he was a breast man, but the way her perfect ass swayed with that white floral skirt was enough to change his mind.

Her hair glowed in the sun, so shiny it

hurt his eyes. Dark, cascading down her back, it was thick and just wild enough to ruin that good-girl vibe she had going on. She shook her head at something the man said to her and started to turn away, back toward the street. The man, dressed in an impeccable suit, grabbed her arm and jerked her back to him.

Ice felt it then. The glacier. That blue well deep inside him, glacier cold, so cold it burned. Need was there — the need to kill. It was . . . overwhelming. It swept over him like a tidal wave, yet deep inside he was frozen. He took a step toward the edge of the sidewalk. Cars rushed by, but he hardly noticed them. Time had tunneled. Pulled him into a cold, dark place he was all too familiar with.

A whistle pierced through the glacier, the sound causing a long, jagged crack to penetrate that deep, dense blue. That note shook him out of his head, and Ice glanced away from the couple. His twin, parallel to him, was already at the crosswalk and headed toward him with the green light. Shit. He'd just made the biggest ass of himself in the history of mankind. His brother was already as worried as hell, and this little episode wasn't going to take any pressure off.

Their quarry was a good block ahead of them. Storm had dropped back to cover him. He gestured toward them and started walking. He couldn't help stealing a glance at the couple. She continued to shake her head. The suit was angry, glaring at her. Making demands. She refused. Good for her. Money didn't make up for lack of character. He should know. He had more money than he knew what to do with, but character? Not so much.

"What the *fuck*?" Storm hissed, falling into step beside him. "We can't lose them."

They picked up the pace, winding through the crowd to catch up with the two men they followed.

"I wasn't planning on losing them," Ice muttered, pulling his cap down farther to shadow his face. "I knew you were on them."

"A woman? You almost blow this hunt over a woman? You need to get laid, Ice, we can pick up a dozen women when we get this thing done."

Ice looked at his brother for the first time, letting him see how close he was to losing his shit.

Storm scowled and shook his head. "You go, I go. That was the deal we made."

"We were seven years old when we made

that deal," Ice reminded quietly. He risked another look at their prey. They were separated by quite a few people. One group of tourists kept stopping in the middle of the sidewalk, and the crowd flowed around them. Because they were close and looked alike, Ice slowed the pace again, staying behind the photograph-crazy sightseers. "Neither of us thought we'd live to see ten."

"You go, I go. That's the deal," Storm insisted.

"Why do you have to be so damn fuckin' stubborn?" Ice asked, keeping his voice low.

"I've always followed your lead, and that's what you'd do," Storm answered with a careless shrug of his shoulders.

Ice couldn't argue with that. He would have done the same. "Don't know, Storm, I'm getting to the point I could be dangerous to everyone."

"Savage is dangerous to everyone, not you. You always choose the right thing to do whether or not you want to do it. Dying isn't the right thing. We've had this conversation multiple times now. You're in a bad patch. We both get them. Fortunately, not at the same time."

That much was true, but damn it to hell, he didn't want to go out hurting innocents, and he thought more and more about just killing a bunch of fucking pedophiles in public. Lining them up and mowing them down. Sometimes he dreamt about it. He couldn't seem to get any relief anymore. Not from booze. Not from women and not from hunting the bastards who stole and violated children.

Mostly, he detested that the men in front of him were upstanding citizens. They had money and prestige, just like the others in the ring Code had discovered online. Auctioning children. They were accepted in society, but he wasn't. He never would be. Never. He was a biker. In a club. Those riding with him were his family, and he would fight and die for them. For his colors. He would never be accepted by society, but they invited monsters into their homes and allowed them around their children because they were dressed properly and they didn't say *fuck* in front of anyone. They just did it behind everyone's back — with children.

One was a doctor. Dr. Hank Bernard. Married with three girls of his own. The problem was, he preferred little boys, the younger the better. Then there was George Durango. He owned a string of spas and retreats for celebrities. He ran in big circles. Bill Churchill was a prominent judge, one with an eye toward moving up in political circles. Paul Bitters was a very respected fire chief. He knew every policeman in his district by name. When he spoke, everyone listened to him. Russ Jarvis and Billy Kent owned a chain of grocery stores together. They'd been boyhood friends and continued to be partners. Most people thought they were a couple. It suited them to let others think that.

Code, with his mad computer skills, had stumbled across the online auction of a little six-year-old boy. It was Paul Bitters who had him up for auction. He had offered the child to what appeared to be a large ring of pedophiles. Torpedo Ink had anonymously bid on the boy, and at first it seemed as if they might get him. They would have been given an address and the exchange would have been made. Unfortunately, law enforcement had gotten wind of the auction, and Bitters had shut it down instantly.

Bitters didn't come back online for nearly three weeks. He sent out an encrypted message: this event was by private invitation only. It was clear the man was nervous and wanted only those he knew and trusted implicitly to show up. He wanted them there in person so he could visually identify each man. Code had managed to break the encryption.

Torpedo Ink hadn't had a lot of time to put together a rescue operation. They didn't just want a smash and grab. They wanted more names. This was no small operation: the original auction had been open to multiple bidders over several states. They wanted to permanently shut it down.

The club and their women were in Vegas for a very good reason. Their vice president, Steele, was marrying his woman, putting a ring on her finger and making that shit real. Naturally, all members of Torpedo Ink would come to celebrate, to witness the event. No one would question their presence in Las Vegas.

Ice and Storm flowed with the little group of tourists, fitting in the way they did, so if the two men happened to glance back, which they did occasionally, they would see them as part of the group. Storm had been wearing a ball cap but when he crossed the street, he switched to a panama hat. It covered his distinctive hair. He walked with a bit of a slump to shorten his height.

Their quarry suddenly turned abruptly and walked straight back toward them. Ice kept walking straight, keeping his head down, while his brother crossed the street with the light. A motorcycle roared past, keeping up with traffic on the street. Transporter had Alena, Ice and Storm's younger sister, on the back of his bike. Her very distinctive platinum hair was tucked up in a helmet. Neither wore their colors.

"I've got them," Savage murmured softly into his radio. *"Switch shirts and hats and come back around. They've got a tail checking to see if they have anyone on them. These fuckers are careful."*

Savage was an enforcer for the club. He was also, along with his brother, one of the scariest men Ice knew, and his club was made up of straight-up assassins. Trained from childhood, each of them knew hundreds of ways to kill. Savage was in a league of his own.

"We made them," Alena reported.

Ice turned the corner the opposite way the two men had gone. Code had narrowed their destination down to two possible buildings on the other side of the block. The lights of the strip faded just a little bit, and a seedier clientele joined those walking along the street.

Storm continued down the street he'd chosen; it was still close to the road Code had identified as the likeliest goal. The taxi Savage had driven up in was at the curb in front of the two men, and he took his time paying the driver, asking directions as he did so. Russ Jarvis and Billy Kent went right past him without even glancing at him.

Their quarry's backup drove past them in a Toyota pickup, giving the two men a quick sign as he did so. Right behind the brand-new Toyota was an old Ford. Mechanic drove the Ford and it was every bit as souped-up as any road rocket out there. Torpedo Ink was out in full force, each member contributing in any way they could, working like a machine together, determined to get the child away from those putting him up for auction.

"I'm on backup with Transporter and Alena," Mechanic said into his radio. *"We'll take this driver for you, Savage, and Alena and Transporter will double back to secure the building while I secure the prisoner and wait for you."*

"Make sure you do. We need one alive," Savage murmured. Jarvis's nod to his backup was nearly imperceptible, but Savage caught it. The driver of the pickup believed no one was following the two men.

"They're doubling back. Now that they think they're clear, they'll head to the live auction. You're on again, Ice. Let's take them down fast," Savage said.

Savage turned the opposite way the two men were walking, heading for the street corner. He crossed with the light and walked purposefully down the strip. Ice turned the corner behind Jarvis and Kent. He was in a dark navy tee and a dark sports jacket, and a fedora covered his head. Storm remained on the same side of the street as Savage. Ice joined the very small crowd at the crosswalk, ignoring his quarry as they waited for the light. Storm crossed at the light.

Jarvis and Kent were the first ones to step off the curb, walking fast now, glancing at their watches and picking up the pace. Ice and Storm fell into step behind them, with only two couples between them. Savage crossed back at the next stoplight, falling into step half a block behind Ice and Storm.

"Backup is ready," Reaper, their sergeant at arms, said.

"Van waiting for package," Czar reported.

"Medic on standby," Steele said.

Absinthe fell into step with Ice and Storm just as Jarvis and Kent turned into the doorway of a massage parlor. The parlor proclaimed twenty-four-hour massages on the doors and windows in gold paint. Ice, Storm and Absinthe were only a few steps behind Jarvis and Kent. Ice glanced up at the surveillance camera. It was no longer recording. Code had worked his magic, taking over the cameras in the building and shutting them down.

Savage was thirty seconds behind the other three. Jarvis and Kent didn't check in at the desk; instead, they started right down the hall. The hostess ignored them but perked up when she saw Ice, Storm and Absinthe. They had that effect on women. Savage made her nervous as he entered, and she avoided looking too closely at him, which gave him the opportunity to keep their quarry in sight as they made their way down the hall.

Absinthe leaned toward her, putting his elbows on her desk, and smiling, looked directly into her eyes while Storm went back to the door. "Hey, beautiful. You really need to go home now. It's late and way past your shift." He pitched his voice low and mesmerizing. "You just want to get out now as fast as possible."

She caught up her purse, frowned slightly and rushed out the door Storm held open for her. He locked the door but left the open sign on so that it flashed right over the words declaring they gave massages twenty-four hours a day.

Savage was already striding down the hall, keeping Jarvis and Kent in his sights. Ice and Storm followed while Absinthe manned the desk just in case someone happened to

31

come by at that precise time to get a massage. He would be shocked at the locked door, taking his time to get to it, and he'd "suggest" they wanted to go to the place down the street. He was very good at making people believe anything he wanted them to.

They'd found the nest and no one could get away, not unless they wanted them to. Once Code had narrowed down the possibilities to two places, they had run simulations for each building. They were good at what they were doing — they'd been hunting since they were children.

Transporter and Alena, after identifying the truck that was backing up Jarvis and Kent, would leave the driver to Mechanic and return to guard the back door. Two other escape doors were built into the parlor as well. One led directly to the shop next door and was usually kept locked, according to the employee Absinthe had chatted up earlier in the day. The second one led straight into the basement. Ice was willing to bet the kid was in a cage in the basement with a camera on him to remind the buyers what they were getting.

Two guards spun around as they approached. Both were armed with semi-automatics, not the usual equipment for a

32

rent-a-cop. These two were definitely private security, paid for by Bitters. No way would the massage parlor pay for obvious mercenaries. The place was classier than most, but they'd never shell out the kind of money that would pay for these two. That meant there were more mercenaries inside.

One guard was directly in front of the door, the other was three steps away, just about to start his walk along the halls in order to ensure no one was near the room he'd been paid to keep secure. He dropped back a little farther in order to cover his partner.

The sentry looked grim as he held up his hand to stop Savage. "You need an invitation to this party," he said. "Everyone on the list has already checked in. Wait at the front desk, and Tabs will find you a masseuse." He winked when he said it, but he had turned slightly, just enough that the weapon was pointed directly at Savage's chest.

Ice wanted to laugh, but he wasn't very good at that. He was better at killing. He didn't so much as glance at the guard in front of Savage. That was Savage's problem. He moved out from behind Savage, Storm pacing along beside him. They didn't even look at the mercenary, the party room or anything else. Storm held up a piece of paper with lines drawn on it. He indicated the hallway the second guard had begun to walk down.

"Hey," Storm said, holding out the paper. "The room numbers don't match what that girl wrote on this. She did write down her phone number, but that isn't helping when we want massages."

"That's not how it works," the guard snarled and brought up his gun.

"I'm so sorry," a female voice came from behind them. It was sultry. Low. Gave promises of sinful sex.

Everyone froze in place as heads turned to see the newcomer. She was tall with a killer body. Her thick hair was glossy black and curved around her face, kissing her neck with every step she took. Not that anyone was looking at her hair. Not with the amazing rack she had on display. Her curves were full and round, pushing to get out of the simple thin tee she wore stretched over them, with a logo for the massage parlor.

"This is my first day and I got stopped by a cop for speeding." She flashed a grin, inviting them to be happy with her. "I got off with a warning. Tabitha at the front desk said I was supposed to meet two customers

34

in room four-oh-seven. It should be down this hall."

She caught up with Ice and Storm, but kept walking to lead the way, pointing to a room at the end of the hall. Her walk was just as sexy from the back as it was from the front, and the man watching Savage kept shifting his gaze toward her swaying ass. She was nearly up to the guard in the hall. He was trying to pull his gaze away from the two breasts nearly falling out of the too-small uniform she was wearing.

Ice could have kissed her. Lana was known as Widow to the other members of Torpedo Ink. She often made widows out of women married to mercenaries. She looked sexy as hell and innocent at the same time. How she did it, he had no idea, but she was a thing of beauty. She always had been, even when she'd been a child, being tortured like the rest of them. She'd come back crying, but ready to do whatever it took to escape.

She walked right up to the sentry as if she were going to walk past him, her eyes staring right into his, a sultry, sexy expression on her face. Savage and Lana stepped into their victims and two blades slammed deep into throats simultaneously. Ice caught the guard in the hall while Lana knocked on a door lightly, opened it and indicated the room was free. Ice hauled the guard into it, took the weapon and handed it to Lana. She rolled her eyes and shoved it onto a massage table. The guard gulped a few times, his eyes wide with shock, choking on his own blood while Storm dragged in Savage's victim.

Ice moved into position with Storm, Lana behind them and Savage bringing up the rear. "If the kid isn't there, we need one alive," Savage reminded softly.

Ice gave him one look and then stepped close to the door, his lockpick out. He was very quiet as he took care of the rather flimsy lock. Those inside counted on their guards just a little too much.

He and Storm each stepped to a side of the door, leaving Lana in front of it. She hovered her palm a whisper from the door, her hand as steady as a rock. Ice admired her, the way she could go from soft and sweet to kill mode just that fast. They'd counted on her when she'd been just a beautiful, dark-haired child, and she'd always come through. She still did.

She held up her fingers. Six men down in front by where they knew there was another exit and four more guards. One on either side of the door. One up high, on a small balcony behind a curtain. One by the exit on the other side of the room that led to the alley.

Savage indicated for Ice and Storm to take the guards out on either side of the door. He would take the one at the far exit and Lana would take out the one behind the curtain. She was the most accurate when there was no clear shot.

Each had the men they were going to kill. Paul Bitters was the man selling the kid, so he would be last to die. They needed to know where the kid was. *"In position,"* Savage reported.

"In position," Reaper said, waiting at the exit directly behind the seller and the buyers.

"Have your package, Savage," Mechanic said, indicating they had taken the driver of the truck and were holding him, so they could extract more information about the ring and move up the chain to the even bigger fish.

"Transporter and I at back door," Alena reported.

"It's a go," Czar commanded.

Ice glanced over his shoulder one last time and then at his twin. Storm. His heart clenched. Abruptly he shoved open the door, stepping through, as he turned and fired through the wood at his target. Storm moved with him, back-to-back, a practiced move they'd done hundreds of times. His gun blazed as well. Lana was right behind them, stepping in front and to one side to give Savage his shot. She fired three times at the curtain. Savage calmly pulled the trigger, and all four bodies dropped to the floor nearly simultaneously.

Savage reached back and closed the door behind them and strode down the aisle toward the six men. "Gentlemen," he greeted them softly.

There was no child in the room. Bitters hastily tried to get to the computer projecting the image of a small boy in a dog cage sitting on the floor holding a blanket to his chest. The four guns went off a second time and Jarvis, Kent, Bernard and Churchill dropped to the floor with very loud thuds.

Torpedo Ink used silencers, but silencers only muffled the sound of a shot. The gunshots could still be heard if anyone was close. Bitters looked hopefully toward the exit that was directly behind him. George Durango edged closer to him.

"I've got money. Whoever is paying you, I can double it," Durango said.

Ice shot him through the heart and for good measure shot him a second time between his eyes. Durango fell into Bitters, who automatically caught the falling body and then dropped it with a small squeak of fear.

Ice and Storm moved together right past Bitters to the computer. "Where is he?" Ice snapped, staring up at the screen. "If you don't tell me the first time, that man right there, standing in front of you, is going to take you apart piece by piece. No one is going to come save you. The back exit is ours. The alley is ours. The front desk is ours. The cameras are not working. Where is the kid, Bitters?"

Storm worked on the computer, using a few keystrokes to allow Code to break in. It wouldn't take long to find the boy on their own if necessary. "Code's in," he said.

Bitters looked around at the dead bodies as if he couldn't believe what had happened. He was clearly still in shock. Killing nine people inside the room had taken less than a full minute. He took two steps back and held up his hands. "If you want him, of course I'll take you to him."

"We have a team that will pick him up. You're going to tell us where he is," Ice reiterated.

Savage had shoved his gun out of sight and pulled out a wicked-looking knife. The blade caught the lights from above and gleamed, drawing Bitters's eye. Savage had no expression on his face, and his eyes were flat. Cold. Dead. It was very clear he could do exactly what Ice had said he would do.

Bitters looked to Lana. She was a beautiful woman, elegant and classy. "Please, I don't know what's happening." He took another step back.

"Look over your shoulder," Ice suggested.

Bitters turned, his face a mask of fear. Reaper, Savage's older brother, filled the doorway, looking like the Grim Reaper. Bitters's frightened gaze jumped from man to man. It was impossible to say which was scarier.

"In the basement, but you'll never get into his cage without me. There's a device —"

Ice's head snapped up. "You fuckin' put a *device* on the cage? Like a bomb? You put a fuckin' bomb on the cage of a six-year-old boy you've been molesting for two years and now he's too old and you want to sell him? You put a bomb on that cage?" He stepped closer. He could kill the bastard with his bare hands.

"You don't understand," Bitters said. He straightened, putting on his public face, the one he gave to the cameras and that made everyone believe. "This boy, these children, they're sexual beings. They want love. They

40

want what we give them. You need to open your mind. I was born to love children. To teach them." He gave that exact rhetoric to the other pedophiles on the website they all visited. Maybe he'd said it so many times he believed it.

Ice hit him hard. He was wearing a thin pair of gloves like his brothers and Lana. Beneath the gloves they wore fingerprints that didn't belong to any of them. He shoved a knee into Bitters's chest when his body went down like a felled tree. Ice hit him a dozen times, smashing teeth and his nose, and breaking his cheekbone.

"Ice is losing it, Czar, with good reason," Storm reported.

"Ice," Czar said softly in his ear. *"We need information. Back off for a minute."*

Lana put a hand on Ice's shoulder. "Get him up, brother," she said softly. "Don't get any blood on you."

Ice glanced at her over his shoulder and took a deep breath to still the beast crying out for more blood. More death. Reluctantly he stood up, jerking Bitters with him.

Bitters wiped at the blood but it kept coming.

"We're at four minutes and counting," Storm reported. *"Move it along."*

"You hear that, Alena? Bomb on the cage.

41

Check it out. Code says the kid's in the basement," Savage said and took a step toward Bitters.

Bitters let out another squeak and held up his hands in surrender. "I've given you the kid. I can give you the code to open the cage. You can have him. I don't need money for him." He mumbled his statement and coughed blood.

Savage slapped him hard. The blow was so strong, Bitters rocked back and to his left. Stumbled. Nearly went down. Blood sprayed across the floor.

"You can't do that," Bitters said, grabbing his face and holding it with both hands. "You have to arrest me."

Ice looked around the room at the dead bodies. "This look like law enforcement to you? We want to know who the man is that sold the kid to you in the first place. He killed the boy's family and took him nearly out of a crib in order to have him without repercussions. He didn't want anyone looking for the boy. He's established quite an MO with his 'kill families and grab the kids' technique. He's a supplier. That's what he does for sick fucks like you. Who is he?"

Bitters glanced up at the camera and then shook his head. "I don't know him."

"You really aren't of any use to us then,

42

but we have to be certain." Ice flicked a quick look at Savage. "Transporter has the truck waiting and the Demons have a small chapter here. They're flying under the radar. They lent us their garage for a few hours."

"I'll get the information we need from one of them," Savage said. "Ice, you're with me on this one. Between the two of us, we can get anyone to talk."

"Wait, wait." Bitters held up his hands again as if he could ward them off.

Lana moved close and Bitters grabbed at her. She caught his wrist, twisted, and he went flying off his feet. She retained possession of his wrist while grinding one foot into his throat. She caught the syringe Savage tossed to her and slammed the needle into Bitters's neck. His eyes rolled back in his head.

"Now I need another shower," Lana said and dropped the dead weight of Bitters's arm. "He's disgusting."

Savage reached down and hauled the man up easily. He put him on his shoulder, so the body dangled like a rag doll. "Leave the computer and all the evidence Code collected on these men. All of it. He has plenty of copies. He's chosen several news outlets to leak the evidence to. Burn your clothes. Everything. Lana, you'll have to get rid of the shoes. There's blood on them. Use the routes given to you."

"Damn it, Ice" — she glared at him — "I love these shoes."

"Sorry, hon, I'll buy you another pair," Ice said. He slung his arm around her. "Really. He just pissed me off. I needed to kill that fucker, so it's a good thing you and Storm were here to give me a cooler head."

"Me too," she said. "I needed to kill him too, but we need to find the one killing families and taking the children."

"Remove all evidence," Czar said unnecessarily over the radio.

"Package is in our custody," Alena reported. *"Poor baby is scared out of his mind."*

"Sedate him if you have to for transport. We'll take care of him," Czar said. *"You all need to get out of there clean."*

TWO

Soleil Brodeur had never actually used the main entrance to the hotel. She used a private entrance, and always had a concierge waiting to give her any little thing she wanted or direct her to wherever she wanted to go. There was a private car to take her places. She had wanted to walk around the strip like a normal tourist and just enjoy the day. Was that asking too much? Did she always have to dress right and talk only to the people Winston dictated she talk to? They were supposed to be having fun. Make that whatever Winston ordered was fun.

She dashed at the tears on her face and stopped to look around her. There were people everywhere. She hadn't used the private entrance because she hadn't wanted the concierge to see her crying like a baby, which was so ridiculous there were no words. She had no idea where to go, which elevator to take or even if she could get one to her room from the main lobby. She'd traveled the world, stayed in hundreds of hotels, but she couldn't find her way to an elevator? She was *such* an idiot.

No one could force another person to marry them. The idea was ludicrous. She'd brought this entire mess on herself. There was no one else to blame. She might let everyone else do everything for her, but she always took responsibility for her own screwups. This was the worst of the worst.

She took a quick look around and caught sight of a women's bathroom tucked behind an alcove filled with gorgeous plants. She hurried across the gleaming marble-tiled floor and ducked into the alcove. The door was opened for her by an attendant in a hotel uniform. She went on through, wondering how many people couldn't open a door. Probably only her. A fresh flood of tears ensured her makeup would be a mess.

As with everything else in the hotel, the bathroom was the epitome of luxury. The door opened to a sitting room with faint music, comfortable but elegant chairs and a sofa, giving women a place to relax if they wanted to hide for a few minutes. A soft fragrance spread through the room, and large, lacy plants of various shades of green added to the peaceful ambience. Once the door was closed, all noise from the outside lobby ceased.

A tall woman with dark hair stood in the midst of the greenery, dragging a dark tank top over a lacy red bra. She was beyond beautiful. Her face was flawless, with dark eyes and an inviting mouth. If Soleil hadn't been crying, she would have stopped and stared. She couldn't stay in the sitting room, not with the most gorgeous woman on the face of the earth casually changing from what looked like a sultry afternoon dress — *not* a girl-next-door sundress.

Soleil went past another concerned attendant to the sink, needing to splash cold water on her face. She had to stop crying, but all she seemed to be able to do was stare at herself in the mirror with tears running down her face. She didn't look at all like the beautiful woman with gold at her ears and a flawless body to go with her flawless face. She probably looked gorgeous when she cried, not all splotchy and red.

There was a faint bruise just on her left cheek where her fiancé had slapped her because she'd insisted on a prenup. There were bruises on both upper arms where he'd grabbed her hard and shaken her, as if somehow, by threatening her, it would make her go through with the marriage.

47

She'd always had a ridiculous fantasy about being with someone a little rough, although they never *hit* her. She never could quite feel that tingle with the men she dated. That spark. Winston hadn't appeared rough. He had soft hands. He always wore a business suit, and his shoes were gleaming with polish. In the weeks she'd known him, he'd never had a single hair out of place. She realized having the real thing wasn't at all what she'd dreamt about. No one had ever put their hands on her like that before.

It was ridiculous anyway. She had known better than to come to Vegas. She'd reluctantly agreed even though, in the back of her mind, she feared Winston Trent was going to try to get her to marry him. They'd argued about it several times before coming. He wanted to marry her quickly to "take care of her." She needed breathing room. She'd told him, and he hadn't listened.

Winston had switched tactics, saying they didn't have to go through with a marriage, but she needed some fun. He'd planned the entire trip and "surprised" her. She should have refused to go. That would have been the adult thing to do. The intelligent thing. She'd done what she always did. She'd drifted. She had let him talk her into it because she wasn't a fighter. She'd never been a fighter. She liked peace. She liked creating peace.

Her longtime lawyer and guardian, Kevin Bennet, had died unexpectedly in an accident just a month earlier. He had always managed her affairs, looked after her trust fund and been more like a father to her, although she didn't really know what a father was supposed to be like. She was grieving. She'd told Winston that repeatedly, but his answer had been to get married and let him take care of things. He had rushed out and hired a lawyer, but she was uneasy around the new lawyer, a man by the name of Donald Monroe, and felt like she wasn't ready to move on. Again, Winston's answer had been to get married and let him handle the lawyer.

She touched the bruises on her arm and shook her head, knowing she was at her lowest point. She'd lost the one man she could talk to, figure things out with. Everything felt so tangled, and she had absolutely no real idea of what to do next.

"Honey, he's not worth it. No matter how much money he's got, no matter how big a ring he puts on your finger, if he puts his hands on you, you should run the opposite way as fast as you can."

Soleil lifted her gaze in the mirror to the woman standing beside her. She had been the one in the sitting room changing. She looked at the woman and then dropped her gaze to the ring. "You're so right," she murmured and pulled it off her finger to shove in the pocket of her dress. "Thanks for the advice."

Up close, the stranger was even more gorgeous. Really, really beautiful. It took some doing not to stare. The woman rinsed her hands in the immaculate bowl and Soleil couldn't help glancing down to see if she wore a ring. She didn't. She wasn't quite as tall as Soleil had first thought but looked it because, although she had curves, she was on the slimmer side. She wore skinny jeans, motorcycle boots and a leather vest over a dark tee. She'd gone from glamorous woman to hot biker babe in about three minutes. Who could do that?

"You all right, honey? I could get you a room if you needed it for the night." Even her voice was sultry.

A perfect stranger in the women's room of a hotel was nicer to her than her fiancé, the man who had sworn he loved her. "Thank you, I really appreciate the offer, but I have a room. I'm going to pack and get out of here fast." The problem was, she was going to have to face Winston. They shared the room.

"Good for you," the woman approved.

"Did you hear all those sirens?" Soleil asked, trying to change the subject so she didn't look so pathetic. "It sounded like half the police force was going somewhere."

The woman nodded. "Around the corner, a couple of streets over. I heard there was a shooting in a massage parlor. Someone said everyone inside was dead."

"What is wrong with everyone these days?" Soleil asked.

The woman shrugged. "Most likely someone didn't pay when they should have." She picked up a small tote, started out and then stopped, turning back. "You have a cell phone?"

Soleil nodded.

"I'm Lana."

"Soleil."

"You here alone?"

"With him." She held up her bruised arm.

"Where's your family? Maybe you should give them a call."

Soleil looked down at the floor. It was absolutely clean just like everything else. She sniffed and wasn't at all shocked to find that even the bathroom smelled good. That citrus fragrance from the sitting room had drifted right in.

"I don't have a family," she admitted in a low voice.

"Friends nearby?" Lana stepped closer to her, concern in her voice. In her eyes.

Soleil struggled not to burst into tears at the obvious sympathy. The few friends she'd had, Winston had managed to alienate. She shook her head.

"Sometimes these things get ugly. You have any trouble at all, you can call me. I have friends. They'll come get you out of any situation." Lana snapped her fingers and held out her hand. "Give me your cell."

Soleil had no idea why in the world she would allow a perfect stranger to take her cell phone, but she did. She pulled it from her pocket, keyed in the code and handed it to Lana.

"I meant what I said. He's already proven he's willing to put his hands on you, so when you break it off, make certain you're not alone with him. Have your cell handy and call the cops. If you can't, you call me, understand?" Lana turned and pointed to her vest even as she programmed her number into Soleil's cell. "It's under Lana. Don't you forget it."

There was a very cool tree with ravens in the branches and skulls in the roots on the back of her vest. A rocker above the tree proclaimed her Torpedo Ink. The one below said Sea Haven-Caspar. Soleil had heard of Sea Haven but not Sea Haven-Caspar and had no idea where that was, or what Torpedo Ink was, other than a club, but it was cool as hell and this was Soleil's first time ever talking to a woman who rode motorcycles.

"We're in Vegas celebrating our brother's wedding to his woman, but you call, you understand? He lays his hands on you again or does anything that frightens you, lock yourself in a room and call." She handed Soleil back her phone. "Someone will come for you, I promise."

"Thanks." Soleil wrapped her hands around her phone as if it were a lifeline. Maybe it was. At least, it was the first truly nice thing someone had done for her since Kevin had died.

Lana gave a friendly wave and walked out.

Soleil stared after her for a long time. She wanted to be like that. Smart. Sophisticated. Independent. She wanted to take charge of her life. Make her own decisions. She sighed. Who was she kidding? She was terrified without her lawyer. Still, she was determined to get herself out of the mess she was in. She knew she'd created it

53

through her own apathy.

Washing her hands for the third time, she took a deep breath. She had been paralyzed with grief since her lawyer died. Her parents had been killed in a car accident when she was four and she'd gone to live with her aunt Deborah. She'd passed away when Soleil was eight.

She went to live with her aunt Constance. That lasted until she was ten, mostly because Constance thought she would have access to Soleil's trust fund, but Kevin kept a tight grip on it. He refused to allow her aunt anything more than it would have cost to have Soleil living with her. Constance had been furious over that and let Soleil know every chance she got how unfair it was and just how much trouble it was to have a brat living with her.

Soleil was put in a series of boarding schools from that time on. She studied abroad. She lived in various hotels because she had nowhere else to go when she wasn't in school. The only constant in her life was her lawyer, and she'd come to rely on him for just about everything, although, truthfully, she rarely saw him. Mostly they talked on the phone or via email, text or messenger. It didn't matter that she hadn't seen him, he was always there.

She could text anytime, day or night, and he answered her. He advised her. He took care of her trust and allowed her to go to art school. She traveled to all the wonderful art galleries all over the world and painted in France, Italy and Greece. When she got into any kind of trouble, he got her out.

She met Winston Trent in London at Sotheby's. They talked for quite a while. He was friendly and knowledgeable about art. Like Soleil, he lived in San Francisco and was on his way back to the States. They were on the same plane and coincidentally seated next to each other. They laughed over that and spent most of the plane ride home talking. She hadn't talked so much or laughed more in years. For the first time in her life, she felt as if she had a friend.

They dated, going to dinner, movies, fundraising events that Winston insisted on. Before she had gone alone and felt out of place. She was just so happy to be with someone. She'd been so lonely. She was so desperate for a relationship that even though he often did and said things that sent up red flags, she ignored them and tried harder to please him. Looking back, she could see how he'd pushed her constantly, even when she'd been uncomfortable with how fast things were moving, but he hadn't listened.

She began talking nightly with Kevin Bennet. Her lawyer wasn't happy with the fact that Winston wanted to put a ring on her finger so fast.

She had always wanted to be wild and impulsive with her man. She actually dreamt of it often, but Winston didn't inspire that in her. She had thought, because she'd met him in Europe, that he was adventurous, but he wasn't. Not in the least. He told her he was a businessman and he wanted her to look a certain way. To dress a certain way. He even gave her a list of people he insisted she "meet" and "cultivate" as friends. When she questioned him, he told her he wanted to make certain she moved in the right circles and she needed to just let him guide her.

Soleil glanced at herself in the mirror one more time. She wished she could be like Lana. Tall. Gorgeous. Perfectly in control. She wore her jeans and vest like royalty. No one would dare lay their hands on her unless she wanted them to. Soleil shoved her phone into the little pocket of the sundress she wore and kept her hand there, holding on for just a minute to the stranger who had shown her kindness.

She had tried to get Winston to be adventurous, at least in bed. Something other than his roll on top of her and roll off again while she lay staring at the ceiling wondering if that was all there was to love and living together. How would she know? She'd never witnessed a real relationship. Neither aunt had been married, and Kevin had talked to her via text most of the time.

She straightened her shoulders and imagined herself to be Lana. Lana wasn't about to put up with a man who didn't satisfy her or listen to her in bed. She would never let him scare her into marriage. She'd tell him it was over. That was *exactly* what Soleil was going to do.

Soleil glanced at the woman who held out a small, immaculate towel for her to dry her hands for the third time. "She's right, isn't she?" she asked her.

The attendant glanced around the large gold and ivory bathroom, making certain no one could see or hear her give advice, and then she nodded.

Feeling empowered, Soleil smiled at her and left. She had to ask the outside attendant the way to the elevators, but she found them. Then she had to talk to another attendant there, and he escorted her to the proper one. She was in a suite at the top of the tower. She slid her flat gold key into the elevator and took the ride up to her rooms.

There were only four suites at the top of the tower. Her room was directly across from the elevator access.

She was used to the best hotels and often had a suite, but this luxury suite was so over the top and ridiculous for the two of them when they planned on being in Vegas just for a couple of nights. Winston had insisted, and she'd found herself going along with his plans, just as she had ever since Kevin Bennet had died.

The suite was nearly two thousand square feet with a gleaming grand piano in the middle of the marble floor. Glass walls gave them a view of Las Vegas that was unparalleled. A fireplace and wet bar added to the ambience in the room. The balcony stretched out for what seemed forever, curving around the building so they could enjoy the sun and breeze. Winston had told her she deserved the best and he wanted her to have it. It was too much.

He'd been rude to the staff at the hotel, complaining about everything. That was the only way to get people to come up to the right standards, he'd told her, and she'd have to learn to deal with those in menial labor positions. They'd argued over that as well until he'd just shut her down by telling her she was too young and naïve to understand how the world worked. In business and politics, one had to assert themselves at all times. Eventually, he planned to go into politics, and he needed a wife trained to handle anything.

Most of this mess was her fault and she had to place the blame directly on her own shoulders. She had let Winston run her life when she'd been without direction. She still had no idea what she wanted to do, but it wasn't marrying a man she wasn't happy with. She was tense all the time and found she was getting headaches when she'd never been prone to them.

When had he changed? He'd been funny and attentive, listening to everything she said in the art gallery and on the plane. She'd thought they had so much in common, but once he'd actually managed to get her to go out with him, the changes had started. At first, they were subtle. He didn't like a certain outfit, and would she mind changing? He didn't like her boots, they made her look too young. Why would she wear that short denim jacket when she had some really beautiful jackets? She should have noticed sooner instead of trying to please him.

Winston was pacing across the long, wide floor as she entered. He looked up quickly as she closed the door, that flat, golden key clutched in her hand as if it were a good luck talisman. He skirted around the piano and rushed to her.

"I was so worried, Soleil. I must have texted you a hundred times. Come in and sit down, darling." Not waiting for a reply, he took her wrist and pulled her across the room to the low-slung couch.

The couch was nearest the door and guest bathroom, but still too far into the enormous room for her to be entirely comfortable. The room made her feel as if it were going to swallow her whole. Still, she sat down, clutching the golden key to the elevator, feeling as if it would see her through the discussion she needed to have with him.

"I'll get us both a drink and we can talk."

Why did she hate the sound of his voice? He always said the right thing, but his tone was condescending, or, like now, when he tried to convey worry and sympathy, he sounded as if he were acting — and he wasn't all that good of an actor. Still, a drink sounded good. She hadn't eaten anything, but a drink might be just the thing to help her explain that she was going to call off their wedding for good.

"I don't know why I lost my temper, but I really am sorry. I was so afraid I'd lose you and I reacted like a madman."

He poured her a small glass of whiskey. She preferred whiskey, and she really needed it, especially as he was giving her his sweetest, most boyish look designed to make her feel bad for him.

"Here, darling, drink that and we'll talk."

He drank half the glass he'd poured for himself in one gulp, so without thinking, Soleil tossed back a good portion of the whiskey and nearly choked. Tears burned and for a moment her throat felt like it was on fire. She could barely catch her breath.

Winston regarded her over the top of his crystal glass, amusement on his face. He did that a lot — laughed at her. Not overtly, but definitely he found her amusing and not in a good way. It was as if she was so young and naïve, and he was worldly, and she couldn't quite catch up. She supposed she deserved his estimation of her. It didn't matter that she knew she could drink him under the table, she shouldn't have tried to throw back half a glass.

"Winston, I —"

He held up his hand. "I know what you're going to say. You're such a sweet, compassionate woman and I know you're going to just dismiss my bad behavior, but it was terrible, and I need to give you my word nothing like that will ever happen again. I feel sick about my behavior. I'll make it up to you, I promise."

Over the course of the last couple of months, there had been numerous promises. She couldn't even remember what they were, but thinking back, he'd never come through. She nodded and cautiously crossed the room to get a bottle of water. The whiskey was doing what she needed though, making her feel as if she could tell him what she needed to.

"Winston," she began again after taking a soothing sip of water and reseating herself. "This isn't going to work between us. I think you know that."

"Of course it is. I made a mistake. It was absolutely stupid of me, but I was so afraid of losing you. Lately, we've been out of sync . . ."

"Exactly." She pounced on that. "I feel as if you don't like anything about me. Not one thing, Winston. The way I dress. My friends. The way I talk. You have to correct everything I do and then I'm still not good enough."

"Darling."

He looked terribly distressed, so much so that her heart hurt. She didn't like hurting anyone. She finished off the whiskey and automatically handed him the glass when he put out his hand for it.

Winston took it from her and crossed to the bar. "If I made you feel like that, you should have told me immediately. I love you with every breath I take. I want to be your husband and go through life with you."

"We don't like the same movies or music." Soleil felt a little desperate. He was looking a little like a kicked puppy instead of a barracuda, and she wasn't good *at all* with hurting people. She kept trying to assert herself even as she took the drink from him.

"Keep going, Soleil. I had no idea you thought I wasn't happy with you. I need to hear this. It's the only way to fix what's broken between us."

"You don't like to dance. You aren't in the least bit proud of the way I look. You want me to change my hair and makeup and wear clothes I consider far too old for me. I don't understand why you think you love *me*, Winston."

"You are so wrong, Soleil. How could you think I'm not proud of you? I told you I wanted to get into politics. I was trying to help you, so you'd feel comfortable when we're attending the kinds of fund-raisers and charity events where we'd need to be seen."

She detested the events he wanted to go to. They were hundreds, sometimes thousands of dollars a plate, very stuffy. She felt everyone was looking down on her. He would sometimes grab her elbow and drag her into a corner and hiss at her that he'd told her to study the list of people he wanted her to talk to. Everyone else there was to be smiled at but ignored. How could an event be fun if she had assignments and failed at all of them, especially when she carefully memorized every single name on his list? She wasn't going to be rude and ignore people who talked to her.

She took another drink and shook her head. "I can't marry you, Winston. That's the bottom line. It isn't going to work. I'm not happy. You're not happy. I'm giving you back your ring . . ."

He went very still, only feet from her, his eyes going from that watchful amusement to dark and a little scary. Suddenly, the large room seemed too small.

"Soleil. Stop right there. Don't make a fool of yourself. We are getting married. It's ridiculous for you to suddenly decide after one small slip to throw me over. You're acting like the spoiled child I know you to be, and I'm not going to put up with it. If this is about that idiotic prenup, I'm not asking

64

you to sign one to protect me. Even your lawyer agrees it's ridiculous. I have far more to lose than you do."

She stood to make herself taller, tilted her chin, narrowed her eyes at him and took another cautious sip of the whiskey. "I am not going to marry you. Prenup or not. It isn't going to happen." And if he was so damned wealthy, why was she always the one paying for everything? She should ask, but something kept her from doing so. It always did.

"I realize you're very young and you're upset over Bennet's death. I found you a lawyer and I told you I'd deal with the businesses and the finances. You don't have to do anything but your art. I didn't realize you were so close to your lawyer, but I should have."

She wasn't certain what to do when he used his reasonable tone on her and reduced her to being a not-quite-bright child. He did it often and now, examining the last few weeks, she realized just how often. She always backed off when he did that, feeling inferior. She had degrees in art and art history. His degrees were all practical, in business and finance. He had said they would work well together, and it had sounded a perfect match. It wasn't.

Soleil took another drink, emptying the glass, and went to the bar herself to pour another short drink before she tried again. The alcohol was kicking in and giving her more courage. "It's true, Kevin's death really threw me. He's all the family I had, as crazy as that sounds. I'm not comfortable with Donald Monroe. He doesn't listen to me and he doesn't answer my questions. He just says not to worry, he'll take care of things."

"Isn't that why we hired him?" Winston sounded as if he was holding on to his patience by a thread. He didn't sound like the man she'd met only a few weeks earlier. What had happened to him?

"*You* hired him. You didn't give me a chance to interview him or even talk to him first. I don't know the first thing about him."

"Someone needed to watch out for you, and you were too grief-stricken to do it."

"We could have waited a few weeks."

Anger flashed across his face. She watched as he swallowed what he was going to say and then he doubled his fist. Deliberately, he clenched and then unclenched his fingers. "Soleil. Is that the reason for all this? You're upset because we hired Monroe? When we get back from our honeymoon, I'll fire him." His voice turned conciliatory

66

and he even smiled benevolently at her. "I can get rid of him just as easily as I hired him."

She had to stop arguing and just insist. He wasn't listening to her, and it was still all about him. Not her. She wasn't going to fire Monroe. He was going to do it. He was going to be very, very shocked to learn she'd already done it.

"Winston, you don't seem to get what I'm telling you. I am not getting married to you. Not now. Not later. There isn't going to be a honeymoon. I've already called and officially fired Monroe. I followed up with the necessary legal papers. I went to someone here to help me. Monroe isn't working for me nor is anyone from that firm." Not after she'd called him about the prenup and he'd said to skip it, it wasn't necessary. Even she knew better.

"You did *what?*" His face darkened with rage. He stepped into her, took the mostly empty glass of whiskey from her and threw it sideways away from them. The glass shattered against the piano.

Winston backhanded her casually, but hard enough to knock her backward. He followed her, slapping her breasts three more times. Each blow made her stumble back more. Pain exploded through her, a shock wave that made her nearly vomit. She knew he was holding back too. He didn't look like he wanted to.

"You little bitch. Do you think I'm going to let you ruin everything because you're so spoiled you want every single thing your way? I want you cleaned up and looking presentable in the next half hour and then we're going to finish up here with the plans we made." With each sentence he hit her again, her ribs and then her stomach, finally knocking her to the floor.

With a look of utter contempt, he reached down, pulled her cell phone from her pocket and tossed it on the couch before he turned away. "Just in case you get stupid. Now go to the bathroom and put some makeup on."

Soleil picked herself up gingerly. No one had ever hit her before Winston. It hurt. Her face throbbed and burned, feeling as if her cheekbone had exploded. Her breasts and stomach hurt with every movement. She recognized that he'd been careful not to hit hard enough to injure her — to make her see a doctor. Her face might swell later, but she'd have some time before it did — enough time to get married.

She made her way to the bathroom, avoiding the master bedroom because he'd gone in there. She didn't want to get anywhere

68

near Winston. The stranger, Lana, had been so right. These things did go badly very, very fast. She didn't even have her phone to call for help. Not the cops, not Lana, no one.

She didn't look in the mirror, what would be the point? She wasn't going to clean herself up and marry Winston. She didn't care how much he hit her or yelled. She wasn't about to tie herself to him.

The sound of male voices made her jam her fist into her mouth after realizing she was crying — making broken sobbing noises. She needed to hear whatever Winston was saying. Maybe, if it was room service, she could call out and let them know he was threatening her. Her fist had the flat golden key in it. She had never put it down, not when she'd drunk the whiskey and not when he'd hit her. At least she had that, the key to the elevator.

She opened the bathroom door cautiously. Winston was in the bedroom. He'd left the door open, presumably in order to hear if she came out of the bathroom. He was pulling on another of his immaculate shirts. He had called someone, and they were on speaker.

"How the hell could you fuck this up, Winston? It was a golden opportunity. We handed her to you on a silver platter. All you had to do was get her to the altar. Monroe would do the rest. Another month and your wife would die in an accident and you'd be a young widower, ripe for so many desperate wealthy women to console, and we could do this again. How hard could it have been?"

"I'll marry the bitch, but she's going to meet with an accident on the honeymoon. Spoiled little bitch, not even a good lay. All she ever did was talk to Bennet like a little baby. He coddled her."

"We cleared the road for you. We're good at accidents, Winston, but if you can't close this deal, you'll be the one dead on the side of the road, like Bennet. You wanted in and we gave you this one chance and you blew it. Get it done."

"She'll do whatever I say," Winston assured. "I made sure of that and she doesn't have the guts to fight back."

Soleil felt the color drain from her face. She actually felt light-headed. Monroe was the new lawyer she'd just fired. She recognized the voice of Harbin Conner. Harbin was a decorated policeman, assistant chief and moving up, one of the many men she had met through Winston. He'd been on the "list." It sounded like Conner had arranged an accident for Kevin. And he kept saying "we," as if there were more of them. They planned to kill her. Winston wanted her dead. Winston and his friends wanted her dead.

She drew in air and told herself not to faint. She just had to make a run for it. Her phone had landed next to her denim jacket on the couch. She'd left the jacket there when she'd tired of their original argument and had just wanted to go for a walk to think. He'd followed her, of course, not giving her time at all, and he'd gotten so angry he'd shaken her. Not once, but several times. He went back to the room declaring she wasn't going to stand him up at the last minute.

She'd called her new lawyer, Monroe, and once again, even after he heard Winston had put his hands on her, he'd advised her to quit making him angry and marry the man. She'd fired him on the spot and then gone to an attorney's office and had the papers drawn up to make it official. That wasn't like her at all. She tended to let things go. Not this time. Kevin Bennet had been such a superb lawyer she felt if she kept Monroe, it was an insult to Kevin.

She waited, her breath coming too fast, and she feared she might hyperventilate. She made a deliberate effort to slow it down. She had to be clearheaded and think out each move ahead of time. She knew if she made it out the door, the elevator would be there waiting. It had to be. There was no other choice.

Soleil peeked out of the bedroom again. Winston had turned his back to her and was reaching down for his gleaming shoes. They were always shined to perfection, but he never passed up a chance to shine them again. It was now or never. She sprinted across the room, scooped up her jacket and phone and ran from the suite. It was only a few steps to the elevator, and she had the key in her hand.

Behind her, Winston shouted expletives and commands, but she didn't turn around. The elevator doors opened, and she stepped in and hit the shut button to override the wait period, her heart pounding. The doors closed, and she caught a glimpse of his furious face as she stabbed at the button to take her to the lobby. Even if he ran down the stairs, he'd never catch her. He would have to wait for the elevator. It was private, just for those four suites. He had insisted on the best and he'd have to reap the consequences.

She shoved her phone into the inside pocket of her jacket and slipped the jacket on before gripping the golden rail with both hands. He would expect her to take the nearest exit, either the private one or the one to the front of the hotel that opened onto the main strip near all the little shops. The back exit of the hotel let one out on the street parallel to the main strip. If she took that one and cut through the next hotel, she would be close to the section Winston had warned her about. The bars and massage parlors. He claimed they were nice enough, just not for her. Hopefully he wouldn't look for her there while she decided on the best course of action.

She ran through the lobby, uncaring of turning heads. One didn't run in a very swank hotel. She wanted to grab security, but Winston had a way of talking that made her look hysterical or childish and him look totally controlled, the adult having to put up with tantrums. She wasn't about to take chances, not when she knew they planned to kill her.

Who would believe her? Her own fiancé? A lawyer? A policeman? All conspiring to kill her? She would look crazy and Winston would explain she'd lost Bennet, the only one she had as family. He would get sympathy and understanding, and they would all look to him to take care of her. He'd probably sedate her. Did he have a doctor involved too? It was possible. She'd met one through him, one he considered important.

She burst out onto the street, her lungs hurting. Clearly, she needed more exercise if she was going to have to run for her life. Her thoughts were wild and a little hysterical. She couldn't have that. It would only play into Winston's hand. She raced to the crosswalk, and fortunately the light changed and there were few people in her way. She was able to cross quickly and get into the relative shelter of the hotel-casino on the next street.

Noise erupted all around her. The concentrated smoke from cigarettes threatened to choke her. For a moment, she paused, a little disoriented. The whiskey she'd drunk was making her feel a lot better. Clearer. She knew exactly what to do. She made her way through the casino with more dignity, not wanting to draw attention to herself.

The casino floor was set up so that the exits were difficult to get to. Every little turn put her in front of card tables, the roulette wheel, craps, or, when she managed to find her way through the maze, machines. A sea of them. They didn't matter. The drinks had finally steadied her, and she was feeling as if she was in control and could do this.

Still, it was a good distance to the exits and it took her a few minutes to make her way to the other side of the room. The casino was enormous, so much so that she knew she'd probably covered a block at least. She had to have. But she walked with more confidence and less panic. Every now and then, just to be certain, she glanced over her shoulder, or paused at a machine to see if Winston was behind her. So far, her plan had worked. Most likely, he'd gone out onto the strip and worried she'd hailed a cab or taken one of the hotel's private limos. She was afraid to do that. He could trace a cab, and he'd talk any driver into coming back for him.

She thought about getting another drink, but she hadn't eaten. Already she was much clearer in what she had to do. She felt very courageous. It only took a couple of times going in a small circle before she mastered the maze of machines and was able to push open the door that let her out onto the street. The lights were much dimmer, but still illuminated the sidewalk.

She looked left and right. She was right in the middle of the block. Across the street, neon blue signs flashed, and the sound of music was loud. Each of the bars seemed to be playing a different song, but she loved to dance and the one on the end at the right blared the best music. She headed in that direction and then changed her mind, a little shiver going through her. She knew Winston. He would hire men to find her. He would call the police and report her missing, saying she had a mental disorder and he was worried for her safety. This street was still too close.

She hurried down the block to the next line of bars. The streets seemed darker, and as she came around the corner, a few men standing on the sidewalk in front of a bar looked up, nudging one another. Alarms went off and she paused to get oriented. Just in front of her was another bar blaring dancing music and in front of it were motorcycles, instantly reminding her of Lana. Her heart jumped. Lana. She hurried toward that one without hesitation. If Lana was there, she would know what to do. She was that kind of woman.

THREE

Leaning against the bar, Ice ordered another drink, wondering, now that Steele and Breezy had left for home, why he hadn't gone with them. He should have. What was he doing there? Drinking? Playing pool? Pretending to have a good time? He could fight. Beat the shit out of someone. That made him feel a little better sometimes. Not often anymore.

He'd been in a thousand bars. Had a thousand drinks. Played pool. Hustled at pool. Gotten into hundreds of fights. Most not of his making, but certainly he had to take responsibility for dozens. Women? Hell. He took the glass and pressed it to his forehead. He couldn't count the women. They all blurred together. To give them their due, they gave their best efforts, but in the end, it had always come down to his absolute control. He had to decide to get hard. Fuck.

He downed the entire contents in one sip and lifted the glass toward the bartender. Unbidden, she floated into his mind. The girl. Not just the girl. *The* girl. The one who had given him a natural, very real erection, and she hadn't done one single seductive thing. Not one. She'd stood on a street corner looking like a fresh summer day, soft skin and eyes promising heaven. That mouth of hers. A perfect bow. Full. And her tits. Shit. They couldn't possibly be real, could they?

He fiddled with his drink on the bar, barely acknowledging the bartender when he gave him a refill. He was too busy remembering every detail of his princess. She had hips and a very nice ass. There was no way to find her and her cute little ridiculous booties that showed off her legs. He could imagine her mouth around his cock, or those tits in his hands, but he was never going to have the real thing. She belonged with the suit, the one with every hair in place and his condescending asshole attitude.

She looked like the girl next door. The one that wanted to make her man her first priority. The one willing to have his children and back him up no matter what. That girl. The one that probably didn't even exist anymore. How the hell would he ever get a woman like that? He had certain proclivities. Even if he got her, she wasn't going to do the things he needed.

Fuck. He should have pulled out his gun and shot those bastards he was tailing and let the police shoot him down like the psycho he was. He had crossed some line and he wasn't certain he could pull back from it. There was nothing for him, and in the end, he had to acknowledge that he was too dangerous to just keep around like some loose cannon.

He'd shaped himself into a weapon. He'd had no choice, not if he was going to get Alena out alive. Storm had done the same, but Ice had always tried to stand in front of his twin. Now, he was expected to act like a wolf in sheep's clothing. Czar knew what he was. Maybe all of them knew, but suddenly Czar had changed the rules of their world. They were supposed to fit in. Be tame. Follow bullshit rules that made absolutely no sense. He couldn't keep pretending. Sometimes he felt that if he had to keep up the pretense one second longer, he'd just implode.

"You okay, Ice? We could go back to the motel," Storm suggested carefully.

The bar was rocking. Three different clubs. Czar and Steele had taken their women and the very scared and traumatized little boy home. Lana, Preacher and Reaper had escorted them. Reaper's woman, Anya, was with them. That left thirteen Torpedo Ink members in the bar. With numbers like that, they could wipe up the floor with any of the clubs. Thinking like that was exactly what Storm worried about.

"And do what?" Ice asked. "Stare at the fuckin' ceiling?"

"You're in a foul mood," Alena, his sister, observed.

She leaned against the bar, very close to him, looking like a seductive siren. She couldn't help it. She was born that way. Trained that way. She knew she looked good and she had no problem flaunting it. She often provided a damn good excuse to fight. Most likely Storm had signaled to her that Ice was on the edge again and they'd need to corral him and get him the hell out of there.

Ice loved her. All the brothers did. She was his birth sister and a few years younger. In those early days, he'd been too young to protect her, too helpless. He hadn't yet shaped himself into a weapon. Now, maybe he was overprotective when she didn't need it. She was sweet, beautiful and lethal as hell. Most underestimated her. They saw a gorgeous woman and didn't think for one moment that she could be trained in a thousand ways to kill. It was a miracle she had survived. Only two women, Lana and Alena, had gotten out of that hellhole they had spent their childhood in.

Before he could answer her, there was a sudden silence in the bar. An actual pause in the many conversations. The music still pulsed through the room, but no one said a word. He turned slightly, angling his body toward his sister, prepared to take her to the floor if necessary. He glanced toward the door and his world just stopped. His vision tunneled. For one moment he thought he had finally gone over the edge and was hallucinating.

His heart thudded. She was there. His little princess. She was beautiful beyond belief, standing there in her little white, flowery sundress with a small denim jacket covering her arms. She wore those little ridiculous boots that showed off her slender legs. He hadn't imagined them. She looked absolutely out of place and, unfortunately, oblivious to the danger.

Ice sent a low whistle into the silence, alerting his brothers. He reacted before anyone, pushing through the crowd to get to her as she stepped inside. "Babe, what the fuck are you doing here?" He took her arm as gently as he knew how, which wasn't all that gentle.

She was breathing hard as if she had been running. The bodice of her dress struggled to hold her tits as she labored to find air. For the first time she really looked around the room and saw the occupants. Most had gone back to drinking and talking now that she'd been claimed, but there were a few watching closely. She was like bait thrown into a sea of sharks. Because he noticed everything, and this was his dream princess, he saw her swallow, but then she glanced back at the door looking more afraid of what was outside than what was in that bar. He recognized fear when he saw it.

"Someone after you?"

His brothers had slowly moved into position to defend her if needed, inserting their bodies between his innocent princess and the rough men and women in the bar. He knew that was why most in other clubs had gone back to their own business. Few wanted to take on Torpedo Ink in a fight. They had a certain reputation.

He lifted his hand shoulder high, tapped three times and then rested his hand again very gently on her arm. His brothers read the code. Transporter, Mechanic and Player slipped out the door, moving into the night, looking for anyone who might have been chasing her.

She looked up at him and those beautiful, lush lips parted. She smiled. Her lashes fluttered, and he nearly went to the floor. This woman had the power to send him to his knees. Holy mother. His temperature went up a million degrees and for the love of God, his cock became a steel spike and then some.

"I'm looking for someone. A friend of mine. She was wearing a vest with a tree . . ." She looked around and then indicated the Torpedo Ink jacket Storm was wearing. Storm was facing away from him, keeping an eye on the room. "Like that." She tried to peek around him, but he kept his body between her and the room.

"Like the one I'm wearing?" He turned slightly so she could see his colors.

Her smile brightened. "Exactly. You must know her. Lana?"

She stood there looking up at him as if he were a good man and would save her. He was debating whether or not he was that good. Unfortunately for her, he didn't think so. When he took a step to the side, keeping a firm hold, the light hit her face and he saw the bruises. Fuck no, he wasn't saving her. He was going to kill the worm that put those bruises on her face and fear in her eyes, and he was keeping her for himself. Someone should be protecting this woman, and *that* he could do.

"Yeah, babe, I know Lana. Let's get you a drink and we're going to talk about whoever put those bruises on your face."

He didn't mean to sound like a hard-ass, but there was frost in his voice. A promise of retaliation. Ice didn't have a lot of social graces, but he forced himself not to pull her close when she hesitated again and looked at the door. Clearly, self-preservation had set in and she wanted to run, but she thought whoever was chasing her was worse than what she faced in the bar. That didn't make sense to him. The suit couldn't possibly be as scary as a bar full of bikers.

"I've probably already had too much to drink," she hedged and tried to step back.

He had his brothers there, and because he was acting out of character, they had already backed his play. Maestro stood behind her, and she bumped into him and whirled around. Maestro had his back to her and was talking to Code. He glanced over his shoulder, murmured an apology, and turned back, but stayed firmly between her and the door.

"What's your name?" Ice said, trying to sound friendlier. She looked like she was close to panic. "Lana isn't here, but we're her family. And my sister, Alena, is here and she's as close to Lana as anyone could be. She'll know what to tell you." Deliberately he used Lana's name and the fact that he had a sister in the bar to soothe her.

She bit her lip. "I'm Soleil."

She pronounced her name with a slight French accent and it sounded like *so-lay.* He liked it. He'd always liked the French language, it sounded exotic and sexy to him. Now he knew why. Soleil. Sunshine. Yeah. He could see that.

He tried another gentle experimental tug. "Let's get a drink and find Alena."

She did the lip thing again and his cock jerked hard. If she didn't stop he might embarrass himself. He changed tactics, taking charge. Circling her back so his arm was an iron bar, he guided her toward the bar. The crowd was tight, and he had to thread his way through, but again, his brothers helped him out, moving in a diamond pattern so they could part the crowd for him.

"Yo, Ice, you gonna share that sweet little piece of ass?" someone called out.

Soleil stiffened. Ice pulled her closer to him. "Fuck you, Sanders, I don't share my woman. Anyone goes near her, they'll be spending some time in the hospital." He put menace in his voice, enough to quiet the room a second time.

Everyone turned away from them. Ice's reputation was lethal, something he wasn't eager for her to know.

He leaned down to whisper in her ear. "In here, you have to belong to someone or it can get ugly. You'll be fine. No one would dare touch you now. My brothers and I will look after you. I give you my word. You're totally safe with me." He wasn't lying.

She was already in the middle of the room. She glanced over her shoulder, looking toward the door, even as he propelled her toward the bar. There was a sea of men and women between her and escape.

He kept his arm firmly around her. "You're safe. I'm not going to let anything happen to you. Lana is a very good friend of mine, and because she's your friend as well, Torpedo Ink will look after you."

Lana's name was like magic. Ice was very aware Soleil had been crying and whoever had hit her face had struck her elsewhere as well. She walked carefully, as if protecting her body. "You need a doc? Steele's on his honeymoon about now, but we can get you to the emergency room or have Alena take a look at you."

She shook her head. "No. I can't go to the emergency room."

Definitely panic in her voice. He wanted to *kill* the bastard who'd struck her. Savage leaned against the bar right over two barstools. Savage was a man no one in their right mind ever called out. No one. Not even some drunk with an entire club behind them. He'd lay waste to most of them, and those he left alive, the rest of his brothers would send to hell.

A few times already, because Savage didn't say much, a couple of young drunks who didn't know his reputation yet and were well past self-preservation thought they could make a name for themselves. Before they got a word out, friends of the two apologized to Savage and dragged them off.

Savage straightened like a lazy panther, his cool blue eyes raking the bar as he turned toward Ice. "This your woman, Ice?"

"She's mine," Ice confirmed. "Name's Soleil."

Savage looked her over. She moved closer to Ice and he tightened his hold even more, tucking her under his shoulder protectively. He wanted to grin at Savage. The man knew how to intimidate.

"What the fuck happened to her?" Savage

87

demanded.

"Some asshole hit her," Ice said. He tipped her face up to him, using his thumb and finger. "That suit I saw you with on the street. He do this to you?" His thumb slid gently over the bruises.

Soleil looked mesmerized by him. He couldn't help himself, he very gently brushed kisses over the bruises.

"You want us to take him out for you?"

Her long, thick lashes fluttered, drawing his attention. Ice wanted to kiss them as well.

"You mean like, kill him?" Her voice was very soft. No more than a whisper, but Savage heard her, and he shot Ice a quick glance. If he was amused by her innocent question, it didn't show, but Ice knew him well enough to know he thought Soleil's lack of street smarts was funny.

"Yeah, baby, like kill him. I don't much like that he put his hands on you. Who the hell is he?" They'd find the bastard and end his days of hitting women. He'd suffer before he died if Savage or Ice got to him first.

"He was my fiancé," she admitted. "He wanted to get married here and I said no way. He wouldn't sign a prenup. Everyone has them these days, right?"

Ice helped her onto the stool and glanced at the bartender to make certain he was paying attention. Keeping a hand on her shoulder, he slid onto the bar stool beside her. Savage stayed at her back and Maestro took the bar stool next to Ice.

"You were going to marry that asshole?" Ice persisted.

"No. He sort of railroaded me. I was in a bad place, and the next thing I knew, he was there running everything. I'm not even sure how it happened. Thank God I woke up." She took the glass the bartender pushed into her hand and started fishing around for her money.

"I've got this," Ice said. "He'll put it on my tab. You were saying this asshole tried to force you to marry him?" He leaned in close and soothingly rubbed along her arm. She wore a short denim jacket, but she would feel his touch beneath the material.

She looked surprised that he was paying. Clearly, she was used to being the one to pay. The suit really was a first-class asshole. Or a con artist maybe, looking for a sugar mama. Soleil seemed too young for that.

"Thank you, Ice. That is very sweet of you."

He was pleased she actually remembered his name. The bar was loud, and she had just walked in alone and afraid. He smiled at her. "Tell me about the suit." Behind his back he signaled to his twin brother, showing his phone and mouthing "Lana." He needed Lana on his side, and she wasn't going to like what Storm was going to tell her.

Soleil took a slow sip of the whiskey and then looked at the glass. "I love the way this burns all the way down." She wasn't slurring her words, but she'd had more than one drink before she'd gotten there. That much was obvious.

Ice nodded his agreement. "Feels good, doesn't it?" She was still looking very nervous and he was afraid if it wasn't for Savage standing right behind her, she might have tried bolting. He was a little out of his depth. He didn't want to sound like her asshole for-sure-to-be-ex-fiancé. He didn't know how to talk to "nice" girls. He tended to just issue orders. Most revolved around sucking his cock. Shit.

He needed to keep this woman with him. He didn't even know why the compulsion was so strong, but that need was relentless, bone deep. Soul deep. He swore under his breath and tried to find the words that would put her at ease.

"It's loud in here, but it will clear out in

90

an hour or two. In the meantime, you think it would be a good thing to give Lana a call, so she can vouch for me? I don't want you nervous. You really are safe with me."

Immediately she put down the glass and all but sighed with relief. "I doubt if I could hear her, but maybe if I text her?"

"Good idea." He glanced back again and saw Storm on his cell talking fast and knew he was filling Lana in. Storm already knew this was the woman who had caused Ice to nearly blow their cover on the street earlier. She wasn't just anyone. Ice wanted her. For whatever reason, he might even need her. Storm would walk through hell to give Ice whatever he asked for — because he'd never asked for anything. His brothers and sisters in Torpedo Ink would do the same.

Ice's body felt cold with nerves. He'd faced guns, knives, all kinds of fights, and he'd done so without flinching. This was different. This was important, and he had absolutely no guidelines. None. He swallowed the whiskey down, feeling the burn. Needing it. How the hell was he going to get her home, where he had a chance of keeping her?

"You know, honey, I've been thinking about this prenup thing. You're right, everyone has them. He was a fool to give you up over that. I would have signed it without even looking at it in order to have you." Deliberately he brought it up again, needing her to want to stay with him in the crowded bar. He needed time. A little time.

"You would?" Her face brightened, and she leaned into him. Just a little, but it was enough to tell Ice he was on the right track.

"In a heartbeat, princess. Any man worth anything would sign one."

"He thought he was still going to get me," she said. "And when he realized I meant what I said, he —" She broke off. Her voice trembled. Her hand shook as she lifted the glass to her mouth.

Ice moved closer to her and rubbed her back soothingly. "You're safe here with us. Text Lana, she'll tell you this is the right place. No one can harm you as long as you're with us." He glanced up as his brothers came back through the door. All three shook their heads. They hadn't found any evidence of anyone chasing her.

He nodded to them and they moved in closer to protect his woman. She looked so completely out of place there, but now they had her surrounded. Alena would escort her to the women's room anytime she wanted to go. Some of the women in the bar weren't looking at her too fondly. He didn't give a shit, as long as she was sitting next to him.

Soleil took out her phone. Ice noted her hand was still shaking. He wanted to cover it, to soothe her, but she wasn't quite yet certain she was out of danger from him. Not even with the liquor. Unashamedly, Ice looked over her shoulder as she typed in her message to Lana.

Came to bar looking for you. Found Ice and others. It was bad. Worse than either of us thought.

What the fuck did that mean? He couldn't just ask her. He waited impatiently for Lana's reply. He knew she'd back him, but to have actually spoken to Soleil, given her contact information when they had just run a huge mission, meant she might know more about her situation. They'd separated, changed, made certain there wasn't so much as a speck of blood on any of them and then gotten back together, everyone wearing their colors, celebrating Steele's marriage to Breezy.

Ice will keep you safe. Don't go back to the hotel. Stay with him. He absolutely won't let anything happen to you. If you come with him, I'll see you soon.

Ice could have kissed Lana. That was put in there so subtly. Stay with Ice. He'd keep her safe. See you soon. Perfection. The seeds

93

were planted. His girl was that scared, and she needed friends. She needed to feel safe after the suit had gotten rough. He watched her carefully text Lana back.

Thank you.

"Here's what we're going to do, Soleil," he said, taking charge, because she might as well know his true nature. "We're forgetting that asshole. He's not coming in here. Even if he did, he can't touch you, there's too many of us. We're going to spend the rest of the evening having fun. We'll dance a little. Play some darts. Some pool. Drink a little. We're ignoring the rest of the world just for tonight. How does that sound? You with me, girl?"

She leaned her chin onto the heel of her hand and looked into his eyes. He was usually the one mesmerizing others with his glacier-blue crystalline eyes, but she turned the tables on him. He was sliding far past want straight to need.

"I think you're making astonishing sense. Absolute sense. I'm with you one hundred percent."

Still no slurred words, but his girl was feeling the effects. "You hungry?"

"I could eat something, but honestly, I don't want to leave yet." She glanced over her shoulder and a little shiver went through her body.

"He'll give up looking."

She shook her head and her eyes darted a second time toward the door. "He won't." Her voice dropped low.

If he hadn't been bending his head very close to her mouth, close enough to feel her lips whisper over his ear, he wouldn't have heard her.

"He has a plan."

The way she said it alarmed him. "What kind of plan?"

She shook her head and straightened, once more lifting her glass to her lips. That told him two things. She was in more trouble than he'd first realized. A fiancé who was willing to beat her was one thing to contend with, but her fear and those four little words said something else, something much more sinister. And his girl had a stubborn streak.

"If you're hungry, we can get you some food. What are you hungry for?"

She flashed him a smile that made his cock come to attention all over again. The woman was beyond his wildest dreams. Nothing made his cock hard unless he ordered it to get hard. She managed effortlessly. She didn't even have a fucking clue what she was doing. Her tits rose and fell with her breath. Pushed against the tight bodice of her sundress. Strained for release. He wanted to pull her into his lap and fill his hands with those soft curves.

"Stop looking like you're the Big Bad Wolf and you're going to eat her alive," Alena said, leaning into him from the other side. She wedged herself in between him and Maestro. "Hi," she added, leaning farther onto the bar so she could see around him. "I'm Alena."

"Soleil."

His girl smiled at his sister. He was a little leery of what Alena might do or say. She could be charming, just as Storm could. Somehow, Ice had missed out, but his twin and his sister could charm the birds out of the trees when they wanted.

Storm was staying in the background. They had a pact. If one of them met the "one," the other would fade until she was hooked. Ice thought Storm wasn't quite as fucked up as he was, so he didn't want to take the chance that his girl did it for his brother or she found out there was a nicer twin.

"I heard Ice say something about food. Pizza sound good to you? We could take over the game room, eat pizza, challenge Ice to darts or pool . . ."

96

"You're not going to hustle my girl, Alena," Ice said.

Soleil laughed. "Has it occurred to you that I might be fairly good at pool? Or darts?"

"Fairly good doesn't cut it around Alena," Ice said. He pulled out his phone and group-texted the others, setting up for pizza orders, and one by one, they headed toward the game room. A few of them going in wouldn't move many of the other clubs out, but all of them together usually sent the players scurrying. "Alena is a genuine hustler. She looks all cute and cuddly and then she takes everyone's money."

"Sounds to me like you lost a bit of money to her," Soleil said, her long lashes sweeping down.

That got him right in the gut. Or cock. Or both. His chest was so fucking tight he could barely breathe. He wanted to tell his sister to go easy. Not eat his little sunshine girl alive. Alena could. She might.

Ice rubbed his chest right over his heart. Soleil's perfect brows came down in an adorable frown. He hoped he hadn't said that word aloud. *Adorable.* He'd have to shoot someone if he had. He'd never hear the end of it.

"Are you all right?"

97

The soft concern in her voice played over his skin like the touch of fingers. Intimate. Anxious. Shit. Alena had noticed as well.

"I'm good. Just hungry."

Both women looked skeptical. He raised his hand for another round, and when the bartender delivered, he picked up both glasses and waited for his girl to slide off the barstool. Her cute little boot things hit the bar floor, and she swayed to the music for a moment before following Alena. He brought up the rear. Close. So there were no mistakes by anyone. She wasn't going to get accidentally touched. Or hit on. Or worse. Some drunken biker tried anything, Ice knew he would turn murderous instantly.

Savage moved with him on his left. Player was on his right. Both were a short distance away, just enough to fight if necessary. The rest of the club had gone inside the game room, one by one, getting the other clubs to drift on out.

"Pizza's ordered," Code called out. He was first at the dartboard.

Alena bumped her hip against Absinthe and took the darts out of his hand. "Ice thinks he can beat me. Want to put money up he can't?"

"No," Soleil corrected, shocking him. "I

98

implied *I* could beat you. Ice had no belief in me."

Code spun around. "You sure you want to take on the champ, honey? She's never lost."

"I've lost," Alena contradicted immediately. "More than once. Just rarely, and never to an out —" She broke off, looking at her brother.

"A what?" Soleil prompted. "And how much money are we betting?"

Ice groaned, put down the drinks and circled his arm around her waist, pulling her back into him. Before she could stiffen, or protest, he put his lips against her ear. "Seriously, princess, Alena is amazing at darts. And pool. Don't play her at pool."

"You're a disappointment, Mr. Ice." Soleil sounded haughty, as only a princess could.

He wasn't impressed. He stepped back. "Let's see what you've got, Miss Confidence."

She laughed and watched as Alena put a twenty on the table. Ice stepped forward to put up the money for Soleil, but she put a hand on his arm and shook her head.

"I don't ever have someone else put up my gambling money. This is on me to win or lose. If you want to bet, that's on you."

Her hand went to the inside of her jacket and she pulled out a matching twenty and set it beside Alena's.

"Girl's got class," Alena observed.

There was a murmur of approval from the other members of the club. Immediately, the real bets began, with Code collecting the money from club members betting on each of the women. Surprisingly, Savage bet on Soleil along with Ice. They stepped back and gave the women plenty of room to maneuver.

"You know the rules, honey?" Master asked Soleil.

"I think so," she replied, using her sweet, not-too-sure bullshit tone. She batted her eyelashes at him. "I'll catch on. I'm a fast learner."

Ice wanted to kiss her. She didn't have a chance in hell, but she didn't back down from a fight either. Alena winked at him and then threw her first dart. Triple seventeen. Two went straight and one landed just outside it.

Soleil took her turn and managed to hit one triple seventeen and two just outside it. The match went that way, with Alena just ahead by a dart or two, but Soleil was always very close. Ice was impressed. It was clear Alena was equally impressed. She hadn't gone easy on her, and the match was very close.

Soleil winced as her last dart was thrown. It was so close to the triple but missed by just a hair. A groan went up around the room, but Code immediately paid out.

"I guess I'll need a rematch," Soleil said. "It's been a while since I played, and Ice is right, you're very good."

"I'm going to concede that you're good as well," Ice said, "but no one is in Alena's league."

"Double down?" Alena challenged.

Soleil hesitated. Ice put his arms around her again, his lips against her ear. "I'm serious, babe, she always wins, it's like some kind of curse on the rest of us when we play her. I think you're probably as good, but she's got this luck on her side none of us can ignore."

"I was so close."

"That's what she does to suck you in," he cautioned.

"Hey." Alena glared at him. "I'm not sucking her in. She played that brilliantly. Give her credit."

He was, but he didn't want her to lose a lot of money.

"I want to play again," Soleil decided.

"Then let me put up the money," Ice said. He glared right back at his sister. "I might have to take you out behind the barn," he added.

Soleil laughed, the sound teasing every one of his senses. "I can tell you really are brother and sister. Aside from the fact that both of you have those beautiful eyes, your hair is nearly the exact same color. And you sound affectionate, even when you're threatening her."

"Pizza's here," Master announced.

Torpedo Ink members weren't shy in the least about grabbing slices out of the box. There were no plates, but they stuffed food as fast as possible into their mouths. Ice had to grab a couple of slices nearly out of Absinthe's hands in order to get any for his woman and himself.

"Do you all have to be fuckin' morons all the time? Get some manners."

Soleil laughed again as she took the slice and ate it just like the rest of them, hands, no plate, napkin barely there. Somehow, she managed to look much more refined than his brothers. That sound, her genuine laughter bubbling up, made his gut twist into a tight knot. He hadn't known laughter. Not real. Not like that. Her laughter was infectious. Ice looked around him and found that all the others were just as affected by her laughter as he was. Maybe not in the same way. He had to adjust his jeans a little to give him some breathing room.

Alena leaned against the pool table, eating a slice as well, grinning at his girl. He couldn't tell what was behind that smile. She gestured toward the dartboard, and to his consternation, Soleil nodded and put more money down. Immediately his brothers began the betting. As before, Savage and Ice bet against Alena. This time Storm and Absinthe did as well.

Soleil stepped up to the line with confidence. Her body posture was different than it had been. She'd been a little hesitant before each throw, but not this time. The darts cooperated. Straight. True. Three triple twenties, dead center. The room went silent.

Alena took her spot. "I can see that first game was more of a practice round for you."

"I haven't played in a long while," Soleil reiterated. She nabbed another slice of pizza and washed a bite down with her whiskey.

Alena scored two triple twenties and one triple six. She stepped back to allow Soleil to take her place. Soleil studied the board while she finished her pizza and then she blew on the end of her dart. The room went quiet as she stepped up.

She hit two triple seventeens and a triple twenty.

Alena grinned. "Finally. A worthy opponent. That's the way it's done, boys."

In spite of the fact that every member of Torpedo Ink left in Vegas was in the room, there wasn't a sound. No one drank. No one ate pizza. They were mesmerized by the two women throwing darts. Alena normally carried her own darts with her, but they were working, and she hadn't brought them. If Soleil had her own set of darts, she wasn't using them. Both women were playing with the bar's darts.

Ice had watched Alena wipe up the floor everywhere she played. He knew she could give the champions a run for their money. Soleil clearly was as good as or better than his sister. She was fast, effortless and confident. He found himself a little in awe of the two women. Alena was used to winning, but she was clearly pleased with Soleil's abilities, and when she lost by one dart, she immediately beamed at his woman.

"That was the best game I think I've ever played against someone," she conceded and scooped up the last piece of pepperoni pizza. "You earned your money."

Soleil flashed a smile that matched Alena's. "I haven't played in a while either and certainly not with anyone who knows how to play."

"You as good at pool?" Alena asked.

Ice smirked as he collected his money. Savage didn't smirk, but he pocketed the cash as did Storm and Absinthe.

"Teach you not to bet against my woman," Ice said.

"Who knew?" Master said. "She looks like she's never been in a bar in her life."

"Guess you didn't notice she was drinking whiskey," Savage said.

"I was too busy looking at her . . . er . . ." He hesitated when Ice glared at him.

"Shoes," he settled on.

The others erupted into laughter.

"Is something wrong with my shoes?" Soleil asked, looking down at the little booties on her feet and then back up at Ice. Her eyes were wide, lashes long and dark and tipped up at the ends. She looked back down to her feet again, frowning a little.

The booties came to just above her ankles, making her look even more delicate and girl-next-door than Ice could almost stand. He was a little in love with her shoes whether Master had actually been looking at them or not. And then she had those eyes. He could stare into them all night long.

Another roar of laughter went up at

Soleil's question. Ice wrapped his arm around her waist. "Pay no attention to them, princess, they're not quite out of the caves yet."

"I suppose you are," Master challenged.

Ice wasn't going to look at the front of his woman and the way the bodice of her little sundress hugged her tits. He would join his brethren in the cave and right now, he was doing his best to gain his woman's trust.

"Seriously, Soleil, don't even look at them. They don't know any better. Do you need another drink?" He glanced at Maestro, indicating he wanted her glass replaced the moment she was finished with her whiskey. He thought a few more drinks would help his cause.

Soleil laughed again, the sound brushing against his skin as if her fingers were touching him, or maybe a thousand tongues tasting him. Champagne bubbles bursting over him. Whatever the analogy, it didn't matter. His reaction was physical. His body worked. All on its own. Without his command. It felt like fucking paradise, and she'd done that with just her laugh.

Just like that all laughter died and the room went electric. Ice turned toward the door to watch the newcomer sauntering through. He was average height but walked like he could handle himself — like he owned the bar. There was no one behind him, no one to back him up. He was absolutely confident, and it showed. He wore his colors like his own skin.

FOUR

"Get behind me and stay there," Ice ordered Soleil in a voice that brooked no argument. He swept her behind him before she could move on her own to obey. He was grateful she didn't protest, but she did lean out to peek around him.

"Pierce. Didn't know you were in town," he greeted. Storm moved to the left of Pierce. Savage slipped in on the other side. The rest of Torpedo Ink spread out behind them. They would take their cue from him. He was Alena's older brother and he was the one calling the shots without Czar or Steele there. He would always call them for Alena or Storm.

Pierce wore his colors with every bit of the same pride with which Torpedo Ink wore theirs. He was Diamondback, one of the largest clubs in the world. One of the strongest. Torpedo Ink resided in their territory and was technically considered a support club for the Diamondbacks.

Pierce nodded at the others as he came right into the center of the room, but his gaze rested on Alena. She was artfully draped on the pool table looking the way only Alena could look. Her jeans fit the curve of her butt lovingly, while her tight tank barely held in her straining breasts. She stood up very slowly, a lazy, sexy move that was all Alena. Ice wanted to shake her. He sent her a look of reprimand, but she was Alena and she ignored it.

"Heard you were in town celebrating. Where's the happy couple?" Pierce asked Ice, but he still didn't look at him. He looked only at Alena.

"They took off for their honeymoon. More to the point, what are you doing in Vegas? Specifically, what are you doing here? This is a little beneath you, isn't it? Slumming?"

"I have business here. Or perhaps a better way to put it would be I have unfinished business, and since she's here in this bar, so am I."

Ice wanted to take three steps forward and end Pierce right there. He could move with blurring speed. The moment he took that first step, his brothers would distract Pierce. He wouldn't need that edge; he had already planned every step out and each counter

Pierce might try. Pierce would drop and they'd be gone. But there was Soleil . . . He could feel her hands gripping the back of his jacket.

Alena was sacred. She'd lived through hell, but she was alive, and that was more than any other female other than Lana could say that had attended their "school." Ice and Storm had managed to keep her alive by bargaining with their bodies. By allowing torture and rape. By agreeing to monstrous terms.

Pierce's club wouldn't welcome her, men or women. She wore another club's colors on her back, on her skin. Just like every one of the brethren, she *was* Torpedo Ink. He had no idea what was really going on between his little sister and the enforcer for the Mendocino chapter of the Diamondbacks, but for Pierce to saunter alone into a bar filled with members of a club he knew were lethal, something big had to be drawing him.

Ice swung his gaze to Alena. She looked cool. Nonchalant. As if she didn't have a care in the world, but she had learned, just as the rest of them, to hide her true feelings behind a mask.

"Not sure why you're here, Pierce," Alena said. She settled once more over the pool table, looking a little haughty.

Ice winced. His sister sounded as sultry as hell. He sent her a reprimanding frown. The only indication that she noticed that he'd gone completely glacier was the small swallow. Her gaze hadn't shifted from Pierce, but she'd seen his frown.

"Just want to talk, Alena. Walk with me."

It was more an order than an invitation, and immediately Ice made a small movement toward Pierce. Alena's breath hissed out. Behind him, Soleil's hand twisted in his jacket, as if she could hold him back. Her hand trembled and he felt it right through his colors. She had no idea what was happening, but she could feel the terrible tension surrounding them.

"You want to talk to him?" Ice asked. He waited. A heartbeat. Two. The room was so still, no one moved. No one made a sound. Waiting, just as he was for Alena's answer.

"Yes."

Ice switched to his native language. "This is a dangerous game you're playing, Alena. It could get both of you killed. This man touches you without your consent or allows you to get hurt in any way, I will kill him. I won't care what club he's in or how many brothers he has. I will kill him. Do you understand what I'm saying to you?"

Alena nodded.

"I did things to protect you. I sold my soul to protect you. No one hurts you. No one, Alena. His club will not want you."

"I know, Ice." Her voice was soft. She spoke in the same language, keeping her eyes on him.

"Let him underestimate you. Let them all underestimate you. But this man will know me. He won't take you without seeing who I am and what I'll do to him if anything happens to you. Do we have an understanding?"

Alena nodded. "Yes."

"And you still want to go with him?"

"I need to," she admitted, her gaze still meeting his.

Ice was glad she was really looking at him. She needed to see him for what he was. What they all were. She needed that reminder. She was theirs. She belonged with them and she always would. He knew if he said she couldn't go with Pierce, she wouldn't. She was a fully patched member of Torpedo Ink. She was a lethal assassin. She was also his little sister and his word was law.

"Storm and Savage will shadow you. Don't try to shake them. That will get him killed as well. Don't go near his club. He tries to take you any place they are, walk away. You get me, Alena? You walk."

"I give you my word."

Pierce hadn't moved during their conversation. Soleil kept her hand on his back, probably because his voice was pitched low and harsh. Ice lifted his gaze to Pierce and waited for the man to look at him.

"You need to see what I am," Ice said quietly. "It doesn't matter that all of us are like me. You just need to see me. She will be safe with you, no matter what your club thinks about her."

Pierce took his time looking into Ice's eyes. Seeing him. Seeing the ice-cold killer that he was. Ice didn't hide a thing. He wanted the man to know what he would be dealing with if there was one bruise on his younger sister. Just one.

"I get you," Pierce replied. "And I saw you back when we first met. She's safe with me. She always will be." He held out his hand to Alena.

She didn't move until Ice gave her a barely perceptible nod. She straightened again, a slow, sensual movement that set Ice's teeth on edge. He believed in equal rights. Well. He didn't mind his sister hooking up as long as it was safe. There was nothing safe about Pierce or his club. Ice had no doubts that

113

Alena could kill him. He wouldn't ever be expecting it from her, but she had some kind of soft spot for the man, and she might hesitate. If she killed him, she'd be running for the rest of her life.

Alena knew Ice. She knew he meant what he said. If Pierce did anything to her, if a single member of his club did, if she tripped on the sidewalk, he would hunt the enforcer down and kill him — and most likely it would be a slow and very painful death, because Ice could be all about that shit when it was called for.

He waited until Alena and Pierce had exited the game room and his gaze settled on his twin. Storm didn't hesitate. He went out the back exit. Savage went with him.

Soleil watched the two men go and then she looked up at Ice. "Who was that man?"

"He belongs to a very big club and he's bad news, especially for Alena."

Instantly Soleil felt guilty. She liked Alena. If she wasn't there, wouldn't Ice have gone after her to make certain no one hurt her? She bit down hard on her lower lip, frowning, trying to think of the right thing to do. Alena had a family and they were clearly worried about her. Soleil had never had a family, but she'd always wanted one. She'd fantasized over that very thing more times than she wanted to admit.

She didn't want to leave. She wanted to stay with Ice, with his friends. Why couldn't she have met him a long time ago, before Winston? Just a long time ago, when she would have thrown caution to the wind and gone with every impulse she'd ever had? He was a beautiful man. Gorgeous. Sweet. He made her feel beautiful and hot as hell. When he looked at her, she wanted to strip right there and wind her body around his. She wanted to go home with him and be part of his very cool family. But she was all about doing the right thing, wasn't she? Shouldn't she?

"Will she be all right?"

Ice tucked a stray strand of her dark hair behind her ear. Just his touch made her heart accelerate. Her breasts ached. She could feel her nipples push against the material of her dress. She *was* worried about Alena. She wasn't trying to be selfish, even if she did secretly want to get Ice so drunk, he'd sign the prenup she had burning in her pocket and take her to a twenty-four-hour wedding chapel. She felt guilty just at the thought slipping into her mind, but it had, and she couldn't get it out. She could seduce him. She wanted to seduce him. She wanted him with every breath she took.

"You saw Savage and Storm slip out after them. Alena can handle herself, but just in case, they'll follow. It's hard to spot them if they don't want to be seen."

It took a lot to force herself to offer, "I can leave, Ice. I put all of you in a very bad position, and that's the last thing I wanted to do. Your sister was very sweet to me. All of you have been." She looked around as if trying to spot the door. She didn't really know what she was going to do if he told her to leave. "If you need to go after her . . ." She trailed off.

Ice slipped his arm around her. "Alena can take care of herself. She's like Lana. They trained with us in self-defense. If Pierce decided to be so stupid as to throw a punch at her, she'd wipe up the floor with him. Two of her brothers went to ensure she is fine just because we do that sort of thing with one another. They'll spend however long it takes on a rooftop watching over her."

Wouldn't it be wonderful to have brothers, a family who would stay on a rooftop for however long it took just to watch over you? She would never have that, but she was glad Alena did.

She tried hard not to let Ice see her sigh of relief. She had a chance of seducing him. She knew he was thinking he was going to get her drunk and get lucky. She was all for that. *All* for it. She wasn't about to tell him she just didn't get drunk. She didn't. She didn't know why, but for some reason, it didn't happen. But she could get to the feel-good stage, and she knew how to make it all work. She'd let him think she was getting there so he could have the fun of seducing her and she could reap the benefits.

She'd have to be very, very careful not to let herself go beyond sex though, despite her longing for more. Just think sex. No prenup signings. No wedding chapels. No I-give-the-best-blow-jobs-in-the-world and you'll-want-me-every-morning-for-the-rest-of-your-life-biker-boy claims. She was going to die soon. Winston and his friends would find her and kill her. She couldn't involve someone else or they might kill them the way they had Kevin. She couldn't be that selfish and take a chance. Just enjoy one night doing what she'd always fantasized about. That shouldn't be too much to ask for.

Ice tapped out code with his fingers on his thigh, letting the others know this woman was his. The one. And he was taking her home. First, seduction. He'd started without her being aware of it. They'd been trained in seduction. They were very, very good at anything sexual. The first step was to get to know what she wanted most. He only had a few hours to pull it off, but he was certain he was up to the task, if his body would leave him the hell alone.

He'd never seduced a mark when it mattered to him. Seduction, as a rule, usually led to assassination. He was always in full command of his body, so it was easy to concentrate on the mark. One didn't make a mistake if one wasn't emotionally or physically involved. They could use any means necessary if their bodies were in control. This was the first time in his life when he didn't have the control over his body — or mind — he needed.

It pissed him off and yet at the same time, he was intrigued and exhilarated. He had to have her consent. Once she gave it, the club would expect her to keep her word, and he would enforce it. One didn't ever go back on one's word. It was their code. She would have to abide by the code no matter what happened.

Maestro handed both of them another glass of whiskey, gave Ice a faint grin and slipped away, although, like the others, he didn't go far, shielding Ice and his woman from other bikers in the main part of the bar.

Soleil stared down into the glass, swirled the liquid and shook her head. "I'm beginning to feel this. Maybe I shouldn't drink any more."

Ice gave her his reassuring smile. He was a good-looking man and he knew it. Women threw themselves at him. He'd never gone without female attention. "No worries, princess. I told you I'd look after you. In any case, we're going to dance, and you'll work it off."

"We are?"

"You said you liked to dance. Or at least you were swaying to the music, and it seems like a good idea."

He led her toward the door but paused just inside the game room. "What is the one thing you want most in the world?" He leaned against the wall, pulling her close, so the two of them were cocooned in their own little world.

Just before she answered, Transporter jostled her back, nearly pushing her into Ice. He immediately swung her to the wall and positioned himself in front of her protectively. He placed one hand close to her head and leaned close.

Soleil's eyes went wide and shone at him. "Thank you, Ice." Her voice was breathless. She was looking at him like he was a knight in shining armor. She didn't see the killer everyone else saw. She didn't see his black soul or his need for the kind of dirty, kinky sex nice girls would run screaming from.

He had to be careful not to fall under her spell. She was sweet. He'd never had sweet in his life. "Tell me the one thing you really want out of life."

"A family." She regarded him over the rim of her glass. "I've never had a family."

"You had parents."

"They died when I was very young, and I spent most of my life in boarding schools or hotels for holidays." She smiled, but there was sadness in her eyes. Reality. Truth. "I think I'm really that proverbial poor little rich girl."

So, she had money. He suspected as much, or she wouldn't have been insisting on a prenup with that suit bastard who was going to die. He deliberately took a sip of his whiskey and she followed the action, but she didn't really take that much of a drink.

"My club is my family," Ice said softly and leaned in closer when Maestro stepped back and bumped him. His face was almost in her shoulder, his lips sliding along her skin

120

as he spoke. She had the softest skin and she smelled liked heaven.

He kept his voice deliberately pitched low, intimate. "My brother and sister are my family. Never had parents that I really remember. Czar, our president, was my parent when he was ten. Looking for a woman who wants to make a life with me. Have my children. Make us a home. I'd die for my club, but I want my own woman, one worthy of living for."

There was so much there to intrigue a woman, especially a woman who craved and needed a family and protection. He felt the shiver run through her body at the touch of his lips on her bare skin. "Been lookin' a long time for the right woman. Not too many women want a home and family anymore." She was compassionate. She hadn't wanted to leave, but she wanted Alena safe.

Her eyes widened. "Ice, that's not true."

He shrugged his shoulders and inched forward, just enough to press his chest against her tits. They were soft. Full. He ached to pull the front of her dress down and expose those beauties, so he could feast on them. She moved her body, and her breasts moved seductively against his chest. His entire body shuddered in reaction. Hell.

He was never going to pull this off if he couldn't control himself.

"It's true for me, princess. I talk rough. I am rough. I don't know how to talk right to a woman." He ran one finger down her cheek to her chin and then pretended to take another sip of his whiskey. "Torpedo Ink has a code. Once in, once you give your word, you're held to that. Scares the crap out of women. They think all sorts of things."

She pushed at the bottom of his glass and he had no choice but to drink it.

She smiled and put her glass to her lips and took a healthy drink. Her face was flushed, and her tits were rising and falling with every breath she drew, nipples hard little peaks, pushing at the thin material of her dress, scraping across his chest. To Ice, they felt like flames, burning through his tight tee to brand his skin. It was all he could do not to strip her bare and take her right there against the wall. He kept reminding himself he was in this for the long haul. This was no game. This was for life.

"Well," she said softly. An invitation whether she knew it or not. "What does it mean?"

"It means you're family. A woman takes me on, she's family to the club. All the way in. She's mine. All the way in. Whatever it takes to work it out."

"No one's like that anymore." Suspicion edged her voice. It was there in her eyes. The hope. The disbelief.

He took her glass and handed it behind him. One of his brothers took both glasses. He was a little surprised that his glass had been empty as well. He put both hands on the wall beside her head and leaned in, creating an even more intimate cocoon.

"Unfortunately, I'm not the greatest catch. None of us are. We're outcasts for a reason."

She was nearly holding her breath. Not quite, but enough so her breathing sounded ragged. He liked that sound. Knew he would hear it when he fucked her brains out. It was all he could do not to take a bite out of her. Her lashes fluttered, drawing his attention to her eyes.

Soleil was staring up at him and his heart accelerated. His cock hurt. Actually hurt. Fuck. He was losing it because he couldn't control his body. He had to get a lock on that immediately. He loved it and he fucking hated it.

"I hear about clubs. They share women, don't they?"

He took a breath as something dark and

ugly swept over him. "Any man touches my woman, he won't be on this earth long. That scare you, baby?" He tucked another stray strand of her hair behind her ear with infinite gentleness. "She's protected. My club will protect her. Every single man. They know better than to touch her." He touched the bruise on her face, just a gentle brush of his fingers. "I don't hurt women or children. That is something you can always count on. The bastard who put these bruises on you had better run. If I find him, he isn't going to be standin' for very long." Ice poured the sound of truth in his statement. He meant every word.

"That doesn't scare me, Ice," she said.

He stared at her mouth for far too long. This was a slow seduction, not slam her against the wall and fuck her until they both couldn't move. That would come much later. He had to make certain she fell hard, fell for everything. Hell. He was falling hard. He didn't even know what was happening to him.

"Come on, baby, they're playing my kind of dancing music. Nice and slow so I can hold you tight." He took her hand, brought it up to his mouth so he could brush a kiss across her knuckles and then led her to the small dance floor, hoping to distract her, or him — he wasn't certain which.

He didn't know shit about dancing, but he could hold her close and move around. The music had slowed down, which was good. He drew her into his arms, pulling her tightly against him so that he could feel her soft tits against his chest again. He was addicted to the feeling. His body reacted of its own accord, and he felt the savage ache move through him like a wave. His blood pooled hotly in his groin. He fucking loved it. This woman could do what no other woman in all the years since he was a young boy had been able to do. His body chose her.

Her arms slid around his neck. She linked her fingers at his nape, swaying with the music. He caught the rhythm and they were moving, locked together in a haze of lust and whiskey. Her head settled on his chest, ear over his heart, and he wondered if she could hear it pounding. She surrounded him with some unidentifiable fragrance, and he was lost in it. She smelled like paradise and sin.

Neither moved when the music stopped, just swaying on the dance floor until the next song started. This was slow as well, and he knew one of his brothers had selected the song for him. He dropped his head to her shoulder, nuzzling close, his breath against her neck. She didn't stop him, not even when he tasted her skin.

Her breath turned a little ragged, and he allowed one hand to slide down her back to the curve of her ass. He loved her ass and the way it swayed when she walked. Looking at her walking away gave him the hard-on of a lifetime. But then there were her tits. She had them, more than a handful on her small frame. Soft. Her nipples were hard and pushing into his chest. His hand slid lower, shaping the curve of her ass. He rubbed gently. Little circles. His palm cupping and then once again rubbing.

His tongue found her ear and traced it. "You're so beautiful." He whispered it, meaning it. "You have the prenup that asshole didn't sign with you?" He felt her heart jump and then pound hard right through the thin layer of her dress.

Her head tipped up until her mouth was against his throat. "In my pocket." Her lips slid along his throat.

"That's my girl." His teeth closed over her earlobe and tugged gently.

He crowded the edge of the floor closest to the game room. His brothers moved around him, forming a wall so they could sway together. So Ice could continue his slow seduction, because this woman was his. She didn't know it, but she was coming home with him.

"You want another drink?" He tipped her face up to his and took her mouth because he couldn't stop himself. He was rough. Demanding. She tasted sweeter than anything he'd ever had. Once he started kissing her, he found himself lost in her taste. Wanting more. Slightly obsessed.

She was pure fire, pouring into him. Sugar. Spice. Cinnamon candy. He tried to tell himself to stop, that it was the whiskey, but he dragged her closer until they were nearly sharing the same skin. If he could have gotten their clothes off right there, and still kept her, he would have stripped her naked and laid her out right on the pool table. Instead, he slid his hand under her jacket, sliding it up gently to first cup the soft weight of her tits, his mouth on hers, lighting a match to all that whiskey.

They both ignited. Hot. Crazy. She didn't stop him. She couldn't possibly be that far gone yet, but she didn't stop him even though they were right there on the dance floor. His heart went crazy, beating triple time. She was fucking perfect. Before he could blow it, he slid his fingers deftly into the pocket of her jacket and lifted her wallet, sliding it very carefully into the pocket of his jeans. His mouth never left hers, and the flames devoured them both.

There was a roaring in his ears. A jackhammer drilling at his head. He was devouring fire, and those flames raced through his bloodstream straight to his groin. Nothing in his life had ever felt like Soleil's soft body melting into his, or the kisses that consumed him with living fucking flames. They rushed through his body like a firestorm completely out of control.

Out of control. His legs felt flickering flames sparking up from his toes to his thighs. His belly had a conflagration rolling in it. What the fuck? Did everyone else in the world feel this way when they kissed, because he'd kissed a thousand women and . . . absolutely nothing. *Nothing.*

There was no way this woman was getting away from him. No fucking way. He had to stop before he couldn't. Already his body was not his own. Still, she was kissing him back. Her arms were wound tightly around his neck, her body was pressed so close she couldn't fail to feel the bulge in the front of his jeans, but she kissed him back. She poured that fire right down his throat, stroked her tongue along his, until he couldn't see straight.

Lightning seemed to be streaking through him, each strike directly on his cock. That particular part of his anatomy seemed to have a mind of its own. Pulsing. Throbbing. Scorching hot, just like her mouth. Like her soft, perfect tits. Hell. He had to stop, or there wasn't going to be any stopping.

Ice forced himself to lift his head. The best he could do was put his forehead against hers and try to breathe through the fire. She was breathing hard too. Her tits were moving with every ragged breath, the feeling like an exquisite fire, flames licking at him, threatening to devour him. It was so fucking perfect he didn't want to let her go. Who knew the girl next door could turn into a fiery, sinful temptress? Maybe, just maybe, he was going to get it all with her. He could lead her down the path he needed her to be on slowly, but with that kind of fire, she might just put up with and even like his needs.

"What were we doing? Do you remember?"

Her mouth curved. He was fixated on her full lower lip. On that angelic bow. Holy shit, his mind was chaotic, filled with all kinds of erotic images. He had a plan, and he needed to have his head clear enough to carry it out. His brothers would help him all they could, but it was up to him to seduce his woman into consenting to everything he needed her to agree to.

"Not really."

"Where the fuck did you learn to kiss like that?" he demanded.

She smiled up at him, her eyes shining bright, her feathery lashes fluttering just a little as she blushed. He loved that she blushed. He could imagine her entirely naked, her skin a soft rose all laid out for him like a banquet.

"That wasn't me, Ice, that was all you. I've never had kisses like that before."

God. Her innocence. Neither had he, but he wasn't about to admit it. "Let's get another drink and cool down. We can play pool. Alena isn't here to challenge you, but I've played a time or two and might give you a run for your money."

She nodded. "Another drink would be perfect."

He took her hand and led her back into the game room and over to the pool table. She looked around, spotted the ladies' room and pointed. He walked her over to it, stepped in first to assure himself no one was inside before he allowed her in. As she started deeper into the room, he caught the front of her dress there in the doorway and pulled her back to him.

He kissed her again, over and over, feeding off her fire, demanding she kiss him back because he needed that firestorm rolling through his belly into his groin to show him there was something human left in him after all. He could *feel.* He hadn't believed it possible, and in a short time this angelic creature had turned his world upside down. Heat rushed through his veins like a fireball. Flames engulfed him. His heart jerked hard in his chest. His arms were steel bars, a cage surrounding her. This woman. This sweet, far-too-innocent woman he was never going to give up.

He knew it was wrong, but he just didn't give a fuck. She didn't belong out there in a world where she wasn't protected from predators like him. He could do that. He could keep her safe, and she could damn well make him feel human when he'd lost that ability too long ago. Every fucking thing in the world had a price. Everything — especially safety.

His mouth left hers and trailed fire over her chin and down her throat. Deliberately, taking a chance, he dragged the front of her dress down to find the curves of her tits. He planned on apologizing later. After all, he'd been so far gone he wasn't thinking straight.

The trouble was, it was the truth.

Her soft curves were fuller than he'd thought. So beautiful. Round and high. Jutting toward the heat of his mouth, wanting freedom. He bent his head and took the left one deep into his mouth, tongue flattening her nipple to the roof of his mouth. Stroking caresses.

Soleil's head fell back, her tit pushing deeper, as if she were feeding herself to him. Her hands came up, one under her breast, the other at the back of his head, holding him there. It was hot. It was sexy. He heard himself groan, and it shocked him. He stroked over and over with his tongue, suckling, and then, his cock pulsing in time to his heart, dared to use the edge of his teeth. Carefully. Almost gently. An exquisite torture.

She groaned, and both his heart and his cock jumped. She was beyond perfection. Beyond anything he could have conjured up on his darkest night, when he was so in need, he didn't think he could make it one more second let alone through the long night.

Abruptly, before it was too late for both of them, he pulled back, using his crystalline blue eyes unashamedly. "I'm so sorry, Soleil. I've never lost it like that before in my life." He poured sincerity into his voice, although for the first time he was telling the truth.

Very gently he pulled the top of her dress up. "Really, baby, I'm sorry. Must be the fuckin' liquor and the fact that you kiss like sin."

She touched his face, a barely there whisper of her fingers across his mouth. His heart stuttered in his chest. "You weren't the only one, Ice. I lost it too."

He could fall in love with her right there in the fucking ladies' room of the bar. "I'll be right outside." Getting her another drink. Making sure his plan was carried out step by step. Losing her wasn't an option.

He stepped back out of the room, giving her privacy and his body a reprieve. The moment the door closed with Soleil inside, his brothers crowded around him.

Soleil knew she was going to burn in hell forever. This was so wrong. It didn't matter that he was trying to seduce her. It didn't even matter why she'd come to the biker bar in the first place. She'd come and she'd chosen to stay. That had been her choice, and she'd stayed because of Ice. She wanted him to seduce her. She wanted to have a night of pure, perfect, tipsy sex with a gor-

133

geous biker like Ice. But more than anything, she wanted to keep him.

She wanted to keep his friends, who thought they were so cleverly helping him with his plan. The hand-off of glasses was almost cute. The bumps to bring him closer to her. The way they chose the music so he could dance with her. They really were like a family, trying to help their brother get what he wanted. She loved that he wanted her.

Ice had almost managed to make her forget what had made her run from the hotel and her life. She hated her life. She really hated Winston. She detested who she'd become over the years. It wasn't who she was inside. She was *this* girl. The one in the bar, plying the gorgeous man with drinks, just as he was doing to her, in the hopes of getting her way.

What were the real chances of riding off into the sunset on the back of his bike, far from her life? Probably zero. She rubbed her temples and looked at herself in the mirror. If she really did seduce him into marriage, how would she keep him? She clearly wasn't all that interesting. She didn't have anything but money to offer him, and he was a biker. He liked being free. Sex? He probably got that on the daily. It wasn't even ethical. Moral. What was she thinking? Was she really that desperate?

The answer was yes. She was so damn tired of being alone. Of hotels. Of silence. Or disgusting, vile people like Winston, and now she was actually thinking of becoming one and tricking Ice into marriage. It wasn't like trapping him. He had a choice, but not if he was drunk. Her conscience wasn't going to let her do it. That had always been her problem. She wanted to be a bad girl, but there was always that moment when she weighed whether she *should* do something against whether she *wanted* to do it.

It had been so hot when Ice had touched her on the dance floor, rubbing the cheeks of her bottom, and then in the doorway of the ladies' room, pulling down the top of her dress. She almost wanted someone to see. It was just hot. He'd been so frantic, as if he couldn't resist her. As if her body were so incredibly seductive, he had to have her right there, right in front of the world to show them she belonged to him. She loved that. She'd always wanted that. Craved it. She wanted to show the world he belonged to her. He was everything she'd ever wanted, and all she had to do was work it a little. Finesse a bit. Flirt. Drink.

She rubbed at her temples, wishing her

life had been different. Wishing just once she had the chance to do things over, to do them differently. Winston wanted her dead. He was going to kill her. Sooner or later it would happen. She hadn't had a chance to live her life at all. To be herself. To laugh and be ridiculous, to ride off with the hottest man in the bar. To do one single thing she'd dreamt or fantasized of doing. She was going to die, and it was going to be ugly, and she was going to do that with all kinds of regrets. She was tired of always doing what was right; it hadn't gotten her anywhere.

She had no one to turn to. This could very well be her last chance to have anything that remotely resembled anything she wanted. She found tears running down her face and wiped them away. She didn't deserve to cry, not when she even contemplated for one moment the idea of matching Ice drink for drink, knowing she wouldn't be drunk, seducing him and trying to get a ring on his finger. She'd lost her mind. She was as bad as Winston.

"You sure about this?" Maestro asked. "She's a fuckin' innocent, Ice. She isn't like Breezy, who grew up in the life, or even Anya, who grew up in a shelter and bar-

136

tended rough crowds. Blythe knew what she was gettin' into. This girl . . . she's like some sort of —" He broke off, shaking his head. "She doesn't belong, brother."

"She belongs with me," Ice said as they made their way back to the game room. "She absolutely belongs with me. She's scared out of her fuckin' mind. Someone's hurt her, and they're still after her. She needs protection."

"We can give her protection, Ice," Keys reminded. "Without seducing her. Or gettin' her drunk. She needs it, she's a woman, we'll give it."

Ice shook his head. "You're not hearin' what I'm sayin'."

"A woman like that, Ice, you take her on like this, there's no goin' back," Maestro reiterated. "You'll end up watchin' over her for the rest of your life. No more women. No more women in the plural. She'll be your only. Hell, she doesn't even get that she's sexier than hell. She walked into a place like this wearin' that dress and lookin' like a fuckin' angel. Everywhere you go, someone is going to be challengin' you for her."

There were nods all the way around. Ice shrugged. His hand closed into a tight fist. "I have no problem with giving up other women. I was fuckin' tired of tellin' my cock to cooperate. Woman goes down on me, the damn thing won't work until I tell it to. With her, my cock is going to stand up all on his own. Fuckin' happy to see her. To feel her."

"We all got that problem, Ice. You don't take on a woman like that just to put a little steel in your dick," Keys pointed out.

"You don't get it, it isn't about my cock, it's about feelin' something. Actually being alive. She makes me feel alive."

"Fuck her, then, Ice," Player said. "But you tie yourself to her and she tries to walk when she finds out we aren't the band of merry men she thinks we are, or that you're not Mr. Nice Guy, you're going to really lose your shit."

"I wouldn't let her leave," Ice said. "She makes that commitment, she's mine. All in. She doesn't get to walk."

"She won't understand the consequences," Absinthe said. "You know she won't. She's probably walked away from everything difficult she's ever run into. She's got money. Anyone can see that."

"It doesn't matter if she understands or not. There's a code we live by. She takes me on, she lives with the code," Ice said. His voice turned hard. Dripped with glacier cold. His eyes had gone hard like twin blue diamonds. He meant what he said.

"It's a trap," Maestro said. "You're fuckin' putting that girl in a trap and she doesn't have a hope in hell of getting free."

"Now you're beginnin' to understand," Ice said. "She's mine, and I'm not givin' her up, so give up arguin'. You all know me when I make up my mind. If I don't have this woman, I don't exist anymore. That's the fuckin' bottom line."

There was a small silence. "I think Ice just put it on the line," Code said. "What do you need, brother?"

Maestro shook his head. "I hope you know what you're doin', brother, but you need help, we're here for you. Call the shots. We'll back your play."

Ice was grateful to his brothers. He knew they would back him when he laid it out for them, although he doubted if they realized he meant every word. He tended to use humor to throw anyone off from knowing he was at the very end of his rope.

He had nightmares and woke in a sweat. He often couldn't find a reason to walk out of his room. He always volunteered for the most dangerous position on any job they ran, a part of him hoping he wouldn't come back from it. He just couldn't feel a thing anymore, not anything worthwhile. At least not until his little princess had walked through the door.

Maestro called it exactly the way it was. Soleil was too innocent for their world. She wasn't like Reaper's old lady, or Steele's. Even Blythe had knowledge of bikers and knew every single member of Torpedo Ink was an assassin. Soleil thought they were all sweet. She was surrounded by a pack of vicious wolves and she thought they were sweet. If there was one woman in the world who needed protection, it was his woman. And she was going to get it.

"Code, I need to know whatever you can get on her between now and midnight."

"You lift her wallet?"

Ice nodded and slid it into Code's hands. It was very slim, a buttery leather that must have cost more than the boots he wore. He slid his thumb over it as he handed it off. Just touching it inexplicably made him want her more.

"She's so far out of our class, Ice," Code said. "You know that, don't you?"

Ice nodded.

"You make certain she isn't just a challenge." Code slid the wallet under his shirt, those too-old eyes staring straight into Ice's.

"She's no challenge, Code. If she was a real mark, I'd have her in bed already." That was the truth, and all of them knew it. "After you get her information, set her up for me. I want it all to happen tonight. Get the paperwork done and make it legit. No backing out. No wiggle room for her. I want her tied to me completely."

His brothers shook their heads, but Code nodded, and he was gone, sliding to a corner of the bar where he could get the Internet and do just as Ice asked.

"Need someone to get her a drink. A screaming orgasm. Want to keep those comin' until I got this locked down."

"I've got it for you," Mechanic volunteered. He followed Code out of the game room.

"Need cameras in here shut down. And no one gets in but one of ours," Ice continued.

He'd been listening, and the water was running in the restroom. She'd be back any minute. "Need her wallet back as soon as possible."

"I'll tell Mechanic to bring it with the drink," Maestro said, "And then I'll guard the door." He gave a good impression of a smile — a shark's smile. "No one will get in."

"Thanks." Ice knew his brothers and they would come through for him, no matter how crazy they thought he was acting.

Soleil came out of the restroom, looking more beautiful than ever. Like an angel. Her skin looked so soft it was an invitation to touch. Her eyes were large, that deep, unbelievable dark chocolate, but more, the color no one would believe if he tried to describe it to them. Her lashes were long and thick, a dark brown that looked black until one got up close. They framed her eyes, giving a man all sorts of needs when he looked at them. Her nose was straight, a little princess nose.

She was born to look fresh and young and way too innocent. The kind of innocent most men wanted immediately to corrupt — or at least he did. He would never tire of looking at her. Every time he did, the ideas that came into his head were dirty, erotic and not for the innocent, yet he knew he was going to try every single one of those scenarios with her.

He could still taste her in his mouth. Feel her nipple on his tongue. That soft, soft mound that was so full and round and perfect for a man like him. He was a breast man. He loved looking at tits, but now that he had found perfection with her very sweet ass, he planned on being very attentive.

Ice held out his hand to her. Soleil didn't

even hesitate. Her eyes were shining, her perfect bow of a mouth smiling, and when she moved into him, she did so all the way, her body sliding up along his.

"I've been holding the pool table for us," he said. His lips brushed her ear. He felt the shiver go through her. "What do you want to bet? It has to be interesting, not money."

Her lashes fluttered. "I don't know, what sounds good to you?"

"You win, you call the bet. I win, I get your panties."

Mechanic set two drinks on the slim side table just below a rack of cues. Soleil eyed them warily. "What's that? I don't usually change drinks midstream. I don't want a hangover."

"You won't get one, and I know you'll love this drink. It's a screaming orgasm."

Soleil rolled her eyes. "Seriously, Ice? There's no such thing. That's a myth. Someone named a drink after a myth."

His eyebrow shot up and he stepped into her, crowding her until he knew she felt the heat rolling off his body. Until he felt every breath she drew into her lungs.

"Baby, I won't even need my cock in you to make you scream when you come for me." He stared straight into her eyes when he told her the fuckin' truth, because it was important she know he meant it. "First game I win, I get your panties. The second I win, I make you scream."

Soleil stared up into his crystal blue eyes, excitement coursing through her. Heat rushed through her veins. He was the one suggesting bets. More alcohol. Did that make her responsible? Or him? He was definitely set on seducing her. And his friends were all in on it, helping him. She loved that, loved that they were willing to do anything for their brother. A part of her recognized that she could be in a dangerous situation, but Ice was too focused on her, and she believed him when he'd told her he didn't share.

He made her forget everything but the excitement of being with him. She needed to forget. She wanted this one night. It wasn't forever, but she didn't have that long. She had this one night, and she was taking it and this amazing, gorgeous, sexy man. She might burn in hell for the things she was going to do this night, but she didn't care. Looking at him, she was certain every single thing would be worth it.

FIVE

Soleil's face flushed, that beautiful rose Ice knew he was going to enjoy seeing all over her body when he had her laid out with his mouth between her legs.

Her chin went up. "You think I'm not up to the challenge? You aren't going to win."

He flashed her a grin. "Princess, win or lose, I'm still going to count myself a winner. You in?"

"All the way," she declared.

He was going to burn in hell for this, but he'd already had a place reserved in the hottest inferno, so he took her fingers, brought them to his mouth, brushed a kiss into the center of her palm, and then put her screaming orgasm into her hand. He took his as well.

"What's in it?" she asked, bringing the glass to her nose to cautiously sniff it.

He took a drink, leaned in and kissed her, sharing the taste of Baileys, vodka and

Kahlúa with her. He couldn't stop his hand from curling possessively around the nape of her neck. The moment they kissed, there was an explosion. Her match to his dynamite. They both went up fast, her mouth moving under his, following his lead, tongue sliding along his, catching every tiny taste left of the drink in his mouth. It was sensual. Erotic. It was the hottest kiss he'd ever had, and he didn't want it to end.

He thought he was playing her. Seducing her. That was the play, but it felt all too real, and he'd never had real. He'd never felt anything at all when he was kissing. He had no idea that one touch could ignite a firestorm that roared and burned through him, leaving him craving more, needing it until her kisses were more important than breathing.

She was supposed to fall in love with him. That was the ultimate goal. His life was an illusion, nothing more. He didn't exist anymore. There was no Ice. There was a killer, and she would be living with that. In return for her love, he would take excellent care of her. And he would have this . . .

The rush that was beyond anything he'd known. The innocence of her to corrupt and protect. If he played his cards right, if he was careful and saw to every detail, this would work. It had to, now that he had a small taste of what it could be like with her. He would have a semblance of a life, and that was all someone as fucked up as he was could ever ask for.

He knew the others thought he was moving too fast, but when a man knew the worst in life, he recognized the best when he saw it. When he had been with hundreds, maybe more, with nothing working for him, he wasn't about to throw away a miracle when someone walked in and handed it all to him.

He pulled back and regarded her with his blue eyes — those blue eyes that tempted so easily. He stayed focused on her, not because she was his mark but because he was fascinated by everything she did. Every gesture. Every expression. The way her fingers folded the material of her dress between them. The way she brought the glass to her lips and sipped. He loved that her eyes widened, and those long, sinful lashes fluttered before she actually took a drink.

"This is good." She sounded surprised.

"Sometimes, princess, you have to take a few chances in life. This is our night, remember? We're going to say the hell with everything and just have a fuckin' good time."

She regarded him over the glass for what seemed an eternity before a slow smile lit up her face. God. That mouth. He wanted her lips wrapped around his cock right there. He needed relief, and thinking about her mouth wasn't giving that to him, especially when her tongue came out and she swiped at a bit of cream lingering . . . He nearly groaned.

"You didn't drink, Ice," she pointed out. "There's no taking unfair advantage."

He was almost desperate to avoid thinking about her lips wrapped around his cock. He picked up his glass and downed the liquid, noticing his brothers exchanging peculiar little grins with one another. He couldn't interpret them because he was too busy trying to get his wayward mind off her lips.

He turned to the cue sticks and hefted a couple of them before choosing the one he wanted while she handed his glass to Maestro. Maestro handed his glass off to Keys.

"You break first."

Her eyebrow went up. "I see you didn't learn from the darts."

"I learned. No mercy, woman. That's what I learned. But I am a gentleman . . ."

There was a derisive snort behind him and he turned to glare at Maestro, even as Soleil burst into laughter.

"He's a fuckin' liar," Maestro said. "He's a hustler with a cue stick."

She flashed a smile at Maestro that made something dark and ugly swirl in Ice's gut. He'd never been jealous in his life, certainly not over a woman, and not when she smiled at his brother. He had no problems sharing as a rule, but he meant what he'd said to Soleil. No one touched her but him. That smile was innocent enough on her end, but hell, she was so sexy without knowing, his brothers were right. He was going to spend a lot of time beating the shit out of outsiders who didn't get the rules. The thought was uplifting.

"So am I," Soleil assured Maestro.

"I think we should keep this game interesting," Ice said. "When you miss, I get to ask you a question. You have to answer truthfully." It was a game they all played, which was also part of a seduction plot they'd learned, and it always, always worked. They needed information to seduce their chosen mark, and the truth game was irresistible and invaluable.

She made a face at him and downed the rest of her drink before putting her glass on the table. Out of the corner of his eye, he saw Maestro glance at her, send the others a small grin, pick up the glass and im-

149

mediately leave for the bar. Yeah. His brothers. He'd fuckin' die for them.

"Just as long as when you miss, you have to answer my question," she agreed.

"No one-word answers," Ice added. "You have to actually answer the question."

Soleil racked the balls and then made the break, sinking a striped ball immediately. She circled the table until she was almost standing in front of Ice. He was acutely aware of her, the scent of her, the way her hair cascaded down her back, that incredible shine under the lights.

She bent slowly toward the table and his heart nearly stopped. She wasn't trying to be seductive, he was absolutely certain of that. She was too innocent. He could see her full concentration was on her shot, but the way the folds of the skirt fell over her ass called his attention to the way she was shaped. So perfectly. A woman's feminine form had always been pleasing to him. She had a perfect, heart-shaped ass, one that just called to a man like him, putting all sorts of dirty, very erotic thoughts in his head.

His brothers said he was an artist. He would never claim such a title, but that said, he did like to look at a woman's body. Her physical form. There was such beauty in the way she was put together. Looking at her, he waged a battle with himself. Let her go, which he knew he should. She was too classy for a man like him. She wouldn't have a clue how to be in his world, and if he was honest with himself, that was half the reason he wanted her.

He cursed under his breath, fighting his protective, selfish nature. He was the very devil stalking her, and she was an angel chased by demons straight to him. Shit. He knew better than to trap her. Those kinds of things never worked out. Never. He'd convinced himself she needed him and so the exchange was fair, but it was bullshit, and he knew it.

While he was fighting to save her, she'd sunk four more balls. She turned her head, still bent over the table, her mouth so close to his groin he nearly felt her breath on the front of his jeans. She looked at him, as serious as sin.

"If I don't remember to tell you again, Ice, thank you for tonight. You have no idea what you've done for me. You most likely saved my life." She turned back to contemplate the table.

He stood there staring at her. Slowly, he lifted his gaze to the others crowded around watching. They'd all heard her. She wasn't being melodramatic. There was a ring of truth in her voice. He looked to Absinthe. He was a human lie detector. Absinthe's nod was barely there, but it told Ice Soleil had just revealed something extremely important. Whoever her ex-fiancé was, he wanted her dead and she was terrified he'd succeed.

A woman like Soleil should go to the cops for protection, yet she hadn't. Why? That didn't make sense, but the fact that she was in that kind of trouble hardened his resolve to keep her. He could keep her safe, make all her troubles go away. He could do that. He was that man.

Her ball spun in the pocket and leapt back out. He whistled softly. "You almost ran the table, darlin', but *almost* doesn't count. You owe me an answer."

She sent him a small smile and a shrug. "I didn't want you to feel bad, you know, a girl beating the crap out of you at pool. What's your question?"

"Never worried, princess. I'm not the kind of man who gets upset if my woman manages to squeak out a win. I'd be proud."

She looked pleased. "Let's see what you can do."

"What's your best and worst trait?" Ice asked as he walked around the pool table, studying the position of all the balls. She hadn't left him much of a shot, and she'd sunk nearly all the stripes.

"You only get one question. That's two."

He flashed her a grin. "Worst, then. Might as well get it over with."

She narrowed her eyes as she watched him line up his shot and then call it. He banked his ball, clipped and then sank it. His grin widened, and he reached for his drink, took a sip and indicated hers.

Soleil sighed and took a healthy drink before pushing a few stray strands of hair out of her face. When she lifted her arm to push her fingers through her hair, her breasts rose, calling his immediate attention to her straining tits. He swore her nipples were hard, pushing against the thin material of her dress, trying to get to him.

He felt around for his glass again, staring at her breasts. Maestro handed him his drink and he all but downed it before he remembered he had to stay in control. He was sweating. Breathing too hard. His cock a fucking spike in his jeans.

"I drift. I'm a drifter. I don't like conflict and I never can make a decision, so I just drift along. I'm working on it all the time, but I still find myself just going along with something when I shouldn't. Like Winston."

153

The bastard's name was Winston. He glanced at Player, and the man nodded and disappeared in the direction of the main room, where Code was busy pulling up everything he could on Soleil.

"I couldn't believe when he hired a lawyer without so much as consulting me. It should have been my decision when to hire one after Kevin died. Kevin was my lawyer from the time my parents died. I wasn't ready to have anyone else come into my life, but Winston decided he was in charge. Nothing I said deterred him. I decided then not to marry him, but I didn't tell him that. Not decisively. I kept saying I needed more time."

Out of desperation to stay on track with his intended agenda, Ice had lined up his next shot as he listened, but he straightened and then stalked her purposefully around the pool table. He must have looked scary because she backed up a few steps. He kept coming. He caught the front of her dress again, this time very gently, and pulled her to him.

"Baby, you don't like something I do, I want to hear about it right then. You don't like something anyone else says or does to you, I want to hear about it right then. You don't tell me, I'm going to be pissed off.

You don't want to see me pissed. You get me? You talk to me. That's how we resolve this shit. We talk. You. Me. You get me?" he repeated.

His voice was pitched low, but it was intense. She swallowed hard and nodded.

"Don't do that. Don't be afraid of me like you are of him. I would never hurt you. Never. I don't hurt women. You need to learn to say what you think, and I can help you with that, but between us, I need to know you're going to always tell me what upsets you. I need that from you."

Soleil nodded slowly. "I'll try, Ice. I don't like being a drifter. I just never learned to be any different. I grew up in hotels. Being alone. I think I wanted to fit in so much I just learned not to say what I thought. I was always afraid it would get me kicked out."

Ice took Soleil's hand and pressed a kiss to her knuckles. "Torpedo Ink welcomes opinions, and we listen to everyone with equal attention. Say what you want, baby. You're free."

She took the drink Maestro put in her hand and took another sip. "For tonight anyway. You have no idea how lucky you are."

He sank three balls in a row and then straightened up to look at her. "You're rid

155

of that parasite, princess. There's no reason not to be free. We're celebrating, remember? What are we celebrating? Your freedom. You're one of us and we've got you safe. You can say or do anything you damn well want to. No one can get to you."

She took another sip of her drink. "That sounds good, Ice, but it isn't exactly the truth. You're going to get on your motorcycle and go wherever it is you go, and I'll still be here, facing him. He's out there, and yes, tonight I can forget him, but he's going to keep coming after me."

"You want to park your sweet ass on the back of my bike, baby, just letting you know, that seat will always be reserved for you."

There it was. The invitation Soleil wanted more than anything. Ice had just opened the door for more. For visiting the twenty-four-hour chapel or just riding away on his motorcycle. She wanted that with every breath she took. More and more she wanted him. The more time she spent with him, the more she wanted to dare to be the bad girl and seduce him. He was there. He wanted her. It was easy so far. He couldn't take his eyes off her breasts or her butt.

Ice was *everything* Soleil had ever fanta-sized over. Everything. Why had she finally met him now, when there was nothing left for her? She could feel the burn of tears at the backs of her eyes. Ice acted like more of a man than Winston ever had. He actually seemed to really care what she thought and felt. No one had ever given that to her before. She could fall hard if she let herself, and she was afraid she was doing just that. Maybe it was the alcohol. She wasn't used to mixing drinks, but she didn't care. She wanted this night with him. She wanted as much time with him as possible. A lifetime. She had this one night to pack a lifetime in, and she made up her mind she would do every single thing she'd ever dreamt of doing — and more — if she could.

If she drank enough, she might just dare to get on the back of his bike and ride off with him. She wouldn't look back. She wouldn't want to look back. He would be enough for her. She could make a life with him, she knew she could.

Ice turned back to his game and sank two more balls. Soleil was coming with him no matter what. She needed someone like him. Someone ruthless and ugly mean, someone willing to beat the shit out of anyone for looking at her wrong. Someone willing to kill an enemy that scared her so badly she'd walk into a biker bar for protection. The sad look she sometimes got on her face had to go.

He heard her soft laughter and couldn't help but look over his shoulder to see her face light up the way it did whenever she laughed. "What?" he demanded, his voice harsh because his body was reacting to that laugh and he couldn't afford not to be in control. The stakes were too high. He was going to get her to go home with him, but their code demanded she give full consent.

"Park my sweet ass on your bike?" she repeated.

He winced. He really needed to learn how to talk in polite society. On the other hand, she might as well know what he was really like. "You've got to admit, baby, you have a very sweet ass."

"I love that you think so. I've never ridden on a motorcycle with someone else. I own one. And I fly planes. I love planes. Have you ever been on a glider? So cool. Especially when the sun is coming up. And then there's paragliding. And parachuting."

His girl was an adrenaline junkie. Who knew? That beautiful little angel face liked to do crazy shit. He was all kinds of crazy. He just might suit her. Hell, he fucking hoped so.

"I think you need the experience of riding with me," he said. "You like all that, you'll love going up the California coast on my bike. What difference does it make if you wait a few days — or weeks — to face this bastard? Come with me when I head back. You'll be able to see Lana again. She went home with the president, his wife and a couple of others."

She didn't answer, and he turned back to the game. She was thinking about it. Out of the corner of his eye, he saw her finish off the screaming orgasm. They went down smooth and tasted even better. He concentrated on his shot. He needed to win this game — and the next. She was a hell of a pool player. He'd probably have to cheat next game and distract her. He grinned to himself, thinking about how he'd do that.

He sank the rest of the solid balls and then went around the table to indicate where he was sinking the eight ball. Maestro handed Soleil another screaming orgasm. She was going to need it. Very smoothly he sank the ball and turned, grinning at her. Maestro had a glass of whiskey ready for him. He was grinning just a little too much at Ice as well. What the hell was up with that look?

Soleil shook her head, her eyes bright, laughter in them. "I can't believe I lost. I was picturing you without your jeans."

"I can do that for you, princess, but I'm commando at the moment, so you might have a screaming orgasm just looking."

Her gaze dropped to the front of his jeans. Her tongue slid out to moisturize her full lips, making his body ache so bad he wanted to groan. She looked like she wanted to drop to her knees and pull his jeans down just to see if he was commando. The stark longing on her face almost undid him right along with her glistening lips. He could imagine them stretched around his cock.

Someone snickered, but he couldn't look away from her long enough to see who it was and mark them for a beating later.

Soleil looked up at him and rolled her eyes. "You're so arrogant." But she was laughing.

"I've got reason to be." It took a moment before he could take a step close to her, subtly trapping her against the pool table. "I think I won those panties." His voice came out nearly a growl. He felt like growling. If he was supposed to be seducing her, he wasn't certain he was the one getting the job done.

She nodded. "I think you did."

He put his hand on her leg, just above her hemline. Her skin was so soft against his callused hand his breath caught in his lungs. Before she could protest, and he wasn't certain she was going to, he leaned in and took her mouth. As before, fire erupted. He wanted to be gentle, but it wasn't happening, not when she went up in flames and just gave herself to him. All in. She tasted like a mixture of screaming orgasm and cinnamon and spice. The combination was an aphrodisiac, and he couldn't get enough of her.

He lost himself in her, kissing her over and over, needing her mouth, the fire he found there, so hot he knew he was burning in hell — or heaven. It didn't matter, he was going to stay there. His hand slipped higher, right to the edge of her panties. Gentle. Completely at odds with his kiss. She should have protested. Stopped him. She didn't do either. Instead, she leaned into him. His heart clenched hard in his chest and his cock jerked and pulsed.

"How the hell do you get your skin so damned soft?" he murmured against her neck.

"I didn't know it was that soft," she said, sounding as ragged as he felt.

He caught her earlobe between his teeth and tugged just before reluctantly pulling back and allowing her hem to drop down again.

They stared at each other for a long moment and then he grinned and snapped his fingers. "Hand them over." He half expected her to renege, or at least try to.

Instead, without looking around at anyone else, keeping her eyes solely on him, she slid her hands under the skirt of her dress and hooked her panties. She skimmed them down, wiggling a little as she brought them over the curve of her hips. His heart nearly stopped. Staring into his eyes, she brought up the sides of the dress rather than front or back. He caught a glimpse of her legs and hips, but that was all. It was the sexiest thing he'd ever seen. Hell. He needed more liquor if he was going to survive this night intact.

She crouched down, still looking at him, stepped out of her panties and, straightening, handed them to him. She'd been wearing a little white floral thong that looked as innocent as she did, until you factored in the sexy little twisted cords that made up the band and fell between her cheeks. His eyes meeting hers, he brought them to his nose without thinking, inhaling the scent of her. He wasn't in the least surprised to find out she had her own unique fragrance.

His body didn't just stir. Hot blood rushed through his veins and pooled in his cock. He wasn't just hard, he was diamond hard, the kind of hard that meant a man could shatter if he so much as took a step. It hurt. A damn good pain that meant he was alive. That meant he didn't have to command his body to respond, it just did it all on its own because his woman was so fucking hot, she was an inferno.

She sent him a smug little look. "Maestro, I think Ice could use another drink."

There was that snicker again coming from someone behind him. Someone else answered, as if his brothers knew something he didn't. He should have turned around to look but he couldn't stop staring at her. He just took the drink Maestro put in his hand and tossed it back, letting the fire add to the steel in his cock.

Soleil racked the balls and picked up her cue stick. "You want to break?"

He should. He was taking a hell of a chance if he allowed her to break and she ran the table. She was certainly capable of it. On the other hand, he wanted the chance to distract her. He needed to see her reaction. She was so focused on him, he wasn't certain if she was aware of the other members of Torpedo Ink moving around the room, and that was exactly what he wanted — what he needed.

He had managed to slip the wallet back into her pocket when he'd kissed her again. Code had made certain the cameras didn't work in the back room. The others were guarding the door and turned away anyone wanting to come into the game room. His woman should be mildly and just pleasantly drunk. Maestro had gotten her a bottle of water, which she'd been drinking between sips of the screaming orgasm. Everything was lining up properly. He indicated with his cue for her to break. Maybe he needed to stop drinking and start paying more attention to what was going on, but between the whiskey and the woman, this could just be the best night of his life.

"You sink four in a row, I'll sign your prenup. I sink four in a row, you sign mine," he said just as she was about to take her shot.

She stopped and turned to him. Her eyes were suddenly pure focus. She didn't look in the least drunk. In fact, she looked stone-cold sober, but as if those beautiful eyes were swimming with tears. "You'd sign my prenup?"

"I said I would. Any man would be an

164

idiot not to. Do your worst, baby. I can take it."

She blinked at him several times, and he swore tears looked like diamonds on her lashes. Then she turned and sank a striped and proceeded to follow it with three more. "I believe you need to find a pen, my man."

She looked very somber, as if Ice signing the prenup was a very serious situation. She bent over the table to take her next shot. Her flirty little skirt slid up the back of her thighs and showed just the very edges of her cheeks. His heart nearly stopped.

"Got one right here, baby."

Ice moved up beside her as if studying the table. He dropped his hand to the back of her thigh, stroking it for a moment before sliding it up under her skirt to find her bare cheeks. He rubbed gently, his palm continuing up until he was cupping one cheek, his thumb stroking caresses. Gently. He waited, his heart pounding, for her to pull away from him.

She felt perfect to him. Every stroke of his thumb over her soft skin sent hot blood thundering with desire through his body. He took his time, stroking. Caressing. Claiming her. He was careful to keep each touch light. He shaped her cheek, palmed it, then went back to those slow caresses.

Soleil pushed back into his hand, her hips moving invitingly. She didn't stop him. She didn't protest or move away. If anything, she moved back into his hand. He followed the curve of her cheek to find her entrance slick and hot for him. He used his fingers to edge all that scorching heat and then he caressed her cheek again before sliding his hand over the back of her thigh, leaving the skirt of her dress to ride up high.

Soleil couldn't believe that on the last night of her life, every fantasy she'd ever had was coming true. If it was possible to fall in love, fast and hard and completely, in just a few hours, she knew it was happening. She loved everything Ice did. Everything he said. He made her feel hot and sexy and desirable. He made her feel as if he couldn't see another woman, would never see one. She loved the fact that he touched her openly in front of everyone. That just made her all the hotter and made her feel even more desirable.

The way he touched her was beyond anything she'd ever known, and she wanted more. She wanted it all with him. She knew he liked her body. It was in the way he looked at her, in the feel of his hands on her. She felt the same way about his. Seduc-

166

tion wasn't difficult when two people were both willing . . . and she was *so* willing. Whatever he wanted. Any way he wanted. Anywhere.

He made the suggestion to sign the pre-nup, not her. Still, she had to keep her mind from going anywhere permanent. It wasn't right to get him drunk, drag him to a twenty-four-hour chapel and marry him, and then ride away where Winston and the rest of the world would have to leave her alone.

She'd make Ice so happy. She'd be happy. She'd never been happy. Not until now. Not until right that moment in a biker bar, bent over a pool table with her skirt flipped up and her very hot bottom hopefully holding Ice's attention while she contemplated whether or not she was going to burn in hell for all eternity after sinking four balls to get her prenup signed. And if she was going to miss the next shot in order to sign Ice's prenup to get him one step closer to the altar or stop the fantasy before things could go any further.

Soleil was gorgeous. Absolutely gorgeous. Ice was dripping with need, his balls so tight he was afraid he might embarrass himself.

It was the most amazing, perfect night of his life.

"Try making the shot, princess," he whispered, deliberately bending his body over hers. He pressed his cock against her inviting, bare cheeks, keeping one hand on her back.

She laughed softly. "How am I supposed to do that?"

"I'm signing your prenup. You don't make the shot, I get the chance to get you to sign mine. I think that's fair . . ." He pressed tighter against her, moving his hips so that his cock slid along the seam of her cheeks through his jeans. "Don't you? Try it. You might make it."

Soleil didn't try to straighten. She studied the table, took a breath and lined up her shot. Ice waited until the exact moment she went to hit the ball and he pressed his cock right into that snug warmth and his hand dipped low to flick her clit. She jumped, and the ball went at an angle, crashing into several solids, sending them flying.

He kept his hand on her back while he fucked her with his finger. She was tight, surrounding him with heat. So slick. So ready for him. He took her just high enough to leave her wanting more before he pulled out of her and straightened slowly, letting her skirt fall back into place.

He caught her hair, tugged until she stood upright and then, deliberately, he licked his finger. Savored her taste. All the while staring into her eyes. Those amazing eyes of hers had gone a little dazed. He knew he'd left her wanting. That was part of the game, but he didn't only savor the taste of her in his mouth; he savored that look of helpless hunger on her face — for him.

She didn't seem to be aware of anyone but him, although when Maestro handed her a drink, she murmured her thank-you very politely. He handed a pen to Ice.

"Prenup, princess," Ice said. "I'm a man of my word. You want the fuckin' thing signed, it's signed."

She nodded solemnly. "It's important." She frowned. "I can't remember why, but I know it's important."

"It is," he agreed.

She pulled the paper out of her pocket, unfolded it and smoothed it out. "Kevin wrote this up for me. Isn't it wonderful?" She acted like it was sacred.

Ice took it just as carefully, pretended to read through it, nodded his head and signed. Maestro witnessed it. "There you go. Signed. Dated. Witnessed. That is a legal, binding document. If Kevin wrote it up for you, you know it's right."

"It is. He always did what was right. Thank you, Ice. I appreciate it." She sipped at her drink and indicated the pool table. "You have to sink four balls, so I can sign yours. That's only fair."

Ice moved around to the other side of the table and went to work. He sank four in a row fast, hardly taking time between the shots. It was Player who solemnly handed him the prenup for Soleil to sign. She did so with a small flourish, adding a little smiley face above her name.

"That was so easy," she said. "Didn't you think so? Why wouldn't someone just sign?" She stumbled a little and had to use the table to keep upright.

Ice put his arm around her waist. "I don't know, baby. He was a fuckin' clueless dick. You're with me now and we're going to forget his ass and have this night for ourselves. Right?"

"That's right. There isn't any use in marriage at all." She sounded like she was trying to convince herself. "Why bother with it when the man isn't going to be worth anything? When he's nothing but a clueless dick. I agree totally with your assessment." She reached for the water bottle.

"There are reasons for marriage, darlin',"

Ice countered. "Quite a few, but the number one reason would be that screaming orgasm. We talked about the importance of that."

She waved her hand in front of his face, shooing his opinion away. "No such thing, Ice. I mean they named a pretty good drink after it and all, but I'm telling you, as a woman, there's no such thing."

Again, she was very solemn, looking him in the eye. Ice couldn't help but brush a kiss along her temple. He still had his arm around her waist, and he eased her back against the pool table. He took her assessment as a challenge.

"You were with the wrong man, princess, I told you that. He wasn't worth marrying for a long list of reasons, but number one is he put his fuckin' hands on you. Two is, he didn't make you scream when you came. You want that, you marry me. I can give that to you a hundred times a day if that's what you want."

She raised an eyebrow and regarded him with a shake of her head. "Ice, you are insane to think it's even possible. If you could do that, you are probably the only man on earth worth marrying. Even Kevin would agree. I'm certain of it."

"Kevin absolutely would agree," Ice said. He turned back to the pool table and took another shot, making certain to miss. His breath hissed out in pretend irritation and then he smiled at her and waved her to the table.

"You're a good man, Ice," she said as she moved around him to study the layout. "I've decided what I'm going to do with my life."

She leaned over the pool table to eye the setup more closely. Ice slipped behind her and put a light hand on her back. He loved touching her. Claiming her. He wanted her for the rest of his life.

"What are you going to do with your life, princess?" He used his palm to rub along her spine, down to the curve of her ass. He was very fond of the way her cheeks were firm globes, round and perfect. He didn't make the mistake of hurrying. Seduction was all about patience. Giving the other whatever they needed or wanted. She responded to him as if born for him — and he was certain she was. More importantly, he was beginning to think he had been born for her.

"Do you know what a vendetta is?" She straightened and turned toward him.

He was so close that when she turned, her breasts pushed into his chest. He didn't move. Neither did she. "A blood feud?"

"*Exactly.* They killed Kevin. I know they

did. They killed him and they think they're going to kill me, but it isn't going to happen. You know why?" She put her lips against his ear. "I'm on to them."

Ice glanced around the suddenly quiet room. His brothers had heard every word Soleil had said. Whatever had made them laugh and snicker was gone. They had all sobered up as well. He glanced again at Absinthe, who nodded. Soleil still didn't seem all that far gone, but drunk or not, she believed what she was saying. Someone had killed her lawyer? That was her belief? This was getting complicated. His woman needed him a lot more than he'd first thought. He was beginning to feel a lot less guilty for what he was doing.

Yeah, he knew what a vendetta was. He lived one every fucking day. They were a wolf pack, spreading out, hunting prey and bringing them down when they were certain they had uncovered the filth walking among the innocent. Vendettas weren't for soft, sweet creatures that were clueless when they stumbled into a pack of wolves.

He swore under his breath. Soleil needed him more than ever. She wasn't going to hunt anyone. That was his job. She was going to stay safe, locked away from predators who killed lawyers and threatened women,

173

scaring them so badly that they ran to a biker bar. What the hell was wrong with the world?

"I was going to get married, have babies, spoil my husband rotten and paint. I'm good at art. Really good. I would love to have a family, but no more. Now, I'm going to go after Kevin's killers. All of them. Cops or not. Lawyers. It doesn't matter. I can get to them." She nodded as if to emphasize what she believed and then turned back to the table.

She bent over the table, her dress sliding up to the backs of her thighs. She had killer legs. *Killer* legs. He could imagine them wrapped around his hips very easily. In fact, if he wasn't careful, it was going to happen right there in the bar. Or he'd put her on the pool table and devour her the way he wanted. She wasn't going to waste her life on a vendetta. She might think she knew what she was doing, but he was taking that off her hands.

His palm slipped to the back of her thigh, and he rubbed gently, soothingly. "I like the part where you spoil your man. Tell me about that. Not sure what spoiling means."

"Haven't you ever been spoiled?" Still bent over the pool table, she looked at him over her shoulder. Again, when she looked at him, she didn't look drunk. Her face was flushed, her eyes bright, but she looked completely and utterly focused on him. "You're beautiful, Ice. Truly beautiful. When I look at you, sometimes I can't breathe. Other women must have spoiled you."

He heard a little snicker when she told him he was so beautiful she couldn't breathe. He sent a glare around the room. His palm never stopped sliding up and down her thigh and then finally, *finally,* slid around to her inner thigh. Very gently he applied pressure until she shifted her weight, spreading her legs for him. He was fairly certain she was barely aware she was doing it, but she widened her stance at his insistence. Triumph burst through him. Another sweet victory. She wanted this with him, right there, anywhere he asked. Was it the alcohol, or was it her? Was she that perfect for him?

"Never once, princess. I don't live in an ivory tower. I live in the gutter, remember?"

She shook her head. "If you were mine, I would spoil you until you couldn't stand it." It was a declaration. A solemn promise. "If I didn't have to go after Kevin's killers, I would find a way to make you so happy you'd never want to leave me."

He already didn't want to leave her. Her

gaze had drifted over his body, stopped and dwelled on the bulge stretching the confines of his jeans. Her tongue touched her lips. The full bottom lip glistened. His cock jerked hard. Throbbed. Pulsed. The monster wanted out, and Ice wanted it out. Her gaze stroked him like the touch of fingers.

"You like giving head, baby?" he asked, one hand still stroking up and down her thigh, and then rubbing along the seam between her thigh and buttocks, while the other cupped his raging cock. Just the thought that his little innocent angel might talk to him about blow jobs sent his dick into a frenzy of pulsing, throbbing and jerking. He was going to spill everything if they kept it up, but he didn't want to stop.

She looked so sexy, with her innocent eyes and that skin of hers that invited a man to touch her just to see how soft it was. Then there was that mouth. That perfect, perfect mouth.

Ice pushed the hem of her dress up to her waist, exposing her gorgeous ass. He continued to use the pad of his finger to trace the seam where her cheeks met her thighs. Back and forth, a hypnotic rhythm. He wanted to drop his jeans and ram his cock home. Her mouth. Her pussy. Her ass. All of her. Claim every fucking inch. He already felt as if she

176

belonged to him.

"Answer me, Soleil." He poured steel into his voice.

She blinked, but she responded to his order. "Depends," she said. "I wanted everything for my man, so I practiced until I thought I was pretty damn good. But seriously, he wasn't worth the effort."

"The right man?" He wanted to yank his cock right out of his jeans and stroke himself for relief. Maybe push her to her knees and have her swallow him down right there.

"On the right man, yes, isn't that spoiling him?" She smiled at him. Sexy. Alluring. "I could spoil you every morning. I bet you taste yummy." She turned her head back to survey the table. "What did you think spoiling a man entails?"

He couldn't move or speak for a moment. He thought dragging her to the altar right then was the only solution. Mornings with her lips stretched around his cock sounded damn good to him. He forced air into his lungs. His fingers danced along the tempting seam between her thigh and cheek. She didn't realize or maybe she just didn't care that he'd pushed her skirt up above her ass, exposing her perfect cheeks. She'd look good with his handprints on that pale skin.

Hell. He wanted to take a bite out of her. Instead, he palmed one cheek, letting the heat from his body warm her. She pushed back into his hand and his heart stuttered.

"Ice?" She kept her eyes on the pool table. "What would it take to keep you happy?"

Was there a little quiver in her voice? He was certain there was, and he wanted to re-assure her that her ex-fiancé was a worth-less dick who didn't know a good woman worth keeping when he saw her. Ice, on the other hand, had no intention of allowing her to get away.

"I want my woman to give me everything anywhere I want it, anything I ask. And it has to be mutual spoiling. I want to give her everything. Including a screaming orgasm."

She laughed softly, and drunk or not, the melody was still pure gold. He could almost see the notes dancing in the air between them.

"I think any woman who belonged to you, Ice, would give you whatever you wanted when you wanted it, whether or not you could actually give her the mythical scream-ing orgasm."

His fingers whispered down her cheeks, slid over her lips to catch the slick honey spilling from her. He rubbed his fingers through the liquid and then did the barely there over her clit. Her entire body shuddered and she pushed back against his fingers.

"God, baby, you're too easy. I love the fact that you think I can't do it."

She turned her head again to look at him over her shoulder. Her face was flushed. Her breathing had gone ragged. "Not you, Ice. I think you could do anything. It's me." Her voice was sad. "I'm just not built that way."

His finger strummed over her lips. She kept herself bare and he liked that. He wanted to put his mouth on her and suck all that honey right out of her. Instead, he placed one hand on her back to hold her down over the table while he pressed his finger into her. She was tight, surrounding him with such heat his finger burned. He let out his breath, just his breath moving over her left buttock while he worked her pussy.

Her body sent him another fresh wave of liquid heat. With the pad of his thumb he rubbed circles around and over her clit. Again, just whispers. His teeth scraped gently on her cheek, tongue stroking a caress and then just his breath.

Her body pushed back onto his hand. She felt like a sheath of silken flames.

"That's it, baby, ride my finger. Just like

that." He whispered the words against her left cheek and then bit down gently and was rewarded with more liquid honey.

A low moan escaped her mouth and she rested her head on the table, her fingers clutching the cue stick as if it could save her. Nothing could. Ice had made certain of that. She needed his brand of care and he was feeding it to her slowly, expertly, making certain she would get hooked. Addicted. She would need him. He wanted her to need him, to be addicted. He wanted that desperately.

He took her up slowly, higher and higher, backing off, taking control, until her breath was so ragged, she was almost sobbing, and her hips were riding his finger in desperate need. He had had no intentions of using his mouth to bring her off, but he couldn't resist her or the terrible temptation. He tried, but his own control was slipping beyond his ability to carry out his perfect seduction. He needed to taste her. He thought he might go insane if he didn't. He kicked her legs farther apart, crouched down and fit his mouth over her pussy. His tongue slid in and dove deep, pulling out her sweet, spicy honey.

She cried out, the sound almost agonized yet at the same time pure bliss. It wasn't the scream he was looking for, but it was close, and he didn't want that yet. It couldn't be over. He needed his mouth on her as much as she needed a catastrophic release. When she was close to exploding, he pulled back, just sending warm air over her clit and pussy, his mouth a breath away. She was nearly crying, pushing back, trying to get to his mouth.

He attempted to stay in control, this was for her, not him, but damn, she was so fucking responsive he couldn't see straight. He couldn't resist those bare lips, licking at them, using his teeth to nip and tug while she writhed and began to press her hips back into him in desperation. And her taste . . . he was already addicted when it was supposed to be the other way around.

She cried out when he fucked her with his tongue, then went to suckling her clit until it was inflamed. He experimented, flicking with his finger and thumb. Each strike sent a shudder through her body and she moaned louder. She was so perfect for him, as if she'd been born to be his. Everything that came before her was gone in that instant. Her taste, her soft skin, her cries, rising for him, wiped out the images of death and torture until there was only Soleil. His sun.

Ice took her over, needing her wild, crashing orgasm as much as or more than she did. Her voice swelled, a crescendo in a beautiful symphony, until there was a long, drawn-out scream of pure pleasure. Ice grinned and wiped his face on her thighs.

He slowly stood, his hand rubbing her perfect ass cheeks gently, bringing her down slowly. "You can have this every damn day, baby. I think we should make us permanent, don't you?"

Her lashes fluttered. She looked up at him as if the stars and sun revolved around him. "Yes," she agreed. "Absolutely yes."

Six

Soleil had never known happiness. She'd never felt a part of anything. She had more money than most people saw in a lifetime, but she had never had anyone to share her life with. She'd lived in hotels, and wandered from city to city, country to country, seeing every sight alone.

It was a strange night. She'd gone from having one of the worst days of her life to having the absolute best. She felt as if she were walking through a dream. A fairy tale. Floating. She didn't ever get drunk, yet she knew, somehow, she was actually tipsy. The combination of drinks, maybe, when she never mixed them? It didn't matter. She still knew exactly what she was doing.

She'd always believed in taking responsibility for her actions, and alcohol or not, she was responsible. She lay over a pool table, very aware of where she was and what she'd done, knowing she was surrounded by a lot of bikers and her body was still rippling with strong aftershocks, sending waves of pleasure spreading through her. She should feel shame, and she tried to, but all she could feel was amazing. Alive. Exhilarated. She wanted more.

She'd wanted what Ice had given her. She'd practically begged him to give her an orgasm. Even with her irresponsible, very risky behavior — so typical of her — she couldn't say she hadn't gotten the best of the deal. Her body had never felt like that before. She hadn't known it could feel that way. She had deliberately seduced Ice into this position, and she actually thought his "brothers" had aided her.

Instead of laughing and walking away, Ice soothed her body with his hands, stroking caresses over her back. Rubbing her gently until she felt like her spaghetti legs could hold her up. His hands went to her waist and he gently lifted her off the table.

She heard him talking to her. She wasn't certain what he said, but he tucked her close under his shoulder, her front to his side, and leaned down to whisper in her ear that they were getting out of that place.

She couldn't look at the others, certain they knew she was seducing Ice and that she was a terrible person. She couldn't make herself look at him; the guilt was overwhelming, but still not enough for her to walk away from him. He was so caring, and she was grateful to him for that. She'd never known caring. They left the bar, going out into the cool night air.

"Baby, you okay with walking? Some of the brothers will ride, but we'll have protection. I don't want you on the back of the bike until I know you can hold on. And I think maybe I drank a little bit more than I should have."

It was the last thing she expected him to say. "I did drink way too much," she admitted. She had. And she shouldn't have mixed her drinks, but she'd do it again. She wouldn't change one single thing of this strange, wonderful night. "You didn't drink any more than I did, Ice." She had to take the blame for that. "I was plying you with liquor, matching you drink for drink, remember?"

"We're both fine," he assured.

He kept his arm tightly around her waist, so it was impossible to feel unsteady. The night air was cool, and she hoped it would help clear her head. She'd gone off the deep end. Just because her life was about to end didn't mean she had the right to screw up Ice's. This was one night. Seduction. Sex.

Fun. Nothing else. She could be the girl she'd always wanted to be. She loved to show off. She craved attention. Was starved for it. She loved to be looked at. Her fantasies had always been safe ones, but the need in her was very real. The only thing that had kept her from being the way she was right now was her sense of responsibility. Where had that gone? Because she was still, in the back of her head, thinking, Would it really be that bad to wake up married to her badass biker?

She heard several motorcycles fire up, the pipes loud, roaring through the night air. She stumbled over an uneven spot in the concrete and staggered a few steps. Ice's arm tightened around her waist. Maestro and Player, two of his Torpedo Ink brethren, steadied her by gripping her arms. She was surprised. Shocked even. They let go of her the moment she had her equilibrium, but their touch had been caring, not at all handsy. Their touch felt respectful. She knew they thought she'd stumbled because she'd been drinking, but was it awful of her to let them think that when it wasn't the case?

They had a group of five members walking down the street together. She was in the center with Ice, and they were halfway down the street when she realized they were protecting her. The members of Torpedo Ink recognized that she was afraid of someone.

She had deliberately let her fears about Kevin's death not being an accident slip out because when she turned up dead in an accident, she wanted someone to know it was murder. Maybe they would remember her and care, maybe they wouldn't, but at least she'd told someone the truth.

Ice suddenly leaned into her and brushed a kiss along her jaw. That little brush of his lips set her heart pounding. Her body had come to life after being frozen for so long. Blood rushed like a fireball, pooling low and reminding her she was really alive and that not only could she respond to a man, but rockets had gone off. More, *he* responded to her. He thought she was beautiful and sexy, and he wanted her. She could see it in his eyes and feel it in his touch. See his body's staggering reaction to her. For the first time ever in her life, she felt everything she had ever wanted to feel as a woman.

"I can't imagine what your friends think of me," Soleil whispered. She didn't care that she'd been bent over a pool table in a bar with Ice's hands and mouth all over her, but he might. She might have embarrassed him.

Ice stopped dead on the sidewalk, turning to block her forward momentum. He framed her face with both hands and bent until his head was level with hers. "You don't worry about what anyone else thinks but you or me, Soleil. My brothers have our backs at all times. They won't judge you. They'll always look out for you. But you're mine. I stand in front of you. Some asshole wants to say something to make you feel bad because we make each other feel good, they better know they're sayin' it to me too — and all of them as well."

His glacier-blue eyes stared directly into hers, mesmerizing. Hypnotizing. She couldn't look away. He had some kind of power or, more likely, he was saying all the right things to her, things she desperately needed to hear. She had told herself a hundred times that she didn't need anyone. That they were after her money, and time and again that had been a proven fact. She'd all but thrown herself at Ice because he was that prince in the fairy tale and she desperately wanted to be a princess — his princess — if only on what could be the last night of her life.

She couldn't help it when tears filled her

eyes. "I don't know what happened, Ice." But she did. She had set out to seduce him and she'd done it. She was still doing it. She wanted him exactly the way he was. She couldn't help touching his face, stroking the pads of her fingers down his jaw. He was so incredibly gorgeous. Maybe when someone only had one night, they were given the perfect gift — and Ice was hers.

"What happened was perfect. You're so fuckin' beautiful I can't believe it." He kissed her eyelids. Brushed kisses down her face to the corner of her mouth. This time, when he kissed her, he was so gentle her heart turned over.

She'd never had that kind of caring from anyone. She didn't remember much about her time with her parents. Aunt Deborah had been gentle and kind with her, but her life after she'd died hadn't been that way at all. Her aunt Constance had made an art out of slapping her, reminding her constantly that she was costing her money. That she was in the way. That she was an ugly, stupid child that no one wanted. She still felt like that unwanted, ugly child, and Winston had only confirmed her aunt's opinion of her.

Ice was physically a gorgeous man. He had scars, but they enhanced his good looks rather than detracted from them. He looked scary dangerous, she wasn't so far gone on him that she couldn't see or acknowledge that, but with her he seemed unfailingly sweet. She needed sweet. She needed someone to be nice to her. To be kind. Gentle. Caring. Not want to kill her just because she had money.

The liquor continued the buzz through her veins. It rushed along with her blood, hotter than ever before. No one had ever treated her so kindly or said the things Ice said to her, and God help her, she needed that tonight.

"You still with me, princess? You going to come with me tonight and let me have you?"

No one, not even Kevin, had wanted her in their life. No one. She ate alone. She slept alone. She was always alone. Ice had turned the worst night of her life into something wonderful. He hadn't complained about what she was wearing, even though she clearly didn't fit in. He hadn't made fun of her when she didn't know something and when she'd gone a little crazy in the bar, throwing herself at him. Rather than act like she would be entertainment for his friends, he'd protected her.

She couldn't keep the stars out of her eyes, or her brain. She wanted it all. She wanted the fairy tale. With him. With Ice. For this one night. Didn't she deserve one wonderful night when not one but a group of people wanted to kill her? She nodded because she would have followed him straight into hell if he'd asked her.

"Say it, baby. Tell me you're with me."

"I'm totally with you," Soleil said decisively. She dared to glance around her at the men surrounding them, waiting patiently while Ice reassured her.

Ice flashed a heart-stopping grin of approval that sent blood running like a hot, steamy river through her veins. He tucked her under his shoulder again, wrapping her arm around his waist, almost at his belt buckle. That put her fingertips dangerously close to his cock and she couldn't help glancing down.

Her heart accelerated. Her mouth watered. There was a distinct bulge in his jeans. Not a small one — it stretched the denim to a danger point. She tried not to be so thrilled. She shouldn't be thinking about how impressive that cock was or what she could do with her mouth to make him want to keep her with him for a long, long time, if not forever. She wanted him forever.

She would be so good to him. So good. She knew Ice was all about sex. He'd relate that way. He'd solve arguments that way. He'd expect and want sex often. She needed that from her man. She needed that to feel he wanted her, that he found her beautiful and sexy. She'd tried telling Winston that. He hadn't wanted her. Their sex had been mediocre at best. It didn't matter what she'd tried, Winston had barely been able to get it up for her. And he'd said he wanted to marry her.

"Why would a man pretend he wanted a woman when he couldn't even manage to get hard around her? Does that make any sense to you?" She slapped a hand over her mouth when she realized she'd spoken aloud.

Ice gently removed her hand. "Baby, if you're saying that limp-dick asshole couldn't perform when he had you in his bed, I'm telling you straight up, he's gay. Nothin' wrong with that, but any straight man is going to take one look at you and get hard as a fuckin' rock. Look at me, haven't been able to calm my monster down since I laid eyes on you."

He casually dropped his hand to the front of his jeans and rubbed, as if trying to ease the ache. His little grin was a bit boyish, as if he was actually happy his cock was hard.

Soleil wanted to rub his cock for him. She

192

dared to drop her hand over his jeans, and he immediately took it and laid her palm over that thick bulge. Heat pressed into her. Hot and inviting. She touched her lips with her tongue. "I can't wait." And she couldn't. She wasn't trying to seduce him. She was telling him the absolute truth. She wanted him in her. Wherever. Anywhere. Just in her.

"That's two of us, baby," he assured.

She looked around her and realized they were walking away from the seedier streets, back toward the main boulevard. She dragged her feet. "Ice, we don't need to go to the strip. Why are we headed in that direction?"

Winston had the cops under his thumb. A lawyer. She knew there were others, she just didn't know where they were, but she knew they'd be looking for her. Winston couldn't afford to let her go, not after what she'd heard.

"There's nothing to be afraid of, princess. We've got your back. Anyone trying to take you away from us is going to find themselves with more trouble than they've ever known."

Soleil had the distinct impression not only Ice but the others would welcome a fight. She was terrified Winston would take out a gun and shoot them. If any were left alive, his cop friends would arrest them and throw them in jail. It would be her fault.

She stopped completely. "Ice, I'm not sure where you said we were going . . ."

The cool night air wasn't helping with those screaming orgasms; instead, walking sent the liquor rushing through her bloodstream to pool low. Hot. Scorching and burning. It didn't make sense that she was so mesmerized by Ice, other than the fact that he had a wicked tongue that could do all sorts of things to her along with his incredible fingers.

"Your fingers and mouth need to be insured. Like for millions, Ice." She pressed her fingers to her lips again, certain she really had blurted that aloud. "I think I might really have had a little too much to drink." She was astonished, because alcohol, as a rule, didn't affect her.

Ice laughed, and this time, the others joined in. He kept walking in spite of the fact that she was very serious about them not going up to the main strip. Having his arm around her forced her to go with him. Or maybe she just went because he was utterly amazing. They had walked past the hotel where she was staying with Winston, but one street down, so she still felt relatively safe.

"Ice, really, where are we going?"

"Shopping. You need clothes. Panties, although most of them will end up in my pocket."

"Do you collect women's panties?"

There was a collective derisive snort and suppressed laughter from their entourage.

"I'm collecting yours. Of course, since I'm going to be buying them, technically, they're mine, right?"

"Not if you give them as a gift," she said.

"Well, I think I'm just going to loan them to you, and you have to give them back whenever — or wherever — I ask for them."

Soleil laughed. That was intriguing. She could imagine him asking in all sorts of places, and she would give them up in every single one of them. Just the idea of it sent more heat rushing through her body. She loved being with Ice. She loved everything about him. She was more aware than ever that they were downtown, very close to those twenty-four-hour chapels. She had the prenup and he had his. She could get her lips around his cock and seal the deal. He would want her the way she wanted him . . . Why hadn't she met someone like him before she'd gotten entangled with every loser that ever was born?

Still, they hadn't slowed down. If anything, they were walking faster. When she stopped looking down at the ground and managed to look up from her fantasizing, she realized where they were. This was the part of the strip that was equal to Rodeo Drive in Beverly Hills. Every store was a very high-end establishment. Worse, most would be closed this time of night. Did they plan on breaking into one of the boutiques? She might be contemplating going to hell for seducing him into marriage, but she drew the line at robbery.

"Where are we going, Ice?" She tried to put demand in her voice, but the sound came out more like a squeak. In spite of her trepidation, adrenaline was beginning to rush into her system, mixing with her need for him. She wanted to push him against the wall and have wild sex right there. In the street. By that upscale hotel. She wished she had a screaming orgasm right at that moment to give her the courage to do it.

"We're heading just up the street. There's a shop the girls always use. Alena called the owner for me, and she'll be meeting us there to let us in so we can get you some clothes. You need a new dress for tonight and a few things for tomorrow."

Tomorrow? Ice used the word *tomorrow* as if they had a future. As if once they had sex he wasn't hopping on his bike and heading off alone. Just like that, she was excited for what was to come that evening, what he had in mind.

"Alena went off with someone for the evening." Soleil gave a token protest, feeling she needed to say something. She was very aware of the tension between Alena and Pierce. It wasn't going to be resolved easily. "She can't want to come back just to make certain I have other clothing." She started to protest further, to say she could make do with her dress, but it occurred to her she wasn't even wearing panties. Ice had them. She could ask for them back, but she liked that he had them. They were hers. They'd been on her. She wanted him to keep them. If she did die tomorrow, something of her would remain with him.

Her hand crept down to the hem of her dress at the backs of her thighs. It was a stretch, and Ice, who seemed to see everything, saw her tug at the hem. He immediately caught her wrist and pulled her arm up to circle his waist.

"You're covered, baby. Totally decent. And Alena is my birth sister as well as a fellow Torpedo Ink. Nothing is going to keep her away tonight. She'll be at the shop waiting for us and she'll stand with you, Soleil. Never think differently. Once we make this official, you'll be her sister. She won't take that lightly. Neither will Lana."

Sisters? That sounded so wonderful. Like in the real fairy tales, where all dreams came true. She loved that. She didn't think too much about the word *official* because if she did, then she would have to ask. If she asked and he mentioned anything that had to do with prenups, she'd have to do the responsible thing and confess she'd gotten him a little drunk and deliberately seduced him, and the night would end. She wanted sex. At least once. Maybe more. Like dozens of times. She was taking a chance on messing that up.

He tucked her back under his shoulder as if she belonged with him and continued walking down the block, turned down an alley and stopped three shops up. A light was on in the elegantly appointed boutique and he was right — Alena was waiting at the top of the three cement stairs. She appeared to be arguing with Pierce. He had his back to them, and Soleil could see he wore his Diamondback jacket. His club was reputed to be 1-percenters, and no one messed with any of them.

As they neared the stairs, two men wearing Torpedo Ink jackets came out of the shadows to join them. One had his face turned away from her, the other was Savage.

Alena smiled as Ice took Soleil straight up the stairs. "Sweet, brother, you pulled it off. I had my money on you all the time. You know a keeper when you see one."

Ice brushed a kiss on her cheek as she held the door for him. "Did you have any doubts?"

He ignored Pierce completely, urging Soleil inside. Pierce shook his head and left, making his way down the alley. Soleil stepped into the cool little foyer that led to the inside of the store. The boutique was extremely high-end. Soleil knew clothes and what they were worth. She knew brands and designers. She'd had a lot of time on her hands and she'd spent it doing adrenaline-filled activities, frequenting art galleries or going through shops like this one, looking for one-of-a-kind, beautiful artworks of clothing.

Ice bent his head close to her ear. "I was proud of you using your money for bets when you were playing darts with Alena, but in here, I pay. There's no argument. It's what I want, and you give that to me."

"Ice." She hesitated and then lifted a hand to stroke the side of his face. She could fall head over heels for him. Just the way he made the statement to her sent her stomach somersaulting. "I'm okay with paying." She always paid. She was used to it. If she was anywhere with anyone, they always expected her to pay. He was capturing her heart. Taking it prisoner. She was never going to get it back.

"I'm not okay with you using your money when we're together. When you're with me, I pay unless we agree ahead of time. I'm not agreeing to that shit tonight. This is our night and you're mine. I take care of you. That's the code I live by, and you're going to live by it as well. That means we live with whatever I can afford. You understand me?"

Soleil knew she should protest and tell him all about her trust fund. She felt guilty making him pay for everything. On the other hand, it was a fantasy, one night she could be Cinderella, the princess he called her. He obviously needed to be the one to pay. She didn't care about the money. She'd learned it didn't buy her anything she needed — or really wanted. She'd felt jaded and sad until she met Ice and the Torpedo Ink members. She could live within his rules, especially knowing she had to give it all up the next day.

"If you're sure." She found herself whispering, holding her breath. Waiting for his answer. He just seemed too good to be true.

She'd paid her way from the time her aunt Deborah had died. After that, all the expenses that had been incurred had been paid from her trust fund. She supposed she shouldn't blame her aunt Constance, but most parents supported their children. She'd been paying her way ever since.

Ice gave her a smile that sent her heart pounding and blood moving through her body from her nipples to her clit. She couldn't have that reaction every time he smiled. It wouldn't be good to just attack him — although it sounded good. She only had one night. She needed to make the best of it, and didn't Cinderella lose everything at midnight? Was it midnight? She glanced at her watch. Not yet. She still had time. For what? Seducing him? Trying to keep him? She couldn't be greedy. She just had to have this one-night fantasy and go along with whatever he wanted because she wanted to be whatever his fantasy was.

Ice took her hand. "Don't like you wearing panties and bras, but figure you'll be a little uncomfortable without them all the time, so we'll start there."

She wanted to laugh and knew she was a little giddy from his attention and her unexpected reaction to the screaming orgasms. Or maybe it was the sex. Did getting off on just his mouth and fingers count as sex? She didn't care. She followed him to the little table where exquisite lace underwear lay on silk.

"Ice." She glanced around, making certain no one else could overhear them. "I do have underwear at the hotel."

"You're not going back there," he said. His forceful tone set her heart pounding.

She didn't like upsetting him, and the thought of her going back there obviously did. She didn't want to go back. The thought was terrifying. Panties weren't worth facing Winston and whatever he had in store for her. She loved that Ice didn't want her anywhere near that place — or Winston.

He suddenly flashed that heart-stopping grin again, his blue eyes turning hypnotic. "And I like choosing sexy panties for you."

His hand dropped to her bottom. He seemed to like the shape of it because he stroked caresses over her cheeks before sliding his hand under her skirt and rubbing his palm over her bare skin. "I love to be able to touch you, princess. I like knowing we're surrounded by people and I can run my hand up your thigh and use my fingers to see if you're ready for me."

Soleil held very still, looking down at the pale blue lace in one of his large hands while his fingers sank into her. Instantly she was slick. His thumb strummed her clit and she gasped. His grin turned wicked.

"I could get you off right here, baby," he offered. "You'd have to be very quiet, so Alena's friend, I think her name is Diana or something close to that, doesn't realize what I'm doin' to you. Wouldn't want to make her jealous." His grin was very wicked.

She'd never heard anything so sexy in her life. His fingers plunged deep, teased and withdrew, only to slide deep again. She couldn't stop her hips from moving, riding his hand shamelessly. She had to hold on to the table to keep from losing her balance as he teased her.

"I love how you look when you're close to getting off, baby," he whispered, his voice as wicked as his grin had been, the lines in his face purely sensual. "You look so completely abandoned, so caught up in the moment, and when you look at me . . ." He shook his head. "You look like I'm a fuckin' god and you'd spend your life worshipping me."

She knew it was true. She did look at him that way. How could she not? She couldn't think straight with his fingers in her and the look on his face. Because he looked at her as if she were the sexiest woman alive. She would worship him. She'd never had any-

203

one. If she had him, a man like him, she would never want to lose him and she'd give him everything.

"I could look at you all day, just like this, your head thrown back, the light surrounding you, so you look like a fuckin' angel while you ride my fingers. Sexy as hell, baby."

She loved his voice, how it had that velvet rasp to it that seemed to slide over her skin, stroking sensually and making her hot, fevered even. She knew she'd always have a response to him, whether it was his voice, his smile, his blue eyes or his fingers. Always. No matter where they were. She'd be slick and ready. More, she'd anticipate his touch. Crave it.

She loved that he was willing to come into a boutique and choose her underwear. She'd never understood why men could be prudish about buying underwear. They liked taking them off yet couldn't walk into a store and buy them? That didn't make sense.

She also loved that Ice wanted to touch her the way he did, wherever they were. She wanted to touch him as well and she hadn't yet had the opportunity. Her gaze dropped to the bulge in the front of his jeans. Ice didn't seem to be embarrassed by any kind of sexy act.

"I think it would be unfair for you to get me off twice when I didn't reciprocate," she said daringly. Her breath was coming in ragged little pants, but she managed to get it out as an invitation — and she meant it. She really wanted to have him in her mouth, this wasn't about seducing him — it wasn't. She was certain of that. She wasn't trying to get him to take her to a chapel. This was about giving him something unforgettable. A gift. She wanted his night to be as perfect as he was making hers.

He studied her face for a few more moments, his fingers moving in her, his thumb circling and flicking until the blood pounded through her sheath and her clit was inflamed. Very slowly he pulled his fingers free and brought them to his mouth. She'd never seen anything as sexy as the way he sucked them clean. Her body was on fire, but it didn't matter, not when he was looking at her like that. Possessively. With such intensity and focus she squirmed, rubbing her thighs together to try to reduce the fire between her legs.

"You'd do that here for me?"

She was mesmerized by him. She knew that. He leaned down and kissed her, sharing her taste, his tongue sliding suggestively along hers. When he lifted his head, still cupping her chin so she could only stare into his blue eyes, eyes that had come alive with a dark, dangerous lust, she nodded.

"I don't think it's very fair that you're still wanting when you took care of me. So yes, if you want me to, of course I'll take care of you." She bit her lip and then decided, the hell with it, she might as well tell him the truth. "I want to. I more than want to."

"Right here, in this store? In front of the window?" He jerked his chin toward the front of the boutique.

She was certain he was testing her resolve. Little did he know she would have been on her knees in the bar for him. "Absolutely."

He slung his arm around her neck and pulled her into him. Tight against his chest. "You couldn't be any more perfect for me, Soleil. Let's get these panties and bras to Alena's friend and then we'll do a little more shopping. You'll need a dress for tonight and some jeans and tees for tomorrow. I think we'll manage to take care of the monster somewhere in all that."

He took her hand and curled her fingers around the thick length of him through the denim. Every step they took had her palm rubbing him. She put pressure on his cock as they neared the owner of the store. Just before they moved out from one of the taller displays, Ice let her hand go and she reluctantly dropped it to her side.

Diana and Alena turned toward them. Aware she didn't have any panties on, and her thighs and bare lips were slick with telltale liquid hunger, Soleil stayed very still beside Ice.

The owner of the shop was a tall, very elegant woman. She wore her hair in a tight chignon at the top of her head. Gold and diamonds dripped from her ears. Her dress was a tight sheath, emphasizing her firm, high breasts and the curve of her hips. She was extremely slender, making Soleil feel chubby beside her.

The cool eyes swept over Soleil dismissively and then she pounced on Ice, smiling at him, her eyes lighting up like a predator's.

"We'll take these." Ice sounded abrupt. "Looking for your jeans and tees. A jacket? Socks. You have shoes here?"

"I do. I can take you into that part of the store if you'd like."

"Point us in the right direction and we're good," Ice said, turning away from her before she could engage him in more conversation.

As they walked down the aisle toward the section of the store the owner had indicated, Ice took Soleil's hand and brought it to his mouth. "Don't like you feeling inferior to someone like that, princess. You're mine. You're my choice. That means I put you above any other woman. That should make you feel confident if you're not already just by being you." He stopped just out of reach of the lights. "What's wrong?"

"I'm almost dripping because I want you so much," she admitted. "I think I might be a little tipsier than I thought I was. And I'm letting you pay for my clothes." She was used to going into boutiques as Soleil Brodeur, a woman of extreme wealth. She was always dressed in the hottest designer clothing and given deference when she entered a store. She didn't know how to act as Ice's chosen babe for the night.

"I love that you're ready for me. That you're so attracted you'll let me touch you or eat you whenever I want. Do you know how rare you are? I never want to give you up." He dropped to his knees and yanked her legs apart. "I'll make sure you're clean and you don't have to worry about that superior bitch. She wouldn't know how to fuck a real man if she ever got one to go near her. The girls spend tons of money in here, so when I said she was their friend, I meant she wants their money any way she can get it."

His tongue slid up her thigh. She closed her eyes and held on to his shoulders. Her legs were shaking. She threw her head back and let herself feel. Just feel. Every stroke of his tongue. His breath. His lips. She had to open her eyes again to look down to watch him. Who could resist the sight of him on his knees?

Soleil found she couldn't stop herself from pushing her fingers into his thick, blond hair. The strands were platinum, gold and a thread of silver. It was unique just like him. She closed her eyes again and let him take her away from her life. Far, far away. She didn't care if everything she was doing this night was considered wrong by anyone else. Tonight, this man was making her feel alive. Packing everything she had ever wanted or needed from a man into one night. Ice. He was so giving, so unselfish. It shocked her that a man could be the way he was.

The tension coiled tighter and tighter until her breath was coming out in ragged pants and her legs were shaking almost uncontrollably. She felt the wave gathering so fast and so strong, she pushed her hand over her mouth hard to hold in the cries that threatened to give them away. Tears burned behind her eyes. It was so good. That good. She'd never experienced anything like it, and she knew she never would again.

The tsunami hit in waves, powerful ones that swept her away from her life of endless loneliness, of always wondering what was wrong with her. Away from Kevin's murder and the fact that a circle of strangers had targeted her for death because of her money. The feeling was almost euphoric, so beautiful she couldn't believe it. She'd never had this. Never had anyone who cared enough to bother to make certain she felt this.

She jammed her fist into her mouth to keep from making any noise. He looked up at her and immediately stood up, a worried look on his face.

"Princess." Ice gathered her into his arms, holding her against his chest, muffling the sobs. "That's not the reaction I was hoping for." His voice was gentle, almost tender, bringing on more tears. No one ever talked to her in a voice like that. No one held her like he did.

He had three teardrops tattooed on his face, dripping down from his eye, while she had unbelievable waterworks going. Just that velvet-soft voice, moving over her skin, made her feel more exposed and vulnerable than ever.

"Baby, look at me."

She shook her head, trying to stop crying,

but the more he was sweet, the harder the tears fell. Could she be any more pathetic? What was wrong with her? She was having a complete breakdown in front of a man she didn't even know just because he was kind to her. She'd been more intimate with him than she'd been with anyone in her life. What was she going to tell him? Sex, without his cock, had been better than anything she'd ever experienced with one? He'd been sweeter, kinder, more wonderful than any other human being had been to her in years? Even Kevin? Her beloved lawyer?

She tried to get air in order to stop crying. She wouldn't blame him if he just left her right there in the middle of the store and disappeared.

Ice caught her chin and forced her face up so that she had no choice but to look into his eyes. "Soleil. Stop. Right now. You're safe. Everything is fine."

She shook her head. "I have to go." Suddenly she was desperate to leave. It was the only sane thing to do. She had to save him, because right there, right then, she knew if she stayed with him much longer, she would commit the worst sin possible and she'd do everything she could to seduce him into keeping her.

His smile was slow. Beautiful. Breathtaking. "You run when things overwhelm you, don't you? That isn't happening tonight. You're going to see this through with me. You're having a little panic attack, but I'm right here. We're going to walk right over there to that table where the jeans you'll need tomorrow are, and we're going to grab a couple of pairs that are your size. Then we'll find a few T-shirts. After that, we're getting you a killer dress."

She found herself drowning in his eyes. His smile. He was so completely confident, and he was sticking with her when she was an emotional mess. It was going to hurt like hell in the morning when he was gone, but she just needed to hold on to the promise of tonight. Instead of falling apart because she didn't have anyone, she had to let herself enjoy the moment. Ice was too good to be true, but she was going to see this night through with him — have her fairy tale, even if she couldn't seem to clear her brain. Give him his because he deserved it.

"Princess, I need you to say you're with me all the way on this."

She was in love with his voice. With him. With everything about him. Maybe he was a fantasy, and in her very emotional state, she had made him her prince, but he was asking her to stick with him for the night, and she was going to give this to herself as a gift. She'd face the mess she'd made with Winston tomorrow, but tonight, she had Ice.

"I'm in it all the way with you." The declaration slipped out, and she meant it.

His smile was worth everything. "That's my girl."

She wanted to be his girl. She even needed to be. She knew he was saving her, because, God help her, she'd run out of strength on her own.

He took her hand and led her to the small table. The jeans were a designer brand she actually wore so she knew the size that fit her like a glove. She chose a pair and Ice added a second one. She had to bite her lip to keep from pointing out how expensive they were. He flashed his heart-stopping grin, almost as if he knew what she was thinking, and then he led her over to the tank tops that were sheer luxury. So soft. Lightweight. Perfect. She let him choose the ones he liked.

Ice caught her hand and tugged her under his shoulder again. He evidently liked her close, and she didn't mind in the least. They made their way back to Alena and Diana.

Ice handed the owner the jeans and tanks. "Where are your couture gowns? Alena told you what I wanted? Soleil needs something particularly spectacular for tonight."

"I do?" Couture dresses? Was he out of his mind? How did he even know what that was? Gowns like that were thousands of dollars.

He kissed her hand. "Yeah, you do. And I want pictures. Lots of them."

Alena blew him a kiss. "We've already got that covered." She glanced at her watch. "You've got about an hour. A little less."

"I'll show you the dresses," the owner said, looking Ice up and down with interest blazing in her eyes.

Ice moved away from her. "Just tell us what part of the store they're in and we'll find them. That's half the fun." Deliberately, he bent his head and brushed a kiss across Soleil's mouth. "Isn't it, princess?"

She nodded, shocked that he didn't flirt back with the owner. She was tall and beautiful. Very elegant. Ice didn't so much as glance at her. He was most definitely wholly focused on Soleil. She couldn't help but feel beautiful and sexy. No one had ever done that for her before. Her money was a draw, but never her as a woman. Ice made her so happy.

She went with him in the direction the owner had indicated, and when she glanced back, Alena was tugging Diana toward the back room. The dresses were toward the front of the store, framed by the windows but back away across the aisle. There were few lights on and those were dim, as the boutique was officially closed. The lights that were on shone on the couture dresses, and Soleil was shocked at the designers represented.

"Ice, these dresses cost a fortune."

"Baby, didn't I tell you not to worry about money tonight? We have an agreement. I like a couple of these. That one there. What do you think about it? It looks your size. Alena said if it needed alterations, Diana could do them." He indicated a dress with white open lace over a silken black slip. It was gorgeous. And pricey.

She moistened her lips but didn't speak.

"Or this one. It would suit you as well. It's about the same length, formfitting and sexy as hell. This one is my favorite."

Like the other dress, this one was white, but one side was completely made up of peekaboo fabric, small diamonds cut out of the material to show skin from shoulder to ankle on one side. The chiffon wrap on the other side covered one breast and wrapped around the waist, colliding with the peekaboo fabric. The slit up the front was wide and bold, with the chiffon dropping to the floor on either side. Concealed beneath the chiffon were panties made of the peekaboo material, so the diamonds showed beneath the dramatic slit when she walked.

"I could push my fingers right through that fabric and keep you wet for me all night," he whispered wickedly.

"Ice, I love it, but it's too —"

"That's it, woman. I told you not to bring up money again." His hands dropped to his jeans and he opened them, sliding them off his hips easily so that his cock sprang free.

They were in front of a long storefront window, one that showcased the couture gowns. The light was dim in the store, but the streetlight seemed to shine right on him. She gasped, staring at his cock. He was gorgeous. That particular part of him went with his amazing good looks. It was hard and thick, standing straight up, and he looked so casual and at ease standing there, waiting. He was . . . beautiful.

She just stared until he caught her by the shoulders and pushed her to the floor, right there, in front of the couture gowns. "Use your mouth for something better than arguing with me, woman."

Soleil was shocked at the way her body went hot and slick at the idea of getting him off there in the store with the owner just a small distance away. He was larger than she'd expected, but she wanted him in her mouth. She wanted the taste of him on her tongue.

She rubbed her hand up his thigh. "I've wanted this ever since I first laid eyes on you." Which was pretty much the truth. This was her chance to give him something back for all the wonderful things he'd given her.

He widened his stance and bunched her hair in his fist. "We don't have all night, baby, so get to work. If you don't want me to blow my load all over these dresses, you'd better swallow me down fast. The sight of you on your knees is fuckin' sexy."

He made her feel sexy. He made her feel beautiful and — his. She couldn't help but be turned on by the way he just touched her whenever he wanted to, almost as if he had to. She loved the demand in his voice and the way, when she looked up at him, his eyes were so blue, so amazing, and so filled with lust.

"You're incredibly beautiful, you know that?" She couldn't help the awe in her voice.

She cupped his balls in her palms and rolled them, hungrily watching his cock as it jerked in appreciation. She licked up and over his balls, loving the velvety feel of them.

He was hot and definitely needed her attention. He was leaking pearly drops and she couldn't resist licking them off and then sliding her mouth over the broad crown. He tasted good. Like addictive good.

"Your cock is amazing," she whispered.

"Glad you appreciate it, princess. I'd appreciate you using your mouth to get me off. I'm about to embarrass myself."

She slid her mouth over him again, feeling him stretch her lips, his weight on her tongue. His cock was scorching hot, and unexpectedly heavy. She used her tongue to map him out, so she'd always remember him. That was important to her. She traced the heavy vein and flicked under the broad head, while she tried to take him deeper. That didn't work out, so she jacked him with her mouth, sliding him in and out while her tongue lashed and danced. She had to get him wetter, and her lips needed to stretch wider. She wanted time with him. Days and nights until she could take all of him. The wetter she got him and her lips, the more of him she could take.

"You love that, don't you, baby?" His hands fisted in her hair. "I can tell."

Her eyes met his, but she didn't stop. She did love it because it was him and he'd been so generous, getting her off twice, teaching her that she could actually have a real orgasm. Treating her as if she was someone special. Yeah, she loved having his cock in her mouth. He smelled good. He tasted good, and his cock was amazing.

He began to move, thrusting gently, filling her mouth, pushing her limit just a little. She worked for him. Determined. She found it sexy as hell to have him looking down at her with those crystal blue eyes, eyes that seemed cold but now had blue flames burning so hot she thought she might actually explode. Was it possible to have an orgasm while giving a man a blow job?

"What's going on back here?" the owner's strident voice demanded.

Soleil made a move to pull back, but Ice held her head firm, thrusting faster now. "No, baby, get me the fuck off, I'm so close." He practically groaned the words.

Her gaze shifted just for a moment. She could hear heels clicking toward them. Outside a man passing by paused and tried to peer in. She was aware of both. Her body clenched hard in reaction. Grew hotter. Her breasts ached. She really was close to orgasm again.

"Don't you fuckin' stop. Your mouth is making this fuckin' for real."

She didn't know what that meant, but

Ice's voice was hoarse. Raw. His grip in her hair made her scalp ache and her sex pulse. His cock seemed to swell and grow hotter. His thrusts went deeper, almost to the point that she gagged, but not quite. She didn't stop because Ice mattered. Not some woman who had already judged her and she'd never see again. Not someone outside a window who couldn't see her face. They didn't matter to her. Only Ice. He mattered. His pleasure. Making him feel as good as she could. She wanted this for him. She would give this to him anywhere. If he needed, if he wanted, she would provide it for him, and she could tell, right then, it was a need.

She hollowed her cheeks. Sucked harder. Took him deeper. Out of the shadows two men materialized, both wearing Torpedo Ink jackets, moving between them and the owner, murmuring to her, taking her arm and leading her away. She wouldn't have cared if the woman saw her with Ice's cock in her mouth, practically down her throat. The woman wanted him. Soleil had him.

Her tongue lashed the crown of his cock, danced and flicked just under it, curled around his shaft as he thrust deep, cutting off her air. She didn't care about breathing either. Everything was for him. She felt his cock expand, pushing at the soft tissues of her mouth, and then he was pulsing, jerking, and she was swallowing, nearly choking as he poured down her throat.

Ice pulled back slightly, just enough for her to breathe. His hands loosened in her hair, so his palm could stroke caresses over it. "Fuckin' hell, princess. I've had a million blow jobs in my time, sometimes with more than one woman trying to bring me off. You did it in minutes. All by yourself. Without help from me. That's never happened. Not one single time."

He sounded shocked. Awed. He didn't remove his semi-hard cock. "Clean the monster, baby, so I'm not a mess. Unlike you, I don't have a change of clothes."

She was more than happy to. She felt the burn of tears behind her eyes, and she hoped she'd given him something to remember her by. She loved what she'd done. She loved having him in her mouth, giving to him what he'd done so generously for her. It was just one more thing to put down in her fantasy fairy tale.

SEVEN

Riding on the back of a Harley in a couture gown wasn't the easiest, although the two long sides of the skirt had been brought up to Soleil's waist and tied there. She sat on the seat in the bodice made of peekaboo chiffon and nothing else, yet she looked as elegant as hell. Her tits were tight against his back, and her bare mound, covered by that peekaboo material, just as tight against his buttocks. The machine roared with life, another sexy monster Ice used to shamelessly entice her into his world.

Ice had pulled her arms around him once Alena and Maestro had helped her onto the bike in her sexy heels. Now he had her so close to their goal. The chapel was just ahead. Everything was arranged. Alena had done exactly what he'd asked and had given his woman another drink while she'd helped her dress and done her hair.

Soleil hadn't asked questions, but she had

drunk the whiskey Alena had supplied. Ice wasn't about to lose her, not after what had happened. He hadn't been lying when he'd told Soleil he'd been blown by countless women, sometimes two and three at a time. He'd still had to command his fuckin' cock to work if he wanted release. They had done their best, trying to suck him dry, yet he'd never once had a natural release, not until her sweet, talented mouth had closed around him. It had been all he could do to stay in control and not shove his cock down her throat. She'd been that good.

Nothing had ever felt like it had right there in that shop with Soleil on her knees looking up at him. Paradise. Another fucking dimension. There was no forcing of his body, no controlling, no commanding his own release. She was his, made for him. How it happened, he didn't have the first idea, but his body wanted hers. Reacted to hers. He had always appreciated the female form, but his body had been taught from childhood never to react on its own. He hadn't been able to overcome that training. Nothing — and no one — had ever ruined his control until Soleil.

She had enjoyed blowing him. It was more than that. She'd wanted to do that for him. She hadn't been thinking about herself at all. That had been all about him. He could tell. He'd had a hell of a lot of blow jobs, and no woman had ever looked at him the way she did. For whatever reason, she looked at him and saw something in him no one else did — but he needed it.

He made the run to the chapel with his brothers surrounding him, taking his back, making certain to show Soleil what family was all about. She needed them every bit as much as she needed him. That was one thing he could provide for her, and as far as he was concerned, Torpedo Ink was the only family they would ever need.

Ice had known, when she'd made that decision to stay on her knees, his cock in her mouth, in front of a window with a judgmental woman coming straight at them, that he would never let her go. He'd seen indecision on her face, but when he'd told her she couldn't stop, desperation — he was certain — in his voice, he'd been too close, she cared more about him and taking him to oblivion than about getting caught by the owner.

She'd chosen him over bullshit moral rules. He'd never thought he'd find a woman who could put up with his needs, and on top of that, get him off without his commanding his cock to cooperate, but she fit every requirement. He wasn't fool enough to throw a miracle away.

She'd let Alena help her dress, but she'd gone very quiet. She hadn't asked questions, nor had she said anything. That alarmed him a little, and Alena had frowned a lot when she'd reported it to him, but she'd said she'd kept very close to Soleil. She hadn't said she wanted out, which, had she, at any time, they would have had to let her go. She wasn't so drunk that she didn't know what a wedding gown was. She had gotten into the gown, the heels, and let Alena do her hair without a word. She'd drunk the small shot of whiskey and climbed onto the back of his bike and held on tight.

The chapel wasn't far from the bar where he'd retrieved his bike, and it was Player who carefully helped Soleil off the motorcycle when they arrived. Alena was there quickly to untie the gown and let it fall to the ground. She fussed over the dress for a few minutes until she was satisfied it was perfect, and then they were all moving inside, surrounding the bride.

"You look beautiful," Ice whispered to her. He took her hand. "Absolutely beautiful."

"It's the dress," she whispered back. "I can't believe you bought this for me. It had to be —"

"Don't say it, princess. After that exceptional blow job, I made up my mind. You give me any nonsense about money, I'm going to occupy your mouth with better things. You're not going to want to accommodate me here in front of everyone."

She laughed. Out loud. The sound played over his skin and slipped deeper, striking inside his chest so that he rubbed his hand over his heart. There was something very real about Soleil, as if she took every moment and tried to live it to the fullest.

"You never know. You tasted amazing, and that cock of yours is worth worshipping."

His heart clenched hard. His cock jerked, coming to attention at the praise. He kept his eyes on her face. Her high cheekbones and the long sweep of her lashes, the generous mouth, the straight little princess nose. Her eyes were almost too big, but the kind that a man could drown in.

"You can't say things like that to me. I don't give a damn who sees me fucking my woman, as long as they know they can't touch what's mine."

"I don't much care who sees me fucking my man, as long as they know they can't touch what's mine," she echoed and laughed again.

She shook her head. Her eyes were dark

chocolate, looking liquid, as if all that chocolate had melted for him. She did things to his insides he wasn't expecting. She had his body, he accepted that, but she was crawling inside him, and that was a little dangerous. She might see things that would scare her to death. Winston was a little pussy, and he scared her. Ice was death coming. He couldn't imagine what she would think.

Storm had told him more than once, when he'd been beating the shit out of someone because he couldn't take forcing his release one more time, that fucking wasn't everything in a relationship. That even if you found the perfect woman, the way Reaper had found Anya, or Steele, Breezy, even Czar, with Blythe, if you wanted to keep her, you had to find a way to live with her. Judging by the rocky beginnings each of his brethren had had, it was true.

At the same time, Ice knew Storm was wrong. There had to be a real physical attraction. One his body recognized. Just looking at Soleil almost hurt. More, she suited his peculiar proclivities. He wouldn't be an easy man to live with, but he would find ways to make that up to her. He knew he had charm. He was an expert at all things sexual. And he wanted her to be happy. He could make her safe.

While he was going through all the reasons in his head to convince himself that he was doing the right thing, Soleil was looking around her, suddenly sobering. She looked at the chapel. The flowers. The way his club surrounded them. Alena holding two bouquets. The strange little man at the front of the chapel with an open book waiting for them.

"Ice." She whispered his name. "What are we doing here?"

"I signed your prenup, princess, and you signed mine. This is all we've got left to do. Almost everyone is here. We're missing a few of the brothers and Lana, but they know about it and are waiting at home to welcome you. They're getting the house ready for us."

"You don't understand what I did, honey." She touched his face with the pads of her fingers. "I deliberately set out to seduce you. I made certain you were drinking too much. You don't know what you're doing."

He stared at her for a long time, shocked that she would think she was responsible for getting the two of them to the chapel. She'd had way too much to drink if she thought they were there because she'd trapped him.

"Baby, I know exactly what I'm doing.

This is what I want."

Her dark eyes searched his. She gave a little shake of her head. She looked so help-less he wanted to pull her into his arms.

"I wanted you so much, Ice. I kept having you drink when I don't get drunk. I seduced you. I know I did. You'll wake up tomorrow —"

"Happy, because this is what I want. I set out to make you mine."

"What are we doing?" she whispered again, her face going pale. Her eyes were enormous, as if she was in shock.

"You're marrying me."

She stared at him as if he'd grown two heads. Panic began to set in. She had to do this of her own free will. There was the code they lived by. All was fair as long as he made certain it was what she wanted, and every step of the way she'd agreed verbally. His club watched for that.

"I am?" She shook her head. "We can't do that."

"Why?"

She opened her mouth and then closed it and shook her head. "I don't know, but we can't. You don't know me. I'm in so much trouble. I don't want that for you. I know you don't believe me, but I put this idea in your head. I did."

His heart clenched hard in his chest. She wasn't rejecting him. She was worried about him. The others were watching. Waiting patiently. No one tried to hurry them. The preacher wasn't as patient, but he didn't voice his annoyance, not with all the bikers crowding his small chapel. Not with the money they were paying him. As a rule, biker weddings could be over the top, and he didn't want any damages to his chapel. He wanted them gone, but that fat paycheck was more than he could resist.

"You don't know me either. I specialize in taking trouble away. That's what I plan on doing for you." Ice brought her hand to his mouth and nibbled on the pads of her fingers. Immediately her eyes darkened with desire. She was so responsive to him. He wasn't letting her slip away, not when he was so close. He had to close the deal. Seal it for good.

"You can't let me down now, Soleil. You promised me. Every step of the way, I gave you an out and you said yes. You said I was your choice. You made me believe that. Are you deserting me now?"

She frowned, biting at her lower lip, calling attention to it. He had a thing for that lower lip, and he wouldn't mind biting it himself.

"But are you sure we should do this?" Those dark eyes met his, asking him. Trusting him to give her the right answer.

He didn't hesitate. "Absolutely. Aren't you? Think about being with me. What I can give you. What you give me. Don't we make perfect sense together? Is it the club? They're my family. They would be yours." Unashamedly he dangled his brothers and sisters out in front of her, knowing she wanted a family.

She stared up at him, her eyes searching his. He wished he knew what she needed from him to say yes. To give herself to him. He had to get her home, surround her with family, give her anything she wanted, be that man every day so she'd never want to leave him. Rule her fucking nights. Put kids in her belly so she'd need him even more. Whatever it took, he'd do it.

A slow smile curved that sweet mouth, the one he planned on using daily. A real fucking erection. A fantastic release he hadn't ordered up himself. Give his woman everything. His world would be right.

"I need you, princess. No one will ever need you the way I do."

"For sex? Anyone could give you that."

They couldn't, but that wasn't the point she was making. Did he want her for more than sex? It was a fair question. He thought about her laughter. The sunshine. He lived in a dark place. Just listening to the sound of her voice took him out of it. Was that enough to reassure her? Or him?

"It's not just for sex, princess. You're the one, the only, for me."

Her gaze moved over his face and then went back to his eyes. Her chin went up. "Let's do it, then," she agreed.

Ice's world righted instantly. Not taking a chance she'd change her mind, he squeezed her hand and nodded to his sister, who came to stand beside his woman. He left Soleil there with Alena and walked down the short aisle to stand beside his brother. Storm was there, his twin, and that added another layer of happiness for him. Ice had done it; he'd gotten his siblings out of that hellhole alive, both intact — at least somewhat. They were alive and there when he needed them to see this through with him.

He turned to look at his bride, and his heart stopped. She was the gift. All his. Soleil looked so beautiful he hurt just looking at her. His lungs squeezed down, burning for air. That dress fit her curves like a glove, the peekaboo material showing that soft, silky skin to perfection.

The slit up the front was almost all the

way to her mound, the material barely showing beneath the chiffon skirt, but it did peek out as she walked toward him. The bodice was a halter top with two thick strips of material covering her tits. The slash was all the way to her waist, and one side was made of the peekaboo diamond pattern. She not only looked beautiful, she looked sexy as well.

She handed her bouquet to Alena and took his hand to stand in front of the strange little man who had the biggest beard and mustache Ice had ever seen. That didn't matter. What did matter was looking into Soleil's eyes to give her courage, holding her hand tightly because she was trembling so hard, he was afraid she might fall.

"Keep looking at me, princess." Ice whispered the command when her gaze strayed to the preacher, who was reading some crap that didn't matter. He wanted the questions asked and the answers made, not something this little man with his squinty eyes and wild beard that needed a trim said to them.

Her gaze jumped back to his. He faced her squarely and took both hands when the little man asked the burning question. Did Isaak "Ice" Koval take Soleil Brodeur as his wife? Hell fucking yeah, he took her as his wife. For better or worse. Sickness and in

233

health until death parted them.

She frowned up at him, wondering, no doubt, how they had her last name. She'd never told him, but they had the papers to prove they'd taken out the license, thanks to Code. Everything would be properly filed by their preacher man.

Then the same question was asked of Soleil, and again, his full name was given. Isaak "Ice" Koval. Did she take him as her husband? The chapel went eerily silent as his entire club waited with him for her answer. Storm shifted closer. Alena did as well. He didn't take his gaze from her, shamelessly mesmerizing her, willing her to say yes. God, he needed her to say yes.

She swallowed. Hard. Her eyes went liquid. His stomach dropped. His thumb slid back and forth over her hand in a small caress that he needed more for himself than for her.

Her voice was shaky, very low, but the room was so silent, there was no doubt that his brethren heard when she committed her life to his, when she took him for her husband. He couldn't help the grin or the triumph bursting through him. He hadn't had a lot of time, but he'd pulled off the most important seduction of his life, and she was just as bound by their code as he was — as they all were.

It came time for the ring and he pushed the one he'd made, drawn in hasty detail on paper and made into a continuous band, onto her finger. He'd done it while she was getting ready. He'd told Alena to take her time. Then he'd had Transporter laminate the thing, so it would stand up in the shower, until he had time to make her the real thing. He pushed the band onto her finger, and his heart jerked hard in his chest just seeing it there.

She looked down at it, gave him a smile and he swore she had tears in her eyes.

"We'll have matching ones, baby. You aren't alone." He wore rings, but they were generally on his fingers for other purposes. He'd wear his wedding ring right along with the other ones that fucked people up when he needed them to.

The preacher pronounced them man and wife, and Ice stepped close, took her into his arms and kissed her as lovingly and as tenderly as he possibly could. A loud cheer went up, nearly shaking the small building.

She turned her mouth up to his and once again gave him everything. She surrendered completely to him, her lips soft and pliant, taking everything he offered, drowning him in fire. It didn't smolder in his belly; it was a raging inferno, starting in that soft, sweet mouth and continuing through his body like a firestorm out of control.

It took a few minutes to remember where they were and that an outsider was watching. He turned his woman away from the preacher and toward his brethren. Instantly, another roar went up. He glanced at Savage and brushed his finger across his watch.

Savage held up three fingers on one hand and his pinkie on the other. Three and a half hours, that's all he'd have with his woman, cementing their relationship, making certain it was legal and she couldn't renege in the morning when she woke up, fully realized what she'd done and went into full-blown panic.

He swept his arm around her waist, locking her to him, where he wanted to keep her forever. He'd had enough of bullshit lonely. Of believing he was the devil walking on earth. He might be a monster, but to this one woman, he wasn't that. He hoped the others could take notice and have hope.

He hadn't believed for one moment this miracle could ever happen to him, not even after Blythe had taken Czar back and Anya had kept Reaper in spite of all his mistakes. Even Breezy had forgiven Steele and seemed to be able to work with him. That hadn't been enough for Ice to think his sins — and his needs — would ever be forgiven enough for him to find a woman of his own. But he had, at the eleventh hour.

Each member of his club had sins and needs that weren't considered normal by society's standards. But because he'd found Soleil, he wanted the others to know they had a chance to find someone of their own.

He fucking loved his club. His brothers and sisters. They'd helped him pull off the seduction he needed in a short time, and a wedding in just under three hours, a record for certain. More, when they'd gone shopping and he'd lost his mind because he couldn't get enough of her and the way she made his body come to life, they'd taken his back and made certain she hadn't been embarrassed or ashamed. He was certain that would come in the morning, when the magic wore off, but he would handle it when it happened.

Now, they had the reception, her party planned. There would be plenty of photographs. She might not like that in the morning, but she would later. Both Lana and Alena had assured him women liked that. He wanted the photos to help ensure there was no sliding out from under him.

He led her out of the chapel and back to

his bike. Alena carefully tied the skirt of Soleil's wedding dress around her waist and Mechanic helped her onto the back of the motorcycle.

Soleil clung to Ice. He turned his head, caught her by the nape of her neck and pulled her in for a kiss. Sweet. Gentle. Filled with promises. Tasting like forever in the fairy tale he was weaving for her. The role was familiar. Prince Charming to the rescue. He'd played it a hundred times. Usually with Storm. The two of them could get a woman of just about any age to fall hard when they played it just right. Most of it was learning what a woman needed or thought she wanted. He couldn't have Storm or anyone else play Soleil. They weren't assassinating her. They weren't carrying out orders. No one but Ice was going to touch her. Still, he'd managed to get a ring on her finger.

Soleil stared down at the ring on her finger. She had jewelry worth a fortune locked in her safe at her home in San Francisco. Not one piece mattered to her the way that laminated, drawn-on paper jewelry did. She wanted time to inspect it. To look at it under the lights and see every detail. She couldn't believe that Ice had managed to make it for her, or that he would have even bothered. Just looking at that laminated ring was one more reason to fall for her knight in shining armor.

She tried to put aside her guilt. She'd told him what she'd done. He insisted on taking the blame, insisted he'd gotten her drunk. He didn't understand that she was one of those rare people who didn't really get drunk. Maybe she was a bit tipsy, or pleasantly feeling the rush of the screaming orgasms, although more likely it was the real thing. But she knew what she was doing, probably better than he did. She was really afraid of what he was going to do in the morning, when he woke up and realized he had gotten married.

She took a deep breath and held on to him as tightly as she could, pressing her face against his back as they rode back to the bar where, apparently, they were planning to celebrate. She was all for that or just skipping the party and going straight for a hotel room and hot sex. This was still the fairy tale, and if she could have Ice for this night, it was going to be the best night either one of them had ever experienced, if she had her way. If she had the chance to keep him, she would move heaven and earth to do so.

Still, she did promise herself, in the morning she would tell the entire truth to him — that she didn't get drunk and that she wanted to run off with him and she would handle the annulment if that was what he wanted. She was always responsible, and she always took responsibility for her actions. Ice was a good man, and he didn't deserve to be trapped into marriage.

Ice liked showing off his woman, that was very, very clear. He wanted her to look sexy. He wanted her to focus wholly on him while others wanted what he had. Tonight was his night, and she was giving him the best of everything if she could. She was going to give him his fantasy, his fairy tale, because if anyone deserved it, he did.

Soleil made a spectacular entrance in her long white gown, walking like a model on a runway. She was used to walking in heels, and these were a good four inches high. The leather cutouts went up her ankle and partway up her calf. The heels made her legs look like they went on forever. With the chiffon skirt parted almost in the middle, her right leg showed all the way up her thigh. Catching glimpses of her left leg was just plain erotic and made her feel that way. She knew how to work a dress. She'd been wearing designer clothes since she was a teen.

Then there was that peekaboo fabric that went down the entire left side of her body. The dress had a halter top, with a dramatic slashing vee down the front so that the rounded curves of her full breasts showed to perfection. The material was draped over both breasts, yet moved as she walked, a sexy, erotic feel the designer had clearly created the dress for.

It was easy enough to feel sensual in a gown designed for that purpose walking in on a man's arm, when that man was as gorgeous and as sexy as Ice, especially when he was looking at her with lust-filled eyes.

Ice thought she was the sexiest woman he'd ever seen. He loved walking into the bar with her, watching the faces of the bikers who were drinking and partying in true biker fashion. One by one they turned their heads and took in his sexy, elegant woman, who had eyes only for him. He stopped in the middle of the room, caught her to him and kissed the hell out of her.

His kiss was all about ownership. Possession. The moment his mouth touched hers, fire leapt between them. He couldn't disassociate from the scorching flames pouring through his veins, a rush that was real. More than real. Heat swirled through him like a storm, racing to his lungs so he had to fight for air, to his heart, so he had to fight to keep from drowning in the depth of feeling she was creating between them.

He hadn't known a man could feel so overwhelmed by a woman, or by his emotions for her. He didn't have them. Not for outsiders. Not for women. He *pretended* to have them. His life was all about pretense, to his brothers, to his sisters. To himself. She was wrapping herself around his heart and invading his mind. This wasn't pretense. This was as real as it fucking got.

No one got close to him. No one, especially an outsider, could see into his soul. That would be a mistake for both of them, yet she was doing just that. How? He didn't know. He had to take control back. She didn't have it. She was his. His possession. She would stay with him and keep the demons at bay, but on his terms. It had to be that way for his survival — didn't it?

His hand slid down the enticing curve of her ass. He palmed the chiffon-covered cheek, knowing she was bare beneath the material. She didn't try to move away from him or stop him. She hadn't since she'd first entered the bar. He kissed her again just because she was so perfect, and he felt far more in control when he turned things between them back to sex. He could handle sex. There wasn't anything he didn't know about sex, and he could keep her under control easily as long as they stuck to the plan.

"Come on, princess, the brothers set up a party for us. Drinks, cake, dancing. We won't stay long." He whispered it in her ear and then stepped to her side again.

The sides of her halter top had slipped just a little when he'd kissed her, when he'd moved his body tight against hers, so he could feel her hard nipples as he rubbed against her. The way he'd shifted his body had pushed one of the strips just a little more to the side, revealing the round curve of her tit and a shadow of her nipple. Just a glimpse. Sexy as hell.

As he walked toward the back room, he slid his hand under the chiffon swath and over that full, round curve. His thumb found her nipple and stroked. She looked up at him and smiled. He fucking loved that she didn't push his hand away or cover up, even knowing her breast was partially exposed and anyone looking could see he was stroking and pinching her nipple. Making a statement. Showing her off. Making cocks hard but knowing she was going home with him. Just thinking about the way other

243

bikers looked at her made his cock so hard he thought he might shatter. She had eyes only for him, and that turned him inside out.

The game room of the bar had been transformed. The cake was there for them to cut and the others to eat. How the hell that had been managed at the last second, he didn't know. Maybe Vegas sold premade wedding cakes twenty-four/seven. Soleil's eyes lit up and she smiled at him as if he were magic and had managed it all on his own.

Taking her hand, he led her inside the game room and immediately pulled her into his arms to dance with her to the blaring music. It was his kind of dance, holding her close, her body moving against his, his cock hard against her soft little mound while her head rested on his chest.

"You know what's a huge turn-on for me, baby?" He placed his lips close to her ear, so his every word brushed caresses over her sensitive lobe. Warm air was a steady assault as well.

She nuzzled his neck. Her teeth teased his throat and then she was pressing little kisses over his neck. "Tell me."

"I like other men seeing what's only mine. I like knowing they want you. That you've got their dicks so fuckin' hard they have to go find their own woman or jerk off alone. Doesn't matter how they get relief, only that they have to. You do that, you know. You're so fuckin' sexy that you make cocks hard as a rock."

Using his hand, he curled hers against his chest, inserting their joined hands between her breasts so he could use a finger to rub over the enticing curve of her exposed tit and then over her nipple.

"You're so hot, Soleil. So damn hot, you're on fire. Anyone can see that. Did you feel their eyes on you when we walked in? All those men, hungry for you?"

"I felt your eyes on me. That was what mattered to me. I like you looking at me. I like when I know you're hard and that you find me sexy."

"You didn't answer my question, baby. It's important. Did you feel them looking at you? Hungry for you?"

She kissed the side of his neck, her teeth nipped his earlobe, sending a small bolt of lightning through his body to his cock. "Yes." She whispered it. "It was hot. I liked it, but I don't want anyone else close to me."

"I wouldn't ever let another man touch you. Not ever. I like them looking, but not touching. We have some crazy parties, babe, not like this one, this is for us, but at home when the other clubs come, that's when it gets hot. Or when we go on runs. You don't ever have to worry, I won't let anyone touch you." He kept rubbing her nipple and then over the curve of her breast.

She kissed the hollow of his throat, a small shiver going through her body. "That feels so good, Ice, so sensual."

"What, princess?" He wanted her to say it aloud, tell him so he could remind her. He also liked hearing the words. From her. Any other woman he wouldn't be giving his attention to the way he did her. He didn't know why it was so important to him that she feel good and that *he* was the one making her feel that way. He needed her to voice it, to tell him out loud.

She didn't disappoint him. "When you rub your finger over my nipple like that. When you pinch and then stroke it. It's like fire arrowing straight to my clit. It's very sexy knowing you're doing that while we're dancing and no one else knows."

"You like me touching you like this? Even in a roomful of people?"

"I love it. No one has ever made me feel the way you do."

He moved slower, finding the rhythm of the music with his knuckles on her tit. "How

246

do I make you feel?"

"Like a princess. Someone beautiful and sexy. I'm not really, you know. I don't want you to ever be disappointed."

"Baby, you got on your knees in a fuckin' clothing store for me. Because I needed it. You could never disappoint me. Not to mention you're the most beautiful woman I've ever met and sexy as hell on top of it. I'll keep tellin' you that until you believe me."

She laughed softly, her breath warm on his throat. "You'll have to tell me for a long, long time. I don't think the night is long enough."

He tightened his arm around her, pressing her body into his. She was finding her way somewhere deep inside him regardless of how hard he tried to make their relationship about sex. He didn't know anything else. He didn't have anything else to give her. She was bright like the sun, like her name. She was truly elegant, a princess stumbling into a monster's path.

His hand pressed hers deeper into his chest, this time over his heart. He was called Ice for a number of reasons, but the biggest was because he was truly ice inside. A glacier. Deep, wide, dense, impossible to penetrate. He thought his heart was encased in ice. He thought his emotions long since frozen, but she was changing everything, including his perception of himself.

He felt protective of her. He didn't have to pretend. There was happiness, and he didn't fake that either. It was there, like a light piercing the darkness in him.

"Do you know what you're doing to me?" He whispered the question, half hoping she didn't hear it above the music.

Her face was turned up to his throat and she brushed another kiss there, and then a series of them, so light, like a feather whispering along his collarbone. Each kiss was so barely there, and yet he felt each one like a brand, burning through his tee straight through his flesh to bone.

"I hope I'm really your princess in the fairy tale we're sharing tonight. I want to be that for you. Everything. I want to be your everything. You make me feel as if I'm somebody special. I want you to feel that, because, for me, you are. You're my everything."

She sounded so sincere. So certain. He was certain she was drunker than he'd thought. He'd pushed the drinks on her. She was still standing, and her words weren't slurred. He was actually quite surprised that she wasn't acting drunker.

She definitely knew how to drink.

Ice couldn't help but love what she'd said to him. He was her everything. He wanted to be that. For tonight, he was going to let her be his. His everything. He'd promised her a fairy tale, she was only giving one back to him. In his fairy tale, his woman didn't mind his needs; in fact, she got off on them.

The song ended, and he was careful, as he stepped back, to make certain the material of her dress was back in place, covering her gorgeous body. Those tits. Hell. He was a breast man for certain. He hated covering her up, but he wanted this night to be perfect for her — not him, although it was fast becoming that. He couldn't remember ever feeling the things he was feeling, especially with such overwhelming intensity.

He had ice in his veins. He wanted to have the emotions he pretended to have, but the truth was, he'd lost all that long ago. He'd traded his soul, and living like a man, for a zombie life. He went through the motions, and that allowed those around him to be happy, but there was only that cold, cold place inside left for him. Until her. Soleil. Somehow her sun extended to him, finding that place inside of him and thawing the ice. He was out of his depths, but willing to go there with her, at least for tonight.

His brothers gathered around them, congratulating them. Ice was pounded on the back until he thought he might have to punch a few of his brothers to get them to stop. They grinned like hyenas, giving him a bad time. A few told him they weren't certain just who had done the seducing. He had to agree. She was so damn sexy, there was no resisting her. A few others thought she'd gotten him a little more drunk than he'd gotten her. Others asked him what in the hell he was going to do with her when she was sober. He didn't quite know. He hadn't gotten that worked out yet, but he was thinking on it.

He found himself enthralled with her. Her laughter. The way she moved. She listened to every single one of his brothers as if whatever they said was important. Through it all, she had eyes only for him. She looked at him as if she could see inside him, past the glacier, penetrate deep and see the man he could have been.

He wrapped his arm around her waist when they called for cutting the cake. "Are you having fun?"

"Way too much. I think I need to stop drinking. You're drinking mostly water while I'm actually having screaming orgasms. They've become my favorite drink."

He wished he could drink screaming orgasms with her, but he had work later on and he wanted her to enjoy her night. More than that, he wanted to make certain he could perform at his best. She wasn't going to be able to say he drank too much and couldn't fuck. Hell, he could do that drunk or not with her.

Her eyes were bright, shining at him with laughter. That mouth of hers — he was never going to be able to look at her again without needing to kiss her or slide his cock in that warm haven.

Ice found he needed to touch her. Every time she'd moved away from him, talking to one of his brothers or playing darts with Alena, he'd found himself slipping back into the abyss. It was cold and dark, that black hole. Touching her warm skin somehow created a way for him to feel sunlight again. It wasn't real. He knew that. It was the night. Their night. All about the fantasy.

Later, after he took her back to the motel and fucked her brains out, he had work to do. The kind of work a man with ice in his veins and a glacier where his soul should be did. He glanced at his watch and then at Savage. Savage barely moved, his nod nearly imperceptible. Ice glanced at Maestro. He

251

gave Ice a faint grin and pointed to his watch.

"You don't have to go this time," Storm said. "I'll take your place."

Ice shook his head. "I pulled the straw, I do the work. Besides, you're going to make certain my wife doesn't wake up and make a run for it." It was stupid crazy, but he fucking loved saying "my wife."

He couldn't take his eyes off her. She was sipping at a drink, her gaze fixed on the dartboard as Absinthe threw his darts and hit three seventeens right in a row. Soleil put her drink down, gave him a smile and stepped up, darts in hand. She looked so coolly confident, Ice's body stirred all over again.

"How am I supposed to do that?" Storm demanded.

"I don't care how it's done, but she doesn't leave," he said, meaning it. "You make sure of that for me."

Storm clapped his brother on the shoulder. "She'll be there."

Ice gripped his arm, his show of affection for his brother. At least that was real.

After that, the photographer was gone, the doors to the game room were closed and the party got wild. He was out of control, and Soleil looked beautiful laid out on a pool table for him to feast on. She tasted even better than he remembered. They had to pose for any number of pictures Maestro took for their private wedding album and then he'd had enough. He wanted to be alone with his bride.

Ice wrapped his arm around her waist and pulled her back against him, declaring to his brethren he wanted his wife to himself. Immediately, because every single one of them knew what was at stake, they prepared to leave. Alena tied up the skirt, and Keys helped Soleil onto Ice's bike.

Soleil laid her head against his back, her body tight against his while the bike roared to life. Her hands were tight around his waist. He dropped his gloved hand to hers and moved one to his lap, right over his cock. The motorcycle vibrated, sending waves of stimulation through him, adding to the ache in his body. Her hand curved over his cock, and she made a small rubbing motion, in counterpoint to the vibration of his Harley.

He loved riding. It was the only way he felt free. Alive. Alone, or with his brothers surrounding him, hurtling down a highway with the wind on his face had always been the best feeling in the world. Now, that included Soleil snuggled up tightly against him, her tits pressed into his back and her hand making his cock very happy.

The motel was two stories, an L-shaped structure with a fenced-in pool in the middle of the L. Six rooms were right next to one another on the second story, with Ice's room second to the end. Storm had the end room and Alena was on the other side of Ice. Keys, Absinthe and Code each had a room on the second story as well. The rooms on the first floor were directly under the ones above them. Seven rooms were taken on that floor. The bikes were parked in a row just outside those seven rooms, so they could be watched. Glitch, one of the prospects, had accompanied them, and he also had a room on the second story.

Keys helped Soleil off the bike and she stood close, waiting for Ice. He liked that. She hadn't even looked at the motel. She clearly had money, but she didn't seem to care that they were staying not in a suite at one of the most luxurious hotels in Vegas but in a small motel a distance from the strip. The moment he backed the bike into his space, Ice had his arm wrapped around her and was walking her to their room. His brothers gave them some good-natured catcalls, which he replied to with a rude finger gesture over his head.

As they walked up the stairs, he slid one hand under that intriguing layer of chiffon covering her tit. He loved how soft she was, how her nipple was already hard. At the top of the stairs, he put his mouth there, pulling her tit right into his mouth, sucking hard, using his tongue on her nipple, flicking and flattening it to the roof of his mouth before using the edge of his teeth. She gave a little broken cry and cradled his head to her, arching a little to give him more. Her soft moaning nearly drove him wild.

He locked his arm around her waist and pulled her tighter against him, forcing her to bend backward just enough for him to have even better access. Everything faded away for him. Everything, until there was only Soleil and her soft body. His demons died down and then stopped tormenting him. He didn't hear or see anything but her. He didn't think about enemies or killing or hear the cries of children. There was only Soleil and her gorgeous tits, his fierce cock and the sounds she made filling his mind.

"Get a room," Storm ordered.

His twin's voice startled him. He was that far gone, and that had never happened to him before. He reluctantly lifted his head, flipped off his brother and took her straight to the room. The moment the door was closed and locked, he spun her around and very gently unhooked the halter top and let it fall in a graceful shimmy of chiffon and peekaboo down to her waist. His breath caught in his throat. She was truly beautiful. He knew the female form. He'd been introduced to it early and taught to admire and revere it.

"Baby, you're so fuckin' beautiful, I can't believe it." He ripped his shirt off with one hand and tossed it aside, his eyes on her breasts, that small rib cage narrowing even more to her waist. The chiffon fell gracefully over the curve of her hips, and he wanted her out of that dress. He wanted to see her body. All of it.

He went to the floor to remove her shoes. He couldn't help running his hand up and down her calf. Her skin was incredibly soft, even on her legs. He removed the classy heels and dragged the dress down her body. He peeled the peekaboo panties off of her, and without the dress she was entirely naked. His breath caught in his throat. Not only was she an elegant princess, but she had the body of a temptress combined with the innocent look of the proverbial girl next door.

"Ice." She breathed his name, and her hand went to his shoulder to trace one of his many scars. "What happened to you?"

He liked the feel of her fingers on his skin. A soft touch, but it burned like a flame. "I'll tell you the story some other time. Now, I just want to eat you alive. Like candy, princess, devour you until you're screaming for me."

He pulled her with him to the bed and indicated she sit on the very edge while he removed his motorcycle boots and tossed them aside. One hand on her belly had her lying down. He dropped to his knees and pulled her thighs apart. Wide. He wanted room. Her little pussy was like a flower. He could never say that corny crap to her, but it was. He opened her with his fingers, rubbing gently. Making little circles, hearing her breath leave her lungs in a rush.

"Should have kissed you, Soleil, but once I start, I can't seem to stop, and I wanted this. I thought about this all the way back to the motel. The way you taste." He licked his fingers. "Eating you out on a fucking pool table. Couldn't help myself. Love the way you taste. Love that you let me, baby. All mine. All for me."

Her hand went to his hair, burying her fingers deep so she was stroking caresses and massaging him, connecting them. "You go right ahead, honey, and do whatever you need to do. You certainly gave me the best night of my life."

"It isn't over, Soleil. Not by a long shot."

He wanted her first time with him to be a memory she'd never forget. He wanted her to feel as if he cared about her. Strange thing was, he did. She'd gotten under his skin very early on, but there was a moment that he absolutely knew what he was doing was right. That moment when she stayed on her knees and risked exposure just to give him paradise. She'd gotten inside him, deep, and somehow twisted around his heart.

He put his mouth on her and again, just like before, the world dropped away completely. One hand on her belly to keep her where he wanted her, he started out with the best of intentions, to drive her up as gently as possible. Her taste was like an aphrodisiac. The addiction grew fast and he found himself lost in a world of pure erotic sensation. Every cell in his body was alive. Every demon was banished because there was no room for anything but his mouth devouring her and the fire running through his veins.

Her breathy moans became soft little pleas that began to rise to a crescendo. She writhed under his hand. He didn't stop, driving her higher. Keeping her right on the edge, licking and sucking and using his tongue like a weapon until she was nearly sobbing his name. Her cries fueled his hunger. She was giving him so many firsts. He wasn't setting her up for seduction, he was totally consumed with lust. With desire. With something else that was undefined in his mind.

She came apart for him, nearly sobbing, her hands fisting in his hair. He wiped his jaw on her thighs, his hands dropping to his jeans, the last barrier between the two of them. His wife. Soleil was his wife.

He liked looking at her, sprawled half on and half off the bed, naked, her skin gleaming in the moonlight streaming through the window. Knowing she was his. His body was on fire for her. He stroked his cock, shocked at how hard he was, how sensitive to every movement of his fist. The woman was fucking paradise, a miracle. She set up such a craving in him.

He lodged the head of his cock between the bare lips of her pussy. Her heat blasted him. Surrounded him. Wet. Scorching. His heart thudded. He looked into her eyes as he pushed deeper, invading that tight tunnel that was his alone. Her muscles resisted, refusing to give way, but he persisted with that slow penetration.

"You're so fuckin' tight, baby. Your little pussy is so damn hot, princess." For him, it was like being surrounded by a fucking inferno, a silken fist full of flames. "What's it feel like, Soleil?" He kept up that deliberate leisurely assault, refusing to go fast as his body urged him to do. "To have me in you. What's it feel like?"

"Burning. You're big and you're stretching me. Full. Watching your cock disappear inside of me is the hottest thing I've ever seen."

He caught her leg and wrapped it around his waist, lifting her beautiful ass with his palms, changing the angle so she gasped. "Wrap both legs around me, princess." His hands slid to her hips. He flexed his fingers.

Obediently, Soleil did what he asked, hooking her ankles behind him. Just that movement sent flames rocketing up his spine. The sight of her on his bed, her tits swaying with every movement, made him want to see more. He buried the last couple of inches in her fast, sliding through those tight muscles so that the friction sent heat waves rushing through both of them.

Her fingers caught the blanket and fisted it, holding on as he began to move in her. Again, he tried to stay slow and gentle, but it was impossible, not with her lifting her hips to meet his every surge. He couldn't believe his body was reacting of its own accord, fire racing through him. Every nerve ending responding.

"Fuckin' paradise, princess, that's what you are, you and this little pussy of yours." He hadn't thought it possible, but that hot, wet, silken fist squeezed and massaged, such a tight tunnel that he thought he might not make it through every time he withdrew and then surged forward, driving through the small, resisting muscles. Streaks of fire burned through him, and if anything, his cock swelled more, forcing her to take his length and girth, pushing against the tight sheath and adding to the friction.

"Look at you, baby," he hissed, "you look so beautiful. Your tits, your pussy. Look at us together." Her skin was flushed a soft rose all over. "I'm going to have Ink tat my name on your tit. He can tat your name on me as well. You want it on my dick? Property of Soleil?"

She smiled at him and shook her head. "Not taking a chance on damaging that beautiful cock. Love it. Love it so much. It's pure magic, Ice."

He grinned at her and watched her gasp when he picked up the pace, letting the fire get just a little out of control.

"Appreciate that, princess."

"It's the truth."

He fucking loved hearing her say that. Every man wanted their cock treasured. She wasn't shy about telling him, and that added to the building hunger in him for her. She was the treasure.

"Love your ass too. Tits and ass. My name might have to be on both." He leaned forward and licked at her nipple before he caught her hips again and began to fuck her the way he needed to.

Each stroke was hard and deep, so that her tits jolted, and her breath turned ragged. Her gaze clung to his face, but he could see a daze developing, that beautiful flush spreading over her face, the haze in her eyes, her mouth open as she struggled for air.

Her body moved with his, harder, faster, the rhythm perfection. Every stroke sent flames streaking through his body. His cock was surrounded by a silken inferno that locked down on him tighter than he ever thought possible. He could feel her body gathering, coiling tight. He didn't want paradise to end, but he couldn't stop moving. It was impossible when every time he buried himself deep, that erotic ecstasy surged through him like an intense wave.

He'd fucked a million times and it had

never felt like this. His wife. Her perfect little pussy. He wasn't ever giving that up. Not ever. He plunged into her over and over until he knew he was going up in flames. Then her body clamped down on his, a vicious vise, strangling his cock, milking with those tight muscles as her orgasm took her. The wave was so intense it took him with her, so they both erupted together.

His cock jerked hard, over and over, coating the walls of her sheath, triggering another huge wave that traveled on the tail of the first one. He rode it out with her, his head thrown back, his cock on fire, bathed in their combined cream. He loved the smell of sex, but now, there was only their sex. That fragrance. That steamy, sexy combination that added to his addiction.

He lowered her legs gently to the floor, triggering a third orgasm. His cock loved it. He loved it. So perfect.

"You okay, princess?"

"I think I'm still alive."

Her lashes lifted and she searched his face. Seeing too much. He couldn't let that happen, especially tonight. Ice pulled out of her a little reluctantly, half expecting his cock to be burned, but he was intact, and he leaned forward to press a kiss onto her bare mound. She immediately dropped her hand into his thick hair and massaged his scalp with gentle fingers. The moment she did that, he didn't want her to stop.

He had no choice. He remained there for a few minutes, savoring the feeling of belonging to someone before he pressed another kiss on her skin and then hurried to the bathroom to clean up and bring her a warm washcloth. She washed herself thoroughly and then suddenly stopped, looking anxious.

"Ice, we didn't use a condom. I can't get pregnant, but . . ."

"I'm clean, baby. You?" What the fuck was wrong with him? Why hadn't he thought about using a condom with her?

"Yes. I always made a partner wear a condom. Even Winston, although it made him angry. I should have been thinking." She scooted up to the pillows.

He flung himself on the bed beside her, framed her face with both hands and kissed her. He wanted more time with her. His cock wanted more time. The moment he had cleaned himself, returned to the bedroom to see her naked and sprawled out, his seed running down her thigh, all of a sudden, the steel was back. He wanted her again. He wanted her in so many ways. He'd like to take her by the windowsill, bend her over and fuck her with her tits pushed up against the glass and her staring out wondering if someone would walk by. Just the thought excited him.

He kissed her over and over, drowning in her, wanting to consume her, to bury himself in her all over again in a million different ways. One hand in her hair, bunching it in his fist as he explored her mouth, demanding her response, he made certain she was only thinking of him, surrendering fully to him. Another orgasm or two and she'd be too wiped out to notice when he slipped out of the room to take care of business.

EIGHT

Ice pulled on his gloves and sent Savage a look that said he'd had enough bullshit. "We know that bastard is at the hotel. He's fuckin' staying in the room she's payin' for. I want to pay him a visit after we get this done. Housekeeping can find him in the morning with his throat slit."

"Ice," Savage cautioned. "You're supposed to be the voice of reason, not me. We can't do him in a hotel. Too many cameras. No way to control it. You know that. We've got his name . . ."

"Winston Trent," Ice said, making the name a bad taste in his mouth. "Who the hell is named Winston? I want to take him apart just for that crap."

"He lives in San Francisco. We'll arrange a match at the fight club and have a reason to go there. A couple of the brothers will pick him up and take him to one of the safe houses and we'll have a friendly chat with him." Savage looked at the two men sitting in the chairs in the center of the warehouse floor. "Like we're doing here. We're keeping it friendly."

Paul Bitters and a man by the name of Rich Marshal sat tied to the metal chairs. They looked worse for wear. Savage and Player had been there earlier, and Savage wasn't gentle by any means. He didn't mind hurting pedophiles, and both these men, fairly high up in a very active ring, qualified.

Torpedo Ink had been hearing for some time that a man would take an order for a child, boy or girl, find a family with no other relatives and kill the parents and take the child so no one would put a tremendous amount of effort into looking for him or her. At first, when Code searched for similar cold cases, he couldn't find anything, but then he widened the search and began to see more than they liked over the last few years, which meant the rumors were true.

Ice walked over to Rich Marshal's chair and toed the front foot. "Got married tonight, you son of a bitch, and I'd much rather be fuckin' a beautiful woman than cuttin' you into little pieces. Don't get me wrong, a piece of shit like you usually is a top priority, but not tonight. So, call me pissed as hell."

"What he's sayin' in a nice way," Maestro said, "is don't pretend to be a hero. Answer the fuckin' questions so he can get back to his woman."

Rich Marshal had been the driver of the pickup truck that had been following Jarvis and Kent to ensure that no one was tailing them before the men met up with Paul Bitters for the auction.

Rich looked at Bitters and shook his head. "I don't know what you want from me. I was hired to tail a couple of guys, make sure no one followed them. Your friend ran me off the road and I ended up here. That's it. I don't know anything else." His gaze shifted from Bitters to Savage and immediately he looked leery.

Savage sat on the edge of a table where all kinds of tools were laid out. He calmly took a bite out of an apple. "Waste of time, Ice. Fuckin' waste of time." He didn't look up as he gave his two cents.

Ice barely moved, but when he did, his speed was blurring. He slammed a knife straight down into Rich's thigh, burying it to the hilt. The blade was only a couple of inches long, but it was wide, and it was sharp, slicing through skin and muscle like it was butter. Rich screamed. Paul Bitters paled and drew back, trying to throw himself sideways out of his chair.

Ice ignored both reactions, shaking his head as he pulled the blade slowly from Rich's thigh. "Don't like lies, Richie. I can hear them. I can feel them. I can even smell them. You like little kids, and Bitters supplies you with them. I already know that about you."

Code had been busy getting as much information on Marshal as possible, even while he was doing the paperwork to ensure Ice and Soleil could get married legally. Rich Marshal was every bit as dirty as Paul Bitters. He might not be as high up the ladder in the pedophile network as Bitters, but he had been working within the ring for some time. He preferred girls, he liked them six to eight. When they got too old, he sold them either in online auctions or to a trafficking ring.

"You're married to a woman with three little girls, ages three, five and seven. You've been molesting the seven-year-old for two years already. Your wife suspects but she's afraid of you, but not so afraid that she didn't try to leave you once. You made certain she didn't try again by making a video of her with two men and threatening to put it online. One of those men is a good friend of yours, Yeger Kushnir, and he, along with Basil Alanis, raped your wife. She cooperated and stayed with you, but you put that video online anyway. A friend of ours found it and took it apart. He saw things no one got to see, such as her fighting and then cooperating when you threatened the girls. What I learned from that, Richie, is that you're a fuckin' liar and you don't keep your word."

Bitters cleared his throat. "You don't seem to understand —"

Ice spun around and backhanded him so forcibly it knocked him over, chair and all. Despite the fact that a tarp lay on the floor, Bitters slammed hard into the cement floor. "I wouldn't speak if I were you," Ice warned. "I don't like you. I don't like anything about you. You locked that little boy in the basement inside a cage with a bomb on it after you molested him for years. You don't want my attention if you can help it, so shut the fuck up."

He didn't right the chair, just left the man lying on the cement floor, because he wasn't kidding or trying to be intimidating. He wanted to fuck Bitters up, slice off his dick and shove it down the man's throat until he choked and suffocated. He'd told Savage and Maestro that before coming. Maestro and Savage didn't make a move to help Bitters either. They left him lying on his side, still tied to the chair. Ice turned back to Marshal, dismissing Bitters as if he didn't exist.

"Let's try again, Richie, and keep in mind, I'm on a time limit here. I ask you a question, you jack me around and I'm going to get creative where I put my blades." He watched the man's eyes widen and he nodded. "I believe we understand each other. I'm looking for the name of the man who is the collector. He scouts for a small family, either a single mother or parents without any other family members. They have a toddler, boy or girl, doesn't matter. He takes pictures of these children and then sends out a little brochure. I know this is familiar to you. If it is to me, then it has to be to you."

Code had discovered the brochure online, little toddlers, both male and female. The collector had their pictures, and if someone put in an order for one of those children in his advertisement, he murdered the parents and took the child. Sometimes there were special orders; he advertised that as well. Twins were rare, very hard to come by. Usually there was an extended family that would continue to raise a fuss, not let the murders fade away, so finding the right child or children was imperative.

Marshal hesitated, his expression betraying him. Ice moved again with blurring speed. The knife slipped in about two inches higher up the thigh. Marshal screamed and screamed. Blood ran down his leg. He stared in horror at the hilt that couldn't be seen when it was in Ice's hand. Now it was sticking out of him. He began to cry.

Ice removed the knife again, very slowly, wiping the blood from the blade on the pedophile's shirt. "Is this brochure familiar to you, Richie?"

Without hesitation, the man nodded over and over. "Yes, I've seen it."

"You know this man is a murderer and he's killing to take these children, so no one remembers they even exist. Isn't that right, Richie?" Ice's tone was low. Mild. All the scarier because of it. His eyes were twin glaciers, so blue they looked crystal — and completely merciless.

Richie nodded over and over. "Yes, yes, I know that's what he does."

"I want his name."

Richie looked terrified, and his gaze once more shifted to Bitters. Ice again moved with that blurring speed, and this time the knife went in very high up, close to

Marshal's groin. The man shrieked, sobbed, screamed — one long, intense wail that didn't seem as if it would stop. Unfazed, Ice slowly removed the knife and again wiped it clean. He sauntered over to Savage and took the bottle of water his brother offered. He drank down a third of the liquid and then capped it.

"He's kinda dumb. Thinks Bitters is gettin' out of this alive and somehow is going to do worse to him than we are." Ice shook his head.

Maestro grinned at him and shrugged. "Got to know who you're dealing with. Guess he doesn't get it yet."

"Say the word, Ice, and I'll start on him," Savage offered. "No fuckin' fun just sittin' here."

He meant it too. Savage was a mean bastard, and he didn't mind in the least hurting someone. Didn't matter if it was his fists or weapons, he knew more ways to take apart a human being than most people ever dreamt possible.

"You're so impatient," Ice said. "I think Richie will cooperate with us. He just has to come to the understanding that Bitters is going to die a very hard death. He's not getting that."

Savage stood up then. He'd been sitting

on the table, one foot on the bench beneath it. When he stood, it was a show of muscle. His chest was thick with roped muscle, his arms big. He looked what he was, a formidable machine with no fat, all stamina and power. He sauntered over to Bitters as if he were taking a stroll in a park. Even that was menacing.

Rich's frightened gaze jumped to Savage. He stopped screaming as if mesmerized. His eyes widened when Savage drew back his heavy boot and kicked Bitters in the ribs, hard, deliberately driving deep, smashing through bone. Bitters shrieked and writhed on the floor; the chair he was tied to looked as if it was thrashing too.

Ice found the sight strangely humorous, with the chair moving all around the floor as if it were alive. He stood over Rich but looked back at Bitters. "He just pissed himself, Richie. That's the man you're afraid of? I think you're afraid of the wrong person. You want to try this again?" He kept his tone mild.

They didn't raise their voices when they did this kind of shit. What was the point? They were in control, and in the end, they usually got the information they needed. Sometimes it took a long time, other times they got it fast. It usually didn't matter to

Ice how long it took, but tonight was his fucking wedding night.

Richie was staring at Savage, swallowing hard, bleeding from three different wounds, the blood running down his leg. He didn't see anything but Savage as the big man crouched beside Bitters, took out a large knife and began to cut off the prisoner's clothes in strips. He wasn't in the least careful. Several times the tip of the knife bit into flesh, so long streaks of blood rose on the man's skin.

"Richie, I suggest you pay attention to me. You don't want that man working on you. I'm the nice one."

Maestro snorted and picked up his coffee cup.

Ice gave him the finger. "You were going to give me the name of the asshole known as the collector. You don't want to tell me you don't know who he is, because if you do that, I'm going to use this knife on you."

Savage cut through the ties holding Bitters to the chair and then sent the chair away with a hard kick. He caught the pedophile by his hair and dragged him to his feet. "You take those little children away from their parents and put them in cages and then you force yourself on them."

Bitters threw out both hands and

275

screamed at the top of his lungs. "Children are sexual beings. They love it, they want it. You don't understand. Let me explain. Don't kill me. Please. Just let me explain." They'd all heard that speech on the website, Bitters spewing his beliefs to other pedophiles to justify their actions.

Savage hit him square in the mouth, driving through his teeth so that the front ones snapped off. He had a big fist and he could hit hard. He'd honed his fighting skills from the time he was a child, and he knew how to throw a punch with maximum force. Bitters went flying backward and hit the cement hard.

Savage followed him up, not hurrying, not paying any attention to the blood and saliva leaking from Bitters's mouth on the cement. He kicked him hard, driving his motorcycle boot into the other side, caving in those ribs as well. He didn't stop there. He systematically began to kick and then punch Bitters, beating him over and over.

"Oh my God." The voice was faint. Richie turned white. "I don't know the collector's name, but I do know who does. His name is Avery Charles. He runs the website for someone in Russia. He makes snuff films whenever the Russian tells him to. If we sell the kids to him, we get top dollar."

The truth came out in a rush of fear, but then he realized what he'd revealed and tried to backpedal. "Not me. I've never done it. Paul makes money that way. Sometimes he just grabs kids off the street and sells them to Avery. We . . . he doesn't sell the kids we . . . he gets from the collector. That price is too steep."

Even Savage had paused in his pursuit of royally fucking up Bitters to listen to Richie. The three Torpedo Ink members exchanged long looks. They had run across a "Russian connection" before. More, most of the children in the "school" where they had been held had been tortured, raped and then disposed of, but a few had been used in snuff films. In investigations, snuff films were deemed to be not real. They knew better. They had lived through such films when other children, friends they'd been in school with, had not.

Ice looked down at Richie without seeing him. Instead, he was back at that school, tied to a pole, whipped, beaten, raped and used repeatedly. That was bad. He thought it was the worst, but it hadn't been, not by a long shot. Not when there was Alena and Storm . . . He wiped the sudden sweat from his eyes and shook his head to clear it. There was no stopping the roaring in his head.

"Richie." His voice was very low. His blue eyes had gone pure crystal. Bile was in his throat. "I think you'd better come clean. It wasn't only Bitters who snatched kids off the street and sold them, knowing Avery Charles was going to have them tortured, raped and killed in a film for other sickos to get off on. You did too. How many? Where did you find them? I'm not fucking around with you. You don't answer me and keep in mind I can hear lies, you're going to be in a world of hurt like you've never known."

The memories crowded in, so that his gut churned, and his wedding cake threatened to come back up. The demons Soleil had managed to chase away returned in full force. His sins crushed him with their weight. Rage burned in his belly. He could barely see through the haze of red across his eyes, but Maestro and Savage looked equally as enraged, not that Richie could tell. It was in their eyes, and he was too scared to look that close.

"From the park. We'd get them in the park. The young ones. Avery wanted them about six or seven. Girls or boys. He paid top dollar when the Russian wanted new films."

"How often did the Russian want new films?" Ice asked. He put his hands out in front of him and spread his fingers wide. Rock steady. He'd learned to always keep his hands steady. It didn't matter how much blood was in the room, or who was giving orders, or if he knew what was coming, he'd learned absolute control. Absolute.

"It wasn't often. Not often," Richie said. "I didn't like that kind of thing, but Bitters wanted us all to be in as deep."

Ice slapped the man almost casually across the face. The blow was hard enough to rock him backward. Blood and spit sprayed out of Richie's mouth. He sobbed and hastily clamped his lips together in an effort to remain silent.

"Richie, I didn't ask for your excuses. You need to listen to the question."

"Yes. Yes." He bobbed his head up and down. "I'm sorry. I should have. About every five months or so. Maybe six. I didn't keep track."

Richie's gaze went again to Bitters, who was moaning and crying.

Savage took scraps of material, wadded them up and thrust them into Bitters's mouth. "Done with your noise. How many times did you make a child scream?" He got to his feet and walked back to the table to pick up a bottle of water.

Maestro took his place, crouching down

beside Bitters, a blowtorch in his hand. Bitters didn't seem to be aware that he was there. His gaze followed Savage. Richie, however, stared at Maestro in absolute horror. He tried to move his chair back away from the three members of Torpedo Ink. The chair tipped but didn't go over backward.

"What's he going to do?" Richie asked in a low, frightened voice.

Ice shrugged. "Ask him, not me."

Richie licked at the cracks in his lips. "What are you going to do?" His voice was still low, almost a whisper. His gaze was fixed on the white-hot blue flame coming from the small torch Maestro held in his hand.

"This is the kind of thing they use in those snuff films, Richie," Maestro explained. "Paul knows, don't you, Paul? You have quite the collection. Code found them. You even have them labeled so nicely, the ones with 'your' kids. The ones you sold. You get off on that sick shit, don't you?"

Paul began screaming around the gag.

"You might want to give me every name in this ring you have going across the country that you know, Richie. Now would be a good time." Ice didn't look at him. He spoke very softly. Very matter-of-factly. He didn't sound like he was making a threat, but it was there, right on the cement floor in front of him, along with muffled agonized screams, and the smell of blood and burned flesh.

"I don't know very many. I wasn't in the inner circle like Paul. I know Avery. A man named Harold McDonald. He lives in a little place near the coast, Occidental, or something like that. He's a cop, a sheriff."

"Small fuckin' world," Ice observed. They had rescued a teenage boy from a desperate situation with a pedophile. The boy now lived with Torpedo Ink's president, Czar, and his wife, Blythe. "We had a little run-in with a man in Occidental. Walter Sandlin, did you know him?"

Richie's eyes widened. "That was you? No one had a clue who did him. Some thought the kid he had did him, but Harry said it was too professional to be the kid."

"Who else?"

"There's David Swcy. He's a vendor. Sells hot dogs out of a truck. Goes all over town in Santa Rosa. Lives in Graton. He's got eyes everywhere. He's close with Bitters and Avery."

Richie frowned, trying to remember others, but his body was shuddering, almost in shock, watching as Maestro shut off the torch and patted Bitters's shoulder as he stood up.

"Stop your whining, Bitters," Ice said. "You're pissing me off. You like this sort of thing, or you wouldn't get off watching it."

Richie began to shake his head. "I don't watch it. I don't. I didn't know they did that to kids."

"What did you think they did, Richie?" Ice asked, once more conversational. "It's called a 'snuff' film."

"I thought they just killed them. Quick, you know. These films aren't for distribution, they're only used for private collectors." He sounded as if that made all the difference in the world. "And each person who asks for a film has to be thoroughly vetted before they're allowed into the circle. It's hard to get in. We're not judgmental. Everyone has different needs and preferences."

"So, you're not judgmental about anyone who likes to hurt a child and then kill him or her," Ice pursued.

"You're twisting my words," Richie whined. "I didn't say that."

"What are you saying, Richie? Because I'm very interested," Ice said.

He walked past Bitters, who appeared to be unconscious, and stopped to nudge him with his foot. The man groaned but didn't open his eyes or move. Ice kept walking to the table where he picked up his bottle of water and downed another third.

"That piece of shit thinks he can escape us by going to sleep. Not going to happen." Fury rode him hard. He despised men like Bitters. They had money and they thought they were above the law. The law would have treated them a lot kinder than the assassins riding after them.

Savage got up, scooped ice and water from the cooler on the floor by the table and stalked over to Bitters. He threw water right in Bitters's face and then stepped on his chest, mashing his foot into the cuts and burns.

"Wakey, wakey, Paul," Ice said. "We're not done with you yet. Until Richie here gives up the name he's protecting, we're going to have to keep showing him what's in store for him if he stays quiet. None of us like you much. We don't mind fucking you up and making sure you feel what those children felt every time you hurt them. So, stay the hell awake."

Maestro grabbed the naked, bloody man by his ankle and dragged him across the cement to place him right in front of Richie. Bitters's head bounced on the cement a

283

couple of times, and the hard surface scraped at his skin. He left a trail of blood, urine and feces behind.

Maestro glared at him. "Fuckin' mess we're going to have to clean up. Should have put a tarp down."

"I had one down. You pulled him off of it. There's one over there," Ice said, indicating the long table under the bank of blacked-out windows where the tools were. "I brought two more." His eyes were on Richie, and he caught the shudder and fearful moan. The man couldn't keep his eyes off Bitters. He was fascinated, repulsed, yet couldn't look away.

"Good thinking," Maestro said. "I hate cleaning up copious amounts of blood." Shoving at Paul's legs contemptuously, he stalked around the man and went to the narrow table to find the other tarps. "Nice, Ice. Big ones."

"They burn well too. My favorite brand." Ice kept watching Richie. "You think you want to give me that name you're holding on to? You gave me a couple of names. A sheriff who we already suspected, a fuckin' hot dog vendor and good old Avery, who runs the website which we already know about and infiltrated. Who are you protecting, Richie? Because I promise you, it isn't going to be worth it."

Maestro and Savage laid out the tarp and rolled Paul Bitters onto it, keeping him on his back, legs apart. He moaned continuously, a steady sound around the material still stuffed in his mouth. Savage pulled out his knife, the big one, the one that had Richie pulling back in his chair and Paul trying to roll over to crawl away. Both men stared at the obviously razor-sharp knife. Paul made horrible gurgling sounds around his gag as Savage sank a knee onto his chest to prevent him from moving.

Richie started a chant calling on a higher power, for what, Ice wasn't sure. "I need that name, Richie. What is it? Not Avery, but the one who really knows the collector."

Richie shook his head, moaning, crying. He didn't take his terrified gaze from the knife, not even when it slashed down through flesh so fast that when it was raised, there was barely a stain of blood on the blade.

Richie watched as Paul's eyes nearly popped out of his head. His skin turned purple. He tried to thrash, which sent blood pumping out of his body. It was a slow, ugly death.

Ice waited until Bitters was dead. He turned back to Richie with a raised eyebrow.

"We didn't like him, Richie. I'm beginning not to like you either. Fuckin' give me the name or I'm strippin' you and laying you on that other tarp. You've got about three seconds to give him up."

Tears poured down Richie's face as he stared, mesmerized, at Paul's body. He kept shaking his head, but when he looked at Ice, there was a defeated look about him. "Terrance."

"Last name, and where do we find him?" Ice snapped.

"Terrance Marshal. My brother, Terrance. He knows the collector. He's helped him a couple of times. He was in the ring long before I came in. He sponsored me." As he talked, he kept shaking his head. "He went to school with Avery. They both were contacted by the Russian. That's what they call him, just the Russian."

The information spilled out fast. Once the dam burst, he couldn't stop. "Terrance helped recruit the ring here. The Russian seemed to know who to send him, and Terrance would get blackmail material on them just in case they didn't want in on the fun. That was what the Russian called it, not me. My brother told me he only had to use the blackmail material on one man and in the end, the Russian ordered him to kill that one, so he did. The others were happy to be part of the circle, so the blackmail material was just filed away. Terrance has it in his safe."

"But he's not the collector?"

"No, no, he just knows him."

Richie began to gag. His stomach heaved and he began vomiting. Savage grabbed the back of his chair and dragged him over to where the second tarp was laid out. He kicked the chair over, stood behind him and cut his throat.

"Fuckin' pussy," he snapped. "What a mess." He stood up, holding up his arm. "I'm showering first." He started to walk away and then turned back. "I was ten years old the first time they burned the fuck out of me, and I didn't even piss my pants, but I cried like a fuckin' baby. Got the shit kicked out of me for it too. Second time I was fourteen and I never made a sound." He stomped off.

Ice was well aware Savage had been burned more than once. He was a twisted son of a bitch thanks to their schooling and the instructors who loved to torture children. None of them were supposed to survive, and out of two hundred and eighty-seven, only eighteen had. They'd banded together, working on strengthening their psychic and physical assets, and had begun to kill off those assaulting them. They had just been children, with no guidance other than Czar, a child himself, and they'd made their own rules and lived by their own code, relying completely on one another. They were still doing it.

Maestro and Ice finished rolling up the two bodies, and they washed off in the deep sink at one end of the room, then peeled off their gloves to add them to the burn pile.

"What made you do it, Ice? Can't be because she knows how to suck dick," Maestro said. He sat on the table eating an apple as they waited to use the shower.

"You mean marrying Soleil?" Ice knew exactly what he meant. "Had to."

"You knock her up when you gave her an orgasm? Hottest thing I've seen in a long while, by the way. Your woman is fuckin' gorgeous."

"She is, isn't she? And hot as hell." Ice knew Maestro was looking for something to hang on to. They all were. They were drowning, trying to fit into a world they didn't understand. The rules didn't make sense. They'd been raised on violence. It wasn't like they could just stop what was second nature — no, make that first.

Ice tried to explain. "She makes my cock

hard as a fuckin' rock. Titanium. I look at her and I'm there. I don't have to have three women suckin' my dick, one after another, while I tell the damn thing to cooperate. I'm not thinking, Maestro. I'm just feeling. It's terrifying, but holy fuck, I never felt anything like that in my life. I'm not giving that up."

"A lifetime is a long time," Maestro pointed out. "What if you can't live with her? What if every time she opens her mouth you want to strangle her?"

"I'll shove my cock down her throat and then she'll be nice and quiet," Ice said with a little smirk. The smile faded. It was get-real time. "She got rid of them."

Maestro raised an eyebrow. "Rid of what?"

Ice leaned against the wall and drank down the rest of his water. "Wanted to blow my fuckin' head off, Maestro. Every hour of every day. Demons were eating me alive. Couldn't stop the memories anymore, and they got inside my head and ate their way to my gut. Nothing I tried helped. Lately, I even thought about forcing the cops to do me, but . . ." He shook his head. "The nightmares were getting so bad sometimes I couldn't always tell reality from my past. I was really afraid of hurting someone. I stopped going to Czar and Blythe's house

289

so often because I didn't trust myself."

He watched Maestro's face. The man didn't blink but continued watching him.

"You know what I need a lot of the time to even contemplate having sex. We're all fucked the hell up. Not one of us is what would be considered normal." He glanced at the door Savage had disappeared behind. "He's the worst of us. How the hell is he going to find someone who'd take him on? Or you? Or me?"

"You just got married, brother."

Ice reached for her. She was inside him, wrapped tightly around his organs. His heart. Maybe his damn soul if he had one. He let himself smile. She was there. She wasn't going anyplace. "She took the demons away. All of them. I didn't feel a fuckin' thing but good. Paradise, man. She let me do whatever I needed. She didn't flinch when she realized she'd had her first orgasm in a bar in front of my club. And when her mouth was around my cock and I was so close and needed her to keep going, that bitch coming to look down on her because she was fuckin' jealous, Soleil kept going instead of quitting. She took me all the way. All the fuckin' way, Maestro. It was a thing of beauty. Never thought I could have it all, but she makes me believe it's possible."

Maestro heaved a sigh. "I hope you're right, Ice, but maybe she really was as drunk as fuck. I didn't think so. I thought she was playing you. Getting you drunk. We all did. We thought it was funny that both of you were looking to do the other. But then you really went through with it. What's going to happen tomorrow morning when you have to face each other entirely sober?"

"I'm taking her back to Caspar with us." Ice made it a statement. "I have to keep her. She's my salvation."

Maestro shook his head. "Face it, Ice, you're not exactly Mr. Romance. You look like it, and the ladies think you are. They want to be with you, but you're not called Ice because you're sweet. That woman doesn't have a clue you're cold and calculating and you're going to rule her life."

Ice shrugged. "Doesn't always work that way in the end. Look at Reaper. He's a cold, scary son of a bitch. Anya's got him wrapped around her little finger. And Breezy with Steele. He might be nuts when it comes to knowing where she is every minute, but she still gets her way in almost everything." He looked at Maestro. "What about you? What kind of woman do you need?"

Maestro avoided his eyes. He jumped

from the table and walked across to the blacked-out window, as if he could see outside. "One who makes my cock work all on its own. I'd be happy with that."

"Yeah, wouldn't we all," Savage said, coming out of the bathroom. He carried a plastic bag with his bloody clothes in it. "Just once I'd like to be close to a woman and have my cock go on full alert without me forcing it to."

"We're talking about what we want in a woman," Maestro said. "I'm not sure, beyond fucking her twenty-four seven, Ice knows what he's going to do with his brand-new wife."

Savage sent Ice a small smirk. "Sounds good. Keep her busy, especially her mouth. She won't say anything to annoy you. Me, I want obedience. The others say that, but they don't mean it. I would have to have it. And she'd better stick damn close to me."

Maestro nodded. "I like certain things from a woman. If she were mine, I'd expect them. Not going to get what I need from someone I pick up."

Savage raised an eyebrow. "I do. When I need it. When the rage is so built up, I'm going to fuckin' kill someone. I get what I need. I find a willing woman to give it to me. Lay it out, so there's no mistakes. She knows what she's getting into." He gave a half smile that never reached his eyes. "She never comes back. There's no going there twice. Fortunately, it isn't all the time." He shrugged his shoulders. "You reach a place where you know you're so fucked up there's no redemption. No way out, and you accept it. I can't change what they did to me. I've tried. It's not happening. So, I live with it same as everyone else."

Maestro headed for the shower. "Sometimes, Savage, that living doesn't feel like I'm alive. Czar brought feral jungle cats to civilization and expected us to be tame. There's no taming us. Sometimes I need shit like this just to breathe." He indicated the dead bodies rolled in the tarps. "How fucked up is that?"

Savage watched him disappear behind the shower door. "We have to clean that drain," he reminded Ice. "The thing is, Ice, you don't need this fucked-up shit. You can get it out by beating the shit out of an opponent. Maestro, he's more like I am, although just cutting that fucker's throat would have satisfied him. He has to know he's making a difference for some little kid. Me, I need to make them suffer for what they did. To me. To you. To everyone I care about. To all those kids out there we haven't found yet."

Ice hadn't heard the man talk so much in his life. Savage tended to sit back, watchful, lost in the shadows. When he came out of them, he'd explode out and annihilate anyone in his path. Savage was a very scary man and the best to have on their side.

"This woman really does it for you?" Savage asked.

Ice thought it over. Soleil's laughter warmed him when he thought nothing could. She moved something inside him, things he thought were dead or never there in the first place. She brought out his desire to be better. She chased his demons away. She was gorgeous, willing, and seemed to be able to put up with his proclivity to expose her body to others. That aroused him unbelievably. And she was the best lay he'd ever had in his life.

"Yeah, Savage. She does it for me. I want a chance with her. I may make a mess of everything because I don't know what the fuck I'm doing, but I want that chance."

Savage shrugged. "Then the rest of us will make certain you have it."

That warmed him. Savage meant it. His brothers would surround him, take his back the way they always did. They'd help him find a way to keep her. He had Lana and

Alena to help him. Anya was still with Reaper, and Steele had Breezy. If they could do it, he could.

"Things get dicey, I can always go to Blythe for help," Ice said.

"Yeah, you might want to be careful there," Savage advised. "She might not approve of getting a woman drunk, seducing her and marrying her, fucking her and then leaving her on your wedding night so you can go fuck up some bastards. She's not going to understand you did all that with the best of intentions because you need the woman."

"Shit, put like that, you got a point." Ice couldn't help his guilty grin.

"Blythe doesn't understand what they turned us into. She looks at us the same way she does those kids of hers," Savage observed. "She thinks we can be saved."

"I love that about her," Ice said.

Savage nodded. "I do too, but I'm just saying be careful." He looked around the room, indicating their talk was over. "We've got work to do. We can start, and when Maestro vacates the shower, you go in and then clean up in there."

Ice nodded. He wanted to get back to his woman and wake her up himself.

It took another two hours of hard work to

clean up the mess and remove every bit of evidence that anyone had ever been in the warehouse. They had to burn their clothes as well as the bodies. Fortunately, the club they'd paid to "borrow" the space from had a nice deal going with one of the local crematoriums.

They were careful. They'd learned to pay attention to the smallest detail. Growing up, if one missed a detail, that meant death for them — or another child. They'd learned that the hard way. They'd spent their teenage years and early twenties as assassins for their country. They'd been considered expendable and had been given impossible assignments, but the training they'd been given as children, trying to survive in an environment of rape and torture, had stood them in good stead. They'd learned how to survive, and whenever possible, one of their brothers or sisters had taken their back.

It had been Czar who'd brought them together and given them hope. He'd been a child himself. He'd seen the dead and dying and knew hope was the only answer, that and banding together. They'd learned to trust one another implicitly — and they still did. They didn't work so well independent of one another. Ice knew that they were somehow woven together, and that was what made them work. That sustained them. Apart, there was no way to survive.

Czar had brought them to Sea Haven to find his wife, Blythe, and they'd made the decision to settle in the nearby town of Caspar. They'd bought up a good deal of the properties and were slowly bringing the place back to life, but they didn't fit in most places. They would never fit in what was considered normal civilization. They didn't know or understand the bullshit rules of society.

Still, they had a great clubhouse and places to live. Their lives were better in some ways. Ice was certain his was going to be getting a whole lot better if he just got over this one last little hump. He had to get his woman on the back of his bike and get her to his home, where he could find a way to convince her to stay with him.

NINE

Soleil had the most delicious, erotic dreams she could possibly imagine. She was used to having sexy dreams, but these were beyond the scope of her imagination, making her want to blush. She'd been woken up four times by the hottest man, with the most amazing body, blue eyes and three intriguing tattooed teardrops dripping down one side of his face. He knew exactly what he was doing with his hands, his mouth and that gorgeous cock of his.

She stretched, arms over her head, and her body protested. Sinfully. Deliciously. Achingly. All in a good way. She'd never felt that before waking. She wasn't a morning person at all. She didn't like getting up to face empty days. Most mornings she covered her head and tried to stay in bed as long as possible, but her body felt different. Everything felt different. So alive.

She pried her eyes open, just enough to

look out. A window faced her, and it was definitely morning — or maybe afternoon. She'd practically lived her entire life in hotels, the most luxurious hotels around the world. This was not one of them. She blinked, trying to change what she was seeing into what she knew her reality to be.

Water running in the shower was the first sound Soleil actually cataloged, then voices and the roar of a motorcycle. Her body felt so relaxed and sated she almost turned back over and went to sleep, but then images began to seep in as awareness blossomed, little bits and pieces floating into her mind.

That gorgeous man with the teardrops dripping down his face. Crystalline blue eyes. Hair, thick and wild, so blond it was almost platinum. A body to die for. His mouth between her legs. Bending her over a pool table.

"Oh my God," she whispered aloud. She chanted it as more images drove through her brain. It didn't matter that she tried to stop them, the floodgates opened. Kneeling on the floor of a shop, the most amazing cock in her mouth. Looking up at him as she knelt, and her entire body going into the most amazing sensations she'd ever experienced. His body moving in hers.

She groaned, turned over onto her back

again and flung one arm up to cover her eyes, trying to push away reality. She'd done some stupid things in her life, but this . . . She would have to call Kevin and confess. He would tell her what to do. This was on her. Completely on her.

What had she done? Guilt assailed her. She'd seduced a very sweet man because he was perfect. Everything she'd ever wanted. She'd trapped him into marriage. She'd gotten him drunk. She'd seduced him in every way a woman could. Deliberately. Boldly. It didn't matter that he'd been attempting to do the same to her; she knew she had made a choice to keep him for selfish reasons, and she would have to confess to him and let him go. The thought made her want to cry. She'd have to call Kevin and make this right for Ice.

It suddenly came to her that she didn't have Kevin. He was gone. An accident . . . She had a fiancé . . .

"Oh my God," she whispered again. Only this time it wasn't about whatever insanity she'd done after meeting the hottest, sweetest man in the world. That she'd take responsibility for. This was about Winston and his pack of rabid killers out to murder her.

She sat up, dropping her head in her

300

hands, pushing at the hair spilling around her face and down her back. She lifted her head and met piercing blue eyes. Crystalline eyes. Her heart clenched hard. Those eyes held amusement, although he wasn't smiling. He just sat in a chair opposite the bed and stared at her.

Something wasn't quite right. He didn't feel right. She was certain she'd connected to him in a way she'd never connected with anyone, yet she didn't feel that way now. She just felt awkward. What did one say to a man they'd spent the night with? Not just spent the night but had the most amazing, mind-blowing sex ever with? She forced herself to focus because no matter how hard she tried to make this man the one who had given her that very first orgasm, and then a hundred more, something wasn't right.

He didn't have those three teardrops dripping from his eye. The drops were tattoos. One couldn't just get rid of them so easily. A chill went through her. This wasn't the same man. They were twins. She stared at him in horror.

"Oh my God."

"You keep saying that."

She became aware that she didn't have a stitch on. Not one. The blankets were pooled around her waist and her breasts were very much on display. She knew because she looked down. There were smudges on her breasts. Red marks. Faint strawberries. She yanked the blankets up to her chin.

"Who are you? I didn't . . ." She gestured, unsure what to say. What to ask. "Not both of you." That would be the most humiliating thing she could imagine.

He drew back. "I wouldn't ever touch my brother's wife."

For a moment her brain froze. Her body froze. She couldn't move or think. She just stared at him. It was all true. She'd really done that despicable act. The worst thing a woman could do to a man. She'd trapped him into marriage.

"Nice wedding in the chapel. Party at the bar. Pictures. Ice couldn't keep his hands off you or you him. I didn't think the two of you were going to make it to your room before the official consummation."

He sounded totally amused. He was laughing at her, and she couldn't blame him. She lifted up her left hand and sure enough, there was a ring. It was laminated paper with a very intricate drawing, but it was there. She remembered the ring he'd slipped on her finger and she wanted to cry. She loved that silly ring. That he'd thought to do that for her.

He'd bought her a dress worth nearly twenty thousand dollars. She'd let him do that. All that money. The chapel. A party with a wedding cake. She'd really done it. She'd gotten him drunk enough that he'd signed her prenup and married her.

His twin sat there thinking it was a huge joke when poor sweet Ice had been taken such advantage of. She dropped her pounding head into her hands. Her head hurt so badly, but she knew she hadn't gotten drunk. Tipsy, maybe, but not drunk. She couldn't even claim drinking as an excuse for her behavior. Fear for her life, maybe, but not alcohol. Guilt overwhelmed her. She didn't have Kevin to sort things out.

She peeked through her fingers, her gaze searching the room. There was a leather jacket over the back of a chair. It said "Torpedo Ink" on it and had a tree, skulls and ravens on it. Ice had that same tree, skulls and ravens tattooed on his back. She'd traced every bit of it with her tongue. It was beautiful on him. Not only had she married a stranger, she'd married a biker. Because when she screwed up, she didn't do it by halves.

"I need to get up. Would you mind leaving?" She used her most reasonable voice. She didn't dare show panic when inside she

303

was shaking like a leaf and wanting to put the blanket over her head.

"Can't do that, honey," he said. "Ice asked me to look after you while he's getting ready. We're leaving soon. Need to get back home."

That was such a relief. She felt like she could breathe. "I'm Soleil, but I guess you know that. You're . . ." she prompted.

"Storm. Ice's twin."

The water went off in the shower, and her heart started pounding all over again. She touched her tongue to her dry lips. "I clearly didn't drink enough water last night."

"Ice left you a couple of aspirin and a bottle of water on the nightstand there."

She glanced over, and sure enough, there was a cold bottle of water and a couple of white pills sitting on a tissue. She stretched her arm out from under the covers. "Where is home?"

He gestured toward the jacket. "Caspar. On the coast."

She'd never heard of it. "I live in San Francisco," she volunteered, because she couldn't think of anything intelligent to say.

"That's about three and a half to four hours from us. You probably know Sea Haven. Little place but very popular."

She nodded. "I've actually been there a

couple of times. It's very pretty." She rubbed her forehead with the heel of her hand. "My head is killing me. I know I didn't drink that much last night. And I don't get drunk. I don't get hangovers."

"Probably mixing your drinks. Does it every time." Storm stood up as his twin came out of the bathroom, toweling his hair dry.

Ice wore a pair of jeans that rode low on his narrow hips. His torso and abdomen were all muscle. And all scars. She could see the white lines and ridges across his skin. They didn't detract in the least from his good looks. No man had the right to be that good-looking. His eyes met hers and instantly her stomach did a slow roll, and a million butterflies took wing. At the same time, she recognized him. Her body recognized him. She felt him all over again, waking her at least four times, his body buried in hers. She had a mini orgasm just looking into his eyes.

She was afraid her makeup was running down her face. It had to be. He looked like a model, and she looked like a wreck. He kept coming straight across the room to her, put his knee on the bed and bent down to take her mouth.

She should have pulled back. She should

have protested. She did neither. She opened her mouth under the coaxing of his and then there was nothing at all but Ice. His mouth. Fire running through her veins. His tongue tangling with hers. His arms sweeping her against him. Tight. Skin to skin. Her breasts pressed into all those defined muscles. Her nipples twin flames dragging over his chest. Her arms slid around his neck of their own accord, and everything but Ice went out of her brain.

His mouth left hers and he kissed and nipped his way over her chin, down her throat to the swell of her breast. His mouth closed over her left breast while he cupped her right one in his palm, thumb stroking her nipple.

"Good morning, princess." His voice was mesmerizing, let alone his mouth. His kisses. His hands.

"Good morning." She was shy, when that was absolutely nuts because he'd had his mouth, his fingers and his cock inside her so many times.

"The shower's all yours. We have to get moving, babe. We're pulling out in under an hour. You hungry? Storm can bring you some breakfast if you are."

Storm? Her gaze jumped across the room. The man didn't even have the decency to look uncomfortable. She tried to raise the covers again, although there was that part of her she couldn't quite control that always thought it was so hot when someone caught glimpses of her. She was ridiculously proud of the fact that she had Ice's marks all over her breasts and someone saw them there.

"I'm not hungry." The thought of eating made her sick. She was going to have to confess to Ice. Tell him the truth. Tell him what a horrible person she was and make the responsible decision to sort it all out. She'd created the mess, and she was the one who had to deal with it, even though she no longer had Kevin.

Ice had the covers in his hand, and he prevented her from raising them. "Shower, then, Soleil. We're really in a hurry this morning."

"We need to talk." She needed to tell him they were getting an annulment *immediately,* that she'd take that responsibility. "I have to talk to you," she whispered, trying not to look at his brother. She didn't want him to see the guilt on her face.

Certainly, Ice wouldn't want to stay married. They were strangers. She didn't fit into a club. She didn't fit in anywhere. And there were Winston and the others, powerful men who wanted her dead. She couldn't take the chance of them coming into Ice's life. That wouldn't be fair either.

"We can talk after your shower." Ice pulled the covers all the way back, scooped her up and cradled her in his arms.

She was totally naked. She wasn't even wearing panties. Worse, just those kisses and his hands and mouth on her breasts had made her slick with need between her legs. She was in such trouble. She wanted him so much. She wanted to keep him. She told herself he wasn't a pet, he was a grown, maybe scary, dangerous man, but to her he was the sweetest, kindest, most caring person she'd ever known.

Ice didn't seem to think anything of having another man in the room while she was naked. At all. Before she could think she should protest, his mouth came down on hers again, and her brain malfunctioned. Her body melted into his. Little sparks of electricity danced over her skin, and lightning seemed to zigzag through her, from her mouth to her breasts to her clit. Her sex clenched hungrily. She seemed to float through the air. That's what he did to her. Then her feet were on the ground and he was lifting his head.

"You all right by yourself in here? I can stay and watch you shower," he offered

308

wickedly. "If I shower with you, we're never leaving the room."

Wrapping her arms around her middle, Soleil backed away from him. Her entire body trembled. Her insides felt shaky. Her breasts ached, and deep inside she throbbed and burned with need. She wanted him to stay there. Her gaze dropped hungrily to the front of his jeans. She loved what he had there. She wanted it.

He let out a groan. "Babe. We're not going to get anywhere if we keep this up."

She knew that. She couldn't think straight when she was with him. She should have been telling him they weren't married, and he couldn't touch or kiss her, but instead, she wanted him to push her up against the wall and repeat all the amazing things he'd done to her the night before. She remembered everything with great clarity. She hadn't been drunk, not even when he'd laid her out on the pool table, her wedding dress bunched around her waist, and eaten her until she'd been screaming for mercy.

She knew she should be embarrassed about her bad behavior, but it was impossible when he made her feel beautiful and special and wanted. When he'd given her the most amazing orgasms ever and when he was still looking at her as if she were the only woman on the face of the earth and he could easily slam her up against a wall and take her a million times without it ever being enough.

Ice brushed a kiss on her forehead. "Hurry, baby." He gave her a swat on her bottom and turned away from her.

She watched him go out before turning to look at herself in the mirror. She nearly groaned. She had bruises on her face. Some swelling. She also had makeup under her eyes with a faint stream of shadowy black running down her face. How could he even look at her when she was such a mess? Especially with the lust in his eyes that was so plain there?

The hot water felt wonderful on all the sore places. She had a lot of them. She scrubbed her skin, although she found herself reluctant to remove Ice's scent from her body. She liked belonging to him — no — she loved it. Even in the light of day, knowing it would be a mistake to carry on with the fantasy fairy tale they'd woven together, she wanted him and the life he offered. His club. His family. She had things she had to face. She couldn't run away and just become someone else — although she'd fantasized about doing just that a million times from early childhood on. And after she told him the truth — that she'd deliberately gotten him drunk — no man would want to be trapped into marriage, especially a man like Ice.

She took her time shampooing and conditioning her hair with the expensive and great-smelling products Ice had left for her. She wondered vaguely where he'd gotten them. Where he'd gotten the money for the dress. The motel was inexpensive, so it was confusing that he'd laid down so much money for their wedding.

Wedding. She groaned and stepped out of the shower, wrapping her hair in a towel so she could see what she could do about her face. She didn't have her clothes, and she needed them. She bent over the sink to study the swelling. It wasn't nearly as bad as it had felt when Winston hit her. Her ribs ached a little and so did her stomach from where Winston had punched her. Actually, her stomach hurt more than anything else, which was probably why she didn't have any interest in food.

The door behind her opened and Ice sauntered in, coming right to her. Before she could straighten, he laid a hand on the middle of her back, holding her in place while his other hand caressed and stroked the cheeks of her bottom. She closed her

311

eyes and just savored the way he made her feel. Beautiful. Desirable. Sexy. Like a woman. Wholly feminine.

"I love the way you smell," he said. "Brought you some clothes, but now that I see the temptation, I don't know." His hand slid lower, fingers finding the instant response he seemed to generate, that slick heat. He buried his fingers deep and then stroked them over her burning clit.

She couldn't help pushing back against his hand. "Ice, we aren't really married, are we?" She sounded breathless. Wanting. She was so addicted to him it was insane. "I mean I know we were at the chapel, but you can't want . . ." She drifted off, because his fingers were magic and it was impossible to hold comprehensive thoughts.

"Definitely married, baby. Have the marriage certificate to prove it. We're locked in nice and tight. Spent all night fucking you. Considering spending the next few days doing the same but not in this dump. You deserve so much better, and I want you to see the house."

"The house?" she echoed faintly. Reality was getting away from her. "There's a house?"

"Yeah, princess. A house. It isn't exactly the castle you deserve, but it's nice. And

Lana wants us to get home so she can see for herself that you're all right." His fingers were gone, and he smacked her on her left cheek a second time. "Get dressed, baby, and let's get on the road."

She leaned against the sink, watching him saunter out with that same easy stride that looked like a leisurely prowl. He was so sexy. So hot. One didn't marry someone just because they could provide endless orgasms, did they? Could you fall in love with a cock? She had. She was in love with everything about him and definitely his cock. Her body was singing. Alive. Happy. She was happy, if she could push away the guilt. She desperately needed to have the talk with him, but she didn't want to lose him.

She took a deep breath and dressed. The clothes were brand-new and fit perfectly. She let herself remember shopping with him. Such a beautiful, unforgettable night. She remembered him making her laugh when she was so scared walking in the open down the street, so afraid Winston or one of his friends would see her. Ice made her feel safe. His brothers and Alena crowded around her, taking her back in the bar, giving her something she'd never had before.

What was she thinking? Even if she could escape into another life, she had no way of fitting in. She didn't know the first thing about club life. Or relationships. She'd blow that right away. She stared at herself as she brushed her teeth with the toothbrush that was left for her on the sink, still in its wrapper. He'd thought of everything, including a brush, comb and hair ties. She braided her hair on the off chance that she lost her mind completely and went with him. She wasn't going to do that. She needed to stop the nonsense before it was completely out of hand, but . . .

Ice was there again, and she realized he hadn't closed the door between the bathroom and the main room. She hadn't even noticed because she was so deep in thought. He caught her thick braid and tugged, pulling her head back.

"You thinkin' of leavin' me already, baby?" He tugged again.

His eyes met hers and the blue was more crystal, more glacier than she remembered. Sexy as hell. It felt as if he were seeing all the way to her soul. Her sex clenched and her stomach did that slow roll. She pressed her hand there. He didn't let go of her hair and she felt the pull on her scalp, a small bite of pain that was more erotic than anything else.

"Well, yes," she admitted, deciding honesty was really the best policy. "You were drinking, Ice. A lot." She cleared her throat. "I did this to you. I took one look at you and you're so beautiful, so perfect, and I wanted you for myself. It was wrong. I know it was. I knew it then but I was drinking, maybe a little too much myself, but that's not an excuse, I shouldn't be making excuses . . ."

"Stop, princess."

"You can't possibly want to be married to me. You don't know anything at all about me. Isn't being in a club all about freedom?"

She tried to make a joke when she didn't feel in the least humorous. Now that she'd made the confession, and told him the truth, it hurt to know she'd have to leave him. Really hurt. That was unexpected. That was how far she'd wanted to believe in the fairy tale.

"I knew what I was doing every step of the way, Soleil. I wanted you from the first time I saw you on the street. When you walked into the bar, I knew then I was going to find a way to keep you. You wanted me to sign the prenup, I had no problem with it." He let go of her hair. "You signed mine. I gave you an out every step of the way. It's done. We're married. You're my wife, and every single club member knows

315

your husband was in here fucking your brains out because you're not quiet when you come for me."

She blushed. That was true. She hadn't believed in screaming orgasms. She wasn't even certain she'd believed in orgasms, screaming or quiet, until Ice. Now, it was the absolute truth, he could make her scream and he had — often.

"Sex and marriage aren't at all the same thing," she pointed out.

"Yeah, well, if all you're feeling is the sex right now, I'll take it."

Ice caught her hand and pulled her out of the bathroom to the bedroom. Putting one hand on her belly, he gently pushed until she sank down onto the mattress. He crouched down and took her foot in his hand, pulling on a sock.

"I'm trying to save you, and you aren't helping." Soleil was feeling a little desperate.

"Save me from who? From what? I was sober, Soleil. I want you to be my wife. Do you even know what you are?"

She shook her head.

"A fuckin' miracle, that's what you are," he said and pulled on her boot.

It wasn't easy. She had to push her foot into it, and she did so without looking at him. He made her want to cry. She was no one's miracle. More like their nightmare.

"I'm not, you know. There's things that could get you hurt." There it was. The truth. She had to keep him safe because he didn't seem to comprehend, she came with too much baggage. "You have a sister. Alena. She needs to be safe. Your brother." She waved toward the window. "All the people you care about. And that's not even getting into the fact that we have no idea if we're even compatible."

He pulled up her other sock and rubbed over her calf before reaching for the boot. "I think we more than proved that we're compatible, princess. As for the trouble you bring, the baggage, if you mean that pussy Winston, he'll find it won't be so easy to take on a club, if he's so inclined. My guess, once you're gone, he'll disappear."

She shook her head. "He won't, Ice. And he has friends, policemen, lawyers. Money behind him. He won't stop."

Ice tilted his head to look at her, and the morning sun fell across his face like a spotlight. His eyes were as cold as their color, a complete glacier. He suddenly looked predatory. Dangerous even. Her sweet, easygoing Ice caused a shiver to go down her spine. That expression on his face should have been a red flag, but instead, it caused her blood to go hot and rush through her veins like a drug.

"Let him come, then, Soleil. We're out of here. The boys are ready. Even Alena's ready. I've packed everything, including your dress. That thing needs to be put in a frame and hung on the wall."

She ignored the hand he held out to her. Someone had to be practical. He might think he could handle Winston and his friends, but the members of Ice's club would be considered outlaws. Winston could harass them — although would he really think she was with a motorcycle club? Even if he found out about their marriage, how would he know where to find Ice? Unless he found out about their marriage and tracked them through the marriage certificate. The final copy would be mailed to Ice's address. She just couldn't do that to him.

She walked to the window and stared out. Below them was the long row of bikes, with men either sitting on them or talking together close to them. She spotted Alena with her platinum hair on her own bike. Heads turned toward the center of the parking lot. A cop car had driven in with another vehicle behind it.

Her heart stopped when Winston jumped

318

out on the passenger side and followed the policeman to the office. One by one the bikes started up, their pipes roaring. Heart pounding, she turned to Ice. Her mouth was dry. She felt as if she'd been punched in the stomach all over again. She knew the color had drained from her face.

Ice silently handed her a jacket and gloves and then stepped up to the window to take in everything happening in the parking lot. The cop, manager and Winston were walking together toward the stairs on the opposite end. Watching them, Soleil pulled on the jacket, zipped it up and tugged on the gloves, already moving to the door.

Ice stopped her. "That him? The maggot? Does he have the cops looking for you?"

She knew he might misinterpret the reason, but she didn't care. They had to leave now. She nodded.

He pushed sunglasses on her nose and handed her a helmet. She stuffed her braid into the helmet and settled it on her head. Ice took her hand and they walked out together, his arm around her waist as they went to the opposite staircase, their backs to the cop. She could hear them knocking on a door and the manager calling out to the occupant.

Ice swung his leg over his Harley, and she

put her hand on his shoulder and climbed on behind him, settling onto the seat, her arms around him. His brothers began to take off, one by one, in formation. Ice followed suit and then they were away from the motel. She could take a breath. Breathe. Elation filled her.

Winston was checking hotels and motels. Some poor woman must have checked in alone and they were making certain that woman wasn't her. Winston hadn't even glanced at the motorcycles. Clearly, it hadn't occurred to him that she would be with them.

She tightened her arms around Ice and let herself be carried away by the experience. The wind was warm, and because there were no doors or windows, she felt as if she were right out with the scenery. It was beautiful once they left Vegas. She loved having the other bikes around them. Somehow, it made the experience more powerful. She loved the feeling of freedom. Several times, Ice put his hand over hers, and she loved that small connection between them.

She should have been thinking about how she had screwed up and needed to end their marriage as quickly as possible, but she loved riding on the motorcycle with him. She loved holding him close and feeling the vibration of the bike between her legs. Maybe it was because she found Ice so sexy that she found the bike that way as well.

Hours passed. They stopped for a water break and to top off gas tanks, but they rode steadily throughout the day. The buzz faded a little, to be replaced by aches and pains — her body protesting the long ride when she wasn't used to it. She didn't complain. She was just grateful she had Ice to hang on to. He continued to do little things that kept her aware of him. More importantly, the way he touched her, dropping his hand to wrap it around her thigh, rubbing the back of her gloved hand, just small things, but they made her feel important to him.

They stopped to eat at a little diner just off the highway toward evening. They parked their bikes and went in, Storm catching the door to allow Soleil and Ice through. Ice had his hand on the small of her back as they walked inside. Her legs were very shaky, and she desperately needed the ladies' room. As if he knew, Ice walked straight to the door. As she went inside, Alena ducked in with her.

"Those boys, they just keep riding no matter what," Alena said, laughing as they raced for the stalls.

"I didn't think we'd ever stop," Soleil admitted.

"I was expecting you to tell Ice to take a rest."

Soleil thought about that. She was tired, and she knew they had a distance to go. Vegas was at least eight and half hours from San Francisco by car. If Caspar was three or four hours from San Francisco, even traveling a different route, they still had a long way to go. She found she didn't care. She washed her hands and looked at Alena through the mirror.

"I like traveling this way. With him. He feels safe."

Alena's smile was slow in coming, but it was genuine. "He's a good man. He wants this, Soleil. I know you're probably freaking out a little . . ."

"You think? I tried to tell him I wasn't drunk, that I was the one trying to get him drunk, but he wouldn't listen. I thought about making a run for it for his sake, but he doesn't want me to. I can handle all the details of getting an annulment, or divorce, but he says no."

Alena laughed softly. "That's so funny. You both were trying to do the same thing. I think that just goes to show you that you're meant for each other."

Were they? She didn't want to leave Ice. She wanted a different life. She always had. But he was a stranger, and his way of life was so completely the opposite of everything she knew. When she let her brain actually work, she knew she was insane not to call a lawyer and get an annulment immediately for both their sakes, but she was already walking out of the restroom and he was there, leaning against the wall.

The moment she spotted him, her heart beat wildly and she could barely breathe. He had draped himself there, appearing casually gorgeous, looking down at his phone and not at the waitresses vying for his attention. The moment she walked out, he glanced up, his blue eyes drifting over her possessively. Just that look sent her stomach on a crazy roller-coaster ride.

He smiled at her. His eyes lit up as if beneath the ice was a spotlight, shining through the crystal so that all that blue sparkled — just for her. He made her feel as if there were no other women in the world but her and she was his everything.

"I have helmet hair," she greeted and then silently cursed herself, wishing she had something scintillating to offer, but looking at him, she was tongue-tied.

"You look beautiful, princess."

Ice took her hand and led her to the booth where his brother, Alena and Maestro sat. Ice waited for her to get in first and slide all the way to the wall. He slipped in beside her and pressed up against her, his thigh to hers. His brethren sat in the surrounding booths, almost as if she was in the center of the club. It was an interesting concept. She was most always alone when she ate — although she didn't frequent diners. She had no siblings, and the idea of having others care enough to look out for her was part of that fantasy she seemed caught in.

The waitress hurried over and handed them all menus. She stared at Ice and Storm. "You must be twins."

Ice didn't look up. Storm answered. "That's what they tell us."

The waitress threw back her head and laughed louder than Soleil thought was strictly necessary. Maestro shook his head and Alena looked bored.

"Anything look good, baby?" Ice asked, leaning into her. He took her hand and rubbed his thumb over her knuckles.

She tried not to be distracted, but that light, back-and-forth motion felt intimate. She pretended to study the menu, but she couldn't think. He could wreak havoc with such a small gesture. Just when she thought she would have to pull her hand away, he dropped their hands to his thigh, pushing her palm over the hard muscle there and holding it to him. That felt even more intimate.

"Princess?" Ice prompted.

She cleared her throat. "I'll have the taco salad." It was the only item she could actually read, and she prayed it would be good because she was hungry.

The waitress wrote down her order and then stood there, staring at Ice and Storm. They both gave their orders, as did Alena and Maestro. The waitress pulled her gaze from the twins to bat her eyelashes at Maestro.

"My woman's hungry," Ice said without looking up. It was a clear order.

His tone made Soleil shiver. He pressed her hand tighter and then threaded his fingers through hers. "We would have stopped sooner, babe, had you said you needed a break."

"I was pretty impressed," Maestro said. "We all expected you to call a stop. Do you remember me?" He sent her a cocky grin.

She tried not to blush. These men had seen her in the throes of passion, Ice's mouth between her legs, her riding his fingers and screaming out her orgasm. Just like that she was hot and slick again, squirming a little in her seat.

"You plied me with liquor all night. Of course I remember you, Maestro. I would presume you like music." She was so glad she hadn't whined and insisted on stopping. If it had been a test, she'd passed it with flying colors.

"You'd be right," Alena said, making a face when she took a sip of her coffee. "Maestro is amazing on the piano. He can play just about any instrument, and when he actually admits it, he can sing too."

"Coffee sucks," Storm said. "But it's all we've got. Alena has a soft opening of her restaurant in a couple of days. That's one of the reasons we're hurrying back. She wants to see to all the details."

She was grateful Alena had needed to go back to their home. What if Winston had caught her in the room with Ice? Judging by the way Ice had cordoned her off from the rest of the room with his body, he would have fought for her. He probably would have gotten beaten up or gone to jail. A little shiver went down her spine at the thought. Did she really have the right to put him in jeopardy? Any of them?

"You're opening a restaurant?" That didn't seem like a club thing to do.

326

Alena nodded. "I was so excited about it." She leaned her chin onto the heel of her hand. "But now that it's close, I want to vomit. It's so scary. What if no one comes? What if no one likes my cooking? I'm the chef, and I won't be dealing that much with the customers, but it's my place and I want them happy."

"I take it you like to cook." That was such a revelation. Alena wanted to be a chef and cook for others. She hadn't thought much about it, but everyone probably needed to work. At least most everyone. She'd tried various ideas, but the moment any employer found out who she really was, everything changed. Most actually brought her business "opportunities" for her to invest in.

The idea that Alena was making her dream come true moved her. She looked up at Ice. He had put his arm around her and was idly massaging her neck. He brushed the pads of his fingers there, massaging and then using the pads of his fingers again, sliding them gently over her skin. She felt those darts of fire running to her breasts. Making her entire body aware of him. Aware of everything about him. His scent. His heat. The way he brought every nerve ending alive. She was aware of the breath moving in and out of his lungs. She didn't know if it was the motorcycle that had increased the connection between them, but it was definitely strong.

"Does everyone in the club work?"

"Pretty much, yeah," Storm answered. "Savage and Reaper work at the club. They aren't the kind of men to work for someone else. We all bring in money. The cash is shared collectively."

Soleil frowned. "You work and any money you make goes to the club? Not to you?"

Ice shrugged. "We've always worked like that. This way, whoever needs it fast has something to draw on immediately."

"The club paid for my restaurant," Alena pointed out. "We have a bar and a couple of apartments over the bar we rent out. Although, at the moment, we're renovating them. We're bringing in a grocery store as well. That's just now getting up and running. Inez Nelson is the owner of the store in Sea Haven, and she's going in with us as partners. Ink has his tattoo shop running, and Mechanic and Transporter have their custom automotive garage."

"That's amazing. I didn't even consider that all of you would have regular jobs." She hadn't, and that smacked of prejudice. She liked them, she wasn't prejudiced against bikers, but she did have preconceived notions about them.

Ice suddenly caught her chin and turned his head toward her. "Kiss me, babe. I don't think I can go another minute. You want to save my life, right? That can be your job."

She didn't think about it or protest. She turned her face up to his without hesitation and kissed him. Butterflies went crazy. Chaos reigned in her head. Her breasts ached and her nipples pushed tightly against her lacy bra, scraping on the fabric. He tasted like sin. Temptation. The devil enticing her down a dark, wicked path. She didn't care. She gave herself to him and was instantly rewarded with the fire rushing through her veins.

It was hot. It was dangerous. It was everything she remembered. Only Ice. Only Soleil. She cupped the side of his face as she kissed him thoroughly. Completely. Losing her ability to breathe so he did it for them. The hand holding hers beneath the table stroked her rib cage and then her stomach so gently, right over the places Winston had struck her. His fingers edged up the material of her tank, so his palm laid against bare skin. It felt as if he branded her. It felt as if he soothed those lingering aches.

The waitress almost dropped their plates onto the table. Ice lifted his head very

329

slowly, uncaring of the noise or distraction. He rested his forehead against hers. "Nice job, baby, you got me through the next couple of hours."

"Is that a real job?" She told herself she should be embarrassed by the public displays of affection, especially the behavior she'd engaged in with Ice the night before, but even thinking about it made her hot all over. She loved that she could be with him and he touched her or kissed her whenever or however he wanted. He made her feel wanted when she never had been.

He nodded. "Need saving, princess, and it seems only you can manage it." He took her hand again and this time, beneath the table, pressed it over his cock. "See what you do to me? That's fuckin' real, baby. That's what you do. Need that. Need to know you can put that there for me."

She rubbed, wishing she could crawl under the table and have him for dinner. She looked up at him so he could see that need and hunger in her eyes. "I have news for you, honey," she said, reluctant to be honest. "Just about any woman can do that for you. You're amazing."

Storm groaned. Alena rolled her eyes. Maestro shook his head. "Now he's never going to shut up about how fuckin' amazin' he is."

Ice brought her knuckles to his mouth. "She's amazing."

"Putting up with you, I have to admit, she is," Alena said. "How did you meet Lana?"

Soleil's heart dropped. She picked up her fork and pretended to find the taco salad interesting. "I came to Vegas with a man who was really nasty. He wanted to get married, I said no, and he got very angry and shook me, left a few bruises. Lana was in the restroom when I came in, and she warned me to be careful when I made it clear I wasn't going to marry him."

She touched the bruise on her face. "I have them a few other places as well. He got really angry when I made myself clear. I took off and remembered she put her number in my phone just in case." She glanced at Ice a little warily.

He immediately leaned into her and brushed a kiss over the bruise. "Thank fuck he was a bastard and I got you. Soleil doesn't need any more questions right now. We don't like them, she doesn't need them."

She sent him a grateful smile. She wanted to fit in. She wanted Alena and the others to like her, but she didn't know what she was doing just yet and she had quite a few things she had to figure out before she went much further.

"Sorry, hon, Ice is right. However you came to us doesn't matter, only that you did. It was a great wedding and we have some amazing pictures. The photographer was awesome. We sent him home when the party was in full swing, but we all took pictures just for you and Ice."

Soleil thanked her. Thanked all of them. "You all were so sweet to pull off a wedding in a couple of hours." She was a little afraid to see the pictures. She knew exactly what had gone on once the photographer had left.

"Your dress was amazing," Alena said. "I can't believe my brother has such good taste. And I loved your shoes."

Soleil loved those shoes too. They were very sexy and went with the dress perfectly. Ice had carefully wrapped the dress and shoes and they were stowed away with her extra pair of jeans in a bag on his motorcycle. Just the fact that he was so thoughtful had her wanting to cry. No one in her life had ever taken that kind of care of her.

"She looks fabulous in heels," Ice said, his fingers once more massaging her neck. He took her free hand and put it in his lap, over that thick bulge that made her want to lick him from head to toe.

She matched the rhythm of his fingers on her neck, slowly massaging the bulge from tip to balls. He was so hard. So perfect. By the time they were ready to ride again, she was fairly certain it was entirely possible to fall in love with a cock. She loved the shape and hardness of him. The promise of what he could bring her — of what she knew she could bring him. His taste. She had that taste in her mouth and wanted more on her tongue and down her throat. It was absolutely possible to fall in love with that portion of his anatomy.

TEN

Soleil stared at the house in sheer shock. It was the last thing she'd expected. The front of the house, facing the ocean, was all glass, from floor to ceiling. A massive covered deck wrapped from one side, around the back all the way to the other side of the house, leaving just a porch and entryway in the front. It was elegant and beautiful and impressive all at once.

Her legs were still shaky from the long ride and she was very tired, but looking in through the glass, she could see a fire going in the fireplace, and that was something she'd always dreamt of when she'd fanta-sized about having a home. Just looking at it made her forget how exhausted she was.

"Ice," she whispered. "Is this really yours?"

He slung his arm around her neck. "Ours," he corrected. "Czar insisted we all have homes of our own. Wanted us to put roots down here and become part of the community." He shrugged. "I liked this house because of all the glass. It still gives you a sense of freedom, not confinement."

Soleil looked up at him. That was a strange reason for buying a house, needing glass so one could feel free versus confined. She leaned into him. He was a strong man and gave her a sense of safety. It occurred to her that he felt safer out in the open rather than behind walls. That was an odd concept to understand. It only brought home to her much more that she knew very little about the man she had married.

Ice leaned down and brushed a kiss over her lips. "Don't look so scared. You're safe with me, Soleil. I swear to you, I won't let anything bad happen to you. I intend to make you the happiest woman in the world." He gestured toward the steps leading to an ornate glass door.

The heavy door had a replica of their jackets' Torpedo Ink logo, only this was in stained glass and very large, taking up a great deal of the door. The tree, the skulls in the roots, the ravens in the branches as well as a few flying away, were very distinct and detailed.

"Someone made this for you," she guessed. The attention to each element was superb. She could look at the door all day.

"Someone you know."

"One of the brothers, Casimir, is married to Lissa, a glassblower. She's famous for her chandeliers. She also does metal and stained-glass work. I pitched the idea of the door to her and she went to work on it immediately."

"The work is amazing." Soleil knew quality when she saw it. Again, her preconceived notions of how her husband lived were completely wrong. She pictured him living in a clubhouse with his brothers and partying every night.

"Haven't really lived here," Ice admitted as if guessing her thoughts. "None of us are comfortable living alone. We spent far too much time together watching one another's backs." He reached around her and opened the door, swooped her up and carried her inside, laughing, his expression happy as he kissed her and then set her feet on the entryway floor.

Soleil stepped deeper into the house, and her breath caught in her throat, the question of why they had to watch one another's backs fading along with her joy at his carrying her over the threshold as she gazed inside. The house felt welcoming. It was large, but not too large. The high ceilings gave it a spacious feel, and the thick, luxurious carpets and long, stone fireplace made the house feel unexpectedly cozy. She found herself clutching Ice's arm in excitement.

"I've never had a home," she admitted, sounding breathless even to her own ears. "This is spectacular."

Ice flashed his heart-stopping smile and gestured to the interior. "Look around, princess, this is your castle. Feel free to do anything you'd like with it. The brothers and Lana hastily added a few pieces of furniture for us. They also stocked the refrigerator. It's nowhere near the things we'll need, so we can go furniture shopping in a few days."

Her heart was pounding, beating way too fast. For a moment she thought she might not be able to breathe. She wanted a family and a home more than anything. Ice was so casual about it, waving his hand around, and telling her they'd go pick out furniture. That was what couples did — they shopped for household items together.

Tears welled up and she looked away from him, not wanting him to see. Naturally he did, because when something involved her, Ice seemed to see everything. He stepped in front of her and tipped up her chin with his finger under it.

"Tell me what's wrong, baby."

His voice was soft and compelling. Her

body reacted the way it did around him, coming to a full alert, every nerve ending springing to life. She wanted to close her eyes and escape his scrutiny, those amazing blue eyes of his that seemed to see everything, but it was impossible.

"It's not wrong. It's all right. Unbelievable." She choked back the tears threatening to clog her throat. "This is like a dream, and I'm going to have to wake up soon and realize it isn't real and I'm alone in an endless string of hotel rooms."

He framed her face with his hands. "You never have to wake up alone again, Soleil. This is your home. You can do any damn thing you want with it."

"I may never leave it." She tried a watery smile.

"That's fine by me. Stay in the bedroom naked. I'd go about my business all day knowing what is waiting for me at home. I'd be perfectly happy with that."

She caught her lower lip between her teeth, anxiety gripping her. "I've never cooked for anyone. I want to learn. I actually took lessons, but I've never had the chance to practice."

"You don't have to cook, princess. You aren't here to be my servant. I wouldn't mind you being my sex slave, just so you

338

know that option of never leaving the house and never wearing clothes is always open," he teased.

Her heart actually fluttered. She couldn't help but laugh. She tried not to look at him with her heart in her eyes, but she was beginning to think she was feeling more for him than the intense physical attraction she'd admitted to herself they had between them. She couldn't fall for him. Not with her heart and soul.

She'd already tried giving her heart completely after Aunt Deborah died and she'd gone to her other aunt — the one who despised her. Soleil had tried desperately to get her to love her. She wasn't the lovable type. Even Kevin, although she loved him because he was the only father figure she could remember, hadn't come out from behind his phone, not even on holidays when she'd begged him.

"Soleil."

Ice's voice brought her out of her memories, although the sadness lingered. Her gaze jumped to his. Those eyes of his saw too much, and she tried to look away.

He kissed her. Long. Hot. Driving sanity away. Driving sorrow away. He left behind feeling. Her body sang, her heart leapt, her sex clenched, and blood immediately heated, rushing through veins to settle between her legs.

She kissed him back. Giving herself to him. Giving him everything she was. Fire burst through her, as hot as the flames leaping in the fireplace. She couldn't hold back when he kissed her like that. She'd had a crap childhood, but she had the feeling his was far worse. She had tried to develop a guarded interior, but evidently, when it came to Ice, the walls tumbled down fast.

It was Ice who slowly, and very reluctantly, lifted his head. "I want you to look around, Soleil. Anything you don't like, we'll change."

"I can't imagine not liking something in this house." The idea of exploring was exciting. She was going to continue the fairy tale they'd started and tell herself the house really was hers and she'd never have to leave. She was there, for whatever reasons, and she was going to take advantage of it. This was her dream, and strangely, the house came close to being her fantasy home.

She moved away from him, toward the other end of the room. The great room was just that — great. It was large with high ceilings and an immense stone fireplace. The room opened into a hallway that seemed massive. Four people could easily walk shoulder to shoulder in that space. She could see why Ice wanted the house if he felt confined indoors. There was no way to get claustrophobia when everything about the design of the house felt spacious.

The kitchen was extremely large. It included a breakfast nook, which, in her opinion, was no nook but almost a separate room. The nook was situated in a rounded glass turret. The view was of a green forest of tall redwood trees. She could look out and see wildlife, trees and shrubbery as she ate any meal.

The setup for cooking was fantastic. She might not be a chef or know much about the inner workings of their space, but she could see how easily one could get from the refrigerator to the oven in a few short steps. Counter space was abundant, as was work space. She really was eager to try her hand at cooking.

The formal dining room had one of Lissa's chandeliers hanging over the table. This chandelier dripped drops of ocean spray captured in crystal. There was color to it, a blaze of light blue. Ice blue. Glacier blue. All of that was captured in crystalline drops.

She swung around to grip Ice's arm tightly. "She's a genius, this Lissa. I've never seen anything more beautiful."

"It is nice, isn't it?" Ice admitted, cocking his head to one side to study the light fixture.

"It's brilliant," Soleil corrected. "Beyond brilliant. She drew inspiration from your eyes. Can you see what she did?"

He shrugged. He was watching her closely, his gaze on her face, a faint smile on his, as if her reactions made him happy. She liked that. She wanted him to feel the happiness he gave to her. She wasn't used to it and she didn't trust that she'd have it long, but she loved being present in the here and now because she was experiencing something perfect and she wanted to capture the memory forever.

"Look at this room." She waved her hands to encompass the large dining room. It held a long rectangular table made of cherry-wood, the light playing over it making it gleam a dark, almost bloodred. The sideboard was made of the same wood, that dark, rich red. The floor was tile, swirls of light blue twisting through a field of white, creating the look of sky and clouds — or the ocean on a stormy day. She loved the floor.

She went on through the archway leading to the other rooms and the stairway. It went both up and down. She looked at Ice for an explanation.

"Upstairs is the master bedroom. Guest rooms and bathrooms are on the main floor and beneath this one, we have the play rooms. Kick-ass home theater, billiards room, as well as a game room with VR, and all kinds of other cool games. And the indoor pool."

"Are you kidding me? There's an indoor pool?"

He nodded, watching her face. "It's more like a spa. A full-sized pool, with a hot tub. It's nice. At least I think it is, I've never actually been in it. I've never slept here."

"You own this amazing house and you haven't lived in it?"

He shook his head. "What the hell would I know about livin' in a house? Never settled down before Czar gave us the big order. What am I going to do rattling around by myself in a house like this?"

She threw her arms out wide and turned in a full circle, joy bursting through her. "I would give anything to own a house like this. It's a home, Ice. A real home. This is the kind of house you raise children in."

He rubbed his chin. "Don't know about that, princess. We have kids, I'd have to block off the stairs so they couldn't go down to the pool. I'd worry about that all the

343

time. Then there's the staircase. What if they fall? If their bedrooms were downstairs and we're upstairs, what if someone tries to kidnap them? Or they sneak out the window and I don't know and can't protect them. There's other houses with different floor plans that might make it easier to raise children."

He wanted children. The relief was tremendous. He had clearly thought about the hazards of raising children in the house. He might be just a little paranoid, but he wanted them protected. She loved that. She loved that children mattered enough that he'd actually given their protection thought.

He gestured toward the stairs and pointed up. "You need to get ready for bed. Meaning a shower or bath to help with the soreness from the ride."

"I caught a glimpse of the flower beds, the landscaping rolling out beyond the kitchen. So many flowers, and I love the little garden."

"The one outside the kitchen is all herbs. The one on the side of the house is flowers. The other side, where we get the most sun, is vegetables. I'm no good at gardening, so someone comes here a couple of times a week."

"I saw a gazebo." She glanced up at his

344

face, hesitating. "There is a child's play yard, Ice. I didn't see much of it, but it seemed pretty amazing."

She didn't want him to think she was making an argument to raise children at the house. If he didn't feel comfortable, then she would change houses in a heartbeat. She wanted to sit on the stairs and weep. This was her dream, dangled right in front of her by a gorgeous man who didn't seem to be able to keep his eyes off her.

She just knew not to invest too much. Not her heart. Not her hopes. She'd been crushed too many times. When she really let herself love, she went all in. She didn't know how to be any other way. It was just that he was giving her every little piece of her dream. Every detail. As if he had seen inside her and turned her fantasies into reality.

"If you keep getting that look on your face, Soleil, you give me no option but to take matters into my hands. If you want that shower or bath, you'd better look happy." He made it a threat.

She turned to him and framed his face with her hands. "I'm terrified of falling in love with you." She didn't know why she'd told him the truth, but she had and now it was right there and he could push her off him and say there was no such thing. Their relationship was about sex, that bright, hot chemistry that sizzled and scorched, demanding they stay with each other until the attraction fizzled out.

"I'm terrified you won't," he answered.

Once again, he kissed her. This was no claiming kiss. Not rough. Not aggressive. This was sweet, gentle, almost tender. Her heart lurched hard and slipped closer to him. She wanted to grab it and pull it back to her, but it was impossible. Ice filled her with him. Her mind accepted him the way her heart did, and she couldn't shut down and protect herself. She just surrendered to that gentle kiss.

The strange thing was, just like when he was aggressive, her blood pounded through her body, racing straight to her clit. No matter what, no matter how hard she tried to keep her emotions apart from the sex, the two things seemed to be intertwined. There would be no saving herself from the consequences of falling in love with Ice.

He kissed his way down her throat to the curve of her breast. She was wearing a tank, and he pulled it over her head, bunching it in his hand.

Soleil laughed. "You're insatiable."

Ice nodded. "Your point is?"

She reached behind her and unhooked her

bra, so her breasts jutted out for him, begging attention. "Are you going to take a bath with me?" Her voice had turned sultry. She was tempting the devil and she knew it. "Or a shower, although I don't want to get my hair wet this time of night. It takes forever to dry. I put it in a braid this morning and it's still damp."

"A bath it is." He cupped her breasts, his thumbs sliding across her nipples, bringing them to tight, responsive peaks. "You going to tell me what kind of trouble you're in?"

She stiffened. He was always so casual about everything. She'd made the decision to get on the back of his bike with him. Winston had seen the club leaving. Sooner or later he would discover the marriage certificate, or his friends would put two and two together.

His body urged hers up to the top of the stairs. She went but stopped again on the landing that was more of a long, wide room, running the length of the great room downstairs. It overlooked almost the entire floor. Ice wrapped his arms around her from behind and cupped her breasts.

"We're walking into our bedroom and I expect you to tell me what you're so fuckin' afraid of. I've been patient with you, Soleil. I hoped you'd tell me on your own, but so far, I don't see you're inclined to do that, so now I'm telling you let's put it on the table. Now."

His hands on her felt good. He had big hands and strong fingers. He kneaded gently, his mouth kissing and then nipping her neck and shoulder repeatedly. Desire in the form of shivers crept down her spine. She didn't want to tell him. Not now, when she had this beautiful house to spend her time in pretending the fairy tale was real. She glanced over her shoulder to see his expression. She wasn't certain she could seduce him into forgetting he'd issued his command.

"I can see that you think I'm going to forget all about this if we fuck, but that isn't going to happen. Just tell me."

Soleil took a breath and looked around the room that was supposed to be the master bedroom. The series of rooms, one opening to the next, were all connected. The bedroom seemed to go on forever. There was a sunken area right in front of a second fireplace. Both fireplaces were gas rather than wood, which she was happy about, because she could wield a remote, no problem, but it was difficult to build a fire. She had no clue where to start.

The front of the room faced the ocean,

348

and like the room directly below them, the entire front of the master bedroom was glass. There were privacy screens, but she couldn't imagine using them — the view of the ocean was too amazing. The bed faced the view, and on either side of it were end tables. The end tables were carved from some type of wood she didn't recognize but thought was beautiful.

The bedroom, like the great room, was carpeted, a thick, luxurious weave. The bed dominated the room. It was king-sized. The headboard had very thick spindles, looking like a fan. When she got closer, she could see the headboard resembled a sea fan. It was quite beautiful and intricate.

Ice left her to open the door on the right. She followed him into the bathroom. She was used to luxurious hotels, but hands down, this bathroom had been crafted so someone could live in it. The bathroom was made up of a makeup room, a long wide area housing double sinks with golden taps, an immense shower, all glass, with benches and so many jets she wasn't certain she'd be able to remember which golden knob went to what. It was definitely a two-person shower.

The bathtub was enormous as well. A claw foot with the same golden taps. Ice was already filling the tub with steamy water and some kind of salts Lana had provided for them. At least she was certain it had to have been Lana. Whatever it was smelled like heaven, and she was done exploring. She wanted to sink into the hot water and get all the kinks and cramps out of her muscles.

She stripped right there. It wasn't like he hadn't seen her entirely naked. He had explored every inch of her body with his lips, tongue and teeth. He'd claimed every inch. She refused to blush when his icy eyes drifted over her, yet she did. It was that possessive way he looked at her. As if she belonged to him. She'd never belonged to anyone so she didn't know how it was supposed to feel, but to her, it felt wonderful. Perfect. Exactly what she needed and wanted from a man. Her man.

She stepped into the tub and gasped at the heat. He grinned at her, already removing his clothes and stepping into the tub. Right away, her attention was caught and held by his cock. She really had fallen a little in love with that portion of him. She licked her lips, remembering the weight of him in her mouth, tasting him on her tongue.

Ice groaned and tightened his fist around his hardening cock. "Baby, you can't be doing that. You're going to soak in the tub so you're not sore from the ride. You aren't used to it, and we were riding for hours."

She stared at him, mesmerized by the growing length.

"Turn around and behave." Ice wrapped his arm around her waist and pulled her back against him. Tight.

She felt every inch of that impressive cock against her back. His palms cupped the weight of her breasts.

"Put your head back and relax. You're going to tell me why Winston scares you so much. I want to know the entire story. Don't give me trouble about this, because we both know you're going to tell me."

"Why would you think I'd tell you?" she demanded, belligerence creeping into her voice.

He kissed her right between her shoulder and neck. "Because I asked you to and you don't lie to me and you give me whatever I ask."

He said it as if it were true. She *wanted* to give him whatever he asked. She wanted to be the one he looked at the way he was looking at her right now. After she told him, he might reject her. That was her greatest fear. Rejection. She couldn't look at him while she weighed the consequences of revealing the truth. She detested the label of "poor little rich girl." She would have given up every bit of her wealth if she'd had a family, parents who loved her, aunts and uncles, cousins. She would have gone hungry in order to have someone care. Just one person.

On the other hand, she'd confessed she'd tried to get him drunk to seduce him into marriage in Vegas and he had glossed over it as if she were being silly. He didn't seem in the least inclined to give her up for any reason. She had to try to start believing him. That was only fair. If they really were going to have any kind of a life, they needed truth between them.

"Soleil. Just start. It will get easier," he prompted.

She took a deep breath and made her confession. "By being with you, I'm endangering the entire club. Every single member. Your twin and Alena. I got on the back of the bike with you when Winston showed up with the cops looking for me. Fortunately, a woman must have checked into the motel by herself. He must have been checking for that sort of thing."

She waited, head bowed, for his condemnation. Ice put his hand on her forehead and tipped her head back until she was leaning the back of her skull against his chest.

His palm stroked caresses over her forehead.

"I was there. I think I got that. That isn't telling me why he was coming after you, Soleil."

She looked around the bathroom. The room was so luxurious, it seemed ludicrous to think Ice was after her money. He didn't seem to know she was loaded — or he knew and just didn't care.

"My parents started a company when they were very young, in their early twenties. The company took off, and in the end, when they sold, they made millions of dollars. That money was set aside in a trust for me at a very early age and continued to make money for me. I was their only child."

She couldn't feel any difference in Ice's body at her revelation. He seemed as relaxed as ever, now lazily playing with her earlobe, making her hyperaware of him.

"Keep going, baby, this is getting interesting."

"The money was invested, of course, and a lawyer was overseeing it. His name was Kevin." Her voice nearly broke. "Kevin Bennet. I told you a little about him. I only met him in person on a few occasions, but he texted me nearly every day and we often FaceTimed. He was the only constant in my life. That's important to make you understand the trouble I'm in."

She wasn't looking for sympathy. Now, she wanted out of the lovely bathtub. She felt too vulnerable in her bare skin. She made a move to stand up, but Ice locked his arm around her waist.

"I'm right here with you, baby. Don't run. Don't try to hide from me or the truth of this mess you're in. We'll figure it out together. Let yourself lean on me."

She'd never had together and didn't know what to do with it. She couldn't lean on him when she expected him to leave. She didn't know how to be with someone when she'd always been alone. She was terrified of falling too hard for him. Of believing. She forced herself to continue because Ice deserved to have her at least make an effort. Maybe he would understand what he was getting into.

"I had no home growing up. I lived in boarding schools and hotels. I was able to travel the world and take any kind of class I wanted, hence the cooking and art classes. There was never a home or a person to go home to. Not even on holidays. I can't tell you how much I hate holidays."

She drew her knees up and, locking her arms around her legs, rubbed her chin on top of her knees. "I would get crazy lonely at times and I'd do things like parachute out of planes, and each jump got riskier. Gliders, paragliding, the scarier the place, the better. I played pool and darts all over the world. Drank whiskey and bourbon and scotch all over the world in a lot of different bars. I found I couldn't get drunk, and believe me, I tried." She glanced over her shoulder and met his gaze. "Lots of risky behavior."

"I can see I'm going to have to watch you if you start to get restless."

She wanted it to be that way. Ice and Soleil. Together. She could do that. She could live on the coast in this gorgeous home with the man of her dreams and have his children. She could be a wife, give him everything he'd ever dreamt of. But reality never matched fantasy. She knew the reality, and sooner or later, rejection always came.

She went back to rubbing her chin along the tops of her knees just because she needed something to do or she would have jumped up and made a run for it, because she was too scared to reach for what he seemed to be offering her — what she wanted most in life. It was too hard to believe it was real. Still, he needed to know the truth.

"I guess I just didn't fit in anywhere." She

355

tried to explain without sounding as if she were having a pity party for herself. "After my aunt Deborah died, no relative wanted me because Kevin wouldn't loosen the purse strings and they weren't getting the money they felt they deserved for having me in their home. Kevin never told me why he didn't want me to come to his house, but he didn't." That had hurt, probably the most.

Ice swept his hand down the back of her head, a soothing, caressing gesture. She wasn't going to tell him about all the lonely nights and days she'd spent wishing and fantasizing about a man like him. It was too pathetic.

"I met Winston at an auction house in London. He claimed to like all the things I liked. He lived in San Francisco, which is where I live, so it was perfect. We dated and then I began to notice little things. He didn't approve of the way I dressed. He wanted me to drop any acquaintances I had and only associate with his friends. He didn't approve of my music. He chose every restaurant. He chose everything."

"Because he's a fucking prick," Ice stated matter-of-factly, and wrapped his arms around her, pulling her back against him. "Relax, baby. It's just me here. I'm on your side, remember?"

Soleil felt a smile welling up and was shocked that she could even find humor in anything when everything she wanted was about to be ripped from her. Doggedly, she went on. She'd started the explanation, and she was determined to see it through.

"He wanted to marry me, and I knew it wasn't right. We weren't at all compatible. Kevin insisted on a prenup. Winston threw a fit. It was the first time I'd ever been afraid. He was so angry. He threatened to walk out, and at first I thought I was panic-stricken because I didn't want to be alone. Then I realized it would be okay if he did. I wanted him to leave. When he saw I wasn't going to relent, he was apologetic and said he'd think about it. Two days later, Kevin was killed in a car accident."

She still had that visceral reaction, the same as when she'd been given the news of his death over the phone. It was soul deep, and her stomach rebelled every time, cramping and heaving. She pressed her trembling fingers to her lips and tried to breathe in air.

"I'm so sorry, princess," Ice whispered, pressing kisses to the nape of her neck. His fingers caressed the side of her neck, right over that little bite that didn't hurt anymore.

He often touched it gently.

She shivered with awareness. She could hear the sincerity in his voice. He was too good to be true. Even Kevin had asked her what the hell was wrong with her that she would allow someone like Winston into her life, yet Ice never once acted like she should have known better.

"Winston instantly hired another attorney, a man by the name of Donald Monroe. I didn't like anything about him, but he told me it was silly to press for a prenup, to just marry the man and put him out of his misery."

Behind her, Ice stirred, his chest expanding and contracting. She heard and felt him take deep breaths, and that helped her breathe and continue.

"Winston had a list of men and women he wanted me to make nice with at charity events. He said he was going into politics and these people were important to his career. I think now, he wanted me cut off from others, and those on his list were helping him. He had a list of powerful people. Cops, lawyers, a city council member. He had a list of very wealthy older women, all widows."

Ice shrugged. "Keep going, baby. Where does the danger to the club come in?"

She knew he prompted her because he was afraid she wouldn't tell him. She had made up her mind he needed to know. They all did. She just wanted him to know the weapons Winston could wield if he chose. He liked throwing his weight around. He'd hurt the club just because he could, and he'd gloat about it.

"I wanted time after Kevin died, but Winston insisted on going to Vegas. He swore he wouldn't bring up marriage, and I agreed to come just to shut him up. It was so stupid of me. I just wanted a little peace."

She closed her eyes and leaned back against Ice, absorbing the feel of him. After she told him, he might be gone, but she'd have this memory.

"He was so angry when I refused to get married, and when I told him I'd officially fired the attorney, he hit me repeatedly. My face . . ." She touched her ribs. "He said to clean up, we were getting married in half an hour."

She looked at him over her shoulder because she needed to see his face when she told him the rest. "I had the door to the bathroom partially open and he had the bedroom door open so he could hear me if I tried anything. I heard him talking on the phone. To make a long story short, he's part of a ring of con men who target lonely women with money. They research their target and then one of them becomes her perfect man. They marry and then, sadly, the wife dies. Usually by an accident. Apparently, I'm such a pain in the ass, Winston couldn't wait to kill me. Kevin's accident was arranged by this con artist ring as well. He was murdered."

Outside, along the bank of windows, the dark sky turned even blacker. Clouds, looking as if they'd been washed in soot, roiled and spun, churning angrily. Winds battered them continually until the moment the clouds broke open, spilling out a deluge of water. The drops battered at the window as if trying to get to them — to get to Soleil.

She could feel the temperature in the water rising. Ice's heart beat so hard she felt it pounding through her back.

"That worthless little dick was really planning on murdering you?"

The words were so low she barely caught them. His face was expressionless, but his eyes were alive with a storm all their own. She had the feeling that all the turbulence outside was being caused by Ice, although she couldn't figure out how.

"Yes. That was the plan. I heard every word. They even threatened Winston. They said I was an easy mark and if he couldn't lock me down, he was the one who was going to pay. I don't really know who they all are, only that there are several. I couldn't go to the police, so I just ran. I'd met Lana and she'd given me her phone number, so when I saw the motorcycles, I just went into the bar without thinking."

"That little fuckin' pussy. He's a fuckin' dead man," Ice spat out. "Fuck him, Soleil. You're safe with me. If that little dick thinks he can kill you, he's out of his mind. Let him try to take on Torpedo Ink. He'll realize he has a tiger by the tail. On the other hand, I believe in being proactive. Tomorrow, we'll go to Czar and the others and you're going to tell us everything you can about the others who might be in this ring."

She tried not to cry. She was so emotional. It had started with losing Kevin, and she'd never quite gotten herself back under control. Gripping the edges of the bathtub, she pulled herself into a standing position. She needed to get out. She just had to. Ice was a miracle, the kind of man she'd dreamt of, and she was terrified she was falling hard for him. The drop would be long and scary, but it would be far worse when he tore her heart out.

She stepped out of the tub and he caught

her arm. "Gettin' tired of you being afraid of lovin' me, baby. I know we belong together. Stop pullin' away from me. You're here, give it a shot at least."

Soleil shook her head. "Ice, you have no idea what you're asking of me."

"You think this kind of commitment isn't scary for me?" he challenged.

He pulled the plug and stood up as well, accepting the towel she handed to him. Once again, she noted that his gaze was riveted to her, as if she were the only being in his world. He had a way of looking at her with complete focus.

"I've never been in a relationship with a woman. I'm not sayin' there wasn't sex. I've had women blow me, sometimes every day, sometimes twice a day. But to get there, to get release, I've had to order my fuckin' dick to work. With you, just lookin' at you, babe, I'm a steel pole. That may not sound like anything to you, but after a lifetime of knowing I can't ever be normal and then finding you —" He broke off, shaking his head.

"It's sex, Ice," she insisted and went to the sink to brush her teeth. She had a thing about her teeth. He wanted to know things about her, he might as well know that.

"It maybe seems like that, but it's not just

362

sex. When your mouth is on me or I'm inside you, believe me, Soleil, it isn't just sex."

"You married me because you were drunk."

"No, you married me because *you* were drunk. I was sober. Stone-cold sober. I wanted you and I was going to get you by whatever means I could. I'm probably as bad as Winston with his ulterior motives. I not only don't have to order my dick to rise and then to release with you, sometimes I need my woman to show me that I'm more important to them than anyone else. Or anything such as moral codes that I can't even understand."

She stopped, toothbrush halfway to her mouth to stare at him. "What does that mean?"

"It means, if you're down on your knees with my cock down your throat and someone is watching through a window, you don't stop, because I'm more important than some bullshit rule I don't understand."

"Well, don't talk about your cock in my mouth when you're not covered up and we're having an important conversation." She glared at him. "And I wasn't drunk. I seduced you into marriage."

"Bullshit. I seduced you." He dried his

hair while she rinsed her teeth. "You chose me, Soleil. I chose you. Let's make this work. You can see I don't need your money. Live here with me and don't spend a penny of yours if that's what you'd prefer. Just give us a chance."

He sounded — and looked — so sincere. She wanted him. Really wanted him. She wanted the house. The sex. His club. Everything he was holding out to her. He didn't seem to be afraid of Winston or the ring of con artists. She wasn't so certain that his club could handle them. Everyone seemed so nice. Well. She hedged in her thinking. Savage looked scary. Maestro did as well, but when they ate together, he was sweet. It was just a dangerous look he got every now and then.

She was just so afraid of being hurt. Or hurting Ice. She had failed at everything she'd ever tried in her life. Ice was . . . extraordinary. Amazing. Worth something. But he was willing to take a chance on her. Didn't that count for something?

"What would a chance entail, exactly?"

"Be my wife."

Her heart skipped a beat and then pounded hard. She closed her eyes and shook her head. "How would I know how a wife behaves? I didn't have any real examples of a man and a woman living together. In fact, I'm more of a one-night-stand kind of girl doing the walk of shame in the morning."

"You'd better never feel shame at anything we do together, Soleil. I mean that. What we do is sacred. Doesn't matter if the world is suddenly watching us. When I touch you, or you touch me, it's us. The two of us and no one else. Don't give a damn if you're looking at someone jacking themselves off because they're staring at your breasts. While I'm fucking you, it's always just the two of us."

She knew there was something seriously wrong with her because it was his speech that made her decide. The use of the word *sacred.* She loved that thought. The idea of someone staring at her breasts and jacking off while he fucked her shouldn't have added another layer of excitement, but it did. The thought of Ice with his hands on her anywhere, anytime, made her scorching hot. Too hot. She burned between her legs. He could do that. His voice. His eyes. His touch. He mesmerized her.

She made up her mind. She'd go all in. One more time. For him. For Ice. She would do it because he was extraordinary and if he was willing to try, she was too.

"All right, then."

His eyebrow went up and he stepped closer, catching at the towel she'd wrapped around herself. He stripped it from her body. "Talk to me, woman. What the fuck does that mean?"

He sounded gruff. Emotional. He looked as cool as ice. "It means, even though I'm going to make all kinds of mistakes and you're going to be very sorry you chose me, I'll be your wife."

"All in?" he prompted. "You'll give me everything."

"I don't know what that means."

"I'll give you everything you want or need, or do my best to make that happen, and I want the same from you. I swear to you, I'll give you everything I am."

She could do that. She already wanted to please him. She just needed to know all the things he wanted so she could make it happen.

"I think that's very reasonable, Ice. I'm all in. I'll do my best to give you everything that I am and everything you want or need. I don't know any other way."

"Better than the bullshit the preacher was throwing out during our wedding ceremony."

He sounded happy. He looked happy, his

expression lighter. That made her glow inside. She wanted him happy. He'd saved her life, and more, he'd given her the best time of her life. He might say he didn't know about relationships, but it wasn't true. He knew, and he offered her everything she could possibly desire.

"Come on, princess, let's christen the bed. I've been thinking about how I want you on your hands and knees right in the middle of it. Not a stitch on. You can look outside into the night and see if you can find a star. See if you can keep your mind off what I'm doing to you, because you can't move."

He was in the mood to play. A shiver went through her body. She loved that he liked her body and wanted to use it for his own personal playground. She benefited every time. She walked to the bed and climbed on, conscious that he was watching her. His eyes on her made her feel sexy and desirable. There was something about the way he looked at her that always reminded her that she was feminine and he was very male.

She deliberately took her time crawling across the bed to the middle and positioning herself on her hands and knees.

"Widen your legs, baby."

He hadn't moved. She could tell by his voice that he was still across the room. The tone he used when he ordered her to widen her legs only made her hotter. She complied. She was already slick with need for him.

"Go down to your elbows, princess."

She did so slowly, and her bottom was up in the air. Her breasts were smashed on the mattress. She felt sexier than ever. The cool air on her inflamed clit only fanned the fire hotter. She stared out into the night, shocked that the storm was gone and she was looking at a night sky. No stars that she could see, not with the wisps of white clouds moving fast with the wind.

Then he was there. Surrounding her with his scent. She felt the light brush of his fingers first. Just that barely there touch. Stroke after stroke, caress after caress. A sudden lick and then his fingers again. It was the start of a very long, beautiful, sexy night with her husband.

ELEVEN

"Stop fidgeting, princess, they're going to love you. You know most of them anyway. We're just going to sit in the common room and have a kind of roundtable discussion. Everyone will throw out ideas or they'll just react to what you're telling them. Names, descriptions, that sort of thing."

His woman was nervous. That was a little shocking to him. She was wearing one of the little sundresses he'd purchased for her from the boutique in Vegas and she looked like a million dollars. The dress was a pastel pink. She wore darker tights, a mauve color, she'd said when he'd asked her. She'd grabbed several pairs of tights at the shop when he'd told her to. He found himself grinning when he remembered how he'd stopped her from arguing about money with him. Just the thought made his cock come to attention all over again.

"I can't help being nervous, Ice," she

pointed out, giving him one of her snippy looks.

He loved when she went all haughty on him. It was that "princess" look he loved so much. She rubbed her hands over her arms and he immediately realized she was cold, not just nervous. He preferred the cool coastal air in comparison to Vegas's heat, and she was from San Francisco, but she didn't have enough clothes. She needed sweaters and jackets. He'd have to get on that, especially since she never complained.

He took his jacket off and had her slip into it. Immediately she got that look on her face, the one he loved most, as if he were her white knight, the only one in the world. She looked at him as if he were a decent man. He'd even confessed that he'd been sober when he'd married her, that he'd deliberately plied her with liquor, and she still looked at him like that. She insisted she'd been the one to trick him into marriage. He was falling harder every day for her.

Ice threaded his fingers through hers and pulled her closer since she was reluctant to take a step away from the motorcycle. "Come on, baby, you'll like everyone. They might look a little intimidating, but you're family. Once you're in, you're not ever out.

They'll all accept you. You're the one who will need the open mind to accept all of us."

She nodded, but he could still feel the tremors running through her body, telling him her nerves hadn't settled. Now that he knew more about her, he understood. She hadn't felt a lot of acceptance in her life. Maybe that was what had made her more tolerant than most people. No one would ever believe a woman with her kind of money would settle for a biker. She had no real idea of their wealth — or where it came from: Code had stolen most of the money from criminals.

They moved in sync together as they walked from his motorcycle to the entrance of the clubhouse. He couldn't help placing his hand on her bottom as she walked. He loved the way the muscles in the cheeks of her ass bunched and released. It was sexy as hell. He'd had her three times in the night. The first time he'd held her on the edge for over an hour. It had been a long hour for both of them, although they'd both gotten the benefit of prolonging the time before the explosion came. When it did, it had been more than spectacular.

He loved that she didn't object to his touch ever. She wore a thong under the dress, and he felt the curve of her bare cheeks as she walked up to the clubhouse. He felt very connected to her. As he reached around her for the door, he rubbed her bottom, trying to convey strength and solidarity to her. He was there with her. For her. He wasn't about to leave her on her own.

He leaned down to press his lips against her ear. "I'm right here with you. You feel afraid, you just look to me. I'll take over until you feel safe again."

She pressed back into him, her cheek in the palm of his hand, her eyes suddenly meeting his over her shoulder. Those eyes held something soft and tender. For him. He was asking her to meet the others, to trust them when she had no cause to, yet she gave him that look. Inside him, there was a curious melting sensation, and he knew he was falling harder than he'd ever thought possible. This woman could break him when nothing that had come earlier in his life ever had.

The common room held all the members of the club. Ordinarily, they would meet in their conference room, but Soleil wasn't part of the club and she'd be much more comfortable in a less formal setting anyway.

Ice took her hand again as they went inside. Immediately he felt the squeeze of her fingers as she walked in with him. She looked regal, very much like the princess he called her, but he could feel trepidation pouring off her in waves. He wanted to wrap her up and carry her out of there.

Alena detached herself from the group and rushed to her side. "Soleil! How are you? Is my brother behaving?" She hugged Soleil to her and gave Ice a look over her shoulder. She felt his wife trembling and instantly blamed him. "Everyone's here to help. We'll find these people and make certain none of them ever come near you."

Then Lana was there. She hugged Soleil as well. "I can't believe you're married to Ice. No one thought any woman could ever tame him. Is he treating you right? I can put the smackdown on him if you need me to."

Soleil laughed and looked at him again, that same soft, tender expression on her face. He hadn't let go of her hand, not even through the enthusiastic hugs of the two women who had full privileges in their club. For a moment he had resented them for taking her attention from him, and then he was grateful to them. The trembling wasn't nearly as bad, and she was still looking at him as if he'd been the one to give her that reassurance.

"There's no reason for a smackdown,

although it's nice to know you could deliver one if needed," Soleil assured Lana.

She smiled at both Alena and Lana. Ice could see it was genuine.

"He's incredibly good to me, although I can't believe he got me to agree to stay married to him."

"He can be very charming and persuasive," Lana said. She looked all sweet when she was facing Soleil, but when she turned to him, she gave him her fierce "you're dead" face.

Ice grinned at her. After all, he had the girl. "Had to get you drunk," Ice reminded Soleil without a hint of remorse.

"I got you drunk," she denied. She twisted the laminated paper ring she hadn't taken off her finger.

Alena caught her hand. "Ice, is this what you'll be making for her? It looks intricate."

"Ice will make for me?" Soleil echoed.

"Didn't he tell you? He's a jeweler. His work is awesome and very coveted. No one really knows who he is, so that makes his custom pieces all the more sought-after."

Soleil's eyes widened when she turned and looked at him. "You're Ice."

He shrugged. "That's what people call me."

"No, you know what I mean. The designer.

I actually have a pair of your earrings." She touched her ears. She wore only small diamond studs. The rest of her jewelry, including the one-of-a-kind Ice earrings, was locked away in the safe at the hotel in San Francisco she resided in.

"I'll make you a dozen pair of earrings," he promised.

"But first, our rings. I'm wearing one as well."

"That will be good," Lana said, an edge to her voice. "When you're at parties, it will warn the women that you're taken."

He knew a threat when he heard it, and he couldn't blame Lana. He'd orchestrated his seduction of Soleil, step by step, and stolen Lana's little chick out from under her safety net.

"I'll know I'm married, Lana," he assured. He glanced at Absinthe, who was standing next to him. The man was a human lie detector. Ice couldn't reassure Soleil using him, but he could Lana. He extended his arm to Absinthe, waiting until the pads of his brother's fingers were on his pulse. "I am not ever going to cheat on my wife, Lana. I married her because she's the one woman I know absolutely without a doubt is mine."

He didn't know how to put it any differ-

375

ently. He knew. It was that simple. Keeping her might be a problem because he had no clue what he was doing, but if he lost her, it wouldn't be for lack of trying — or because he cheated.

Lana hadn't been the only one watching. His brothers had gone silent and had watched his declaration. He wanted them to hear it. He needed them to know how important Soleil was to him. And he wanted them to always take care of her if he wasn't around.

Storm came from behind them, wrapping an arm around both. He kissed the side of Soleil's cheek. "You're taming the beast, woman. Glad to have you as a sister, although the girl club is getting too big, now that Reaper has Anya and Steele, Breezy. And there's Blythe."

Alena nudged him with her foot. "Alena and Lana," she added, glaring at her brother.

"You don't count. I'm pretty sure you're half —"

"Don't you dare say it." Alena shoved him. "Don't fall for anything he has to say, Soleil. He thinks he's charming."

"I *am* charming. Now that Ice is taken, I'm going to be the hot one."

"You've always been the hot one," Ice said hastily.

Soleil had tensed, just a little, when his twin had wrapped his arm around the two of them. Ice was certain it was because she hadn't liked waking up thinking she might have been with both of them. Storm had relayed what she'd first said when she'd woken. His twin had thought it was funny, and he had as well, but now she was uneasy in Storm's company and he didn't want that — not ever.

Ice leaned into her and put his lips against her ear. "I don't share. Storm would never touch you. He thinks of you the way he does Alena. You're mine, Soleil. Storm will love you like a brother, but you're my woman. My wife. He knows and respects that. They all do."

Some of the tension left her body. She smiled up at Storm and shook her head at the teasing his sister was giving his brother. Ice slipped his arm around her and led her to Czar, the president of their club.

Czar had been the ten-year-old boy who had masterminded the plan to keep them all alive in the hell they'd grown up in. He'd given them hope in their darkest times. He'd driven them to perfect their abilities. Czar had always believed every human being had some small psychic talent, but they hadn't just worked on developing them. He'd made each of them work on theirs daily for hours.

Along with sharpening their assassin skills, he'd had them practicing whatever talents they had, small or large. He'd organized them to work as a pack, much like wolves, each with his or her job, so in the end, they'd turned the tables on their brutal instructors. They'd been children, but they'd been lethal. Now, as adults, they were even more deadly.

"Czar, Steele, this is my wife, Soleil. Soleil, Czar is the president of Torpedo Ink and Steele is the vice president."

She smiled at them both and offered her hand, again looking like a princess. She made Ice's heart stutter.

"I understand you just got married as well," she said to Steele.

He nodded. "My woman's name is Breezy. She'll be excited to meet you. She's home at the moment with our son. He picked up a bug while we were gone. Nothing scary, just the flu, but he's definitely uncomfortable."

Ice knew it was a sacrifice for Steele to leave his son when he was sick, especially since Steele was a doctor. He liked both his wife and his child close if possible. He was still getting used to having to allow Breezy out of his sight.

"That's terrible. I hope he's better soon," Soleil said.

Czar took her hand and smoothed his fingers over hers. Ice had seen him do that many, many times in the past. Czar was somewhat of an enigma. He had many talents, but Ice didn't know what all of them were. He found himself tense, wanting to snatch her hand away from Czar, but the man had always been the one who led their way. Ice had no idea why he felt so protective of Soleil in that moment.

Czar looked gallant as he smiled down at Soleil. "So, you're the woman who stole Ice's heart." The president of Torpedo Ink suddenly looked straight at Ice. Those eyes hit him hard. Penetrated, like an arrow, warning Ice not to ever hurt this woman. Whatever Czar could read by taking her hand, she had his approval. Ice let out the breath he hadn't been aware he was holding. His club had his back, which meant they were all going to be vetting Soleil.

"I understand you're in a little bit of trouble, Soleil," Czar said. "I think we can help you with that."

Soleil gave a slight shake of her head and took a step back. Ice's heart dropped. All of them were rough-looking, scarred and products of their childhood. He couldn't imagine how afraid she must be surrounded by complete strangers, all of whom looked like what they were — killers.

"I know you all think you can help me. Ice said the same thing. I really appreciate your kindness. I've never had anyone be so generous to me before as all of you have offered to be. It's just that when I overheard them talking, I could tell they'd killed many times. I wasn't going to be their first. They definitely killed my lawyer, and I have no idea how many are involved. I do know they have at least one cop and probably more than one. I tried to tell Ice, but he's adamant that it doesn't matter."

She looked up at Ice, and that softness was there again. The look that said he was the only man in the room. Perfection for her. He wanted to melt at her feet. He looked over her head to Czar, hoping his president could see why he was falling for her so fast. It wasn't all sex like they thought. Like he thought. She was getting to him, getting under his skin and twisting around his heart.

Czar's gaze held amusement. "I can see why you'd be concerned."

She nodded. "All of you are very nice, and

I don't want these people to find you. I have no idea what they'd do to you, but I can imagine they would manufacture evidence and throw you in jail or something."

Czar glanced around the room. Ice followed suit. Lana and Alena looked amused, in the same way Czar had. The rest of his brothers looked shocked, the way he felt. He was beginning to know her, and he shouldn't be surprised, but he was. His little princess was determined to protect them. Protect his entire club.

"You're all very important to Ice. You're his family. The last thing I want is to be responsible for any of you getting hurt," she continued.

Ice pulled her back against his body, his arms locking around her. He dropped his chin on top of her head. He had to hold her, or he'd carry her off to one of the rooms in the clubhouse and bury himself deep in the haven of her body. In his wildest dreams, he hadn't conjured up a woman anywhere near as good as Soleil.

"I understand your concerns," Czar said and waved them to the chairs. "But I think we can handle this group of con artists. We've had a little bit of practice in that area. Since they seem to be working out of San Francisco, that even makes it easier."

381

Ice got the silent message and led Soleil to the armchairs that had been set up in a loose semicircle. The other members sat as well, with the exception of Reaper and Savage, who separated and positioned themselves in the shadows near the walls where they just seemed to blend in. Maestro remained behind Steele, draping himself against the wall as well. It was no coincidence that Absinthe sat on the other side of Soleil.

Ice found himself looking around the room. There were twenty of them now, fully patched, not a big club as clubs went, but every man there had been trained from childhood in the brutal schools, as assassins. They were all looking for a new life and trying to figure out the rules of society. They knew they'd never fit perfectly, but they were doing their best.

He started the explanation, of everything Soleil had told him about meeting Winston, his trying to groom her as well as cut her off from anyone who knew her and guide her toward his approved list.

Code interrupted to ask for the names on the list and anything she could remember about their jobs. Soleil answered, her voice a little shaky, but she complied. There were several she hadn't mentioned to Ice. A detective. A judge. An assistant police chief. A medical examiner. A highway patrolman.

The club members exchanged long looks. The ring was well set up. She gave every name easily and described each man.

Czar nodded to Absinthe, and Ice found himself tensing. He kept his gaze from traveling to Reaper. Absinthe had questioned Reaper's woman, Anya, and it had been a disaster.

"When you answer, princess, make sure everything you say is the exact truth," Ice said.

Soleil frowned. "Why wouldn't I tell the truth?" She sounded genuinely puzzled.

"Soleil, why would you be able to remember these men so clearly?" Czar asked. "You say you met them at fund-raising events. The events must have been crowded."

Ice found himself holding his breath. His heart accelerated until it was pounding hard. He wanted to snatch Soleil up and run with her. Soleil ran her palm down his thigh, keeping her other arm right where it was so Absinthe could loosely wrap his fingers around her wrist. His touch was light, but it was deadly. She didn't ask why he was holding her wrist, or why the room suddenly became filled with palatable tension, she just rubbed her hand up and down

Ice's thigh as if to soothe him. He fell even harder. His heart did that weird clenching thing, and if he could have, he would have kissed her.

"Winston insisted I memorize all the names of the men he wanted me to befriend. We attended four events in the two months I was with him. I had to know those names. Winston would quiz me on them, to make certain I knew who I was supposed to talk to. I needed to put names with faces, so I looked them up on the Internet, and I also, at each event, made certain to study them before I went over to them. I didn't want to make a mistake."

Absinthe let go of her wrist and nodded his head. Ice continued the story with her lawyer's "accident."

"They would have arranged the accident when the highway patrolman was on duty so he could pronounce it an accident," Steele mused. "The medical examiner would concur. They would all be useful in making murders look like genuine accidents."

Czar indicated he wanted Soleil to tell the rest. Absinthe once again took her wrist. She glanced at him this time and then to Ice as if for reassurance. He nodded his head and placed his hand over hers, pressing it into his thigh muscle.

She told them how Winston hired a lawyer and she was upset about it. She thought it was too soon, and she needed to interview the lawyer herself so she could feel comfortable with him. Kevin oversaw her trust and the financial portfolio that was maintained for her. She lived on a very healthy budget, but if she ever needed anything, she had only to ask. She was so uncomfortable with the new lawyer she officially terminated him. That infuriated Winston, as had her refusal to marry him.

Absinthe nodded and some of the tension in the room dissipated. It didn't for Ice. The churning remained in his gut. As long as Absinthe had his hand on Soleil, he was going to be nervous. If Czar touched on anything Soleil didn't want others to know, she could be hurt if she chose to lie.

"Soleil, did you break off the engagement because you didn't want to marry Winston or because he refused to sign the prenup and you didn't want him to be able to get to your money?"

Czar slipped the question in so smoothly, Ice almost didn't notice. He scowled when he realized what had been asked.

"That's more personal, Czar, and has nothing to do with this ring of con artists who have targeted her for murder." Ice tried to push down his anger and instant resentment. He didn't care if the president was asking. He didn't want Soleil to have to answer personal questions with Absinthe touching her, or even in front of all of them.

"I don't mind," Soleil said. "I made up my mind I wasn't going to marry him before we ever went to Vegas. I told him several times it was too soon, and I needed time, but he refused to listen. I mostly needed the time to figure out how to break the engagement off for good. I knew he'd be upset, although I didn't realize he would resort to violence."

Absinthe nodded and the terrible tension in the room dissipated along with the churning in Ice's stomach. His woman. She spoke matter-of-factly. He brought her hand to his mouth and kissed her knuckles before pushing her palm into his thigh again.

"How did you end up in the bar, meeting Ice?" Czar asked.

"Winston and I were walking along the strip and he wanted to go directly to a chapel and get married. I told him that wasn't happening. That we agreed we weren't going to get married. I mentioned the prenup. He actually had it with him and shoved it in my face and then he grabbed my arms and shook me. Hard. It scared me."

Ice clenched his teeth. He wanted two minutes with Winston Trent. He'd show him what pain was. He could tell by the sudden stillness in the room that the others agreed with him.

"I had bruises and I was crying. I didn't want to give him the satisfaction of seeing me cry, so I detoured and went to one of the restrooms on the main floor. Lana was in there changing. She was beautiful and confident, and I wanted to be like her. I imagined that no one would ever be allowed to treat her the way Winston had me."

Soleil smiled at Lana. "She was worried about me. No one had worried about me in a long time. She programmed her number into my phone and told me to call if there was a problem. She showed me her Torpedo Ink jacket and said she had lots of friends and that they'd help if Winston got rough with me."

Czar's gaze flicked to Lana. She shrugged, uncomfortable with the others hearing the admiration and respect in Soleil's voice.

"When I told Winston I wouldn't marry him, he went crazy, hitting me, and then he told me to clean myself up, we were getting married in half an hour. I went into the bathroom but left the door ajar just in case he was coming back. He left the bedroom door open and I heard him talking. I thought it might be room service and I could yell for help. That's when I overheard that Kevin's accident wasn't an accident and that they could easily kill me, but if he didn't finish what he started, it would be him."

"Thank you, Soleil. I'm certain that wasn't easy reliving." Czar nodded to Absinthe, and he removed his hand from her wrist.

Soleil gave him a faint smile. She seemed to have such a natural compassion for everyone. "I still want all of you to see how dangerous they must be. I'm not the only one they tricked. It's a little humiliating to know I was taken in by Winston."

Steele shrugged his broad shoulders. "They studied you, found out everything you liked, where you would most likely go, and then Winston had to memorize those things, much like he wanted you to make friends only with those he trusted. If he cut you off from others, you would have no one looking to find out what really happened to you. That's the way a lot of these cons work, although murder isn't necessarily a part of them."

Ice threaded his fingers through hers.

"Code, can you find these people?" Code was always their go-to man, a genius on the computer.

"I've located nearly all of them. I've gotten into Winston's private email accounts. He had four addresses. He's already corresponding with another woman. She's older. A widow. Her estate is large, but not nearly as large as Soleil's." He whistled, still not looking up. "Nowhere in the ballpark. They aren't going to let this one go, Ice. They thought they had that money in the bag. Now it's gone. I've got demands from four others in the ring insisting Winston find Soleil fast, marry her and dispense with her. That's the word they use. *Dispense.* I guess they're too sophisticated to use the word *murder.*"

Ice felt the little shiver go through Soleil's body and he tightened his hold on her hand, wishing he was holding her in his arms. "No worries, Soleil. You're safe here."

"This is so wrong, putting it off on you," she said. There were so many emotions crowding into her voice. He could tell she was close to tears and he didn't want that, not in front of his brothers and sisters. He'd act like a pussy for certain. Her tears could bring him to his knees.

"We've got this now," Czar decreed. "I

don't want you to think about it anymore. Alena put together lunch for everyone since we're celebrating. Blythe was upset that she wasn't around to witness the wedding, Ice, and you're going to have to explain to her what the hurry was. I want to be there when you mention you plied her with alcoholic beverages until she said yes."

Laughter swept through the common room at his expense. Ice didn't care. Soleil was laughing too. That was all that mattered.

Soleil opened her mouth to protest Ice's innocence, but he just brushed a kiss over her lips to silence her and happily took all the blame. "I thought I'd skip that part."

"Are you afraid of my wife?" Czar asked.

"Damn straight, I am," Ice admitted instantly. "Anyone with a brain would be. Am I right?" He looked around the room for confirmation.

The others nodded soberly. Czar gave a little snort of derision and whispered, "Pussies," under his breath.

"Nice try, Czar," Reaper said from the shadows. "You forget who's on you day and night watching you with her." Reaper was the president's guard. "That woman looks like something's wrong and you crawl over hot coal to make it all better."

"You've got a woman," Czar pointed out when the others finished laughing.

"Yeah, but no one's watching me," Reaper said.

Another eruption of laughter. Ice wanted that for Soleil. She wanted a family. This was his. Now it would be hers. They were coarse and crude. They made rude finger gestures to one another and they wore their scars like badges. They were a family, unbreakable, loyal and absolutely powerful when they stood together.

"Just so we're very clear," Soleil said, and the room went silent.

Ice waited, thinking she was being very brave, but not knowing what she planned on telling the others.

"Ice didn't get me drunk. I wasn't drunk. He was. I was the one making certain he was drinking. I seduced him. If your wife or anyone else is upset with him because they think he did that, please tell them it isn't true. It was all me. Maestro knows it's the truth." She held up her head; color had swept into her face. "He was kind enough to take the blame and keeps insisting, but it isn't the truth."

It was all Ice could do not to fall to his knees and worship at her feet. She was wonderful standing up for him. He could barely comprehend that she was trying to take the blame and get him off the hook with his club.

Czar studied her straight-faced. "Let me get this straight, Soleil. You got Ice drunk and seduced him into marrying you? Why would you do that?"

Ice glared at his president.

She nodded. "He's so amazing. I tried very hard to resist, but he's —"

Ice caught her by the nape of her neck, desperate to stop her before she said anything he'd never live down, planted his mouth on hers and kissed her until she melted into him and kissed him back.

The others erupted into laughter, roaring at his expense. When he finally let his woman come up for air, he looked at his sister, and as always, she came through for him.

"Need someone to help carry trays," Alena called out. "I have four trays."

Storm stood up immediately. Ink did as well. Keys and Player followed suit. Ice leaned down to whisper in Soleil's ear, although he made his voice loud enough that the others could hear his mock whisper.

"They're volunteering, making themselves look good, but they're really doing it in the hopes of getting in Alena's good graces.

She's made several berry pies for dessert. No one makes them quite like Alena."

"Well, I'd give them extra helpings for volunteering," Soleil said staunchly, raising laughing eyes to Storm.

Storm gave her the thumbs-up. "Hope you're listening to the voice of reason, Alena."

Ice tugged on Soleil's hand. "Stand up, baby. Come sit with me. I'm lonely."

She didn't hesitate or look embarrassed. She got up immediately and turned to sit on his lap. He pulled up the back of her dress at the last moment, so when she sank down on him, her bare cheeks were on his denim-clad groin. When she sat, she wiggled a little to get comfortable. The sexy movement went straight to his dick. He loved the way she made him feel. After nothing for so long, after feeling dead, as if that part of his anatomy wasn't working, to come alive felt even better than it should have.

He dropped his hands to the sides of her hips, feeling her soft skin. He began to rub gently. "Has Bannister moved all the way into the apartment over the bar?" he asked everyone and anyone in the room.

Transporter nodded. "Yeah. We fixed up the apartment as fast as we could. He's tough. That son of his tried pushing him around, even hitting him. Bannister took a few punches, hoping that would satisfy the kid, but when it was obvious it didn't, he knocked the boy out."

"That boy is our age," Mechanic said. "He's gambled his life away. He owes everyone and has been trying for some time to get Bannister to sell his bike."

"That's some bullshit right there," Transporter said. "He thinks he can use the money to gamble to make back what he lost."

"That's always what addicts think," Maestro said.

"Who is Bannister?" Soleil asked, leaning back into Ice.

"He comes to the bar. Looks to be a nomad. He's been in the life with a club at some time, but he doesn't wear colors. He's in his sixties. Good man. Solid. Wish he had a woman," Ice answered.

"He's good friends with Anya," Reaper said from the shadows. "When there was trouble in the bar a time or two, he stood with us. He looked after her."

If Reaper endorsed him, Bannister had to be a good man to have at their backs. "We still have someone stealing?" Ice asked. He filled in Soleil. "It was small stuff gone missing over time. Tools. A bottle of vodka. Food from the small kitchen behind the bar. We changed the locks, but it kept happening. We have cameras but so far no one has been caught on any of them. There were glitches occasionally, the screen going white for a moment, but even Code couldn't see that the recording was tampered with." He shrugged. "We were hoping Bannister might catch whoever is stealing from us."

Czar smirked a little. "The great Torpedo Ink. We can't stop a thief. Anya kept finding an occasional bottle of liquor missing. It showed up on the inventory. We thought the distributor was shorting us. Turns out, they weren't."

"You don't seem too upset that someone's stealing from you," Soleil said.

"Small shit," Ice explained. "Whoever is taking things, other than the liquor, they probably need it to live."

"We'll catch them eventually," Steele added. "In the meantime, we've left items out to entice them. When I say *items,* things that cost a lot of money. They never took the bait."

"Yeah, they're either clever or they really aren't after money, just things for survival," Maestro said.

"At first when you were talking about it, I was upset that there was a thief around,"

Soleil said. "Now I feel bad for them."

Ice rubbed along her bottom under her sundress, feeling the soft skin on the pads of his fingers. He loved the feminine lines there, the two indentations just above the curves of her cheeks. It soothed him just to feel her skin. Just to have her close to him. She kept his demons at bay. After meeting her, it was the longest he'd gone without the nightmare of his past crowding in.

He held her forward so he could press his face against her back. She was a shield of some sort for him. She thought she needed him. He'd let her think that. He'd encouraged that need, as if it were the truth. She thought he was saving her. Sooner or later, he'd have to come clean, but not yet. Not until she was really in love with him. He'd hooked her. He had to find a way to keep her.

Storm, Player and Keys came in with three of the trays and laid them out on the very long curve of blond wood that was the bar. Ink and Alena followed. Lana helped Storm take the plates and silverware off the trays and put them to the left of the food.

Ice nudged Soleil and shared laughter with her that his twin and the other three were already getting their plates. Lana rolled her eyes as she took her plate and waited while the four men mounded food onto their dishes.

"See what I mean, princess? They had their own best interests at heart the entire time." He helped her off his lap, making certain her hem was down as she stood. "We need to get to the front of the line, or there'll be nothing left."

Soleil went with him to grab a plate. She stared at the various dishes. "Ice, there's tons of food here. They can't possibly eat it all."

"Alena made it. Wait until you sample it before you decide it won't be eaten. No one cooks like she does." He raised his voice. "What's your secret, Alena, to making all these dishes taste the way they do?" He put his lips next to Soleil's ear. "I know what it is. Let's see if she does."

Alena looked at him, color moving into her face. She shook her head. "I have no idea."

"Love, little sister. That's what makes the difference," Ice told her.

The others broke out into grins, all of them nodding their heads. Alena gave him the finger. That was his sister, trying to be tough and failing when she was with her family.

"Eat that, Ice," she said rudely.

He blew her a kiss. "Love you so much, little sister."

Alena narrowed her eyes and started toward him.

"Quick, babe," he counseled Soleil. "Get as much food on your plate as possible and then protect it." He scooped up several healthy servings of the various dishes and heaped them on his plate and then hers. "She'll yank our plates away and toss them in the garbage. She's famous for that, and we're not missing out on her food."

"I wouldn't throw Soleil's plate away," Alena clarified. "Just yours."

He refrained from pointing out he was only telling her the truth. He kept moving down the line until both of them had plenty of food and then he found a table for them to sit. Czar, Savage and Reaper joined them. He didn't think anything of sitting with them until he felt Soleil's hand stray to his thigh under the table. He'd chosen the corner table because it was mostly in the shadows and set a little distance from the others. He thought she might be more inclined to talk to whoever sat with them.

"How's the kid, Czar? He must have been scared out of his mind."

Soleil sat up straighter. "The kid? Someone scared a child?"

Ice wanted to curse. He shouldn't have brought it up.

Czar, however, was as smooth as ever. "Blythe and I have four adopted children and we've just brought a fifth into our home. This boy's parents were murdered in order for a pedophile ring to acquire him and keep him. No one would be looking for him that way. His life has been very difficult, so it will take time for him to trust his environment."

Soleil looked as if she might cry. She glanced at Ice and then away, but not before he caught the sheen of tears in her eyes. His heart clenched hard. She really was compassionate. She seemed to feel the pain of others.

Czar leaned close to her. "Soleil, you're gifted, did you know that? You take others' emotions into you. Ice, you're going to have to shield her from things for a little while, until we can get Jimmy to settle and feel safe."

Ice knew that meant not to bring Soleil to his home for a little while. Everyone went to his home. Blythe was there. The kids were there. All of them were "uncles" to the four children. He wanted to meet Jimmy, the newest addition, the little boy they'd rescued in Vegas. He also had seen Czar work his magic on victims. He'd been doing it since he was a little boy and they'd been thrown down in that dungeon, broken, bleeding, and terrified out of their minds.

Ice nodded to show he understood. He ate, listening to Reaper and Czar talk about an upcoming run they were supposed to go on. He was looking forward to it. His bike. His woman. The open road. They were just getting settled, but he knew Soleil would go with him if he told her he wanted to go. She wouldn't hesitate.

He leaned in to kiss her. She tasted the way Alena's cooking did. Like love. Wincing at the word, he went back to eating.

"You're right about her food, Ice," Soleil said. "Your sister can cook better than any chef I've ever experienced. I've been around the world to some of the best restaurants and eaten great food, but this is amazing. When word gets out, she'll have more people coming than she'll ever imagine."

He turned to look over his shoulder. "Alena, Soleil loves it. Says she's eaten all over the world in some of the best restaurants, and your cooking beats them every time."

Soleil nodded, looking over her shoulder as well. "It's wonderful."

Alena beamed. "Thank you, Soleil, that

means a lot."

"Since I had the good sense to get her drunk and marry her, do I get first dibs on the berry pie?" Ice asked with a quick, superior grin around the room at his brothers, and ignoring Soleil's sigh of protest.

"Soleil can have the first piece," Alena conceded. "You, however, after your nasty little crack, can wait."

"I was giving you a compliment," Ice protested, when the laughter died down.

Soleil leaned into him. "Is her pie that good?"

"Better than the food you're consuming."

"I was going to say I'd give up my piece for you, but after knowing her pie is that good, I'm going to have to keep it for myself." She said it straight-faced.

Ice stared into her laughing, dark chocolate eyes. He watched her lips curve into a smile that lit up her entire face. Around him, laughter erupted, but all he could see was Soleil. He pulled her hand to his mouth and bit down on the tips of her fingers. Hard. She mock-scowled at him and yanked her fingers away.

"Ow."

"You remember last night?"

She blushed. Appropriately. She nodded.

"That's nothing compared to what I'm going to do to you when we get home."

TWELVE

The house was quiet. Soleil could hear the ocean in the distance, as the waves swelled and then folded over, collapsing against rocks, stacks and cliffs. Beside her, Ice slept. He'd woken her only a couple of hours earlier, his mouth between her legs. It seemed to be his favorite way to wake her. He was the sexiest man she'd ever met. He seemed to need to touch her. To kiss her. To be inside her. She needed it as much as or more than he did, that affirmation that he wanted her, that he found her sexy.

When he looked at her, there was something stamped deep in his expression that made her heart pound. Possession? Lust? Affection? More than affection? She wasn't certain, but she knew she wanted to see him looking at her like that every day. He clearly liked being with her. There was a part of her that feared he'd grow tired of her. She expected him to want to leave her for long periods of time, but he didn't. When she was in the kitchen, making a mess of recipes, he was right there with her, laughing over the disasters and making them fun instead of letting her sit on the kitchen floor and cry over them.

She loved the sex with him. It was always an adventure. She had never felt sexy until she'd been with Ice, although she'd tried to be a few times. With him, his eyes were always on her with hunger, as if he were a wolf and she was his prey. She loved knowing his gaze followed her everywhere. If his friends came over, he had his arm around her or his hand on her. Sometimes he'd throw her up against a wall and have wild, crazy sex as if he couldn't wait one more minute to be inside her. She *loved* when he did that.

That morning, sitting on the terrace, they'd had breakfast together. He'd sipped at his coffee, looked up with his amazing eyes, and instantly her nipples had gotten hard, forming twin peaks beneath her thin top. She'd worn no bra and he'd noticed. He noticed everything.

"Been thinkin', babe. Great morning. Feeling good. You know what would make me feel even better? You takin' that pillow over there and putting it just between my legs, crawling under the table and suckin' me dry the way you do. You have an objection to that?"

He could make anything sound hot, but the way he looked at her, and the way he spoke, so raw, his voice already gravelly with need, there was no resisting him.

She immediately got up and positioned the pillow beneath the glass table top and then crawled under the table between his legs. Before she could touch him, he swept up her hair into his fist and looked down at her through the glass.

"Take off your shirt, princess. I like to see your tits, your nipples hard like candy and your lips stretched over my dick. Love the way you look. You're so fuckin' hot."

She didn't hesitate, although she was very aware she was outside with him and anyone coming up their drive might see her. Just the possibility made what she was doing even hotter. The nearest house facing them had terraces that wrapped around the house as well, but that house was situated to the side of them, providing a similar ocean view. Ice had told her Storm had bought the place but hadn't yet moved in.

Her shirt on the ground, she was entirely naked. He put pressure on her head, tilting it back so he could guide his cock to her lips. She loved the scent of him. The taste and weight of him. She loved the hand in her hair, the bite on her scalp. He caressed her breast, his free hand kneading and then tugging at her nipple until fire darted straight to her sex. Lavishing love on Ice's body was so easy.

Soleil brought her hand up to her throat. She'd said she'd try with him and she was doing just that. She'd thrown herself into the role of wife. She had taken cooking lessons, and she utilized those as well as watched shows to learn more. She'd gone to Alena to ask as well, and every day Alena gave her a lesson. She enjoyed that. She'd learned how to make a bed from Ice. He always helped her in the morning. They had house cleaners come in once a week to thoroughly clean. Life was good. Too good. She didn't trust it because Ice was fast becoming her world, and if she lost him . . .

She got up slowly and walked across to the windows to stare out at the ocean. In the dark, the white foam almost glowed. She touched the glass, feeling a little battered by her thoughts. She was falling in love. She knew she was. She loved everything about Ice. He seemed completely devoted to her. She knew he couldn't be in such a short amount of time.

He was a gorgeous man. She'd been with him a few times to get groceries, and women stared at him. Sometimes openmouthed. He was that good-looking. He could have any woman he wanted. He might say he wouldn't cheat on her, but why stay with one woman when he could have an entire buffet? She heard the talk of parties, of women all over him and Storm. So many wanting him. She didn't blame them.

A soft groan escaped. She pressed her fingertips to her lips and turned away from the window, tears blurring her vision. She'd invested so much in him so fast, and she was going to get her heart torn out. Glancing at him, she hurried out of the room to the wide expanse of carpet overlooking the first floor.

At night, with the lights out, the house was different. It seemed much more ominous. Shadows played through the glass and danced through the great room. She went halfway down the stairs and sat, dropping her head into her hands. She hadn't taken care of business. She needed to find a lawyer she could trust, and figure out her life, because, really, did she think a man like Ice would want her forever? She was a throwaway unless she was wanted for her money, and Ice certainly didn't need that.

She didn't realize she was crying until a sob welled up and she had to choke it down. She wiped at her wet cheeks over and over. She'd been called that by her aunt. A throwaway. She'd been told no one wanted her and if she wasn't coughing up money, what was the point of caring for her? The worst was, Winston had said nearly the same thing to her when he'd been angry with her after a fund-raising event. He'd told her she was useless and that if she didn't have the money, what man would be interested in her?

Soleil had been so hurt. She'd refused to talk to him and had cried herself to sleep. He'd been very apologetic and told her he loved her, but that she really needed to make more of an effort to do as he asked. It was such a simple thing to avoid those people he knew wouldn't help further his career. Was that so much to ask? At the time, she'd been desperate not to be alone. She'd been alone far too much, and she wanted a relationship. She'd done everything she could think of to please him, and it hadn't been enough.

Was that what she was doing with Ice? Doing everything she could to please him? Unfortunately, that was who she was. That was what she did. She loved pleasing the people she loved. She wanted them happy. That was what made her happy. She rocked herself gently, terrified of losing him. It wouldn't be like losing Winston. She'd wanted out of that relationship. Losing Ice would just about kill her. She wanted to be with him.

He'd shown her his workroom he'd set up to make jewelry. It was kept locked and gems were kept in a safe. He'd laughed and told her before they'd come to Caspar, he'd made jewelry on the road and those same very expensive gems were just in one of the compartments on his bike. He'd been so free. Now, he was tied down to her. What did she really have to offer him? She was certain the explosive chemistry between them would wear off. Then what?

"Soleil?"

Her breath caught in her throat. He was at the top of the stairs. Ice. Her heart began to pound the way it often did when he was near. She turned her head slightly to acknowledge his presence, but she couldn't stop the tears running down her face. She could only suppress the sobs, so no sound emerged.

He came straight to her, his body entirely naked. He seemed so at ease without clothes, as if he was more used to going

409

nude than dressed. "Princess, what is it?" He sat down beside her, his arm sliding around her shoulders to pull her close to him.

She shook her head. How could she explain that she knew sooner or later he was going to want another woman? That he would see she was a fraud and didn't know how to sustain a relationship? That he would grow tired of her and leave her? That he would see her attempts at pleasing him as desperation?

"All right, baby, cry it out and then we'll talk," he said. "But the stairway isn't the best place to hold you." He took her hand and tugged, forcing her to rise, and they went down together to the very comfortable seats in front of the fireplace. He sat on the couch and pulled her down to him, fitting her head on his lap as she stretched out. "That's better, Soleil." He stroked her hair, comforting her.

She let herself cry because there were so many things in her life to cry over. She wished she was a stronger person. She was learning, especially since she'd been with Ice. He liked her to make household decisions. The hand in her hair was soothing. He didn't try to stop her tears, he just held her and ran his fingers through her hair, massaging her scalp.

"I don't know how to cry," Ice said suddenly. "I lost that ability when I was a kid. Crying's good when you need to do it. You can get to a place where anger and rage turn to ice. It builds and builds and gets uglier and uglier. So thick and dense it becomes like a glacier and then you're frozen inside. You can't cry. All you can do is tattoo fake tears dripping down your face to remind you that you're supposed to be human when you know you're not."

He was talking about himself. Soleil's heart clenched hard. Ice couldn't cry. Her Ice. He spoke matter-of-factly, as if he wasn't giving her something big, but she knew he was. Did he really see himself that way? Not human? Those teardrops, the tattoos, were one of her favorite things on him. She'd spent time kissing and tracing each one.

Soleil sat up slowly and framed his face with both hands. "Ice, you're human. You're a better man than anyone I've ever known."

His incredible blue eyes searched her face as if looking for something. What? Whatever it was, she wanted to give it to him. Acceptance maybe. He seemed to like whatever he saw because he smiled. It was one of his slow, sweet smiles that he reserved only for her.

"Baby, you're a fuckin' miracle. I don't know what I did to deserve you, but you have no idea how glad I am that I found you. I saw you, you know. I was on the street when you were there with Winston. You were across the street, standing there in that sundress, looking like a million dollars."

His hand dropped casually to his cock, fingers curling around it. He didn't seem to notice and Soleil found that sexier than ever.

"My cock was as hard as a rock looking at you. Your tits in that dress, your little waist, those booties on your feet. Then you turned your back to me and took a few steps away. Your ass was swaying, and I couldn't decide whether I was in love with your tits or your ass. Maybe both. Then that pussy Winston grabbed your arms and shook you. I wanted to rip his head off and throw it down the street for all the cars to flatten."

She found herself smiling, because Ice could do that so easily, turn her world from tears to laughter. She turned her head and licked up his shaft as if that thick rod was an ice-cream cone. He caught her hair and pulled her head back.

"As much as I want your mouth on me, I want you to talk to me. We're in this together, and we fix the things that are wrong. Something's wrong or you wouldn't be sitting on the stairs crying at two o'clock in the morning."

For some reason, the fact that Ice wanted to work things out rather than have sex made her cry all over again, but this time from hope. What man would do that? He loved when he was in her mouth. He often initiated oral sex in the strangest places, as if he couldn't wait another minute to feel her mouth. He was equally in love with being inside her.

"You're going to make yourself sick. You were done cry-in', babe. You're safe. It's dark enough. Tell me what's upsetting you."

"I'm not certain I have that kind of courage," she admitted reluctantly. She knew he heard the hesitancy in her voice, because he tugged on her hair until she looked up at him.

"You're the most courageous woman I know. You married me and committed to me. I was a stranger, yet you decided to make that leap of faith alone. You're courageous, Soleil. The longer I'm with you, the more I know it was the right choice for us."

She took a deep breath and let it out. She might be able to tell him the truth there in the darkness. But what if she did? She pressed her eyes closed tight. "Ice, I'm falling in love with you, and it's going to hurt so bad when this all falls apart. So bad, I'm not certain I'd survive."

There was silence. She could hear only the beating of her heart in time with a clock ticking loudly in the distance behind them. Probably the new grandfather clock they'd found together in one of the furniture shops they'd visited.

"Why would you think what we're building is going to fall apart?" He chose each word with equal the care she had chosen hers.

Soleil couldn't tell from his tone what he was thinking. Sometimes Ice retreated behind a wall and she felt she couldn't get to him. It wasn't often that it happened but when it did, that was another thing she feared. Another reason to think he was withdrawing from her.

"You're . . . extraordinary." She sat up slowly and forced herself to face him.

He gave a slight shake of his head, as if in complete disbelief, and she nodded. "You are, Ice. You're this amazing man. The way you treat me is unbelievable, like we're living a fairy tale. The world isn't really like that. I may have been an outsider looking in, but I watched people. Because I didn't

414

have a family, I watched others. They seemed to start with love or wild passion, but it always ended fast. Like they just stopped caring about each other. It was so sad."

He took her hand and pressed it to his chest, right over his heart.

Before he could say anything, Soleil continued. "It was so sad, and they were strangers to me. You've gotten inside me in such a short time. If we're together longer, you're going to take me over until I can't breathe without you. I know everyone would say it isn't healthy to love that way, but I don't know any other way. If I'm with you, I have to give you everything. It terrifies me to see ahead —"

"Stop, Soleil." There was pure steel in his voice. "We're not going to break up. I told you that when you signed on. We live by a code. You're part of that now, and by marrying me, you consented to live by that code. We fix anything broken between us. You're my first priority and I'm yours. I give you my everything, and I expect that same level of commitment from you."

He sounded more like a dictator than a lover, and somehow that reassured her more than his words. He meant them. The air in her lungs that refused to release rushed out

415

of her all at once. She watched his eyes grow even more crystal blue as he lifted her hand to his mouth and gently scraped his teeth back and forth over the pads of her fingers. It felt erotic. Sensual. Strangely, as if she belonged.

"Baby, you think I'm extraordinary, and I'm fuckin' glad about that. I'm not. I'm not even a nice guy, but you go ahead and think that of me. Maybe it will make me have to live up to your standards and I'll be a better man for it. To me, *you're* the extraordinary one. You're beautiful and funny and you want to please me. Believe me, that's a new experience for me. You take care of me in ways I love. I think you're sexy as hell, and when I ask you to do something, you do it with no hesitation. You've given me your trust and that's priceless to me. Bottom line, we aren't going to end this."

Soleil wanted to believe him. She touched her fingers to those three perfect teardrops. She loved them. They belonged on him. "I don't think I could ever love anyone else the way I do you, and it's growing every single day we're together."

"You're not alone in that. You aren't, Soleil. What I feel for you is enormous. So much so that I can't look at it sometimes. Talk about terror. Let's just live. We're good.

Don't worry about things that aren't going to happen. This gets broken, we fix it. You get upset, don't like something, you tell me and trust me to do the same. We don't hold shit back from each other. That's what fucks up relationships."

She held his words tightly to herself. Whatever he felt for her terrified him, and she knew that emotion. She nodded. "I'll try. Sometimes I can't help what creeps into my mind. I'm used to being thrown away because I'm not good enough. That I was lucky I had money."

He studied her face, seeing too much, and she looked away. He caught her chin and forced her to meet his furious gaze. "Who the fuck told you that, Soleil?"

She shook her head, feeling humiliated, just as she had when she was a child. "Ice . . ."

"No, I want to know because someone said it to you."

She shrugged, trying to be casual, trying not to let him see how much it hurt. Or how much she let it color her life. "An aunt who took me in for a short while, and Winston said something similar."

"Well, it's bullshit. We haven't touched your money and we're not going to. I pay. I told you that. As for Winston, that little pissant is going to reap his rewards. We've got eyes on him and have almost since we came back from Vegas."

Her head jerked up. "What? You didn't tell me that."

"You didn't need to know. He's not your problem anymore. But I will say, it might be time to get a lawyer you trust to take over your business. Code says you have a lawyer trying to file to 'protect' your trust as you've gone missing. You'll need to surface soon."

A shiver crept down her spine. She wrapped her arms around her middle. "The moment I do, they'll come after me."

"By *surfacing,* I mean file papers of your own. That's why you need a lawyer."

She frowned. "I have no idea who to hire."

"There're a million lawyers who deal with your kind of trust. Choose one. Or you could use Absinthe. He'd eat them alive. He's that good."

"Absinthe is a lawyer?"

He nodded. "Yep."

She liked that he didn't push her. She was intelligent enough to know that when Absinthe had sat next to her in the clubhouse when they'd asked her questions, that he had some special talent. Since then, she'd heard several times that he was a human lie

418

detector. She liked him. He was quieter than most of the others. Sometimes he seemed apart from them. She knew Ice not only liked and respected him but also admired him. Still, Ice hadn't insisted she choose Absinthe as her lawyer.

"Don't you think that if I hired Absinthe as my lawyer, he'd become a target? That it would be painting a huge red bull's-eye on his back?"

He grinned at her, and for a moment, the way the light shimmering off the ocean hit his face, he looked a predator, like a hungry wolf eager to bring down his prey.

"We have to draw them out. Code has gotten to them, found them online. They exchange emails all the time, and they have a private group chatroom they go into sometimes. There appears to be eight of them and Winston. He isn't very popular right now. The others are holding him accountable for you getting away. He got very angry at one point. It seems he doesn't have a handle on his temper at all. In the heat of the moment, he admitted he believes that you overheard the conversation with Harbin Conner, and might have heard another name, but you know they're plotting to kill you."

She pushed her hair back behind her ears

and drew her knees up, wrapping her arms around them. "His temper is a lot worse than they realize."

"This is your business, Soleil, but you need to let the world know you're alive and file papers to stop Donald Monroe from stealing your trust out from under your nose. We may not need it, but our children might be grateful to have it."

"You keep saying that, Ice, and you don't know how much I appreciate that you want to pay, but I'm in this too, and I'm capable of contributing."

He caught her chin between his thumb and fingers. "Really? You're going to go there again while we're having a serious conversation?"

"I am serious. You give me everything."

"I like buying you things. I like clothes shopping with you." She blushed. He'd gone shopping with her just a few days earlier. He was especially fond of dresses. She obliged by trying them on. Each time she came out of the dressing room to show him, he had her turn around in front of his chair, then he stood and reached down the bodice to caress the upper curves of her breasts before sliding his hands up the backs of her thighs to cup her bare cheeks. He preferred her to wear thongs or no panties at all. She went with the thongs most of the time.

He made everything they did together fun and sensual. She looked forward to every day. She looked forward to just being with him. Her heart hurt sometimes just looking at him.

"Do you think Absinthe will have time to meet with me?"

"First, Absinthe only works for Torpedo Ink. You're now property of Torpedo Ink because you're my wife. That means he works for you."

"Whoa. Back up the bus, Ice." She couldn't admit that little thrill that shot through her at his casual statement. She wanted to be his in every way, but *property*? "I'm Torpedo Ink's property?"

He slung his arm around her neck and pulled her to him. "You're *my* property, but Torpedo Ink will protect you. Every member. Every prospect. I'm having your jacket made. We'll be going on a run with the Diamondbacks and a few other clubs and I'll want you wearing it or the denim vest I've had made up as well. That's important. You can't just walk around unclaimed in that situation. You have to stick close to me."

"I always stick close to you." She did. She loved being with him, and she didn't care where they were.

He nodded his head. "So, talk to Absinthe later this morning and we'll get the ball rolling. Once he files the papers, and proves you're alive and hired him, we'll be able to take these fuckers down. Three of them are 'married' to their victims and looking to kill their spouses off soon. They joke about it. Code said it made him feel sick reading their dialogue. These women think they love them, when their 'husbands' are really after the money. If it hadn't been for Lana . . . I'm so fuckin' grateful to her."

"Me too."

"I've got some other business with the club to take care of before the run, Soleil. I'll be gone for a day or two at the most, but it hopefully won't be long. I'll want you close to the house or clubhouse. You can visit Breezy or Anya. Both places are very protected. If you need anything like groceries, give a list to whoever is here looking out for you. I'm not certain who we're leaving behind this time."

Another shiver slid down her spine. "I don't understand. Where are you going?"

"Club business is something we don't talk about, babe. I didn't explain that and I'm sorry. I should have before hitting you with it. We take jobs and work them out, that's how we make our club money. Only fully patched club members are privy to what we do. It's to keep things confidential. It's no big deal."

"I couldn't care less what you're doing, Ice, but I don't like the fact that you're going someplace where I won't know where you are."

"You'll get used to it." He stroked a caress down the back of her head as if that could fix things.

Soleil wasn't buying it. "How would you feel if I disappeared for a couple of days and you had no idea where I was or what I was doing?"

"That isn't going to happen."

His voice had turned pure steel again, something that sent butterflies winging in her stomach. His eyes had changed again, going pure glacier blue. Pure ice. He was dead serious. She put a hand defensively to her throat.

"Can you not see how unfair that is?"

"I don't give a flying fuck whether it's fair or not, Soleil," he snapped. "You don't ever disappear on me."

His eyes blazed with blue flames. She found that fascinating and kind of hot — a bad thing because he really meant what he said. There was a razor edge to his voice. Suddenly he wasn't the easygoing man she'd married.

"Honey" — she tried to be reasonable — "I've been on my own for a very long time."

She could see the effort he made to push down those hot, blue flames. She almost didn't want him to, fixating on them. He was *such* a beautiful man, even angry. She didn't like him upset with her. That didn't sit well, but the way his eyes looked as he ran his gaze over her . . .

There was possession, as if she belonged to him. There was that dark lust that was never quite gone when he looked at her. There were those blue flames that leapt in his eyes and focused on her as if she were the only woman in his world and he burned for her. She'd heard angry sex was explosive . . .

"You're not on your own anymore, Soleil, and you have a pack of murderers looking to kill you. You aren't being reasonable. Why the fuck aren't you being reasonable?" He raked both hands through his hair, messing it up more so he looked like a wild surfer instead of a biker.

She tried not to smile, knowing that wouldn't make him happy. She couldn't help rubbing her finger over his lips, tracing that little intriguing frown, trying to soothe him because he was genuinely upset. Suddenly it was no longer about sex, angry or otherwise; it was about fixing the problem and getting him to understand so he wasn't upset and neither was she.

"You could try asking, Ice. I pretty much would do anything for you. I don't want to be treated like I'm ten and not quite bright. What would be the point of me going anywhere without you? I have a million things to do in this house, or I can go visit the other women. I want to get to know them. What I don't want is to be treated like a child. I may have made a few mistakes, or maybe even a lot of them, but I did learn from them."

He froze, his turbulent eyes completely focused on her face.

She nodded. "I was making a point that you wouldn't like me to disappear for a few days without your knowledge of where I am. You had a rather visceral reaction, so I'm fully aware you wouldn't like it. But you're doing the same thing to me and expect that I'll be okay with it. Do you see my point?"

"I see it," he conceded. "I can't change my work, baby. It's what I do."

"I've heard what men do on runs. Whatever happens stays there. I don't like that, Ice, and I'm not living with it. You do that and we're done." She stated it irrevocably.

"First, princess" — he cupped one side of her face with his palm, his thumb stroking gently — "I told you, I don't cheat. That's not who I am. I would never disrespect you that way. Second, we aren't going on a run. If we do that, I'll take you with me. We're working. It's going to happen that we have to leave every now and then. This is one of those times. I need you to be okay with it whenever I'm gone on club business."

Her eyes searched his. She didn't really care about knowing his club's business, but she didn't like him somewhere she couldn't reach him. "Can I text you?"

"Sure. I might not be able to answer right away. You can send me nude pictures too."

Immediately she felt hot in her stomach, as if a fire smoldering there suddenly burst into flames. Color crept up from her stomach to her breasts, heating them to an aching point and then moving up her neck, framing the pulse beating so madly there, to her face, coloring her a soft rose.

He grinned at her. "You like the idea."

"I like thinking of you hot and bothered looking at the pictures. I don't think I could actually take pictures of myself to send you." She turned her head to face his hardening cock. The size and shape of him were beautiful. She circled the girth with one hand, making a fist.

"I love how perfect you are. So thick and hard, yet like velvet." She licked up his shaft and then swirled her tongue over the head, collecting pearly drops. "I also love how you taste." Her eyes met his as she turned over onto her stomach, her mouth inches from his groin. "You have no idea how beautiful your cock is, Ice. It suits you perfectly."

He reached down and smacked her on the bottom. Heat blossomed and spread. She let out a little mock cry, but truthfully, it didn't matter what Ice did, she was always turned on. Instantly.

"Get up for a minute."

His voice had turned wicked. She sat up and watched as he got up. "I'll be right back." He raced up the stairs. She found it extremely exciting to watch his body move, all those delicious muscles she'd traced with her tongue. The scars on him that only made him look awesome. He came down with his phone.

Soleil started laughing. "What are you planning?"

"I want pictures."

"Once you have them, anyone can see them."

"No, they can't. I'm not sharing them. I want them, though. My sexy wife. I love saying that. I love that you're mine. Come on, pose for me."

"I'm not a model. I'm too self-conscious to pose nude or fully clothed. I never look that great in pictures."

"I'll direct you."

He sounded so eager she found herself smiling, suddenly uncaring that he wanted nude photographs of her, no matter how awful they turned out. He pointed to the thick rug in front of the fireplace. He turned the flames on low with the remote and they danced to life, a long line of them recessed into the wall.

"Sit and let your shirt drape off one shoulder and unbutton all the buttons so your tit peeks out. That's sexy as hell."

"Is hell sexy?" she teased, complying with his instructions.

"Look up at me with your innocent face. That little angel face."

She wasn't sure she had an innocent face. She certainly didn't have an angel face, so she just looked up at him under her long lashes and hoped that was good enough. She parted her lips and then looked directly at him as he snapped away. When he didn't give her further direction, she swept the shirt open and cupped her breasts like an offering to him, throwing her head back so the line of her throat showed.

"Shit, baby, I'm getting as hard as a rock."

That was nothing new, but it inspired her. She lay down on her stomach, legs bent into the air, a distance apart. She turned her head to look at him, propped up on one elbow, so he caught her breast hanging down, nipple rubbing the warm, thick carpet.

He tossed her a pillow and she thrust it under her bottom, lifting her butt for him. "That's so beautiful, princess. Turn over and lie back, arch your back and bring up your knees. Legs apart so I can see all that wonderful honey you feed me in the morning."

He devoured her at least twice a day. She didn't contradict him because she didn't want to sound as if she were complaining.

"Get yourself off, Soleil."

She slid her hand down her belly and then curled her fingers into her slick heat, her eyes on his. With one finger, she circled her clit. She couldn't believe how hot it made her having Ice watch her with hungry eyes while he took pictures.

"You're my little exhibitionist, Soleil." There was laughter in his voice, humor in his eyes. He kept snapping pictures. "I love that so much. I'm switching to video, because you're so fucking sexy I've got to have this for myself when I'm all alone."

The dancing flames from the fireplace threw shadows around the room and played over her body. Her lashes fell, that long feathery fall, and his body responded. Her gaze was riveted on his cock. She wanted it and she brought her finger to her mouth and sucked, closing her eyes for a moment, pretending she had the weight of him on her tongue.

"I fuckin' love this, Soleil. I want more of these sexy pictures. Kneel up in front of that ottoman. I want you to lie over the top of it so your tits are hanging down. Wait. I'll be right back." This time he disappeared down the hall.

Soleil sat up shaking her head, finding herself laughing, wondering how she had gone from tears to laughter so fast. It was Ice. Life with him was an adventure. She never knew what he was going to do from one moment to the next. When he returned, he looked so pleased with himself she just shook her head. She was already so in love with him.

"Come here, baby."

"Abandon the ottoman?" But she crawled across the floor to him, using her sexiest crawl, eyes on his cock, that delicious part of his anatomy that always seemed to keep her enthralled.

When she was kneeling in front of him, he crooked his finger so she knelt upright. He bent his head, captured her left breast in the hot cauldron of his mouth and sucked hard, flattening her nipple and then tugging at it with his teeth. She gasped as he elongated it deliberately and then fastened a clamp with sparkling jewels swinging off it. Her breath left her lungs in a long rush. He grinned at her and then his mouth was on her right breast, repeating the same exercise. A double chain hung like reins from one nipple to the other.

"Was going to save your surprise for later but couldn't resist. You look so beautiful."

Soleil looked at him suspiciously and then down at her breasts. The jewelry was beautiful, and she could see his signature design on it, but she wasn't altogether certain yet she was a fan, although the way his face was so lit up it made her want to give him anything he wanted.

"What are we doing?" Her nipples burned and then when she moved, it was as if he were stroking and tugging all over again, causing her to gasp.

"We're making a video for me. An extremely hot one."

"I take it you have ideas." She didn't dare move. When she did, the jewels swung and the clamps tightened, sending streaks of fire straight to her clit. She was afraid she might have a climax just from that and then he'd want to play with clamps all the time. She'd heard taking them off was painful, and she wasn't into any kind of real pain.

He grinned at her, kissed her until she couldn't think straight and then had her kneel up, legs wide apart. This time he had her bend backward over the ottoman until her back rested on it and her head was over one side and her bare mound on the other. The jewels pulled her breasts to both sides, causing her to gasp again as fire streaked through her. Her sheath clamped down and a fresh wave of liquid heat told her she was getting very needy.

"Ice." She nearly wailed his name.

"I'm turning on the video feed so we're recording. You just follow my instructions."

She nodded, her eyes on his. She loved him like this, happy and laughing. Playing. Ice didn't seem a man to play often, and he was playing.

"Bury your fingers in your pussy, princess. I want you getting yourself off. Open your mouth and I'll feed you my cock. It's going deep this time, but you can take it. I'll work it in slow. You can work my balls and your pussy, but not my cock, you understand?"

She nodded, her hand already sliding down her soft skin, feeling the touch like a flame. Shadows played over his face, giving him the look of a warrior. His eyes were blue steel, like hot crystals demanding her compliance, and she would have given him anything in that moment, just to see that the lines of strain he always carried were gone.

"Open your mouth for me, baby."

His voice had gone hoarse and she knew he was becoming as aroused as she was. She wanted his cock, but she made a show of wetting her lips with her tongue, before slowly opening her mouth. He pressed the broad crown against her tongue, and she tasted the salty mixture of masculine flavor that was unique to Ice.

Her own body was on fire and when he lifted the chain so casually off her belly, she barely noticed until he tugged, and her breasts rose upward at his command. She gasped and his hips thrust gently forward, so that his cock slid deeper than it had ever gone.

"That's it, baby, squeeze down on me. So fucking hot. Look at you. Get yourself off."

She couldn't breathe and she looked up at

him, trying to tell him, but he was already sliding back to give her air, then he tugged again, and the flames shot through her and he was thrusting deeper, swearing, one hand in her hair so tightly her scalp ached. She thought she was going to explode.

Soleil backed off riding her own fingers deliberately, not wanting this to end too soon. It was too good, too perfect. It didn't matter that it started off in tears or play, the expression on his face was what she wanted to have for all time. He could have the video. She could have the pleasure beyond measure and that expression.

She focused on the coiling tension in her body and the beauty of his cock. The weight of it. The shape and size of it. The way he tasted. She loved it because it represented him. Every stroke of her tongue, her hollowed cheeks, sucking him hard, using a flutter motion, not breathing and trusting him to give her air, all of that was telling him how much she loved him. Saying it without words. All the while she looked up at him, into those blue flames that never left her face. Never left her eyes.

He tugged on the chain and sent fire rushing through her, thrusting his cock deeper until she had no choice but to relax her throat, but he didn't push her into a panic.

He was careful with her. And then, before she could stop it, her body exploded in fierce, wild waves that overtook her, even as his cock swelled and jerked, pouring his seed down her throat, forcing her to swallow over and over.

"Don't move, princess," he ordered, his voice ragged, as if he couldn't get enough air. He started to retreat from her.

She reached out behind her and caught at his hips to stop him from rising completely. The action lifted her breasts and sent another streak of fire racing through her body, straight to her sex, so that another powerful wave rushed through her.

"Don't move yet," she ordered. "You know I don't like to leave you like this." She did her best to glare at him. "You're mine and I take care of you." She did. Unless he was in a huge hurry, she always spent time making sure she got every little bit of his seed. It belonged to her. That taste. That was Ice.

She loved to watch his face as her tongue tenderly licked at him. As she gently sucked. He always closed his eyes, his hand in her hair, fingers moving in time with her tongue, the connection between them feeling sacred to her. When she was done, his lashes would flicker and then he would lift them and look at her with something close to worship. That was the time she most could believe he felt for her what she felt for him.

"I have to get those clamps off you, baby. They can't be on too long."

She'd almost forgotten, she'd been so wrapped up in his look. She didn't move as he bent over her. Her breath hissed out as he removed the first one and replaced it with the warmth of his mouth. It wasn't as bad as she'd feared, but it was definitely more intense than she liked. Because she knew what was coming, she just nodded and he was quick, once again using his mouth to soothe her nipple.

He helped her to sit and then he was kissing her, over and over, driving out any remaining worries she had. There was no way to think when he was kissing her. When she stood a little shakily, he smacked her bottom and grinned at her. "Come on, princess. We're going for a ride. We need the wind in our faces. We may both be just fine or damaged beyond repair, but we belong to each other, and riding always makes the world perfect. You already did that for me. I'm going to do that for you."

He'd already done that for her, but she definitely wanted to go for a ride. She liked the idea that the sun wasn't up and they'd be riding in the dark along the coast, with the ocean so close.

"I love every minute with you, Ice," Soleil admitted. "And I want a copy of that video on my phone too. I love to watch your face when your cock is in my mouth. You're so amazing." She had to tell him, because it was the truth.

"You know what I love? You look like the sweet little girl next door, baby, and then you say *cock* and you definitely claim ownership of it, and it blows my mind. I fucking love that." He caught her hand. "Let's get dressed."

THIRTEEN

Highway 1 was a ribbon of curves and switchbacks, with few straight stretches. Ice loved the winding road. His woman wasn't used to the bike, but she was on it with him, no complaints, dressed warmly for the early morning hour and the coastal highway. This was what he lived for, his woman, his Harley and the open road. He'd not gone more than fifteen miles when two bikes came up behind them. He sent his brothers a quick grin and a wave.

Savage and Absinthe moved neatly into position behind them. That was the way it often was, one would decide to ride, but others were already on the open road. The ocean stretched out to their right, and the mountains rose to their left. It was a beautiful sight. The sun wasn't yet thinking about rising in the east.

They could find a little diner for breakfast in an hour or two. Soleil was bundled up —

gloves, scarf, warm clothes, jacket — and her arms were tightly around him. He hated that she was worried he might leave her — that people in her life had led her to believe she was worthless other than for her money. He wanted her to see that he valued her for the person she was. For every part of her, including the little exhibitionist in her. She didn't know it, but he needed that. He wasn't being fair to give her only a part of who he was.

He thought about that for the next few miles. She was giving him everything. He could see who she was. So sweet. Cooking for him in their kitchen, poring over recipes she thought he might like. He didn't give a damn about the food, just about her. He loved sitting in the kitchen watching her look so serious as she attempted some recipe that was probably far too complicated for an amateur. It didn't matter. She was doing it for him. To make him happy.

Ice had never had anyone go out of their way for him in the way she was. He couldn't remember his parents. They'd been murdered and he'd been taken to the school, supposedly to turn him into an asset for his country. There were four such schools, three of which trained children using torture and brutal methods but expected those children to serve their country. The fourth, the one he'd been taken to, was made up of criminals, pedophiles who were given a virtual smorgasbord of children to abuse in any way they could conceive. The children weren't expected to ever leave the school alive, although each had been trained as a very lethal and skilled assassin so Sorbacov, the man who had put them there, could use them if he wanted to kill an enemy.

Soleil's hand began to rub up and down his abdomen, as if she knew his thoughts had taken a sudden turbulent turn and she was soothing him. He dropped his gloved hand over hers in a silent show of gratitude. He knew he was far past falling and had actually fallen in love with her. He just didn't know exactly what that was yet or what he was going to do about it.

A car came up behind them. It had been traveling at a high rate of speed, but it slowed to drop in directly behind the three bikes. Savage gave a low hand signal to Ice to pull to the side of the road when possible to allow the car to pass. It was an Audi, and there were four men inside.

Something about the way the car moved up on them, like a hungry predator, set off not only Ice's warning system but Savage's as well. Ice glanced at Absinthe. He wore an expressionless mask. Yeah, he felt it too. Whoever was in that car was specifically targeting Torpedo Ink. It wasn't a random car just happening to slide in behind them.

He would have welcomed the action, and he knew the others would have as well, but there was Soleil to protect. And were the men there to kill her? Was this about their enemies? Or hers? Savage suddenly dropped back, signaling to Ice to take off. He didn't bother to look, he already knew Savage had sent him forward to protect Soleil. Those in the Audi were making their move.

His Harley was a road rocket, and it shot forward at his command, Savage and Absinthe using their bikes to provide cover, weaving back and forth as they sped down the road. Ice heard the whine of a bullet as it zipped past him. That thoroughly pissed him off. Soleil leaned into him, tightening her arms and curling her fingers into his jacket. She didn't panic or try to ask questions. She did what she normally did when she was with him. She gave him her complete trust, her body moving with his and the bike as if born to do so.

Just ahead, around a curve in the road, was a switchback. They knew the road and knew it was there. He gave a hand signal to Savage and Absinthe just before entering the switchback. The moment they were out of sight of the Audi, he slowed the bike and pulled off the road.

"Off, baby, run for the brush." He had her arm and all but yanked her off the motorcycle. Soleil obeyed him, taking off for the heaviest brush.

Savage and Absinthe were there, bikes down, running with them for either side of the road, weapons out. They'd had seconds to set up. They were used to that, used to moving fast in a fluid situation.

The Audi swept into the switchback. Savage stepped out from the left side of the road and fired directly into the car. Absinthe did the same from the right. Ice had taken up the position just at the very apex of the curve. Savage must have hit the driver. The car went into a slide, and the smell of rubber burning was strong. The car spun and then hit the mountainside hard.

Ice sprinted to the rear door of the Audi, yanking it open, his elbow slamming into the bearded man on the passenger side, knocking him sideways. He pressed the barrel of his gun to the man's head.

"I'll fucking end you. Put your weapon down." At a glance, he could see the driver was dead, slumped over the steering wheel, his foot a dead weight on the brake.

Absinthe had torn open the passenger door behind the front seat. He'd struck the man there a couple of times, ensuring he was dazed as he dragged him out of the car, taking him to the ground on his belly while he searched him for weapons.

Savage had the third passenger out, the shooter from the back seat. Ice had been busy trying to get Soleil out of harm's way, but it was Savage and Absinthe who had been fired on. Savage wasn't taking any chances with his prisoner. The man was dragged out of the vehicle and taken to the ground. Savage was rough as he inspected the man for weapons, but he didn't bother collecting every gun and knife on his person. He left one. Just one, because that was the kind of bastard he could be — and there was Soleil.

"Who are you?" Absinthe asked his prisoner.

Ice dragged the bearded man around the car, uncaring of the rocks and branches that the body bumped over. He threw him down beside Absinthe's man.

"Ed Charles." No sooner had he gotten the name out than he began screaming, grabbing his head.

Absinthe smiled grimly. "I can make it hurt worse. You tell me the truth and it all

443

goes away. Your name?"

"Phil. Phil Roberson." The man took in great gulps of air. There were actual tears in his eyes.

"Why did you attack us, Phil?" Absinthe continued.

"Don't you answer him," Savage's prisoner snarled.

Savage instantly retaliated, his gloved fist smashing into the man's mouth over and over, breaking teeth and driving them back into his mouth, nearly pushing them down his throat. Blood sprayed and then ran down his chin and throat.

"Go ahead, Phil," Savage said. "You're going to want to answer the question." He spoke calmly, matter-of-factly, as if he hadn't just destroyed a man's face.

Phil looked horrified. "If I answer —" He broke off screaming, grabbing at his head.

"If you choose not to answer or you lie, your head is going to hurt like that, Phil," Absinthe said, sounding perfectly reasonable. "And it will get worse."

"The girl. We're after the girl."

Ice stiffened and glanced across the open space to the brush where Soleil stood watching, a distance away. He didn't like her seeing what they were doing; on the other hand, they needed the information

444

they were quickly extracting. *He* needed the information. These men were after Soleil. They had to be fast and then get out of there.

"How did you find her?" Absinthe asked.

"Winston remembered the club at the motel. She was seen going into a biker bar. A biker gave her up."

"Name and club of the biker." Absinthe nearly spat the demand.

"Fred something. His club was Venomous."

Ice remembered them partying at the bar that night. He didn't remember Fred. Of course Fred had noticed Soleil. When she'd walked into the bar, everyone had gone silent and turned toward the door in shock. Ice filed the name of the biker away. They'd come back with Soleil in her wedding gown. She'd looked like a princess and she'd been memorable.

"Who are your friends? The man with his mouth gone?"

"That's Yeger. Yeger Kushnir."

Ice stiffened. He recognized the name. They all had flawless memories. They had to. That was how they'd survived the hellhole. Yeger Kushnir was one of the two men who had raped and frightened Rich Marshal's wife to keep her in line. He was

445

heavily involved in human trafficking, taking the children that weren't sold at auction to remain in their trafficking ring until the children died. How had Winston connected with the pedophile ring and the men Torpedo Ink was after? Was it some kind of a coincidence? He didn't believe that for a minute. What the hell was going on?

Yeger spit blood toward Phil and then launched himself at Savage, swinging his fist up, his gun spitting bullets. Savage flung himself to the side, slamming his arm hard against Yeger's as the weapon came up. Yeger rolled and turned the gun toward Soleil. Savage was on him before he could fire, his punches fierce. Hard. Relentless. Not giving Yeger the chance to get off another shot. Yeger fought, trying to pound Savage in the face with the gun, trying to turn it back on him. Ice could have told him that was a bad idea.

Savage caught the wrist and snapped it back all in one motion. The weapon went flying and Yeger howled. Savage punched him several more times, taking the fight out of him.

"And the other one."

Ice's prisoner had been stoically silent. Now he glared at Phil, as if somehow he thought he was going to frighten the man.

446

Phil had eyes only for the violent beating Savage had given to Yeger.

"Basil Alanis."

Again, Ice remembered the name. He was the other man who had raped and intimidated Rich Marshal's wife in order to force her to stay with Rich in spite of the fact that the man was molesting her daughters. He was also part of the human trafficking ring that took the children deemed too old for the pedophile ring.

"And the collector. Give me the name of the collector." Absinthe spoke softly, but Phil continued to stare at Yeger's bleeding body.

They needed that name above any others. He was the man targeting and murdering families in order to fulfill his orders for young boys or girls.

Yeger tried hard to speak, but his mouth was so fucked up it was impossible. Clearly, he didn't want Phil to continue. Like Torpedo Ink, Yeger knew they couldn't afford to keep up with the interrogation. They had found out quite a bit in the three minutes gone by, but a car could be along any minute and they couldn't afford to be seen.

"I don't know! I don't know!" Phil shrieked.

"Shit," Ice spat. "Time's up. We can't

stay." He wanted the connection between Winston and the pedophiles.

"We can't take them with us to interrogate them," Absinthe said, regret in his voice. "We're on bikes. And they know where Soleil is."

Ice shrugged. "Let them bring it." He shot Basil in the head.

Savage did the same for the mess that was Yeger. Absinthe pulled out his gun and executed Phil just as quickly.

"We've got to get out of here," Savage said. "Did either of you touch anything?"

"The door," Ice said. "I was wearing gloves."

"I'll wipe down the car," Savage said. "Get her out of here."

He glanced over to Soleil. Absinthe and Ice did as well. She was pale, her hands over her mouth as if covering a scream. Ice knew Soleil wasn't used to sudden violence. This had to be a thousand times worse than anything she'd witnessed with Winston. She was probably scared out of her mind.

He straightened up and shoved his gun into the side holster before starting toward her. Soleil backed up a couple of steps. He stopped and picked up his bike, running his eyes over it to ensure it was in good working order.

"Baby, get over here. We have to leave before we're seen."

She was used to giving him what he wanted, and she took several steps toward him but then she stopped, shaking her head. "You just shot them. In the head. You just shot them, Ice."

"We had no choice. These men were here for you. Now get the fuck on the bike now. We're running out of time." He took his colors off, rolled the jacket and pushed it into a compartment on his Harley. "Now." He hissed the last command.

Soleil came to him, albeit reluctantly, but she came. She put her hand on his shoulder to steady herself while she straddled the machine. Her hand was trembling. The Harley started with a roar. He reached back, gripped her hands and yanked them to his belly, forcing her arms around him.

She was shaking nearly uncontrollably. He couldn't blame her. She wasn't a woman exposed to violence. Immediately, he had them speeding down the highway, looking for the first road that would take them on a circular route back to Caspar without actually riding along the coast where they could be seen and identified.

Savage and Absinthe would remove evidence of their being there, particularly the spots where they'd dropped their bikes and Soleil's footprints running to the brush and coming back. Like Ice, they would remove their colors and find an alternate route so few people would ever see them. It was the best they could do to cover their tracks in the minutes they had to get things cleaned up and them gone.

Savage would have to search the car to ensure there was nothing to lead back to them. That would take an extra minute, time they might not have. Ice cursed and slammed his fist against his thigh. If Savage was compromised because he didn't wait and help, he would lose one of his brothers to prison. Savage wouldn't do well in prison. He'd pick fights every day. They knew that because he'd been sent to prison to take out a threat to the government. He'd been in several weeks and had spent quite a bit of time in solitary. He had gotten into fights many times and come close to killing with his fists. It hadn't been easy getting him out.

Ice hit his thigh again. Off to his right, across the highway, was the road that cut through the mountain. He turned off immediately to get off the main highway. The first few months they'd settled in Caspar, they'd learned every back road, even the ones that were dirt. There were so many logging roads that every part of the highway was connected somewhere. As they'd learned the ones close to Caspar, they'd begun spreading out, going farther and farther from home. They'd made certain they had escape routes set up everywhere along the highway.

He slowed his Harley, not wanting to draw attention to himself. The others would be riding after him, minus their colors, just two men riding together in the early morning hours on back roads. Bike enthusiasts did it all the time. As long as no one looked too closely, they'd be fine — if Savage had gotten away safely.

The road was mostly shadowed by trees, which meant it was wet in places and covered in pine needles in others. He maneuvered through the various "danger" zones easily and kept them moving in the general direction of Caspar.

"Stop." Soleil put her mouth against his ear. "Stop right now, Ice."

He tried to pat the back of her hand, but she jerked it out from under him. "Can't do it, babe. Too dangerous."

"Savage will have left DNA back there! They'll arrest me as an accessory! You *killed* those men!" She was shouting, saying every thought crowding into the chaos of her mind.

He could feel her entire body trembling. He dropped his hand to her thigh and rubbed. "He knows what to do. He wore gloves and he'll leave evidence behind that points elsewhere. Nothing that will jump out. Take a breath, Soleil. We're on the way home and we'll talk this out when we get there."

"I want to stop. I need to breathe."

"You're having a panic attack." Ice flinched inwardly. Sooner or later, the cops could find a tie between Soleil and these men. The men might have stopped and asked questions. They'd searched for her and gone to the bar in Vegas, although if Fred had talked to the cops, even his own club would turn on him. "Just breathe. We're not stopping, and you're going to pull yourself together."

"You killed those men," she repeated. "I think Savage beat that one to death. Or at least came close. You *killed* them."

"They were here to kill you. If you're dead and you haven't filed any papers, that lawyer Winston hired can say just about anything he wants!" Ice had to shout to be heard above the pipes. Even going slow, communication was difficult. "Damn it, Soleil, pull yourself together. This is serious. All of our lives are in your hands. You'd better know you can handle it."

She went instantly silent, too still. She also held herself stiffly, away from him. Her hands crept from around his waist to fist in his shirt at his sides. He was in a shitload of trouble with her and he probably should have handled the situation with care, but he was worried that Savage and Absinthe hadn't gotten away cleanly.

He couldn't call them to ask because he didn't want his phone to have any evidence that they were out riding in this direction. His locator was off, but he knew if he called, the cell tower would be instant evidence. Soleil's cell phone was still in the end-table drawer beside the bed. Winston had blown up her phone with his "worried" calls. He was already setting up for the cops to think she'd had a breakdown. He'd been very solicitous. Ice had told her not to answer until they knew what they were doing.

He cursed again. He had to have Absinthe file papers immediately, but after this fiasco, persuading her to use him as her lawyer, and to trust Torpedo Ink — and Ice — was not going to be easy. He couldn't take the time to stop until they were miles from the scene, and even then, he would prefer to keep going so they couldn't be seen at all. He would wait until they were at the clubhouse before he texted Czar and Steele to come as well so they could put a plan in place if and when the cops came sniffing around.

They kept to the back roads, moving slowly. Once, a car came along, but he heard it before it got to them, so he pulled into deeper shadows and angled the bike away from the road so the license plate couldn't be seen easily. The moment the car was a good distance away, they were back on the road, traveling toward Caspar.

The sun had climbed into the sky by the time he made it into Caspar and their clubhouse. Soleil was off the bike without help, backing away from him, wrapping her arms around her body and looking around her as if she might make a run for it. Ice gave her a few moments to make up her mind, pretending to tinker with his bike before sliding off. He looked at her. She'd been crying. He didn't blame her. The scene must have been shocking to her.

"Soleil." He used his gentlest voice and held out his hand to her. "Let's go inside. We'll get some coffee and warm up."

She held up her hand. "I need to think. I have to get past panic and think."

"You can do that inside where it's warm." He stepped closer to her, using a very subtle glide he'd perfected when he was a boy, learning to kill. He could inch within striking distance and his prey never realized he had done so until it was too late.

Soleil looked so pale her skin was nearly translucent. Her eyes were wide with shock, giving the illusion that they were too big for her face.

She looked at the clubhouse and then around the grounds. One hand crept protectively to her throat. He wanted her to come to him for protection.

"Baby, I know you're scared. That was a very violent and scary, fucked-up mess. It happened so fast. We were on the main highway where anyone could have come by at any moment." He couldn't help glancing up to the highway, not that Savage or Absinthe would come that way. Like Ice, they would use the old logging roads to make their way home.

"Just come inside with me and we'll talk it out." He inched closer, seeming not to move. He didn't want her running. He wanted — even needed — her trust. He didn't deserve it. They'd spent a month together, and most of the time he'd related to her through sex. He was afraid to talk too much to her about himself, to give too much of his life away. He should have, though. He should have done more than just have sex with her at every turn; he should have given her something solid to hold on to.

"I'm not going anywhere, Ice." She took a deep breath and ran her hands down her thighs, rubbing up and down as if to warm herself. "I just need to walk around for a few minutes and sort things out in my mind before I'm inside, where I might have more trouble breathing."

She meant before she felt trapped and unable to run if she needed to, Ice was certain. She was still trembling so hard he was afraid she might fall. In the distance, coming from the north, he heard the sound of pipes. Even fainter, coming from the south, on Highway 1, he heard more. Soleil heard them too, and panic set on her face.

Reaper was the first to arrive, coming in from a back road north of the property. Anya was on the back of the bike. As soon as the bike was parked, Anya jumped off and went straight to Soleil as if she didn't notice that Soleil was close to running.

"Honey. How terrible. Ice texted us about the men who were after you. I know what that feels like." She threw her arms around

456

Soleil and hugged her close. "You're shaking." She glared at Ice. "She needs to be inside, where it's warm."

Soleil immediately shook her head. She wasn't the type of woman to let someone else — especially Ice — take the blame. "Ice wanted me inside, I just couldn't breathe."

Anya ran her hands up and down Soleil's arms as if to warm her. "I overheard things I shouldn't have at my work, and the next thing I know, my roommate is dead and I'm on the run. That's how I ended up here, in Caspar. They were looking for a bartender." She took a couple of steps toward the clubhouse, her hand still on Soleil's arm.

"They killed your roommate?" Soleil's voice sounded faint.

Ice made a move toward her, wanting to wrap her in his arms, but the moment he did, Soleil stiffened and looked frightened. He detested that look on her face.

Anya sent him a quick flick of her lashes, a veiled reprimand, and he stopped immediately. Czar and Blythe were next, coming from the south, and Steele and Breezy had wound their way through Caspar to park beside Reaper's bike. Both women went straight to Soleil while their men went to Ice.

Czar indicated the clubhouse, clearly

457

wanting Ice to move ahead of him. He knew Savage and Absinthe were probably close. He didn't want Soleil outside when they drove in. He shook his head.

"They'll get her inside," Czar said. "Let them take care of her."

"It got messy. If she sees Savage, she might freak out and then I'll have to force her inside, and that will just get ugly. She's really shaken up, Czar. It isn't like she's been exposed to this kind of life before."

"You have to trust them, Ice, just like you trust us."

"Where's Lana? Or Alena? She trusts them."

"They left this morning to pick up supplies in Ukiah for the restaurant and club-house."

Ice swore and reluctantly went with the men inside. The moment the door swung closed, he went to the window to watch the women with Soleil. Blythe was the one they all counted on for calm in the middle of the storm, but he could see both Breezy and Anya were equally as composed.

It took only a couple of minutes before the group was coming up the walkway to the door. Ice hadn't realized his heart was working overtime. He glanced at his twin, Storm, and shook his head. Storm placed a cup of coffee on the table.

"Got your text. I'm sorry this happened, Ice. You must be worried that they found her."

Ice was more worried that she would want to leave him. He had no idea how he'd react. Everything in him rejected the idea of losing her. She'd been getting comfortable with the club. He'd made a point of making certain she knew his married brothers and their wives.

Reaper had been first, Savage's brother, who pretty much scared the crap out of anyone who looked at him, much like Savage did. Reaper was married to Anya. She worked as a bartender for the club. Soleil liked Anya quite a lot, and they spent time together.

Breezy was married to Steele, their vice president. Breezy had been born into the life and was very comfortable with their ways. They had a son, and she rarely went anywhere without the boy. He'd been kidnapped and taken from her by her former club and she still had a difficult time having the boy out of her eyesight. Steele was the same way. Breezy took point at every party and helped ease the other women into the club life. Ice was grateful that when they got the call-out, they'd both come.

Lissa, married to Casimir, and Lexie, married to Gavriil, were rarely available, as both worked long hours elsewhere. She hadn't yet met either of them, but he hoped those introductions would come soon.

Then there was Blythe, Czar's wife. There was something peaceful about Blythe, but she also gave off the aura of being able to solve any problem. She was the kind of woman that could be counted on. She was accepting, nonjudgmental and thoughtful before she spoke. The men and women in the club looked to her in a crisis.

As far as Ice was concerned, this was the biggest crisis he could have. It had to be handled delicately. Soleil had somehow become his world, and it wasn't the sex, as much as he'd like to make it that. It was her. The woman. He needed her in his life.

"I can't believe this shit. It had to happen right in front of her."

The door opened and the women came into the common room. Storm had lit a fire in the stone fireplace, driving the chill from the large space. As soon as they were inside, Keys brought hot coffee to one of the tables, placing mugs out for the women. Soleil looked surprised as she thanked him.

Ice found himself relaxing just a little bit. His brothers and sisters were rallying around him, taking his back, making certain his woman felt the loyalty and strength of family.

"Why are these men after you?" Blythe asked.

Ice knew Blythe was fully aware of Soleil's situation. Czar rarely kept her out of the loop and never if she asked him a direct question. She was keeping Soleil's attention centered on the fact that someone wanted her dead and the club was protecting her.

"I got entangled with a con artist. He's part of a ring of con men who target wealthy women. They marry them, murder them, and get the money." Soleil blurted out the truth, her hands cradled around the coffee cup.

Her face was so pale, again, it was all Ice could do not to go to her. He wanted to be the one to comfort her. She needed comfort. She looked too fragile for their life. What had he been thinking bringing her into a world of violence when she couldn't possibly understand it? He'd been selfish, thinking only of himself, not of her. He thought sex would be enough to satisfy her. He could make her feel special. Feel beautiful. Desirable. He hadn't thought about the rest of it, the way she would have to live. An actual relationship. The others had warned

461

him, but he hadn't cared, thinking only of what he needed, and now she was paying the price.

"That's so awful," Breezy said. "I don't understand people. My own father and brother kidnapped my son, Zane, and beat me up when I tried to stop them. They threatened to kill him if I didn't kill Czar and some others. That was my *father*, Soleil. Thank God I found Steele again." She gestured around the room with a faint smile. "They're all a little screwed up, but they have a code they live by. They take care of family, and they're good at it. I'm so thankful Savage and Absinthe were with you."

Soleil's hands shook so badly she had to put the coffee cup onto the table. "Savage beat this one man horribly. It was terrible to see. I'd never seen anything like it. Not even on television. He was brutal."

Ice winced, not wanting Soleil to relive the experience. He wanted her to shut the door on it and never talk about it. Never think about it.

Anya rubbed her shoulders. "Honey, what was going on? Why did he do that?"

Ice realized, again, they were allowing Soleil to sort through the images to get past her shock, past the blood, and see what had

462

actually taken place.

Soleil glanced at Ice, who gave her a faint, encouraging nod. "Everything happened so fast. Like seconds. The man was angry at the one Absinthe was questioning and he had a gun. He tried to shoot Savage."

Ice knew Savage hadn't taken that gun on purpose. They had no choice but to kill the men. They knew that. Knowing Soleil was with him, he had to give them an excuse to do so. He'd deliberately gone up against an armed man with his bare hands in order to give Ice an explanation for his woman. He also knew if he tried to thank Savage, the man would just look at him with his flat, cold eyes, shrug his shoulders and act like he had no idea what Ice was talking about.

"He had a gun?" Breezy echoed, wanting to make that clear, to keep the image uppermost in Soleil's mind.

Soleil nodded, a frown on her face. "Yes, and he tried to shoot Savage. I was so scared for all of them. Everyone. And if they were hurt it would be my fault. He shot off several rounds, I think. I'm actually not certain because they were struggling. Savage kept hitting him, especially when he turned the gun toward me."

"Oh no, Soleil," Blythe said. "You must have been so frightened."

463

"I could barely see or think. I was frozen to the ground and couldn't move. I actually thought about it, that I should move, but I couldn't. Savage kept punching him until the man turned the gun back on him. It was awful."

"Czar," Ice said very softly, making certain that he drifted completely across the room, away from Soleil and the women. "There's some connection between Winston's con men and the pedophile ring we've been hunting."

Czar frowned and turned to look at Soleil. "You're certain."

"Absolutely. The men there were members of the pedophile ring, yet they were hunting Soleil. Absinthe questioned one of them, and he stated they were looking for her. They even told us who gave her up and what club he was in."

Czar stared out the window for a few minutes, his fingers drumming on the bar top where he stood at the very end of the curved bar. "This isn't good, Ice. Even if the ring we're after stumbled across Winston's search for her and put her together with us, that means she has both rings hunting her."

Ice nodded. "Exactly. Whatever the reason, she's in more danger than I first realized."

Czar turned to face the room, watching the way his wife gently touched Soleil's hand to comfort her. "Women are magic, Ice."

Ice wasn't going to argue with that. "I have to agree. I don't want her to leave me over this. I don't honestly know what I'd do."

"She isn't going to leave you," Czar said. "But it might be uncomfortable for a while." He turned his head to look back at Ice. "If you want advice, I would say spend a little time on your relationship. You married her, Ice. You can't just take. You have to let her know who you are. You have to give her that. Eventually, it isn't all about sex. There are going to be times you might not be able to have sex. Or the spark wears off for a while and it fades to a slow burn. You have to have something else. Give her something else."

Ice stopped himself from shaking his head. Czar was right. He knew it, but the idea left his insides tied up in knots. He couldn't look at the reasons too closely, so he turned the subject back to what he was most comfortable with. He was a hunter, and he was at his best when he was hunting.

"We need to find the connection between the two rings, and I need to pay Fred from the Venomous club a little visit."

"The run is coming up," Czar reminded. "Their club will be one of the clubs there. You want to take care of Fred before the run or during? We'll have to put that on top of the list just due to time constraints."

"During. We won't chance cops singling us out, putting us in the same space as his fuckin' dead body."

"Sounds good."

Ice nodded. The door opened, and Savage and Absinthe walked in. Savage glanced at his brother first and gave a small nod, letting him know he was fine. Both men immediately came to their president to report.

"Were you seen on your way back?" Czar asked.

"We were riding together on an old logging road not far from here, and a man in an SUV was out cutting wood. He wasn't supposed to be there, and we kept going and he pretended not to see us," Absinthe answered for both. "Even if he's asked, we were close to home and just out riding the roads like we normally do."

"That's good," Steele said. He'd joined them. The other members were pushing closer as well.

"Let's take this into the other room," Czar said. He signaled to Fatei, one of their most trusted prospects, to watch the door, ensuring Soleil suddenly didn't take it into her mind to make a break for it, and then went into their meeting room.

"There's a tie-in between the ring we're looking to take down and these con artists that target wealthy women," Czar announced to everyone when they were seated around the table.

"What in the hell would pedophiles and men looking to murder wealthy women have in common?" Keys asked.

"I can start looking," Code said. "Get the computer to search any commonality between the names we have. Soleil gave me a few names, and we have a good number in the pedophile ring. I've started a database. The search might turn up a connection somewhere."

"How's Soleil holding up?" Master asked.

"She's shaken up," Ice conceded. He didn't want the others to think she wasn't a good old lady. She was. He had known she had no experience with violence. They'd grown up in it. Brutality was a way of life for them. "She's never witnessed anything like that before."

"You killed them right in front of her," Steele reminded. "Each of you put a bullet in one of their heads. If the cops come around, and a good investigator might

467

uncover that they were searching for her, will she be able to stand?"

Ice honestly didn't know. He wanted to believe that she would, but how could he know? If she told the cops the truth, he and Savage and Absinthe would be going to prison for a very long time. Inwardly he cursed. He needed to do what Czar said. He should have already been giving himself to her in the way he'd insisted she give herself to him.

"I don't know." He was honest. He had to be. It wasn't just his life, it was the lives of the two men he called brothers.

There was a long silence while most looked down at the table. There was a pretty big threat hanging over their heads, and normally the club removed all threats. Ice's stomach began to churn. No one was removing Soleil. If the suggestion even came up, he was walking out, grabbing his woman and taking off.

"Hopefully the women will do their jobs," Czar said. "Ice, you get a handle on this — and fast. We can't expect her to know our ways just because you've been fucking her brains out for the last month. You instruct her. Teach her. Her loyalty has to be to you and the club. You get me?" There was a ruthless note in Czar's voice. One all of

468

them recognized immediately.

Ice nodded. "Absolutely. Consider it done." He'd been the one to make the mistake, not Soleil. She hadn't done anything wrong. He had to make certain that she didn't.

"Have Lana and Alena help you. Soleil seems to trust them, and they like her. Alena is already hoping for a niece. That's another thing," Czar continued. "You were big on telling Steele to keep Breezy knocked up; get it done if that's what it's going to take. Soleil is married to you, that makes her one of us. No one wants anything to happen to her, but I can't have a sword hanging over the heads of any of you."

Ice stood up slowly. "Nothing is going to happen to her." He put his hands on the table and leaned toward his president, ignoring the restraining hand of his twin. "I hope you understand me. All of you. Nothing is going to happen to my wife."

Savage stood up as well, immediately drawing the attention of all of them. He rarely spoke. "Soleil is innocent in all this. She actually did very well. It all happened in the space of less than five minutes and she didn't throw up. She didn't run. She didn't start screaming. She just needs a little time to adjust. I'm the one with the sword hanging over my head and I'm willing to risk it."

"I am as well," Absinthe agreed.

The knots in Ice's stomach began to relax. Czar put both hands on the table and shoved his chair backward until he could stand. "Well, I'm not. Clean this mess up with your wife, Ice. No one is going to take down three of my brothers because she was brought in before she knew what she was getting into."

The knots were back in full force. Ice turned on his heel and left the meeting room.

FOURTEEN

Ice stood for a long time staring out the window of the pool room. He'd brought Soleil home and they'd had a quiet lunch together. She'd said she wanted to swim. He knew he was going to have to talk to her. Break the silence between them. He'd put it there, not her. This was one of those defining moments when he was going to make it work or everything was going to fall apart. He turned back to look at his woman.

Soleil cut through the water like she was born there. Whatever she chose to do, she did very well. She'd told him that she had lots of time to practice the things she was interested in. Swimming appealed to her, and every hotel she stayed or lived in had a pool. It was significant to him that she wore a bra and underwear instead of swimming naked. She didn't have a suit because he hadn't thought to buy her one. They still didn't have her things because they hadn't

471

gone near her place in San Francisco.

"Come on out of there, princess, before you turn into a prune," he called.

She glanced up at him, did another lap and then swam to the stairs. He handed her a towel and watched her dry off.

"I'm sorry about this morning, Soleil," he said quietly, meaning it. "I've never told you about myself. I should have given you so much more. Something for you to hang on to so you'd trust me to do whatever was necessary to protect you at all times from anything, including being an accessory to any kind of violent or criminal act that takes place anywhere near you."

She stopped in the act of drying her leg, looking up at him. "They were after me. They clearly said so, Ice. I put all of you in a terrible position. Savage could have been killed. All of you could have been killed. I've shot a gun. I'm very good at it, but after watching what unfolded so fast, I realized I wouldn't have pulled the trigger. I was horrified when I saw all of you kill them. It was so terrible. And it happened so fast. So unbelievably fast." She shook her head and her hands trembled again. "I need to get dressed."

He knew she felt vulnerable without her clothes. He'd felt that way a long, long time

472

ago, when he'd *been* vulnerable. Before Czar. Before they'd taken back control. He trailed after her as she took the stairs back up to their room. He liked being behind her when she walked, especially since her panties were see-through and showed her firm cheeks to perfection. It took restraint not to reach out to claim what was his. He wasn't going to allow himself to get off track or diverted because he didn't want to go where he knew he had to.

Ice waited until she had rinsed off in the shower and come out fully dressed. He gestured toward the comfortable chairs positioned in front of the fireplace. "It's very understandable that you would be horrified by violence, Soleil. Especially that brutal, that fast."

"None of you hesitated, not even for a second. I blinked and there were three dead men. Then you all were ready to leave, and I was still trying to breathe."

"You grew up very sheltered. You didn't think of it like that because you were alone so much, but no one would dare touch you. You didn't have to worry about where your next meal was coming from, you just had everything there."

Ice rubbed his thigh, back and forth, trying to stop the churning in his stomach. He rarely opened the door into his childhood. He felt it creaking open, his personal nightmare. Immediately, his temperature dropped, and his heart began to race. Cold sweat broke out on his forehead and trickled down his chest. He took a breath. He just had to get it done. Get it over.

"My parents were murdered by a man who felt very threatened by their political views. His name was Sorbacov and he was a very powerful man in Russia. At the time, he backed a certain candidate for the presidency, and he got rid of any opponent to his choice. When he killed the parents of his political enemies, he took their children to one of four schools to train them to become assets for his country. That was really code for assets for him. He oversaw the schools and directed his agents — us — where he wanted them to go, to those he wanted them to kill."

Ice kept his gaze fixed on her face. Her chair was angled toward him and her eyes had jumped to his. He saw trepidation there, but mostly compassion. Soleil was all about that emotion. She had gone very still.

Shit. He'd been such an idiot not sharing anything about his life with her. If he gave her anything, it was done so casually, as if the tidbit meant nothing. This meant something to her. He reached for her hand and immediately brought her palm to his thigh, his thumb sliding back and forth across her knuckles. He needed that connection to her.

"Alena was a baby, an infant really. Storm and I were toddlers. Unfortunately, we were striking, all three of us. Our unusual eyes and hair made us prime targets for the pedophiles running the school Sorbacov sent us to. He liked little boys. More, he liked to see little girls hurt. The school was the perfect playground for him, and with our looks, he wasn't going to give us up."

She was beginning to register what he was saying, the vile truth of his past. Her breath caught, and her expression was one of horror. He kept doggedly on.

"They ran the school as if we were being taught to be assets, but they didn't expect us to live, so we weren't taught much about society outside the walls of the schools. The first thing they did was take our clothes."

He leaned back in the chair, closed his eyes and tried not to let that little, terrified boy out. There were so many things to be terrified over, but losing her was the worst. He kept rubbing his thumb gently over her knuckles, needing the contact.

"I want to tell you about my past, Soleil, because I want to spend my life with you. If you want that as well, you have to know me. You have to know who I am and what shaped me into being this person." He took a deep breath. "I don't want to lose you, Soleil. It's taking a big chance giving this to you. The things I had to do to survive and to make certain Storm and especially Alena did will turn your stomach. They also shaped me into a pretty fucked-up mess of a human being."

Soleil moistened her lips and then nodded. "I married you, Ice, without knowing you, but I made a commitment to you when I knew exactly what I was doing. Did today shake me up? Yes. I had several things to think about. One, I put you in jeopardy. But two, how easily killing came to all three of you. I never thought of you like that. Savage, maybe, but Absinthe or you, not at all."

He understood. He hid the killer. Taking a life was instinctive in him. A survival trait. "We were 'pretty' and favorites of the instructors. They would rape us, pass us around. Beat us. Throw us back into the dungeon, broken, bloody and traumatized. Little Alena. She was just a baby. We couldn't stop them." He shook his head and looked away from her, not wanting her to see the rage that sometimes consumed him. "Czar was only a kid as well, but older by a few years, and everyone looked to him to find us a way out." He shook his head, trying not to allow the bile to rise.

He couldn't look at her now. He could only stare into the flames dancing in the fireplace. "There was no way out. They began to teach us how to have control. They did that by arousing us while we were being beaten. We were supposed to force our bodies to cooperate no matter how much it hurt. Sometimes it was the opposite, we weren't supposed to react when someone was arousing us. That training continued for years, day in and day out. Depending on who the instructors were and what type of sex they got off on, we were used and taught to be proficient at their games until those games were normal to us."

Her hand went to her throat in that defensive way she had. When he glanced at her, her eyes were wide with shock.

"Ice." She just murmured his name. Softly. Lovingly.

The sound of it wrapped him up in something safe. He wasn't used to that feeling, and it nearly undid him. He needed distance from his past. He expected her to reject him for many reasons, one of the biggest that he'd been a victim of pedophiles for years. He knew there wasn't a lot of sympathy for male children, regardless of the fact that they were helpless and the act was rape. He forced himself to continue, to get to the worst. There was a lot of the worst.

"Along with sexual training, they trained us to be assassins, how to kill in a thousand different ways. To slip in and out of homes, crowds, over rooftops, vehicles, whatever it took. If we blew it during training, the beatings were horrendous. We used every kind of weapon. Learned about explosives, how to use them, how to build bombs and take them apart."

"I would think they would have become a little afraid of you."

Her statement gave him some hope. He wasn't coloring in the details because he couldn't look at them. He had to make her see just how desperate they were without opening those doors too wide and letting the monsters free.

"So many children died in front of us. We all were freezing. There were rats, bugs, little food, no medicine. It reeked. The longer we survived, the more they devised brutal, cruel tortures to use against us. The more children died and the worse our captors got, Czar decided we had to fight back, and he had us work on various skills or talents we had. He wanted each of us to contribute so that we all could get out of there alive."

"You said he was a child."

Ice nodded. "He was maybe ten or twelve, I don't know. He and Reaper had begun devising a plan even before we arrived. Reaper was around five at that time, I think. He and Savage were extremely popular, the way Storm, Alena and I were. I don't know if when we came, it took some of the pressure off them, but I doubt it. They were much more savagely beaten than us."

He fell silent, lifting her hand to his mouth, his teeth on the pads of her fingers, scraping back and forth gently.

"Savage and Reaper appear to be very scary men."

He nodded. There was no denying that fact. "They are for a reason. They had to be so the rest of us could get out of there alive. All of us had to be."

He was watching her out of the corner of his eye, and he caught the moment when knowledge was beginning to blossom. She went very still, and she briefly closed her eyes. Her expression was cautious.

"The instructors liked to force us to do different things in these sexual training sessions. One of the things I was supposed to do was get a girl excited sexually and show her off to others so they could get off. A group of pedophiles liked that kind of thing. I was getting older then, meaning twelve or thirteen, and the girls were thankfully a little older, not the usual six or seven, but still, it was abhorrent to me when I knew that all these men would be watching her and getting off. It sickened me. Still, if that's all they'd done, I could have taken it better."

He shook his head, looked down at her fingers and then brought them up to press them over his forehead. He just sat there, breathing hard. He couldn't look at her. He had never acknowledged his shame to anyone but Storm, who'd often been forced to participate.

"Ice, it's all right," she whispered softly, compassion in her voice.

He shook his head again, refusing to look at her. "It's not. I refused at first. They beat me. They beat Storm, but I wasn't going to do that to any of the girls. Then they took Alena from us. We fought them, but they were grown men and they stomped the hell out of us. She came back so broken. She was so little, and they used her like that . . ."

He looked at her. He had to. Right in the eyes. "I would have done anything to save her, including selling everyone else down the river. I traded my soul for my sister. I felt like I had no choice. I agreed to do what they said. The worst was in the beginning it sickened me, but then, after a while, it began to arouse me. I liked seeing whatever girl I was given excited, knowing what we were doing could arouse others. That she could do that with her sexuality. I don't know, it all got mixed up in my brain. We were turned into killers — and sexual beings. Not much else. That went on for too many years, Soleil, and it fucked me up permanently."

"Because you still like other men to see you with a woman."

Her voice was neutral. He couldn't tell if she condemned him or not, and there was a lot to condemn him for. He'd learned to arouse the girls to a fever pitch, wanting it to be easier on them when they had to be with the men waiting. He hated himself for that. He despised himself for ever becoming aroused when it was taking place. He really hated himself that he was forever fucked up beyond saving. He swung back to look into the flickering flames.

"Yes." She might as well know the truth. "I *need* other men to see my woman when she's sexy as hell. I want them to want her. To know she's only mine and goes home with me. Not all the time, but I need it some of the time. I need to know we're in risky

481

places and she'll still get on her knees and let me do her."

"So, it's about what she's willing to do for you as well."

He thought that over. It was. He needed to know she would risk everything for him, do anything, the way he'd done for his family. In a weird convoluted way, he felt less alone. He nodded his head.

"You do realize that you had no real choice, Ice. Alena was your sister. Your choice was to allow monsters to hurt her over and over until they killed her or do what they said. If you didn't do it, they would have forced someone else to do it. More, they would have hurt those other girls anyway. They were monsters. There was no good choice. You wanted Alena to survive."

"She survived. Lana survived. No other girls. Not one of them." His voice shook, and he cleared his throat. He hurt all over, as if he'd been the one to fight with someone, not Savage.

"Alena did survive, Ice. You did that."

"We did it. All of us together." He did look at her then. Once again, holding her gaze. "We began to kill them systematically. One by one. We crawled through vents. We went into sewers. We laid in wait and we took

482

them out, the worst ones first. Reaper and Savage did most of the killing, but all of us had to. All of us did our part to contribute information and help select each target. But we killed them one by one."

She didn't make a sound, nor did she look as shocked or as surprised as he'd thought she would. He went on determinedly because he was getting it all out at once. Everything. He didn't want her to leave him, but if she was going to, he had to find out now, because she didn't know it, but there was a definite threat to her from the president of their club.

"Sorbacov suspected it was the children killing the instructors. We thought he'd wipe us out, but instead he put in cameras everywhere. We learned to bypass those cameras. He took Reaper and nearly killed him, torturing him to see if he would give up those doing the killing. You have to remember, it was one dead instructor here, one there. Planning took time. Making certain not to leave any trace evidence took time. Sorbacov really didn't know if he had a vindictive serial killer in the school or if it was us."

"He tortured Reaper?"

"For days," Ice confirmed. "When he didn't break, he brought in Savage. It was far worse for Savage. And they did that shit right in front of Reaper. I knew I could be next because I had Storm and Alena. I tried to think what I would do if they took Alena. I might have killed myself. I wouldn't have given up the others, but I couldn't stand the thought of what they'd do to her. Preacher was in the same boat. He's Lana's older brother. He was as concerned as I was. I think all of us were. We didn't expect Sorbacov to let it go without killing Reaper and Savage, but he did. None of us thought they'd live, but they have wills of iron."

Silence filled the room. He could hear her breathing softly. She hadn't pulled her hand from his, and he rubbed her palm back and forth on his thigh. She let him. She had told him she liked having time to think things through, but he wanted her to say something immediately. If she was going to pass judgment, he was going to fill in details. He didn't want to relive them, but he would. To try to hold on to her, he would. His heart beat too hard. He could barely force air through his lungs. He brought her hand up to his chest and rubbed in an effort to try to get his body working again.

"I'm so sorry you went through all of that, Ice. That all of you went through it. It certainly explains why you're all so strong. I don't think anyone could have survived such an ordeal if they weren't strong."

"We're all fucked the hell up," he said, his heart accelerating more.

"Honey, don't you realize every single person in the world is screwed up in some way? You fought back in the only way open to you. I would have hopefully found the strength to do the same. The fact that you're alive is a tribute to you. To who you are."

Her voice. Soft. Intimate. Telling him more than the words she uttered. She wasn't going to leave him. She was going to stay and be there with him.

"I can see why all three of you were so skilled and fast at what you did. I would still be making up my mind on what to do."

"Czar is trying to get us to live within society as best we can. The problem is, none of us know or understand half the rules. Blythe tries, but the rules don't make sense to us. We spent a good part of our lives naked. When we had sex, it was safer to do so with one another around. We protected one another. It's difficult to change the conditioning. All of us were trained in some sexual way, or the trauma has given some of us disturbing traits society says are kinky or wrong. It makes it difficult to ever feel as if we can assimilate into a civilian population."

He wasn't going to say what those things the others had were because he was only giving her himself. He wanted her to accept him regardless of his past, or that he was also conditioned to thinking first to kill if threatened, not to talk or call the cops. They would never get used to dealing with the police. They were a closed society, and they protected one another vigorously.

He wanted her to understand, he had tried, at first, to fight that conditioning when it came to sex, but it was too in-grained, and it had been the only way to get his cock to cooperate with him when he tried to force himself to feel something. Maybe because it was natural to have an erection around her, he might not need it every time. So far, he hadn't.

"The cops might come asking questions, Soleil. You're not just my wife. You're part of this club. We don't talk to law enforce-ment. If Czar wants them to know some-thing, he'll tell them. We try not to lie if we can help it, but we don't ever give one another up. You have to understand, that's a sacred rule. It's part of our code. We never give one another up, no matter the cost. That's what got us out. We did it by sticking together. If one was going down, we all were."

She nodded. "I understand. I've never had a family, Ice. I never had anyone standing for me. I've never been a part of anything. Or anyone. I see the value of your club and the loyalty to one another. Why you're such a strong family. It's something I've always longed for. All of you have had one another for years. I'm just seeing the care you give one another. Blythe, Anya and Breezy were wonderful to me. Being treated like family is something I treasure, and I don't take it for granted. Believe me, I want to be part of that. But mostly, I want to be with you, and I want to be someone you can be proud of."

He could breathe again. The air moved through his lungs, in and out. His heart slowed to a normal pace. He tightened his hand around hers. "Savage and Absinthe stood for you today, Soleil, and if you knew Savage the way I do, you'd know that's huge. He stays apart from everyone else. He's quiet, rarely speaks. But he's always there for the rest of us."

"Why is he always a little apart, Ice? I've noticed the way he is."

Ice shrugged. "The things we endured in that place shaped us. There's no getting away from it, no matter how hard we try." He looked at her. "You quiet the demons for me. When I told you I didn't have natural erections before you, I didn't. One look at you in that little sundress, standing across the street, with your tits and that ass, I thought I was going to embarrass myself right there on the street." He couldn't keep the awe out of his voice. "I know I can't keep my hands off you, and that has to get old for you, but seriously, baby, it feels like the first time every time we're together. Sometimes it's so fuckin' good I think my head is going to explode."

Her laughter surprised him. "Well, don't let that happen. I like sex with you. Actually, I love it, but an exploded head might put a damper on our sex life." Her fingers twisted so she could hold on to his hand. "Baby, let's go downstairs. I want to show you something."

"Got a couple more things to discuss, and they're important."

He had his phone in his hand and was texting Czar, sending him a thumbs-up. If their phones were ever checked, there was nothing to connect them to the crime that had been committed miles from where they lived. He sent out a call to Absinthe and Code. He needed them to come as soon as possible.

Ice wanted whatever papers were needed filed on Soleil's behalf. The moment they did, no doubt Winston's lawyer would insist on a well checkup and they would try to get a hearing in front of whichever judge owed them favors or was part of the con artist ring. They had to have someone on their payroll.

"We can talk downstairs," she insisted and stood up.

He kept possession of her hand, even when she tried to pull away from him. Soleil only tried once, and then she sent him a quick grin, shaking her head. The stairs were wide enough for the two of them to walk down the sweeping staircase to the first floor together. She went through the dining room to the kitchen, and right on past the refrigerator to the door there. She opened it and stepped back. The pantry was fairly empty, just rice and potatoes as well as flour jumping out at him.

Soleil closed the door and went to the fridge. Inside, fresh vegetables were over-flowing, along with a couple of cuts of meat, different types of berries and melons as well as other food items, all fresh. She closed that door and pointed to the counter where more fruit was in a bowl.

Leaning one hip against the center aisle, she looked at him. "What does that tell you, Ice?"

He knew his face had to look as blank as he felt.

"You aren't paying attention. You think I have one foot out the door, that I'm not fully committed to you or to your family. I told you I didn't cook. Where do you think the groceries came from, and how do you think I got them?"

He frowned. This was obviously a trick question, one women conjured up just to make men crazy. "Sorry, babe. Not following."

"I've been taking cooking lessons from Alena. What did you think I was doing with her when you were doing whatever mysterious thing you do that I'm not supposed to know about?"

Like tracking down the pedophile ring in San Francisco. Or the ring of con artists. No, he wasn't about to talk to her about that or what they planned to do to them all.

"I don't know, princess. Talking? Women like talking together."

She rolled her eyes. "And the meals that have been improving? Did you think they were just getting that way with luck?"

Definitely a trick question. "I didn't really think about it."

"I spent several hours at least three times a week on cooking lessons, honey. For you.

For us. For our life together. I want to make a home for you. I've been doing that. Today scared me, but not for the reasons you think. I'm a processor. I needed time to run through everything that happened. When I do, I'm used to pacing. It helps. I'm really used to being alone when I do. You have to remember, you're the only person in my life I've ever spent this much time with. The point I'm making is, I have no intentions of leaving you. You have to learn to trust in that, just as much as I have to learn to trust in you."

The relief was tremendous. He rubbed his chest again, right over his heart. "I'm going to piss you off, baby. More than once or twice."

"I'm well aware."

She sounded so droll he couldn't help but laugh. Love swamped him. He put his arms around her and pulled her tight against him, nuzzling her neck. "We're going on a run. Have I explained what that is?"

She shook her head. "You haven't exactly explained, but I've seen bikes riding together."

"This one will be particularly large. Several clubs will be riding. It's a charity drive the Diamondbacks put on every year. We'll be riding behind them. You have to wear the jacket I give you with our colors. You never go anywhere without us. You stick close to me at all times. We'll have fun, so don't look alarmed, but you have to follow the rules I lay down."

She nodded. "Of course, Ice."

"You have to remember, our entire club will defend you. We're very good at what we do. If we have to defend you against a Diamondback, that will bring their entire club down on us. That's the way it works, even if their member is at fault. We'll be running for the rest of our lives if that happens."

"I understand."

He caught her hand and led her away from the kitchen back toward the great room. He liked the furniture there. They sank onto the comfortable couch. She leaned into him and put her head on his shoulder.

"What else did we have to talk about?" She reached out to thread her fingers through his.

He liked that. Liked that after everything he'd told her, she was matter-of-fact. It wasn't like he didn't know how compassionate a woman she was. He did. Everything he'd told her was the truth, but he'd chosen his words as carefully as possible. He'd told her the least amount that he could, even while looking for the best way to lay it out for her to elicit that deep empathy he was counting on to keep her with him.

"We need to establish Absinthe as your lawyer immediately. These people are playing for keeps. They found you, and they're going to make every move possible in order to keep you off-balance. The best way to get at you is to have a doctor or someone imply that mentally you've had a breakdown and you need care. They'll do that by saying you're under my influence and you would never marry a man like me."

"I didn't think about that," she conceded.

"The lawyer will file papers to have you go before a judge, and that judge will be his judge, the one in his pocket. You'll be remanded into the loving arms of your fiancé while they unravel the paperwork and annul our marriage or declare it invalid."

Her face had whitened with every word he said. "Ice. Oh my God. I don't want to be anywhere near him."

"That's not going to happen. Absinthe will see to that. He's amazing at what he does. Let's just start with the necessary paperwork. You have to make certain the world knows that Absinthe is your attorney and anyone else acting in your name is doing so without your consent. He'll find the lawyer in Vegas you used to help you get rid of Monroe, in fact I believe Code has already done so, and he'll back you up that you fired Donald Monroe."

"When are we doing this?"

"Absinthe is on his way."

"Do you think they'll try to kill me before I can file these papers?"

He ruffled her hair. "Baby, they did try. They tried this morning. That was their attempt. They sent four killers after you. I think you're safe for at least today. Winston doesn't strike me as the type to think that fast on his feet. He has too bad of a temper."

"He isn't the boss," she reminded. "They threatened him, Ice. They said if he screwed up, he would be dead, not me."

"Well, that's something. Maybe we can get the boss man so angry with good old Winston, they do him in."

"I can only hope." Soleil rubbed her face against his arm like a little cat.

He cupped the side of her face and turned it to him. He'd needed to kiss her since early morning. "You're always going to be my princess, Soleil."

"I want that, Ice," she admitted.

There were stars in her eyes. That look he craved — as if she worshipped him and the ground he walked on. She looked at him as if there were no other men in the world, certainly not worthy of her. He was it. The only one. Her only one.

He brought his lips to hers. Gently. Reverently. Just a brush. A whisper. His tongue touched that curve along the bottom. He knew it intimately. Knew the taste and texture of her. He felt that touch all the way to his soul. She parted her lips for him, and his tongue swept into the velvet heat. That place that took him away from his past and the dark demons that were always poised so close, waiting to devour him.

Kissing Soleil was like stepping into a different world. Fireworks played behind his eyes, as sensations poured through his body. He was gentle because his woman deserved gentle, but as always, that rapidly developed into a firestorm of flames and need, until he was devouring her. He loved the taste of her. He loved the way her body melted into his and her mouth gave back that scorching-hot fire until he was burning from the inside out.

When he lifted his head, Ice knew he was so far gone, there was no going back. His relationship with Soleil wasn't about sex anymore. He hadn't kept it there. There was no keeping their bond to that, not when just looking at her made him happy. His thumbs rubbed gently over her beautiful cheek-bones.

"You're going to have to surface, baby."

"I know. But this has been a beautiful dream, Ice. You gave me this last month, and it's been the loveliest time I can ever remember having."

He heard Absinthe's Harley come up their drive. He wasn't alone, which didn't surprise Ice. They were all trying to get Soleil used to them, especially after what had happened that morning. At least the attack site was a good distance from their compound. There had been too many disappearances lately, and the sheriff kept coming back to the bar with questions.

They all liked Jonas Harrington, the local sheriff. He appeared easygoing. He knew just about everyone up and down the coast. He knew their families. He was well liked for a reason. He was a good man. On the other hand, he was very intelligent and good at his job. Outwitting a man like him wasn't easy. They didn't need him to find a connection between the dead men and Soleil — or their club.

Absinthe and whoever had come with him parked their bikes outside and came to the front door. As a rule, no one bothered knocking, and they didn't now. They just walked in. They were used to nudity, to anything, even private moments they might stumble across.

Ice used his arm to keep Soleil in place when she would have stood up and probably put distance between them. He wanted her to get used to the club members' ways with one another so that she'd eventually be just as easy around them as he was.

"Absinthe, Code, Mechanic, come on in." Ice waved them toward the chairs. "We were just talking about filing the papers and making certain Winston and his crew don't get ahead of us."

Absinthe pulled one of the comfortable chairs around to face them, seating himself opposite Soleil. Code set up close to the end table so he could set his computer there. Mechanic stretched out, legs in front of him, looking for all the world as if he were lazy and about to go to sleep. It was a very deceptive pose.

"Princess, you're comfortable with Absinthe, Code and Mechanic, right?"

"Of course." She sat up straight. "Thanks for coming here, instead of me having to go to the clubhouse. It's been a little shocking today. I needed . . ." She looked around her.

"Something familiar. I just needed to be home."

Ice's heart clenched hard in his chest and his stomach did a slow roll. She thought of their house as home. He couldn't have asked for a better gift. He'd needed to hear that. He had been secretly worried that after he told her about their past, she might think less of his brothers and treat them differently, but if there was a difference, she was more open to their friendship than ever.

"Any opportunity to get on my bike is a good one," Absinthe said.

"I'm sorry I freaked out on all of you earlier," Soleil continued.

"Babe. Really?" Absinthe returned. "There was every reason to freak out. Glad you're feeling better."

She smiled, and Ice threaded his fingers through her hand. Absinthe got down to business, taking her step by step through the process — and extensive paperwork — of hiring him as her personal lawyer. His credentials were impeccable. Code had seen to that. From hiring him, they went next to making certain to file papers stating that Donald Monroe had been fired as of the date a month earlier she'd officially terminated him. Then more papers declaring he was to cease and desist from acting falsely on her behalf and that he had no authority whatsoever to act on her behalf.

"You're going to have to make a public appearance soon, but let's give it a few days so we can see what their reaction is," Absinthe advised.

"Ice said it was possible they would demand some kind of competency hearing and they might have a corrupt judge and they'd get them to turn me over to Winston."

Absinthe's eyebrow shot up. He turned his head to look at Ice with cool eyes. Absinthe's eyes were so light blue they were like two crystals. At times they were strangely opaque, as if they could see through things, rather than their outward appearance. "You told her that? I can assure you, both of you, that won't happen. They can try. I even expect them to try, but they won't get away with it."

"But, Absinthe, if they have a corrupt judge . . ." Soleil looked and sounded scared.

Ice put his arm around her and pulled her close to his body. "Seriously, Soleil, do you think I'm the kind of man to let someone take my woman from me?"

Mechanic didn't open his eyes. "Or that we're the kind of club that allows some jack-off to take one of ours away and mess with her? Not happening."

Code looked up. He'd been busy ensuring everything Absinthe wanted was done. "Babe. Really? The first mention of a judge's name and I've got all I need to find out everything about him, especially if the name is the same one you gave us. We can take him down before he can put on his robes. And when we take someone down, we do it hard, so it's very difficult to get back up."

Ice sent him a look that said to shut the hell up. "You don't have to worry about those things, princess. Absinthe will do that for you, and he's very good at his job. I know because he brags all the time." He got the smile he'd hoped for. Soleil seemed to relax a little, the tension easing out of her slowly.

"Thanks, everyone. I honestly can't see what they think they're going to gain by running to authorities and making the fight public. When they kill me, won't people be just a little bit suspicious?"

"No one's killing you," Absinthe said. "Honey, I need you to let me take your wrist, and I want you to answer as truthfully as you can. Really think about your answers. This is important. I'm not expecting you to lie, there's no reason to, but sometimes your brain retains something buried deep, and I'll know and I can ask you more questions. That's why I said to really think carefully."

Soleil looked at Ice for direction. He nodded. Now, he was the one who had tension coiling deep, although he knew this wouldn't hurt her, no matter her answer. Absinthe leaned toward her and she extended her arm. He was careful to keep her comfortable, not making her stretch too far or lean forward. Absinthe loosely circled her wrist, but two fingers were over her pulse — that lifeline.

"Have you ever heard the names Yeger Kushnir or Basil Alanis before this morning? Have you met them? Did Winston ever mention them?"

Soleil frowned and nodded her head slowly. "Winston liked to go to fund-raising events, and he always wanted me to meet the right people. He gave me a list of names to memorize so I could be nice and smile and pretend we were all going to be friends. Kushnir was on the list. This morning I didn't mention it because, honestly, I didn't recognize him. When I first saw him, he was wearing a tux and looking — and acting — very sophisticated. But he was on the list."

She ran her palm up and down Ice's thigh,

revealing her nerves. "I'm sorry, Ice, I should have remembered. I couldn't hear what you were saying most of the time. I was pretty far away, and it happened so fast."

"Babe, look at me," Absinthe said. "No one's upset with you. The circumstances weren't the best. How did Winston know Kushnir?"

"They didn't really interact much. They stood next to each other at the bar, and I know they exchanged at least pleasantries. Kushnir looked at me a couple of times while they were talking."

Absinthe glanced at Ice. It was possible Winston was bargaining with Kushnir to see if it was worth his while to spare her life and sell her into the world of human trafficking. He'd make money on her as well as get rid of her, although it would be more complicated to get her money out of the trust.

"What do you know about him?" Absinthe persisted.

"Only that he owns a string of real estate businesses as well as an export business in San Francisco."

"Perfect for human trafficking," Mechanic muttered.

Absinthe ignored him. "Did Winston ever

talk about a connection with him? School? A past of any kind?"

She shook her head. "No. He actually didn't reveal much about himself at all. What he did tell me was never about his friends, only how difficult his childhood was."

"Difficult?" Absinthe pushed.

"He was very broken up when his parents divorced. He was seventeen, and he said it tore him up and he's never been over it."

"Tough life," Absinthe said, straightening up in his chair and letting go of her wrist. "So grateful I didn't have his problems growing up."

"Yeah," Mechanic confirmed. "I'm with you there."

Code made a rude noise and Ice laughed, leaning in to brush a kiss along Soleil's temple.

FIFTEEN

The roar of pipes was extremely loud as fifteen hundred motorcycles went down the highway and through small towns and large cities in formation, with more clubs joining them along the way. The entire Torpedo Ink club rode together. There were forty-five members and seven prospects. Ice had forgotten to tell Soleil the club had a second chapter in Trinity, and they came down to be supportive of the run. The Demons, a club they were allied with, rode directly behind them.

It was strange to ride with so many others wearing their colors. The twenty-five newer members had come from another one of the schools in Russia. Theirs had been brutal, but it had been a legitimate school to train the students as agents. Casimir Prakenskii, birth brother to Czar, had gone to Trinity to oversee their club, as the entire club had been patched over. Now, there was at least

504

one more club asking to be patched over as well. Czar hadn't met with them yet. He was leery of growing their club too fast. He didn't want any more attention called to them than was strictly necessary.

Each of the schools was different, but all trained the children of their political enemies to be assassins and spies for their country. Ice liked knowing those riding with him could handle themselves in any situation. They'd taken the time to get to know one another as well. That helped to make him feel comfortable enough to go on a run with them wearing the Torpedo Ink colors. They couldn't afford a hothead who would start fights that ended up in wars with other clubs.

Torpedo Ink did their best to stay under the Diamondbacks' radar. That had become impossible when they'd helped the club get back the Mendocino chapter's wife from kidnappers. Now, they all knew, the club was watching them closely.

Ice reveled in the roar of the pipes as they made their way down the highway. There was nothing like riding on a hot afternoon, surrounded by family and friends, knowing the party started when you set up your camp. Behind him, Soleil was wrapped around him, her tits pressed tightly into his back. He felt them in spite of the jacket he wore. He grinned remembering her little sniff of disdain when he showed her the "Property of Ice" on the back of her jacket and vest. Torpedo Ink. He fucking loved that.

She hadn't fought him on it, and he caught her twice running her hand lovingly over the patches on the back. She'd been on safaris before, but she hadn't actually roughed it camping. Czar had sent Fatei and Hitch ahead of them in the RV he'd acquired from somewhere, in the way Czar seemed to be able to get whatever he needed. If worse came to worst, Soleil could always sleep in the RV with Blythe. He hoped not. He had plans.

Ice patted Soleil's hand as he drove through the city with the formation of bikers. The lights were blocked off so there was a steady stream of motorcycles going through, instead of having to wait for lights. There was something majestic about all the bikes moving together. He loved being a part of that.

Soleil could quiet his demons just by being around him. Just with her smile alone. When he fucked her, she drowned out every vile act he'd ever committed or seen until there was only her soft skin and her hot body squeezing his like a silken vise, taking him to paradise. Riding with the others, her at his back, the vibrations of his bike going through him, he was having the best of his world.

It took hours for them to reach their destination. They stopped a few times to eat and use the bathroom, but for the most part, they kept going to reach their final goal. When they got to the massive campground, each club broke off and claimed their site, some as far from the Diamondbacks as possible. Ice didn't give a damn about them. He'd come to party. To have a good time. To show his woman they could have fun no matter where they were. To find the Venomous club and Fred, who Torpedo Ink had a very big score to settle with.

"It's hot," Soleil observed as she spun around in a wide circle, taking in everything.

Fatei had claimed a good space for them. He'd set up quite a few places for them to sleep, around each of the firepits. Ice deliberately chose a section for them toward the center, but just on the right edge that bordered another club's camp. He set up their sleeping bags and then snagged her hand so they could walk around, and he could show her where the bathrooms and showers were.

The sun was sinking, bathing the sky into all shades of orange, red and pink. He liked watching his woman when she walked. She looked classy. There was an innocence about her, even though she wore a tank where the lace just edged the top of her nipples. The tank was tight, but it had pulled down some in the front on the ride and there was no mirror for her to notice. He wasn't going to tell her because she looked sexy and he liked that.

Storm came up on the other side of Soleil and they walked her to the ladies' room. The line wasn't that long yet and she was able to get in fairly quickly. Alena and Lana appeared out of nowhere and slipped inside with her — just in case. Women could pick a fight just as easily as men. The bathroom was the one place Ice worried he couldn't protect her, but he had family, and they helped.

The three women returned together, talking softly, laughing at something Soleil had said, giving Ice plenty of time to look at what was his. She hadn't yanked up her top. He couldn't imagine that she hadn't looked into the mirror, but she'd left the lace right where it was — for him. He knew she had. She knew he liked showing her off, and she didn't mind being seen.

His body tightened. His cock became steel. His heart reacted, pounding in his chest. That part of him that he'd held aloof crumbled like tumbling bricks. He loved her. Loved everything about her, and he didn't even know when it had happened. He held out his hand to her, waiting to see her expression. Needing it.

Her gaze touched on his hand and then jumped to his face. His cock jerked so hard he was afraid of embarrassing himself. It throbbed and pulsed along to his heartbeat. That look was there. Reverence. Almost worship. The tip of her tongue slid around her lips, moistening them, making him ache even more. Her hand slipped into his and just that small touch of her skin against his nearly shattered him.

They began walking around all of the back campsites, taking a circular way back to theirs. More people had already set up, and they had to weave their way around the large groups. Fires sprang up. Laughter and the continual buzz of conversations were loud. A few men walked around with bottles of alcohol, tipping them up to drink healthy doses. Music was loud, vying for space in the air from various campsites. Women began to dance, swaying and laughing as they drank. The sky had darkened, but the first stars were out along with half of a moon. It was perfect.

Ice turned Soleil's head toward his and kissed her, letting her taste his need. His building lust. The desire running like molten lava through his veins. He slipped his hand inside her tank, feeling her tit. Her nipple. He tugged and pinched, rolled and twisted, all the while walking with her. When he lifted his mouth from hers, he touched his mouth to her ear.

"You're so fuckin' sexy, baby. I could do you right here." He meant it too. Right on the picnic table in the camp three sites out from theirs.

She smiled up at him, her heart in her eyes. "You know you can have me anytime, anywhere, honey."

His heart pounded so hard he thought it might burst through his chest. His cock echoed the pounding beat. It felt damn good to be alive. He kept her walking, but he didn't remove his hand from her tank, caressing and kneading that perfect breast. He lifted it free of the lace, amazed at the size and shape of her, exquisitely feminine.

Abruptly he stopped and turned her around to face him, his mouth hungry. He devoured that soft offering and instantly she cradled his head to her and arched her back to give him everything he wanted. He took the offering, sucking hard, flattening her nipple to the roof of his mouth, using the edge of his teeth, delivering little stinging nips to the top of that curve and around the curve to the side.

He lifted his head and grinned at her. "Goin' to leave some marks on you tonight, princess. You nice and bare for me like I like?" His hand slid between her legs to rub his thumb back and forth over the denim covering her mound. At her nod he continued. "Might write my name on you. Nice little strawberries right across your sweet little pussy."

He slung his arm around her neck and kept walking, enjoying the way she didn't put her tit back into her tank but left that round temptation out where anyone looking could see. Not only could they see how perfect it was, they could see his marks of possession all over the soft skin. Sexy as hell. He loved it.

When they reached the firepit closest to their bed, Ice snagged a bottle of whiskey and a place for them to sit by the fire. He positioned her between his legs, facing outward, her back to his chest, her hips wedged between his legs. He took a drink of the whiskey and then held the bottle to her mouth. She drank and then leaned her head back against him. When she did, her breasts jutted upward, so that the one uncovered seemed to glow in the firelight spilling over it.

He reached around her with both hands, pushing the tank down below her tits, freeing them from the bra she had insisted on wearing as they made the trip to the camps. Idly, listening to the music and the talk swirling around them, he caressed both breasts.

"Did you see Pierce?" Storm asked. "He's here and I heard he was looking for Alena."

The others looked at one another. Ice stilled inside, but he refused to allow anything to interfere with his enjoyment of the evening — or of his woman. He passed his twin the bottle. Storm took a drink and handed it to Soleil.

She tilted the bottle to her lips and some streamed down over her tits. "Oops. What a mess. I can't believe I did that."

Laughing at her ploy, Ice tilted her backward over his arm and bent his head to lick at the whiskey covering her left breast, the one without a single mark. He remedied that immediately, using his mouth, his teeth and tongue. He made certain to get every drop; after all, it would be a sin to waste any.

She was panting and squirming by the time he let her up. The firelight played over her body, exposing the high lift to her breasts and the marks on them. His hands framed them as he joined in the conversations going on around him.

Every now and then, just to keep her aware of him, he tugged and rolled each of her nipples, sometimes elongating them until her breath would catch. He went back to talking. The night wore on and more women shed their clothes. In the next camp, one woman was on her hands and knees with three men taking her at the same time. As entertainment went, it was pretty spectacular. The four were really into it.

One by one, his brothers and sisters drifted away to find their own amusement for the night, leaving him with Soleil. The music grew louder, and the whiskey tasted better. His cock went from aching to hurting. Ice eased his zipper down, freeing himself. He put his lips next to his woman's ear. "Jeans off now, princess. I'm in the mood to play."

He caught the hem of her tank and removed it easily. Her bra was next to go. She stood up and began to slowly push the denim from her hips, watching his face the entire time. She was beautiful in the light of the fire. She looked exotic, exactly what he called her — a princess offering her body to her conqueror.

His little exhibitionist. He loved that a part of her liked to be safe, but was turned on by being seen by others. She danced slowly for him, her body sultry as she shed her clothing, the firelight playing over her soft skin. He slid his jeans down his thighs, releasing his hungry monster and the tight balls that seemed to be burning out of control.

"Straddle my lap, princess," he whispered. "Facing away from me."

"You're so hard. I could suck you, Ice. I love the taste of you. The shape and feel of you. You're always so hot, and the weight of you on my tongue is sexy." Deliberately, she tempted him, crawling up his legs.

"You're sexy. I'll be fucking your mouth, but later. Right now, I'm going to give you something you're going to love. Do what I tell you."

Facing away from him, she straddled his thighs. He opened his legs farther, so that her thighs were forced to part wide, and her little pussy glistened in the firelight. She was already wet and slick with her liquid heat. He laid his hand on her belly, stroking caresses over her soft skin, his fingers creeping down to her bare lips to find the hot moisture so he could taste her.

"I love the way you look. All soft skin and tits." His hand came up under her right breast, sliding back and forth, rubbing and then kneading. "Look at you. So needy." He took another drink of whiskey and held it to her lips until she drank it down as well.

"Do you feel that burn, baby? It goes all the way down to your little pussy, doesn't it?" He licked her ear, then bit down on her earlobe. "Lean your head back against my shoulder, but I want you to look around. See if you can find someone watching us. Some man who might have a woman sucking him dry, or maybe he's all alone, but he needs to watch. He needs to see you just like this. So fuckin' sexy. Look, baby, tell me what you see."

His hand moved between her legs, rubbing up and down against her sensitive, already inflamed clit. He pushed something over it, a little button that buzzed ferociously. It was soft at first, that little stimulant, but it began to vibrate faster and harder. She bucked and gasped, her tits swaying with each jolt of her body. He pushed a finger into her tight channel and began to slide it in and out. A deliberate, slow burn.

"Tell me what you see."

"A man directly across from us in the other camp. He's got his cock out and he's masturbating. Watching us. He can't take his eyes off of us."

"Anyone else?"

"More than one. But one man is watching while a woman is going down on him just like you said. His face is all flushed now and he's pumping into her mouth faster."

"He's paying more attention to you than to her, isn't he?" He whispered it in her ear, more like a sinful temptation, leading her down that road while he pushed a second finger into her and turned up the vibe on her clit.

She gasped and arched.

"Look straight at him. Let him know you're watching him get off while he's watching you get off. If he connects, don't look away. Bring your hands up and play with your nipples the way I do. I want you to be a little rough."

He kept his voice low, like velvet, giving her the instructions and watching her get off on them. Her body was hot silk, scorching him, her firm cheeks squirming around his cock. He pumped his fingers in and out of her, feeling the tension coiling tighter and tighter.

"Is he watching, baby? He thinks you're the sexiest woman alive, doesn't he? He can't take his eyes off of you, right?" His mouth wandered down the side of her neck, stopping so he could use his teeth on her. He loved how her body sent fresh waves of liquid around his fingers when he bit down on her.

"Yes." She gasped it.

She was bucking her hips, riding his fingers frantically as he turned up the vibration on her clit. Just before she came, he stopped the clit button and pulled his fingers free, making a show of licking them and then holding them in front of her mouth so she would finish licking them clean. Her hand crept down her belly toward her pussy and he stopped her.

"I have more surprises, for you. You'll come hard for me, I promise." He bit her earlobe again and then collected her liquid, the gold he craved. He coated his finger and the small little vibrator he'd brought as a surprise. Once more, he started the clit button on the lowest setting and then shifted her so he could slide his finger between her cheeks.

"Ice." She panted as he pushed the vibrator into that forbidden little star.

"You'll love this, baby. I promise you." Once more he began to bring her up slowly, turning both vibrators up so that ripples moved like waves through her body, until she was nearly undulating with need and a fine sheen made her body glow. He gave her his fingers, three this time.

"Watch him, baby. Is he looking at you? Can he see the strain on your face? That desperate need? That's what I see. You're lost in the feeling. Nothing matters, does it, but this. How I make you feel. How your body is desperate for what I can give you. He can watch you. He can want you, but only I have you. Ride my fingers and let him pretend it's him you're riding. Let him wonder if my cock is in your ass and you're riding it while I'm taking you apart. You're all mine. Every single part of you. Pussy. Mouth. Ass. He knows that now. He wishes it were him."

He kicked up the vibrators and her body nearly seized as she came apart. She cried out, oblivious to anything around them, only feeling the orgasm tearing through her. It roared through her body, spreading like a wildfire out of control. Those tiny beads of sweat made her body glisten in the firelight. She was beautiful, her lips parted in a shocked O and her eyes wild and dazed. Her body shook over and over, one orgasm swelling into another as he relentlessly kicked the vibrators to high and pumped harder with his fingers. She screamed. Her head thrashed. Her hips went wild, and her sheath gripped his fingers like a vise.

Ice looked up and unerringly found the man watching his woman thrashing in the ecstasy he'd given her. The stranger was emptying himself down a woman's throat, but his eyes never left Soleil's body. Deliberately, Ice pulled his fingers free, sucked them dry and then cupped her breast, his thumb strumming. She was his. She was beautiful. And he was so fucking hard he was going to shatter.

He turned off the vibes, to give her clit some rest, but he vowed he'd spend a night teasing her. Leaving them in her, he shoved the whiskey bottle into her hand, rose abruptly, lifting her into his arms, and carried her to their bed. It was all laid out under the stars, just a few feet from two other firepits. They were caught in the middle, just the way he liked.

She rolled off him as he sank on top of the double sleeping bag and began to yank off his boots so he could remove his clothes. "Need your mouth on me, baby. Hurry."

She crawled back to him, looking for all the world like a wild temptress, and he shoved a rolled-up blanket under her hips to push her ass into the air. He liked looking at her tits and ass when she took him in her mouth. She had a shape that appealed to everything in him. He could watch the shadows playing over her cheeks and he could just see the end of that little vibrator right where he'd put it.

Soleil kissed his belly and then licked up his shaft. He let out a long sigh of pure pleasure and reached down to turn her, positioning her the way he wanted her, adjusting the pillow to lift her ass, those perfect tempting cheeks. He rubbed the closest one to him.

"Get to work, baby." He turned on the vibrator between her cheeks and she jumped.

He smacked her ass, his hand coming down hard. She lifted her head and glared at him.

"Mouth on me, baby. You love it. You think I don't feel you getting all slick against my thigh? It's your fucking favorite thing. If you don't start, I'm going to yank you up to your knees and then I'm going to be in control. You might not like it as well as this."

He was beginning to feel desperate. His

cock throbbed. Burned. Pulsed with urgency. All he could think about was the fire in her mouth. That tight throat. The way her brown eyes looked up at him as if he were the only man in the world and she worshipped at his feet.

She touched the tip of her tongue to the head of his cock, teasing him as she brushed it back and forth. He smacked her hard again, bunched her hair in his fist and stood, pulling on her hair so that she had to rise to her knees to avoid a painful scalp.

He caught her jaw and forced her mouth open when she would have laughed. Her eyes laughed even when he pushed his aching, painful erection halfway to her throat. He was wide and stretched her lips. Usually she got used to the size of him but he didn't let her, pulling back and pushing forward. The sensations were unlike anything he'd felt. So good. So fucking good. Her mouth was scorching hot, silken fire, surrounding him, sucking at him while that wicked tongue danced and flicked and fluttered until his brain wanted to explode.

He'd almost forgotten he had the control for the vibrators in his other hand. "That's right, princess, take me down. It feels so good. That mouth of yours is pure gold. Harder. Suck harder."

Feeling eyes on him, he glanced around. He was used to runs. Used to parties. Used to others watching when he had sex. It never bothered him. In fact, it simply turned him on more. He knew the exact moment he spotted the man Soleil had connected with. He couldn't take his eyes from her and was mirroring everything Ice was doing.

"The man still can't stop looking at you, baby, but you're all mine. You only look at me. You understand me, Soleil? You only look at me." He wanted her eyes. She belonged to Ice all the way. "You're *my* wife. My woman. You get on your knees for only one fuckin' man."

He pushed a little deeper, and when she tried to put her hand on the base of his cock, he shoved it away, but he did turn up the vibrators to the next speed. She gasped and he took advantage, pushing deeper, holding himself there in that tight paradise while she looked up at him helplessly, liquid swimming in her eyes while he pulsed in her mouth. While his heart beat in her mouth. It took effort to give her air. The feeling was that good.

He pushed deep again while her hips began to move urgently back and forth, desperate to fill the emptiness. He smirked down at her. "Do you need my cock again, baby? You feel empty and you need me to fuck you until you can't breathe? You can't think?"

While he asked her, he pumped in and out of her mouth, until he finished his query and shoved deep, nearly choking her. She took him though, relaxing into his thrust, letting him push far past her comfort zone. He didn't kick up the vibrators to high. He didn't want her to come. He wanted her desperate. Begging him.

He gave her a wicked smile, holding himself right there in that paradise, his cock caught in that vise, squeezing him until he felt his seed want to rise like boiling magma. Immediately he withdrew and pointed to the sleeping bag. She dropped to her hands and knees.

"Hurry, Ice. You have to hurry." She panted the words.

He turned her around, so the firelight played across her firm little ass. He loved seeing the vibrator between her cheeks and he pulled it in and out as if he were fucking her with it. She gasped and pushed back into him.

"Such a needy girl."

He gave her a couple of swats, hard enough to drive her forward just a bit. Her breasts swung with every movement, an enticing, erotic sight when the firelight touched her, caressing her nipples and highlighting the rounded curves.

He knelt behind her and used his fingers to coat her liquid between her cheeks and over his cock. She didn't protest. She didn't do anything but pant with lust. He leaned forward, bit her perfect little ass, kicked up the vibrator covering her clit and the other pushed deep into the star, and then he thrust into her sweet little pussy almost at the same moment.

Soleil let out a wail as he caught at her hips and pulled her into his plunging hips. He set a ferocious rhythm, hard, deep, and fast. Fire streaked from her body up his, the flames rolling in his belly, his chest, roaring for more and igniting his brain. He was lost in the fiery sensations, unable to process anything else. His entire being was centered on her body. In her. The way they came together.

"So good," he whispered, chanting it. "So fucking good, baby."

He never wanted it to end. She was squeezing him. Milking him. A silken, scorching-hot tunnel so tight that each movement sent the friction up another notch. He wasn't certain he could survive, but it was the perfect way to go out. He was climbing higher and higher. Everything was perfection. Her body gleamed there in the firelight, with the shadows adding to the beauty of her form. Her body gripped his. The swing of her breasts with every hard jolt, her smooth ass cheeks and the sight of the vibrator he'd slid between those perfect cheeks added to the rushing fire burning through him. Everything came together in complete perfection.

Mostly, he knew, it was Soleil and what she gave him. She made him know she was his and that he mattered. What he needed or wanted mattered to her. As much as Ice had known about fucking and was an expert in ways to give pleasure, or take it, Soleil had brought the one thing to him he'd been missing.

His balls drew tighter and tighter. It was rising, that terrible, brutal release that was going to kill him but also take him somewhere out in the universe where nothing could touch him. He jerked her hips to his, feeling her sheath bite down hard, pulsing with energy, pulsing with life, muscles working like fingers to milk his seed from his body.

She cried out, something he couldn't hear because the roaring in his ears prevented any sound from entering. He could only yell hoarsely as she ripped the seed from him. He exploded, there was no other word for it, his body jerking violently in hers, splashing hot semen on the walls of her sheath, triggering another massive orgasm in her.

He collapsed over top of her, smashing her under him, unable to think. He felt as if he were floating in space, the stars flickering around him, while behind his eyes colors burst like rockets. He never wanted to move. Or think. He lay there, panting, his lungs bursting for air. Raw. Real. Perfection.

"Ice." Soleil wailed his name. "You have to turn them off."

Shit. The vibrators. He couldn't remember what he'd done with the remote. He couldn't move. Not even to roll off of her. Besides, he liked being buried in that snug tunnel. He rubbed her bottom and then forced his eyes to work, peering around on the ground. He caught up the small remote that Mechanic had programmed for him and hit the universal off button. Her hips had been frantically bucking but once he had them off, she lay quietly under him, her breathing ragged, almost labored.

"Can't move, princess. I'm going to have to sleep just like this. Can you breathe?" Her face was turned to the side and one eye peered at him. He rubbed her bottom.

"No, but I don't need air right now."

Her voice was so soft he could barely hear. He kept rubbing, trying to soothe her. She'd come multiple times. "What do you need, then, baby?"

"Right at the moment, not one little thing. I think I'll just lie here for the rest of the night."

They lay quietly together, just trying to find a way to breathe. The night breeze helped to cool the heat and sweat on their bodies. Around them, the music and sounds of conversations and laughter once more began to register. Finally, Ice could actually see straight. He found himself smiling and pressing kisses onto the back of his woman's shoulder.

"Storm and Transporter were going to grill something for everyone. Fatei brought the side dishes in the RV. Are you hungry?" He kissed the nape of her neck. He really felt a little like an animal. Animals could stay erect, couldn't they? His fucking cock was still hard. Not like before he'd fucked her. Not when he was pure steel, but the ache was building. Didn't lions go at it every fifteen minutes or so? Didn't they stay connected the way he was with Soleil?

"I was hungry for you," she pouted.

That mouth of hers was making that little

moue, the one that gave him all sorts of ideas. He shut it down, looking at the exhaustion on her face. It was just that, this was his absolute nirvana, the place where he could have everything come together in a perfect storm of lust and love. That was what Soleil gave him. Love. That had been the missing ingredient, and shockingly, it worked.

"I'm sorry, baby. I promise I'll feed you dessert after dinner, but you need to keep your strength up. I'm planning to fuck you until you can't walk."

"I can't walk now."

He kissed the nape of her neck again. He wasn't altogether certain he could walk either.

"Besides, I wouldn't count on dinner too soon, honey." She didn't lift her head, but nodded in the direction she was looking. "I think Storm and Transporter are otherwise occupied."

Ice turned to look. Storm was on the picnic table with a woman he'd never seen before swallowing him down. She looked as if she was very eager. Storm said something to her and moved his hips aggressively, pushing deeper. Transporter was using another woman, or she was using him. Ice couldn't tell which, but they both looked happy as he fucked her mouth.

Shit. He shouldn't have looked. He turned his head away to see that the stranger in the other camp was seated on a ground sheet, stroking his partner's hair. His gaze kept straying to Soleil. Cold fingers crept down Ice's spine. It was one thing for the stranger to watch Soleil in the throes of something so sexy as an orgasm, but to keep it up, that was just plain stalker mentality.

For the first time, Ice didn't like someone else looking that closely at a partner of his. He'd never cared before. Not before, not during and certainly not after. Sometimes he had as many as three woman all over him. He always made it clear it was for a night. That was it. Now, he wanted to tell the man to go fuck himself. If he kept it up, he might lose his life. The urge to get rid of him was fast becoming a need.

There was Fred too. Fred had noted her walking into the bar in her sexy wedding gown, seeing the shadow of her nipples, seeing Ice as he caressed her tit and teased her nipple. He'd never once considered that might be endangering her. Not one time. Now, it was twice. Fred had given her up to killers, and who knew what the creep in the next camp might try?

"Honey, what's wrong?" Beneath him, Soleil turned her body slightly to push up on one hand so she could look more fully at him. The action revealed far more of her breast.

Ice cursed. "Lie down, baby. Just lie there for a minute." He waited until she obeyed him, and he rolled off her, clenching his teeth against the waves of pleasure engulfing him as his cock slid out of her. Immediately he pulled a sheet over her body, hiding it from the pervert. The moment he had her covered, the urge to kill faded to a persistent nagging thought at the back of his mind.

"Talk to me, Ice," Soleil said. "What's wrong? You were feeling great and then you got tense. I could feel your entire body go stiff."

"Nothing, princess. Sometimes I think shit up just to make myself crazy. It happens."

"Do you want me to start the grill? I looked at it when we chose this site. It's quite big enough to cook most of the meat at the same time, and it was surprisingly clean. I can scrub it down fast and get moving on that. Alena might help me."

He'd forgotten that Pierce was there and might come looking for his sister. He sat up abruptly and looked around. She was nowhere in sight. They stuck together, no one going without a partner anywhere in the camps. They were always careful. They often had a third person shadowing the first two. Just to be safe. They'd learned they were never safe unless they were with one another.

"Come on, honey, please take out the toys you brought so I can get up and cook. In a while everyone's going to be hungry. Even if Alena isn't around, I can get started."

Soleil's soft voice was a clear breath of fresh air, blowing away the last of his anger. He took a deep breath and let it out. She silenced monsters. She did it with her body. She did it with her voice. Mostly she was able to drive the monsters and the nightmares far away and replace them with happiness because she loved him.

He took another breath and looked around the campsite. Alena was missing, but so were Savage and Maestro. He should have known they were looking out for her. He hadn't thought about anything but the way Soleil made him feel.

"All right, baby, I'm removing the little button. Are you supersensitive?"

"Yes." She gave a little shiver as he reached around and tugged it loose. She gasped and clenched her ass cheeks. "Very sensitive."

"You'll feel my mouth tonight," he said.

He smacked her ass. "I'm leaving that one in. It acts like a plug."

"You are *not* leaving it in." She sounded shocked.

He grinned at her. Because she was always so willing to give him whatever he wanted, or try anything he suggested, he kept forgetting she didn't have the experience he did. He kept the sheet over her, reluctant to expose her any further to any other man's gaze. It was a strange feeling to be protective of her body when he'd never considered that to be an issue with him, but he detested that his need to play the way he liked might have put her in danger.

"Roll over, baby, but stay under the sheet. I'm getting your clothes for you. You can pull your jeans on right there." He handed her his shirt. She could put on her sexy tank in the morning, but tonight, he was going to make certain he didn't have to kill someone when he'd been the one to provoke the man in the first place.

He'd never thought much about what kind of feelings exposing the beauty of his woman when she was in the throes of ecstasy would bring out in another man or if that might set up some kind of obsession with her. He might have put her in danger. That didn't sit well with him either. Ice let his gaze slide toward the other camp. The man was still staring at Soleil. He didn't seem to notice Ice watching him. Yeah, he should have been more careful.

He certainly had put her right in Fred's path. He had never considered that another club would sell his woman to killers. She was wild. Sexy. She liked exposing her body. She didn't mind getting on her knees for him anywhere or letting him fuck her where he wanted. He was going to have to be the one to learn a little control in order to protect her better — and that was laughable.

"I don't want you going anywhere without an escort. I need to know where you are at all times," he said uneasily.

She dragged her jeans up her legs and over her hips, lifting to pull them over her bottom. She gave him a small smile. "Honey, you've laid down the rules. I'm not going to do anything that would upset you. This isn't an environment I'm familiar with, so I'll follow your instructions to the letter."

She tossed the sheet to one side and stood up, looking toward the grill. "Come help me clean it and get the fire going."

He was right behind her, matching her pace, his hand cradling her bottom possessively. His thumb slid over the rounded curve, and he couldn't help but glance over to the other camp. The man was still staring at Soleil, watching her walking over to the grill. Shit. Now what? The grill was close to the edge of the two campsites' borders. Instead of making her safe, he was putting her in more danger by allowing her to be that close to the neighboring camp.

The club was called Twisted Steel. They tried to come off like badasses, the worst kind of club. The larger legitimately badass clubs looked down on them, so they were always trying to prove themselves. They wore the 1-percenter patch to indicate to the world they were outlaws and followed their own rules. That wasn't smart of Twisted Steel; if they started something, the other clubs would eat them alive.

Ice cursed under his breath.

Soleil reacted immediately. "What is wrong? You have to tell me. I mean it, Ice. If I was upset about something, you'd insist on me telling you. We're supposed to be in this together. Did I do something wrong?"

Now she sounded hurt. He slung his arm around her neck and pulled her in close to him. "No, princess, this was all me. I like sex the way we just had it. It makes me as hard as fuck, but I didn't think about the repercussions. From now on, we're saving that experience for times I know the others are around us and can control the environment and the aftermath better. I just don't want anyone fixating on you."

Her eyes searched his and then she smiled, righting his world. "I think I'm desperately in love with you, Ice. That fall is longer and deeper than I ever imagined."

"I don't know what I did to deserve you, but I'll take it."

Together they scrubbed the grill. Ice kept his body between Soleil and the other campsite as best he could. He ignored the other camp, although he was always aware of it. Still, she pushed the sights and sounds far away with her soft, intimate laughter and the way her eyes danced when she looked at him or talked to him.

She still had that soft look, eyes only for him, never straying to look at any other man. He knew, because he watched her carefully. Twice when she wasn't expecting it, he turned on the vibrator and she yelped and jumped. He grinned at her when she glared at him. Playing wasn't something he was familiar with, but with her, he found he was really enjoying himself.

After the grill was scrubbed clean, he got the necessary coals going. Bags of it. The good stuff. He was better at it than he'd let on. She looked at him suspiciously and then when it caught fire and spread rapidly through the large grill, she flung her arms around his neck and pressed kisses up his throat to his chin where she nibbled.

"You've done this before."

"You could say that," he agreed. Hell, if lighting a barbecue grill had gotten him her kisses, and her tits pressed tightly against his chest, he would have told her far sooner. That was as far as his skills went. He could spread out the coals and get them lit. After that . . .

He reached down with both hands, cupped her ass cheeks and pulled her tight against his body. "Kiss me."

She did. Without hesitation. Her lips found his and her tongue slipped along the seam, temptation itself. His cock jerked hard, coming to attention. He used one hand to turn the vibe on again and then he rubbed her ass, wishing it was bare. His other hand slid inside the shirt to find her bare breast. He loved her tits almost as much as her ass. Maybe more. Maybe it was the same. He didn't know. Didn't care. He just loved the way her body fit with his. Loved the way she made him come alive.

"Hey, you two." Lana came up behind them. He knew before she spoke who it was because he was familiar with her energy. "Enough of that."

They broke apart, both laughing. He remembered to turn off the vibrator to give his woman a little relief.

"I thought I'd help with the cooking, at least until Alena gets back. Pierce showed up and off they went together. I don't know what's going on there," she added.

Ice didn't believe her for a minute. "I've got this."

"You've got that thing, remember?" Lana stated, holding up her watch.

He had no idea what "thing" she was referring to. He frowned and she tapped out their code on her thigh. Her hand was down low, up against her leg, so few people ever noticed the small taps of her fingers.

Fred. Venom. Of course. The club had come as well. He didn't have to make a special trip to find the son of a bitch who'd given up his woman to murderers. They'd found him. He nodded. "I don't want Soleil out of your sight. She's got a couple of men watching her, and I don't want them getting close to her."

He didn't want to leave his wife. He was having fun with her. He couldn't remember there ever being a time when he was reluctant to go with his brothers and deliver a much-needed lesson. He was now. He would choose Soleil over fighting any day of the week. Shockingly, he'd fallen that far. But this was important. This kind of betrayal wasn't acceptable, and Torpedo Ink had to get that message across to the Venomous club.

He caught Soleil's chin, turned her head toward him and kissed her. He took his time, establishing the fact that she was with him. That he loved her. That she was protected. "Stay with Lana at all times."

"I'm good, Ice. Nothing is going to happen to me."

Ice looked up to find Absinthe and Storm close. They nodded at him. His brothers, ready to teach Fred a very hard lesson before he died and remind the Venomous club that no one put one of theirs up for murder. He stalked off, leaving his woman with his very lethal sister. Anyone who tried to touch what wasn't theirs was in for trouble.

SIXTEEN

Ice smiled. It wasn't a nice smile. He'd perfected that look over years of beating the shit out of his enemies. "Hello, Fred. We met in Vegas. You remember? My wedding day. My woman looked like a fairy-tale princess in her dress. You were staring at her tits, as I recall. So, if you don't remember the dress, you might remember the perfect tits she has."

Fred's smirk faded and he turned slowly around, trying to look nonchalant as he searched the bar for his brethren. None of his club members appeared to be inside the bar. He gave a quick shake of his head. "Don't know what the hell you're talking about. You must have the wrong man." He made a move as if he could get around Ice.

Ice blocked him. "You can't go yet. I want to talk about old times." He stepped in close to the man, put a friendly hand on his shoulder and then punched him three times in rapid succession in the gut. The punches were fast, hard, and delivered with Storm and Absinthe blocking the view from the rest of the bar.

Ice put a solicitous arm around Fred as he bent over, gasping for breath, his drink coming back up as he spewed it onto the floor.

"Freddie, you had too much to drink. Let me help you." Ice appeared to help him as he staggered toward the darkest corner of the bar. Three men sat at the table there but moved quickly when Storm and Absinthe stood over them and just stared.

Ice shoved Fred into a chair, his back to the wall, the table in front of him — close. "Let's get acquainted. We're going to be friendly now. Really friendly. If you don't want me to slit your gut open right here and let your intestines spill out into your lap, you're going to give me everything I want. Tell me everything I want to know."

He shoved a very sharp blade against Fred's straining, heaving gut. "You feel that, you fuck? You gave up my woman. You went against the code. You're a piece of shit and you're going to answer any question I ask."

Fred was no hero. That much was certain. On top of that, he'd been drinking heavily. He nodded over and over, sweat pouring down his face. Absinthe took the chair next to Fred on his other side. That left only Storm to block any view. Fred immediately lunged to the side, toward Ice, to get the attention of the others in the bar.

The noise level in the bar was extremely loud. It was crowded and fairly dark. Liquor flowed and music blared. Dozens of conversations took place from every direction. A few couples even attempted to sway to the music. In one corner, a woman stood on a table, her tits out as she danced drunkenly. No one paid attention to the men sitting in the corner, and no one could hear if Fred called out.

Two more people blocked the view and he looked up and groaned. He'd run into the blade of the knife and it had cut through his denim jacket as well as his shirt to score a long, painful laceration across his stomach.

Standing in front of him was a woman with a wealth of blond hair and the same blue eyes as Ice and Storm. She wore a Torpedo Ink vest over her tight tank. Beside her was a man with flat, cold eyes, and Fred recognized him immediately as an enforcer for the Diamondbacks, and no one messed with them.

"Thought we'd join the party," Alena informed her brother. "Saw you come in."

It didn't surprise Ice in the least that he hadn't seen his sister. They all tended to fade into the background, a trick they'd learned as children that had often saved their lives. The bar was packed and dark inside. The strip outside was being used for bike tricks. Across the way, in the main common area of the campsites, wet T-shirt contests and mud wrestling along with a massive party were taking place. Inside the bar, the noise level was loud in order to hear above the motorcycles used in the street tricks as well as the music blaring from multiple speakers outside. That would all be helpful if Fred got noisy.

Ice waved Alena and Pierce to the chairs at the front of the table. Pierce would not want his back to the room. That was a sweet kind of triumph, to have the enforcer of the Diamondbacks seated facing them. He didn't take the chair. He glanced at Absinthe and Ice, realizing neither was going to give up their seat, and he stepped to one side, standing rather than sitting. Ice didn't like him there when Absinthe was questioning Fred, but he needed to get on with it, and Pierce's appearance would ensure no one would come near them. In any case, Pierce wouldn't have a clue what Absinthe was doing.

"Answer Absinthe with the truth, Fred, or you're going to be hurting," Ice cautioned. He really didn't give a flying fuck if Fred hurt himself, but he didn't like leaving Soleil alone for too long. Lana's presence might serve to bring more men around. She was beautiful, and any man could easily see that.

Fred dribbled down the front of himself, still coughing up his last drink. "What do you want?" He tried blustering, but it came out scared.

"You contacted someone to tell them Soleil Brodeur had been in the bar and that she was with a member of Torpedo Ink, didn't you?" Absinthe asked. His voice was pitched low, but it resonated through the brain, almost as if that tone could actually shake the brain.

Fred shook his head, but then clutched it, moaning. "My head hurts. It hurts."

"It will keep hurting until you tell the truth," Ice said, sounding bored. He was bored. They'd repeated this exact same scenario a million times. He'd much rather be with his woman, her mouth on him, his hand smacking her ass, sucking on her gorgeous tits. He could slice Fred's belly open just for forcing him to be away from her.

"Yes. Yes. I called a friend of mine."

"Who did you call, Fred?" Absinthe asked.

Pierce leaned closer, and Ice clenched his teeth and gave his sister a look of pure reprimand. Alena put a restraining hand on Pierce's arm, forcing him back.

"Yeger. I called Yeger Kushnir. He knows everybody and he lives in San Francisco. Some people were offering a huge reward just to know where she was."

"Why didn't you just call them yourself?" Absinthe asked.

More sweat broke out on Fred's face and trickled down. Ice could smell the fear. He glanced at Storm with a raised eyebrow.

"I — I didn't care about the money, but I knew Yeger would."

Ice expected him to grab his head again, but evidently, he was telling the truth.

Absinthe sighed. "What did you care about, Fred?"

Fred covered his face with his hand, shaking his head, refusing to answer. Immediately he was holding his head, rocking and moaning. Tears began to trickle down his face.

"What could Yeger get for you that Winston, who was offering a huge reward, couldn't?" Ice said. "You know it's going to keep hurting and get worse if you don't answer."

"He could get me a woman." Fred choked, and then nearly screamed. A thin trickle of blood slipped from his right ear. His face turned red. "A girl. A little girl," he corrected. "He's got connections, and he could get me what I wanted. One I didn't have to worry about."

Ice was sick to death of meeting men like Fred. "One he didn't have to worry about" meant no one was looking for the kid and Fred could do whatever he wanted with her when he was finished with her. He took a deep breath and concentrated on not slitting the man's belly open. The roar in his ears prevented him from hearing Absinthe's next soft question. Screams, so many surrounded him until he couldn't drown them out. Blood. So much. A lake of it on the floor.

"Ice," Alena whispered his name. "Honey, look at me."

Her voice, that sweet, sweet voice, meant she was still alive. He hadn't failed her. He had done things, made decisions based on keeping her alive, and there she was. He lifted his gaze to hers and took a breath. When he did, he took in Fred's disgusting odor. He'd smelled so many men and women like Fred. Corrupt. Vile. Base. It was all he could do to keep the knife from going in. The temperature in the room had lowered by several degrees. He took a deep breath and let it out, forcing himself under control.

"Yeger gets you the kid in exchange for you giving him the information so he can get the money from Winston?" Absinthe persisted.

Fred started to nod and then stopped abruptly, clearly afraid of lying. "Turns out Yeger knows this Winston. He's involved with a lot of heavy hitters in San Francisco. One in particular, Yeger wanted an introduction to. He wanted to trade the information. A few days later, he called me and told me they were looking for a couple of shooters to help make sure the woman doesn't surface. They wanted it permanent." He looked at Ice. "I said no."

That had to be true. "Who does Yeger associate with?" Absinthe asked.

Fred shrugged. He was beginning to breathe again, thinking himself safe as long as he answered their questions. Ice could have told him he wasn't safe in the least. That he wouldn't live to see the morning sunrise, not after his admission that he was looking for a little girl.

"He's got a lot of friends. He knows people. Avery Charles. He's got this job with the cops. Right there every single day. He can tell Yeger if places are going to be raided. Or if evidence is being moved. He's a good man to know, and Yeger keeps him very happy. Then there's a couple of cops in Occidental. See, the key, Yeger says, is find out what a man or woman likes and supply it to them. They'll tell you anything you want to know."

"Like you do for him?" Absinthe asked.

Fred nodded. "He does that for a lot of people."

"But not Winston or his friends."

Fred shook his head. "Winston got introduced into some circle of men who had something big going. They'd covered everything they needed from the judge, attorney, cops, and even someone at a mortuary." There was a little bit of a sneer when he said the last. "Yeger wanted that kind of coverage, I guess."

That explained a lot. Yeger was into human trafficking. He didn't care if they were old or young, male or female, but he did want to be secure — to know even if he was busted, he would get off. Yeger saw an opportunity to use Winston to get to the others in the con ring.

"Do you know the names of Winston's friends? The ones Yeger wanted to meet?"

Absinthe persisted.

Fred shook his head. "He never said."

"Did you get paid for the information with a girl?"

"Not yet. He said after they took out the woman, he'd bring one to me." Fred avoided their eyes.

"You mean, after they killed my old lady, they'd bring you a little girl to rape. Isn't that what you mean?" Ice demanded.

Fred remained silent, staring down at the table until he had to grip his head with both hands, gritting his teeth. His eyes bulged. Tears ran down his face. He opened his mouth to scream but no sound emerged.

Ice signaled for Alena to take Pierce and leave. Alena stood up and reached for Pierce's hand. He threaded his fingers through hers, but he stayed stubbornly watching. She wrapped herself around him as only Alena could. When he still didn't respond, she shrugged, turned, and left the table, moving through the bar with complete confidence, her hips swaying. She didn't look back once.

Pierce glanced after her and then back to the table, clearly fascinated by Fred's odd suffering. There was no way to connect him grabbing his head to anything the Torpedo Ink members were doing. Storm sat passively. Absinthe was looking at the Venomous club member, but as far as Pierce could tell, he wasn't doing anything to him. Ice sat closer than any of the others, but he wasn't touching the man that Pierce could see. He swore, once more looking after Alena.

Ice wanted to smile, knowing his dilemma. His sister would be lost in the sea of bikers. So many clubs. So many parties. So many men. She was beautiful and mysterious and elusive. In the end, Pierce turned and went after her.

Ice removed the threat of the knife and put it back inside his jacket, out of sight. Blood was dripping from Fred's ears and trickling from both eyes. His head went down on the table and his body began to seize. Storm stood up and walked casually to the bar as his twin and Absinthe worked their way toward the door.

"Just wanted you to know, that man over there looks like he's having some kind of seizure. I'm not a medic, but it doesn't look good." Storm patted the bar once and turned his back, threading his way through the crowd to the door where the others waited.

The bartender glanced over at Fred, who was slumped over the table. He could barely make him out. Several voices rang out demanding drinks, and he shrugged and went back to work.

"Are you happy with Ice?" Lana asked.

Soleil glanced up from the long rows of chicken on the grill and met Lana's eyes. "Very happy, Lana. Thanks to you, I'm still alive and happier than I'd ever thought possible. I never had a home or a family. Torpedo Ink has been amazing, the way they've taken me in."

She turned back to eye the chicken. She'd never actually grilled anything before. She waved the long tongs toward the chicken. "Have you ever done this?"

Lana stepped back, throwing both her hands into the air. "No way. Alena can do this with no problem. She'd make it all perfection. Me, I'm the queen of burning things."

"You ladies need help?"

Both spun around. Soleil recognized the stranger, the man who had watched her earlier in the evening having sex. She struggled to keep the color from rising under her skin. She refused to be embarrassed, but her skin crawled. She'd liked him watching when she'd felt safe with Ice with her, but now she felt a little dirty, and not in a good way. He had participated by watching, by getting off on it. His gaze seemed to burn into her, making her feel more uncomfortable than ever.

"We're fine," Lana said, flashing him a smile. "Just making some food for our club." She shifted slightly, gliding to put her body between Soleil and the newcomer as if she sensed he had come for more than helping them.

"Name's Stallion," he said, grinning, gripping the front of his jeans suggestively. "Bet you can't imagine why."

"Bet I can," Lana said, glanced at Soleil and rolled her eyes.

Soleil hid her smile by staring down at the chicken. So far nothing looked as if it was burning. She just hoped Alena would come, or one of the men.

"You haven't told me your names," Stallion pushed.

"I think that was on purpose," Lana said.

The smile faded from his face. "Don't be a bitch. You don't want to get your club in trouble. Mine has a certain reputation, and no one's heard of yours."

Lana burst out laughing. "Are you honestly threatening the club because I didn't tell you my name?"

He took a step toward her, his face going

red with anger. Soleil held up the tongs threateningly. Lana just remained looking cool, the way she always did, although her eyes had gone cold and watchful.

"I'm going to give you one warning, Stallion. If you lay one hand on me, I'm going to hurt you like you've never been hurt. They won't call you Stallion anymore because you're never going to be making babies." She spoke very low, but her voice carried absolute truth.

"Everything all right here, Lana?" Ink asked, as he emerged from the shadows. He was a big man and covered in a multitude of tattoos. He spoke softly, like most of the Torpedo Ink members did.

Preacher, Lana's older birth brother, came up on the other side of her, both men blocking Stallion's view of Soleil. "Hey, sis, sorry we're late. Got caught up in the wet T-shirt contest."

Lana rolled her eyes. "Of course you did. You can't tell fake from the real thing." Her gaze went past him to lock onto Ink. "Neither of you can."

"Is that where Ice went?" Soleil asked. It took an effort to keep her voice very casual. She was used to pretending everything was okay. She'd been doing that most of her life.

She hadn't thought of all the parties going

on everywhere all around them. She knew there was anything he might want to do right there for him, and he was very, very sexual. Women fawned all over him. She'd been with him only a month, but in that time, she'd noticed that everywhere they went, women looked at him, flirted and tried to entice him. How had she ever thought someone like Ice would be satisfied by a woman like her?

She turned her back on the others, fussing over the chicken. Ink reached around her to take the tongs out of her hand. "Babe. Really?"

He ignored Stallion's posturing. The man could bluster until the cows came home, but he wasn't going to fight them. Eventually, with no one paying him any attention, Stallion slunk back to his campsite, stomped over to one of the women, caught her wrist and yanked her with him as he stalked away.

"I don't know what that means." Soleil raised an eyebrow toward Lana. "Does 'Babe. Really,' actually mean something?"

Lana shook her head. "No, but they pretend every time they say it that it means something defining. It really means they have no vocabulary. Don't pay any attention to them. The minute you do, you're encouraging their bad behavior."

"Talk about bad behavior," Preacher said. "I saw that little smile you gave good old Stallion. You were egging that poor boy on. You wanted to kick his balls up to his throat."

Lana shrugged. "That could be true. He was looking at Soleil like he was going to eat her for dinner and then he threatened the club because I wouldn't tell him my name. Both offenses deserved his balls meeting his throat."

Soleil wouldn't say so out loud, but she kind of agreed. The man gave her a creepy feeling. She wasn't choosing someone to look at next time. If Ice wanted that, he would have to do the selecting himself.

She looked around her. There was a sea of bikers. Hundreds in every direction she gazed. Fires danced in pits. Music vied for the airwaves. The sounds of motorcycle pipes as bikes were revved and tires smoked before taking off for difficult and dangerous tricks. Laughter and delighted screams could be heard. The scent of weed was prevalent. The smell of alcohol. If she wanted to walk off the panic welling up in her, how was she supposed to do that?

Panic was sliding up her throat, choking her. She didn't look at the others. She couldn't. She needed to be alone to think.

She wrapped her arms around her middle and took a step, immediately feeling the vibrator between her cheeks. It had felt playful and sexy and fun when he was close to her. Now it felt dirty and tawdry and foolish. Ice was out there somewhere in that sea of bikers, and she was locked here in this place, afraid of taking a step in any direction. She didn't have Lana's or Alena's confidence to just strut around and feel hot and desired.

She would do anything for Ice. She knew he could make her feel like the only woman in the world. He could make her want to leave a vibrator between her cheeks and take off her top and dance for him in a crowd. But he'd gone off and left her so he could watch other women in wet T-shirt contests.

She looked around again. There were so many fires going it was fairly light in spite of the time of night. It wasn't like she could just call for a ride. Where could she go? Winston wanted her dead, and he'd even gotten some friends of his to try to kill her.

"Soleil." Lana said her name sharply. "You've gone off someplace in your head that clearly isn't very pleasant. You look like you're going to cry." She indicated the lawn chairs. "Come sit down with me and we'll talk about it."

Soleil needed time to think this all through before she made a fool out of herself. She knew her number one problem was self-confidence. She had been trying to work through that, but looking around at all the beautiful women everywhere surrounding them, and knowing Ice's appetites, it was hard to think he wasn't somewhere with a couple of women right at that moment. She'd heard the rumors.

She eased into one of the chairs that was set in a semicircle around the firepit and flashed a fake smile at Lana. "Did I look like that? I guess I do that. A leftover childhood thing. Everything is great here, a little scary because it's different and I don't know exactly what I'm doing yet, but I'll catch on."

Lana studied her face. "Honey, you don't have to do that with me. I'm your friend. In the club, we're sisters. We look out for one another. This has something to do with Ice. You know he didn't go to a stupid wet T-shirt contest. If he wanted to see boobs under a wet shirt, he'd spray you with a hose. There was some club business he had to take care of tonight. Storm and Absinthe are with him." She glanced at her watch. "They should be back any minute."

Soleil didn't know whether to let herself

believe Lana and be relieved, or to hold on to her fears and be miserable. She'd never been happy until she'd been with Ice. Never. Not really. She glanced at Lana. Lana was confident in herself as a woman, as a member of Torpedo Ink. Soleil had promised herself she was going to be like her — to get to that same place as a woman, as Ice's wife and as part of the Torpedo Ink family. Maybe she was making a total fool of herself, but if she was going to make a choice, she wanted to choose happiness, and that meant believing in Ice. She had to make a conscious choice to believe in her husband.

Two more of the Torpedo Ink men joined them. She recognized Mechanic and Transporter, brothers who owned a garage. She liked them both and gave them a shy smile. She didn't have confidence in her place in the club without Ice there — everything was too new — but she was determined she would.

Mechanic joined Ink at the grill. "Not bad, Ink. You got everything ready. Czar and Steele are on their way. Breezy and Blythe are bringing the side dishes. The prospects are helping carry them. Since when have you been doing the grilling?"

Lana kicked Soleil's foot to get her attention. "That's what they do. You do all the work and they take credit for it."

Soleil couldn't help but laugh at Ink's expression. He pointed the tongs at Lana. "Woman, you are a pain in my ass. I didn't take credit, and Mechanic, for your information, I can grill."

Lana laughed. "You're just making shit up, Ink. No way do you know the first thing about cooking or grilling. I've known you since you were a little scrawny kid. I never saw you behind a stove or in front of a grill. There were no secret lessons in the middle of the night."

Ink managed to look so affronted, Soleil nearly fell off her chair laughing. Feeling eyes on her, she glanced up and everything inside her stilled. There he was. Ice. He took her breath away. He was such a gorgeous man. That build. That hair. Those eyes. Beside him, Storm stood talking in a low voice to Absinthe. Storm looked just like Ice other than the three teardrops tattooed onto Ice's face. They were stunning when they were together. She knew they must have caused a sensation when they walked through the throngs of biker women to make their way back to the campsite.

Ice came right to her, took her hands and pulled her from the lawn chair into his arms. His mouth settled on hers. He swept her away, swept every doubt away. How could he possibly kiss the way he did if he didn't feel anything for her? He tasted the way love should taste. His hands swept down her back and pulled her tighter against him.

"I missed you. Were you good while I was gone?"

"No, she wasn't," Preacher said. "Neither was Lana."

"Lana was flirting her cute little butt off with some asshole named Stallion," Ink informed them.

Mechanic had just taken a drink of beer and he spewed it out onto the ground. Transporter stopped the beer can in midair, staring at Lana. Lana tapped her fingers on the arm of her chair, giving Ink the death stare.

"He was after Soleil," Lana informed them haughtily. "I had plans to ruin him for life. He was hideous."

A roar of laughter went up. Soleil smiled, but it faded quickly when she found herself looking into a glacier of blue. Her heart skipped a beat.

"It was him, from the site next to us, wasn't it?"

She ran her hand up and down his arm.

"It was nothing. Lana handled it. And then Preacher and Ink came along, and he took off."

"What did he say to you?"

"He talked to Lana mainly. He said if she wouldn't tell him her name, the club could have trouble, or something to that effect. He left, Ice."

Ice turned to look at Lana. "Thanks, Lana. Means the fuckin' world to me, right here." He swept his hand down from Soleil's head to the curve of her butt. "You want to walk around before we eat?"

She could tell he wanted to be alone with her, so she nodded. He threaded his fingers through hers, and they began moving through the pathways between the camp-sites. The grounds were packed. Everywhere she looked, people were dancing, gyrating, drinking, laughing, catching up with one another. Very few women were wearing tops, and she was feeling a little overdressed in Ice's shirt.

"This is actually far different than I pictured it. It's wild and fun."

He sent her a little grin. "I'm glad you're having a good time. Thanks for getting the grill started. By the time we usually get around to it, we start eating around three in the morning." He pushed her deeper into the trees. "I fuckin' missed you. I had things to do and all I could think about was getting back to you." He cupped her face and bent to brush his lips over hers. Gently. A barely there kiss that sent butterfly wings fluttering through her stomach. "Did you miss me, Soleil? Did you miss my hands on you?"

"So much," she admitted. "I always miss you, Ice, when you're not with me."

He kissed his way over her chin, down to her throat. "Open your shirt for me."

She obeyed without hesitation. There was a small picnic table set to one side of the long sweeping strands of a willow tree. He backed her right up to the table so that the edge pressed against her lower back. His lips continued to travel down her throat to her chest and then over the top curves of her breasts.

Everywhere he touched her, kissed her, little flames lingered. He ignited every nerve ending without trying. She was always acutely aware that she was female and he was male whenever they were near each other. Her breasts ached for him, for his touch, for his mouth. His hands were gentle, his mouth even more so. It was so unexpected she found tears burning in her eyes.

"Hold your shirt open for me."

He framed her breasts with his hands and steadily bent her backward over the table. His mouth followed her down, finding her left nipple as she pulled the shirt out of his way. It took a moment to realize he'd left her shirt on to protect her from the top of the table. His mouth was powerful, sucking at her breast with a strong, steady rhythm that instantly made her go damp. Without warning the vibrator began to buzz, stimulating the nerve endings inside her butt. She gasped and squirmed. His fingers tugged at her other nipple, rolling and pinching until her breath hitched in her throat.

"Open your jeans, princess. Push them down your legs."

He whispered the order and somehow that soft intimacy sent a shiver through her body. It wasn't easy to obey him. He didn't let up with his hands and mouth, and the sensations were growing until her legs felt like rubber. The vibrations seemed to move through her body like waves of heat.

He kissed his way down her breasts to her belly button, his tongue tasting every inch of her skin between. He took his time, his hands gentle on her, whispering over her skin, the way his mouth was. Her breath hissed out of her lungs, and she tried not to thrash. Tried to stay still. It was beautiful, what he was doing to her. Amazing. She was drenched in desire for him, the need for him so strong she couldn't stop her hands from stroking his shoulders, his back, from moving through his thick hair.

He dragged her jeans down to her shoes. She'd worn her pull-on boots and was thankful she had when he pulled them off and set them with her jeans on the bench. He was precise about each movement but very fast, as if every detail was already seen to in his mind. He kept one hand on her belly, pinning her to the table almost the entire time.

Then he simply lifted her legs and settled them over his shoulders. She watched his face. He looked like sin itself. Sensual lines were carved deep. His eyes moved over her, burning his name into her thighs. His tongue slid up the inside of her left thigh, and her entire body shuddered.

She couldn't stop moaning. Then his mouth was there, right in her burning center, and the vibration hitched up another notch and she was gone. The moaning turned to wails. The wails turned to screams.

Soleil had no idea how long Ice spent using his mouth and fingers to bring her to orgasm, over and over, but she thought a few times she might not survive. He seemed to know just when she was too sensitive, and he'd use his teeth to nip along her inner thigh and then spread kisses over her bare lips before using his expert tongue so wickedly she could see colors bursting behind her eyes.

She had no idea how many times those waves rushed over her, but they kept coming even when he lifted his head and slowly lowered her feet to the ground. His hands guided her around until she was bending over the table. Just before her front felt the surface, he reached around and drew the edges of her shirt together, so her skin didn't touch the wood.

He kept his hand on her back, keeping her bent over the table. "I love your ass, Soleil. It's so perfect." He rubbed her cheeks. "I love how responsive you are to me."

He smacked her, spreading heat across her bottom that erupted into fire, burning straight through her center, sending the little vibrator crazy. It felt like flames licked continuously at her insides, touching her everywhere until she was crazy for him.

Soleil gave a small sob of need and pushed back against his hand. "It feels so good when you do that." It did. He never smacked hard, just enough to spread that heat everywhere.

"I like to see my handprints on you," he admitted. "Sexy as hell." He added several more, always rubbing to keep those flames burning inside her.

Then he shoved her legs farther apart and, without warning, pushed into her with his cock. It felt massive. An invasion. Perfection. He drove through tight muscles that were hot and slick, coating the thick shaft as he surged into her. He buried himself deep, forcing his way so that those muscles had to give way for his entrance.

He threw his head back and roared. He sounded so sexy. Hoarse. Husky. His hands kept moving over her back, stroking down her spine. Smacking her cheeks, rubbing there. The vibrator sent waves of fire rushing through her. It was all too much. Pressure coiled tighter and tighter. She could barely breathe. She reached out with both hands and grasped the sides of the picnic table.

He kept pistoning into her. Lust grew sharper. Spread through her until she couldn't think of anything but his cock moving in her, claiming her, taking her so high she was afraid to let go but desperately needed to. Her world narrowed until there was nothing but that perfect instrument of lust, driving into her, over and over, her inner muscles inflamed and drenched in fire.

She felt him grow, his girth stretching her. It suddenly felt as if his cock were pure steel, white-hot. Her breath caught and then she was screaming as he erupted, dragging through the bundles of nerve endings, flinging her out somewhere distant, so that her entire being became pure feeling. There was no Soleil. She was gone and in her place was a writhing, sobbing mass of pleasure. The vibrator went off and she got her vision back.

Ice bent over her, holding her as he fought for air. "Holy shit, babe. We may have just found outer space." He whispered it against her back.

She laughed, her lungs protesting, burning, but she didn't care. She'd never been so happy. Never. The tears burning behind her eyelids were happy ones. He just made her feel special. It didn't matter that now she could hear the loud music and the voices surrounding them. Their little oasis seemed remote, as if there were only the two of them in the world.

"I love you, Soleil."

She closed her eyes, her heart stuttering. He whispered it against her back, his lips touching her skin, as if he could sink the declaration through skin to bone. Her throat closed, the lump so big she was afraid she might choke. He managed to surprise her, shock her, doing and saying the most unexpected things.

"I love you very much, Ice," she whispered back.

"Hold still, baby." Very gently he removed the vibrator.

She closed her eyes and then slowly pushed up as he stepped back to give her room. He handed her a small cloth he'd pulled from a ziplock bag. It was damp. She cleaned herself off before handing it back to him. As she pulled up her jeans, she watched him clean himself and then drag his jeans up.

Soleil perched on top of the picnic table, mostly because she wasn't certain her legs would keep her up. They felt like jelly to her.

He grinned at her as he sprayed the vibrator with antibacterial spray and dropped it into the small plastic bag.

She narrowed her eyes at him. "Clearly, you've done this a lot, being so prepared and all. The washcloth, the spray, the plastic bags."

He shoved the bag into his pocket. "Never cared that much one way or the other about getting a woman off. I want you to feel everything. I want you to have any sensation I can give you, as long as it feels good to you. No, baby, all this preparation, it's only yours. Only for you. And yeah, I thought about it before we ever came here."

Her heart stuttered. His beautiful blue eyes moved over her with a kind of reverence that made her stomach slide.

"Walking back tonight, I scouted for a place we could be alone, found this and knew it was secluded. Asked a few of the brothers to make certain we stayed alone, to watch our backs because it was important to me to show you how I feel about you. When I touch you, princess, every time I touch you, I'm showing you how I feel." He fished around in his pocket and brought out a jewelry box.

Her heart began to pound. She looked from it up to his face. "Ice." She just breathed his name. His face. That beloved face. So sensual. So hers. He didn't give that expression to anyone else. She brushed his jaw with her fingertips because she couldn't help herself.

With his thumb he flipped open the box. Her wedding ring was nestled there. Made of platinum, the etchings were infused with dark chocolate diamonds to match her eyes. He took her hand and slipped off the laminated ring to push the platinum one in its place.

She just stared at it, knowing it was one of a kind. "What does it say?"

He kept her hand, his thumb sliding over the ring. "In my language, 'Soleil was born for Ice.' Mine says 'Ice was born for Soleil.' Then here, 'For Eternity.' " He brought her hand to his mouth and kissed the ring. The paper one he put in the box, and that went back into his pocket.

She had to blink back tears. "It's beautiful, Ice. I really love it." She wanted to just stare at it, to fling herself into his arms and hold him tight. She couldn't move. She could only look at his face. Into his eyes.

He curled his palm around the nape of her neck and pulled her into him so he could kiss her. She loved when he did that. It always felt to her as if he was being possessive, as if he was telling her and the world that she belonged to him. And then he could kiss like a dream . . .

She cupped her hands around his face. "Thank you for finding me, Ice. You changed my life. I love being your wife."

"I love that you're my wife," he answered and caught her hands in his so he could kiss both of them. "Technically, you found me." He jumped down from the table, pulled her boots on her and helped her off. Raising his voice, he called out, "We're coming out."

She tried to pierce the veil of darkness and the long, sweeping limbs of the weeping willow tree, but it was impossible, and the members of Torpedo Ink were too quiet to ever hear them coming.

"Let's get back and eat. I'm starved," he said. "Tomorrow will be fun. There're vendors, rows and rows of them. The girls will want to visit them all."

"I'll be able to use my bank account," she said. "We filed the papers, they know I'm alive and I don't have to hide. I can actually use my own money instead of living off you all the time. I've hated not being able to help you out."

Ice stopped dead, just before he pushed back the weeping limbs of the giant tree. He caught her hair in his fist and pulled her head back, forcing her to look into his eyes. "Are we fucking married?" With his other hand he lifted her hand to hold up her ring.

She blinked, her stomach dropping in trepidation. At the same time, a wicked little flame sprang into life, flickering hotly between her legs. "Yes."

"What did I tell you?"

"I don't know. About the money?"

"We don't argue about money. Not ever.

My money is your money. You want money, you just use it. We don't talk about yours or mine. I hear you talk about money, what are you supposed to do with your mouth instead?"

"Umm." She squirmed a little, the flames spreading, which was insane after what they'd just experienced together.

"You can use your mouth to swallow me down."

"Now?" She could hear the murmur of voices growing louder.

"You just talked about money again, didn't you?" His hands dropped to his belt buckle. He jerked his head toward the ground.

"What the fuck is the holdup, Ice?" Maestro asked, stepping through the weeping tree limbs. He wasn't alone. There were two others with him, but she could only see their boots.

Soleil would have pulled back, but Ice pushed his cock into her mouth. It was semihard. Hot. Delicious. He gave a small groan. She loved the taste and feel of him, and she was already lost. She loved that he was using their ridiculous money argument as an excuse for her to blow him. It was her favorite thing. Absolute favorite thing.

"Just stopping the bullshit money talk.

We're not ever going to be arguing about that shit. I've been reading how many marriages end because of money fights."

"You found a good way to stop it," Maestro said, amusement in his voice. "I think I'm going to have to do more reading."

"I'm never giving her up, so I'm finding ways to keep her occupied so she doesn't think about trying to leave me."

He was growing right there in her mouth, and the sensation was so good. She closed her eyes, no longer hearing more than their voices off in some distance. She decided the first step was to want to give him the best experience of his life, so good he wouldn't be able to talk or even think, and to do that, she had to drown out everything but him. She concentrated on the shape of him, the taste and texture of him. She simply worshipped him. She loved him with everything she was. She lavished attention on him, using every technique she knew aroused him the most.

Next, she had to make this so good for him that he could no longer see or hear anything but her and her mouth and what she was doing to him. She knew he had gone beyond the point of no return when he groaned. His fist tightened in her hair and he began to talk dirty to her. His hips thrust deep, and she forced herself to relax. He let her breathe and then surged forward again.

"Look at me, princess. I want to see your eyes."

She loved that. She loved when he looked into her eyes. She lifted her lashes to all that startling blue and saw what she was doing to him — shattering him. So perfect. She lashed him with her tongue and took him deeper.

His strangled cry was the sound of ecstasy to her ears. She loved that sound and wanted to hear it again and again. It helped to keep her from panicking when her air was cut off and she thought he might not let her breathe. Even then, she felt him pulsing on her tongue, his heart beating against the roof of her mouth. She forced her throat to relax as he pushed even deeper. Then he was helpless, emptying himself into her, groaning deeply, mindless because she gave that to him. She took her time making certain he was clean before she let him help her up. She had done exactly what she'd wanted to do, and she'd never been happier. She loved him with every breath in her body. With every beat of her heart. She chose this man, and she was determined to be happy and confident in herself as his woman and just as confident in their relationship.

SEVENTEEN

Czar lay on the rooftop of the apartment building across the street from their target. His honor, the renowned judge Bonner James, one of the main members of the con ring, had his elegant luxury condo facing the ocean so he could have his view. The back side of his condo faced the apartments were Czar had positioned himself so he could direct his pack.

The judge had a visitor tonight. His bedroom was in the back of the house, and he kept his curtains open. Never a good thing for a judge who sat on the bench and wanted an impeccable reputation. Most likely his proclivity of having Mistress Scarlet visit him was what had gotten him in trouble in the first place. Czar had never understood why others gave a damn about what a man or woman preferred in the bedroom, but apparently society liked to pass judgment. As far as he was concerned, that was what was wrong with half the world.

They'd have to wait until Mistress Scarlet finished collecting her tools of the trade and left. She was very businesslike, patting the judge's face as she unstrapped him and gathered everything up, including the money on the bedside table. They exchanged a few words and then she breezed out of the condo.

The judge wrapped himself in a short silk robe and went to the small bar he kept in his bedroom to pour himself a nightcap.

He's alone. Awake. Move in.

In answer to his command, Transporter rappelled from the roof to the front of the condo and knelt by the door. Around him, the rest of the team dropped from the roof, spread out, staying still; it was always the unexpected that got one in trouble.

He's turned on his stereo and appears to be settling. He's in bed, Czar told his team.

That was good. They could hear the music. Classical. The judge liked it loud. Hopefully the neighbors were used to it.

Transporter had the door unlocked and he cautiously pushed it open. Ice took lead, entering first. The room, as expected, was empty. He was a little shocked that the judge didn't have a better security system than the crappy one they'd found and disabled. It was more for show than real, probably because the judge didn't want to take a chance that anyone might be able to get a shot of him on camera doing what he loved best, so he'd bought a security system off the Internet rather than having one installed by an actual company.

Ice moved into the room, padding across the floor, careful not to touch anything. They had Winston's prints and a few hair follicles they'd gotten from a brush in his bathroom. They had decided that Winston would take the blame for the deaths of the other members of the con ring. It was known that he had a bad temper, and when he was angry, he was clearly capable of murder. More than once he'd been seen yelling at a couple of the others. Ice had been in his home several times in the last week, collecting everything they would need.

The story had broken in the news, and it had been huge. The missing heiress was married to a biker. That was exactly the kind of news that seemed to appeal to everyone. Winston had insisted she was ill, and her marrying a biker only proved his point. He wanted her seen by a doctor and remanded to his custody. He had been very specific about which doctor she was to see. Dr. Cyrus Mills had to be involved with the con artist ring, and when Code looked closer into his financials, it was very clear that he was.

Ice had been shocked at how many upstanding citizens were involved. Code began to go back several years and found more than fifteen women who had died under what he considered suspicious circumstances, and that was just in the Northern California area. Perhaps if they'd all been married to the same man, their deaths would have raised an alarm, but only a few times had the same man been widowed there in California. Code said the pattern was repeated in other places.

Winston had wanted in on the scheme, and he'd been given his chance. No one was very happy with him. Now, he had drawn attention to them. Even if they got Soleil back, it wasn't as if they could just kill her right away, unless they could make it look like a suicide.

Ice and Storm crossed the room to the hallway. Czar sent Mechanic and Transporter to check the other rooms while Savage walked boldly into the bedroom, the twins behind him, immediately spreading out. Absinthe followed them in.

The judge had his eyes closed but, sensing the menace, opened them and tried to grab for his phone. Savage yanked it from him. He didn't say anything, just put the phone in his pocket and stepped back.

Ice smiled at him. "Good evening, Judge. I'm so glad you had a nice relaxing evening with Mistress Scarlet. I always like to know a man's last night is a happy one."

The judge put his sternest face on. "What do you want?"

"You had to know, sooner or later, your lifestyle was going to catch up to you, and I don't mean the lovely Mistress Scarlett. Your friends have been murdering women for several years now, and you help them do it."

The judge shook his head and pulled back, looking innocent. "No. No. Absolutely not. I have no idea what you're talking about."

"You don't want me to let Savage loose on you, Judge. We already know you're a part of the con ring targeting very wealthy women."

The judge hesitated, started to bluster and then changed his mind. "Those women are dying. The men make their last days very happy ones. They choose to let those men in their lives and are glad for them. They're grateful. No one suffers. The money has to go somewhere."

"Some of those women were in their early forties or late thirties. And then there's Soleil. She's not even thirty. They weren't dying, and you know it. You may try to justify it, but in the end their lives don't matter to you, only the things you can have with the money they pay you."

"What do you want? Tell me what you want!" The judge fisted his silk robe as he shouted his demand, his face twisted with anger and fear. He was used to commanding authority, but no one seemed very impressed.

"I want to know the name of every single person working with you. *All* of them. You shouldn't leave anyone out. This gentleman" — Ice indicated Absinthe — "will know if you're telling the truth. He is going to check your pulse while you tell us."

"Don't you touch me," the judge snapped.

Ice produced a gun and shoved it in the judge's mouth. "Or I could just blow your fuckin' brains out right now. It's all the same to me."

The judge nodded, and Absinthe took his wrist loosely. Ice removed the gun. "Start talking. Just names. Be clear."

"Dr. Cyrus Mills. Detective Danny Sullivan, San Francisco PD. Officer Paul Bailey,

California Highway Patrol. Dr. Ronny Tiptree, medical examiner. Simon Overfield,
Evergreen Mortuary. Donald Monroe, he's
a lawyer. Harbin Conner, he's an assistant
police chief." The judge coughed, his eyes
darting around the room as if looking for a
miraculous escape.

Ice shook his head. "You're doing great,
just keep going."

"Darrin Johnson. Ben Thurston. They go
after the women."

"How many others? Who are they?"

"The widowers. There's six of them.
Originally five. Winston makes six. Cooper
Knight, Bob Flannigan, Peter Daniels."

"That's the entire ring?"

"Yes, yes. I think they have others helping
them in other places. They're branching
out."

"Nice. Must be lucrative."

"They want to recruit some women to
help them," the judge offered eagerly, seeing that everyone appeared much more relaxed.

"How'd this start? Who's the boss?"

"We all are. It just kind of evolved. We got
talking over poker. All that money at the
charity events we have to go to. The women
dripping in diamonds. What a waste." He
looked around the room at the grim faces.

"It is, isn't it? So much money we could all share."

"Would be nice if all of you lived through tonight, wouldn't it?" Ice asked. He caught up a pillow, thrust it over the judge's face and fired three bullets into him.

Paul Bailey, an officer with the California Highway Patrol, sauntered out of the diner where he stopped every evening to get his coffee before he resumed his patrol. Driving the choked highways could get both boring and dangerous if he didn't keep up the fuel. He was on the lookout for bikers — the scum of the earth, as far as he was concerned. He didn't like that they could ride legally through traffic when everyone else had to sit and wait for the lanes to open. He didn't like a lot of things about them.

And now, Soleil Brodeur, the woman Winston had targeted, was *married* to one. Sleeping in his bed. She was beautiful. Sexy. There were photographs of her in every news article and magazine everywhere he went — even the diner. Shit. Winston had that. Could have kept it for a while, and he blew it. Now some biker had it while he was stuck driving the highways and listening to people bitch all the time.

He opened the door to his patrol car, slid

in, and froze. There was a file taped to his dashboard. He ripped it down and opened it. Names jumped out at him. Dates. His heart began to pound, and he looked wildly around him.

That's when he saw that his rifle was gone. He kept it strapped right where he could pull it free if needed. It wasn't there. Not quite believing it, he looked on the floorboards and then on the seat again. He started to call it in but hesitated. Even after destroying the file, there would be so much paperwork. So many questions. An internal investigation. He couldn't afford to be looked at too closely.

Cursing, he stepped out of the car and looked around. Above the diner, on the roof, something moved. He squinted, looking for focus. A man seemed to be standing there, just looking at him. And then he saw the other one — the one holding the rifle. Flame seemed to blossom from the barrel, and something knocked him over. The sound reverberated loudly through the night and he found himself on his knees, and then his face hit the dirt, and everything went black.

"You know we've got to get rid of that son of a bitch," said Harbin Conner, assistant police chief of the San Francisco Police Department, dealing the cards to the others at the table. "He's all over the news." He glared at Donald Monroe, a very high-powered attorney. "And you advised him. Now we're in a hell of a mess."

"Winston had already gone to the cops in Vegas to help him look for her and then taken it to the newspapers. We were left hanging. I thought it would get to the judge and he'd quietly handle it and we'd get off scot-free."

"It didn't work out that way, did it?" Detective Danny Sullivan snapped. "She's become this romantic heroine. The heiress with the biker. What a crock of shit."

"You have anything on this club? I've never heard of them," Monroe asked.

"I've got our people looking into it," Harbin Conner said. "They're up north, on the coast, three or four hours from here. They're a small-time, nothing club. Even the Diamondbacks don't think they're worth pushing around. Very small. Probably a bunch of weekenders wanting chicks to think they're hot."

Dr. Cyrus Mills picked up his cards, discarded two immediately and tapped the table. "This will blow over. No one needs to panic. If necessary, we can lie low for a while. I agree, Winston needs to go. He's a weak link. We let the woman live for a while with her biker, and she'll get sick of slumming and be ready for a wealthy man who wants to spoil her."

Harbin Conner nodded at the assessment. "I've never understood why these women want the bikers to debase them and treat them like servants. Why get beat up and carry their drugs for them, taking all the risks?"

The detective nodded. "Most of them won't turn on their man for anything." He shrugged. "I don't get it either. And this chick, the heiress, she's young and damned good-looking."

"Maybe after Winston, she needed a real man," Dr. Ronny Tiptree ventured. He was a medical examiner and best friends with Mills. "He's got a foul temper."

"Who brought him in?" Sullivan asked.

Monroe pushed chips into the middle of the table. "Cooper Knight. He's delivered two big scores for us. I'm not putting this on him."

"Still, maybe we should serve him notice so that he works all the harder for us," the assistant police chief said. He tossed his chips into the middle of the table, indicating he was in. "We started this with one widower, and we should have stuck with five. Let's pull back in and wait this out."

Monroe tossed back his drink. "Over cards. Funny how playing cards can always have you coming up with the best ideas, Harbin."

Harbin raised his glass toward Monroe. "Here's to all of us. We get rid of Winston and leave the little biker bitch alone for a while. Tell the others to lie low and then when we know we're in the clear, we can resume business as usual."

"What did the honorable Judge James have going tonight that was so important?" Detective Sullivan asked. "He rarely misses poker night."

Monroe winked at him. "Mistress Scarlett had to cancel her last two visits, and this was her only night open for him."

"He told you that?" Sullivan raised his eyebrow.

Monroe shook his head and indicated Harbin. "He did."

"Got her phone bugged," the assistant police chief said. "I like to know who in our little community likes to use her services."

They all burst out laughing.

"My wife wants to head to Paris in the next couple of months," Mills said. "If she hasn't already been talking to your wife,

Ronny, she will be."

"Yeah, I've been hearing nothing else for the last week. Was going to warn you."

"Your wives spend more money than half the old biddies in San Francisco," Monroe accused.

"True, but they put on the best fund-raisers and attract the richest widows as well," Tiptree pointed out. "I'm out, gentlemen." He tossed his cards facedown on the table. "Without the two of them, we would have a much more difficult time finding out about our marks. They're better at gathering information than detectives, present company excluded."

Sullivan raised his glass to Tiptree.

Czar looked around at the team spread out in front of him. "There you have it. Our great minds. Whiskey and cards, they plan to kill innocent women for their money. Nice. Really nice. And they think bikers are scum."

"Do you think the wives know?" Reaper asked. "I couldn't tell from their conversation."

Czar thought it over and then shook his head. "That doesn't feel right to me. I doubt if the others would trust them to that extent. I think the poker friends thought the scheme up and that it started with one, they got away with it and then they got greedy."

"We have to be certain we got the head of the snake," Ice said. "I don't want any of them coming after Soleil."

"And nothing can tie back to her," Storm added.

"The cops might look at her because her name's been in the news tied to Winston, but there isn't a tie at all to any of the others. The file we left in the highway patrol car didn't have any reference to this scheme. Bailey liked to blackmail people. The others didn't know about his side business. Code found his money and the damning entries in his computer. That will explain his death. It will appear that someone got very tired of being blackmailed."

"Are you certain blowing all of them up is a good idea, Czar?" Transporter asked from under the Mercedes Dr. Mills drove.

"We were very fortunate in that Winston was in the military and handled explosives for four years," Czar said. "It's a fitting way for them to go, and when the cops find Winston, he'll have the evidence of all these bombs in his apartment. We used his credit card to buy the materials as well."

"Nice," Mechanic said. He pushed down

588

the hood of the matching Mercedes Tiptree owned.

Ice glanced at his watch. "They'll be out in about eight more minutes."

"Harbin Conner will be up in his room, like every Friday night. It will take him about four minutes before he turns on his television set. The explosives are set to go off near simultaneously," Transporter said and rolled out from under the Mercedes. He grinned at Mechanic. "Nothing fancy. We didn't want anyone to think this took brains."

The men gathered tools, making certain to leave nothing behind. All four cars gleamed under the parking garage's lights. Code had dealt with the cameras, but it didn't matter, they stayed to the shadows. The entire team slipped back into the night and waited.

The four poker players came out together, laughing and exchanging quick good-byes. Dr. Mills and Dr. Tiptree slid behind the wheel of their respective Mercedeses. Monroe broke off to climb into his sporty Aston Martin. Detective Danny Sullivan preferred his SUV. He couldn't look as if he had a shit-pile of money, and the SUV was good for off-roading.

Waving, they started out of the parking

garage. Once on the street, Sullivan turned to the left while the other three turned right. A window blew out in one of the condos above the garage, a wall of flames shooting out. Monroe slammed on his brakes and looked up as a body on fire followed after shattered glass and dropped like stone toward the street. Behind him, Tiptree's Mercedes exploded, and immediately, Mills's vehicle in front of him did the same. In the distance, he could hear another explosion and he sat still, his heart slamming loudly, waiting. Two heartbeats later it came. The blast rocked the car, blowing up from under him, driving him right through the roof, smashing every bone in his body.

Czar didn't leave anything to chance. They waited, now across the street on the rooftop, watching to make certain every one of those involved in the planning of killing socialites for their money was dead. When the last body was accounted for, Ice and Storm looked at each other with satisfaction.

"Alena's got Overfield at the bar. She's looking pretty hot as a redhead. She's all spiked out, rock-and-roll style. He can't stop looking at her legs. Savage and Absinthe are covering her," Czar said. "Let's get moving. We still have all the players to get to before anyone, especially Winston, gets wind that his entire ring is gone."

"Come on, baby," Alena whined, rubbing her hand up and down Simon Overfield's thigh as if she couldn't stop touching him.

He owned and worked in the mortuary where all the bodies of the murdered women had been taken. He'd gone to school with both Tiptree, the medical examiner, and Mills and had remained close friends with them. His mortuary had become a very important piece of their business together.

"Don't you want to dance anymore?" Her fingertips came very close to his groin.

"I worked all day, darling," Overfield complained. "You've had me dancing for the last hour."

She would have shot herself had she danced with him that long. He couldn't dance. Mostly he turned in circles and stepped on her feet while he rubbed his body against hers.

"Do you want another drink?" he asked hopefully.

Alena was dressed in high boots, a miniskirt and a camisole that pushed her generous breasts up so they were nearly falling out of her top. She wore a bright red wig that was short with spiked hair, dark brown contacts and long gloves that matched her boots.

She leaned in close to Overfield, one hand sliding around his neck while the other slid up his thigh to his crotch. "What I really want to do is take you into the alley and fuck your brains out. I've been wanting to do that all night."

His breath hitched. His cock jumped under her hand. She squeezed it through his trousers.

"Please, baby, you've been teasing me all night." She batted her lashes and parted her lips so the tip of her tongue touched the top of her teeth.

Overfield grabbed his drink and tossed it down his throat so fast he coughed. "Come on, Mary, I wouldn't want to keep you waiting." He caught her hand and tugged until she slipped from the bar stool. He grabbed his suit jacket and led the way, nearly pulling her out of the bar. He stood just outside for a moment, looking around as if he didn't know the proper direction to go. Alena let him, wanting him to feel desperate.

He turned to her and she smiled and took his hand again, tugging to take him around the corner of the building into the alley. She kept walking until they were all the way in the middle of the narrow lane. A homeless man sat with his back against the wall several feet from the other end, wrapped in a blanket, talking to a second homeless man who was stretched out, looking as if he was trying to sleep.

"They can see us," Overfield whispered.

She laughed. "Isn't that hot? Don't you want to fuck me up against the wall with them watching? How hot would that be?" She put one hand on his shoulder. "I forgot to tell you something, Simon. It's really important."

"You need money?" He sounded a little disappointed, but willing.

"No, I'm not the one taking money, that would be you," she whispered, keeping that same smile on her face. Keeping her tone the same. "You take money to keep quiet about the murders. All those women murdered. Their voices cry out to me for justice. You wouldn't give it to them, so I have no choice."

He stared at her a moment, uncomprehending. Then he began to sputter, bringing up his hands to push her away. It was too late. The long, thin dagger went right into his heart. He opened his mouth to yell, and the dagger went through the jugular in the side of his neck. Alena knew enough to stay to the opposite side so the blood spray wouldn't get on her. She waited until he slowly collapsed to the ground, and she crouched beside him, helping to lower him almost gently.

While he bled out, she peeled off the gloves and clothes, and then pulled off the thin plastic she had covering her clean clothing. That was crumpled up and stuffed inside her tote, which she'd already turned inside out so that rather than a bright saucy red, it was a muted mushroom. She carefully inspected her body and clothing to make certain not one speck of blood was on her.

She wore a dark dress that fell well below the knee and sandals rather than heels. She walked to the entrance of the alley where the two "homeless" men were. Absinthe and Savage had shed their disguises, fitting them into the briefcases each carried. They were now dressed in suits and they emerged together, the three walking toward the upscale hotel in the distance.

Once they'd passed it, Alena dropped the rolled-up plastic into one of the large hotel dumpsters and continued walking without missing a beat.

Cooper Knight and Bob Flannigan were doing what they usually did on a Friday night when they weren't working. Both were very good-looking, in their early fifties but could pass for late fifties or early sixties if they needed to. Some older widows refused to look at men they considered much younger. Knight enjoyed his work. He threw himself into the role of the adoring and attentive male finding an older woman who "understood" him. Often, he had money; other times, he didn't. Once he was officially widowed, women felt sorry for him and he was fair game. In his role he cared for the woman, and when she died, however that was — he preferred an accident — he felt sorrow for her passing.

Tonight, like most Friday nights, they sat in Bob Flannigan's apartment, watched porn and discussed acting technique. Knight believed himself superior. Flannigan had difficulty closing a deal with a rich widow, whereas Knight could tell when he was first introduced how big of a challenge the woman was going to be. For him, the thrill was in that challenge. Flannigan felt differently. He just wanted the job over.

"That's why you have so much trouble, Bob," Knight said, leaning back and taking a handful of popcorn. "You don't appreciate the actual work. You're an actor. You have to view yourself as an actor. You take on a role. We go to these charity events in that role. We get the list of names from Harbin and then we just walk around and talk to the various women. Sooner or later you'll feel a connection, not between you and the woman but between whatever role you've chosen, that person, and the woman."

Bob rolled his eyes. "Seriously, Knight? You think like that? No wonder it takes you so damn long to get the job done." His gaze jumped to the screen as he watched two women working a man's cock. He sighed. "You ever have that? Because those old ladies aren't going to give you that."

"Those old ladies have experience, Bob. Some of them are very, very good at what they do. You never look at the larger picture."

Bob grunted but he didn't take his gaze from the screen. "I do my job."

"But you don't enjoy it." Knight was on a roll now, completely into the argument. "I want my woman to have the best time of her life with me, for however long that lasts. I know she's going to die, but she doesn't. We laugh and talk together. She falls in love. She has it all. A man who adores her. Is completely attentive. When she dies, she dies happy, not alone and sad and ill. She goes out the way she should. Then I'm not up at night thinking I'm doing something wrong."

"You *are* doing something wrong, you moron. You're murdering a woman for her money," Bob pointed out.

"Not really. I earned the money. And I don't murder her. She has an accident."

"Don't get offended. You always want to talk about this, but you get offended when the truth comes out. Shut up already."

A voice came out of the shadows. "I was very interested in his point of view. Weren't you, Ice? Storm?"

Another voice answered, "I've never met anyone who could convince themselves that murder wasn't really murder. When I kill someone, I know I fucking murdered them." Ice stepped out of the shadows and knocked the phone from Knight's hand. "Don't be stupid, you've got several guns pointed at you."

"What do you want? Money?" Knight sounded snide.

"I don't need money," Ice said. "I want you dead. Those women didn't even matter to you."

"They didn't matter to anyone but me," Knight corrected. He narrowed his eyes as the others stepped out of the shadows. "You're the motorcycle club. The one that took in the bitch Winston was supposed to deal with."

Ice casually slammed his gun across Knight's face, opening a cut that began to bleed profusely. "No one gets to call my wife a bitch. You can apologize or I can keep going. I don't much care either way." He sounded bored.

"I apologize," Knight said immediately, reaching for the roll of paper towels they kept close. "I didn't mean that the way it sounded."

"Knight," Bob hissed. "Shut the hell up." He turned to Ice. "Just tell us what you want."

"Well," Ice said, "I want to know how a man with your background, Bob, a man who came from a good family, with decent parents and all, thinks murdering women for money is perfectly okay. I'm very interested."

"Just get it over with," Bob snapped. "I don't need the bleeding-heart lecture from a fucking biker."

"I'm a fucking biker assassin, Bob. I've been killing since I was five years old. Grew up doing this shit, and I'm still doing it. Always envied those houses with real parents and then I come across scum like you and wonder what the hell happened."

Bob gave him the finger, and Ice shot him between the eyes. Knight screamed, a high-pitched sound the bullet Ice fired cut off.

They left the movie playing with the scattered popcorn soaking up the blood, disappearing into the shadows just as they'd come in.

Peter Daniels entered the club feeling as if he were on top of the world. It was a good night. The best. He was good-looking and knew it. Already pushing sixty, he looked like the proverbial silver fox. He was the perfect age to appeal to both young women and older women. He'd brought in forty million dollars for his group, so he was being hailed as a hero, and now he wore the coveted title of widower, the most sought after of all men.

Those who'd thought up their scam were pure genius, and he was willing to give them their due. It hadn't been difficult to arrange for his "sweetheart," a really lovely woman of seventy-eight, who was still very active, to work out, drink champagne, have sex and sit in the hot tub. She'd taken some pills to energize herself for their incredibly adventurous romp. He'd left her only for a few minutes to fix them some caviar on her favorite crackers. During that time, she must have tried to exit the hot tub, slipped, hit her head and fallen underwater.

No one had been more distraught than he had. They'd only been married three months. The detective, Danny Sullivan, had pronounced it a terrible accident. The medical examiner had confirmed it and the insurance people had made everything smooth and easy for him, feeling so sorry that he'd lost his dream wife just when he'd found her.

He was on a high that didn't seem to fade as he surveyed the room. So many women. So little time. He went to the nearest bar, looking down the row of bar stools to see who might catch his eye. He felt intensely powerful and wondered if it was because he had gotten away with murder. If this was how it felt every time, he was going to work overtime to find the right woman and make her fall for him. It hadn't been that difficult.

There was a beautiful dark-haired woman sitting alone at a small table looking sad. She was drinking what looked to be a cosmopolitan. Perfect. She had a really good body. An amazing body. He liked what she was wearing. It showed just enough, not too much. She wasn't putting herself on display. She wore gloves, delicate little things, to go with her perfect little black dress. He had to make a move on her before any of the other men eyeing her did.

He ordered two drinks, one for her, one for himself, and walked over with complete confidence. "Would you mind sharing your table? There's nowhere to sit and I'm afraid I'm not as young as I used to be."

She glanced up, looking annoyed at first, and then when his words sank in and she checked out his gray hair, she waved him toward the seat. He put the drinks down. "I figured the least I could do was order you a drink."

"Thank you."

She sounded shy, and the smile she gave him confirmed she must be.

"What's your name? I'm Peter, Peter Daniels."

She hesitated again. "Alice, Alice Burns." Alena gave him her sweetest smile. Her hair was a dark mane of chestnut and her eyes were that dark chocolate she'd used earlier. It was just easier to leave the contacts in.

"What are you doing here all alone?"

She swallowed and looked down at her hands. "I lost my husband recently — well, it still feels recent but it's been over a year. He . . . we . . . I own a tech business and we took our first vacation in a very long time. There was an accident and he . . ."

She trailed off and then looked at Peter Daniels with her tragic face that could bring a room to tears. "I just lost him. My friends told me to quit moping, that it was time I got out of the house, but I still think it's too soon."

"I recently lost my wife as well," Peter said. "You're right, friends push and push and they don't understand."

Alena reached for her drink, knocked into his and then managed to save them both, a small embarrassed smile lighting up her face. "I was going to suggest we toast to our friends, but I'm a bit of a klutz. It might not be safe."

He grabbed his glass as she lifted hers. "To our friends who we both let push us around."

"I'll drink to that," Alena agreed, and lifted her drink toward her mouth, her eyes beginning to dance with amusement.

Peter took a healthy drink and looked at her over the rim of his glass. "You didn't drink."

"I was just thinking about what I said. About it might not be safe, and how I'm a klutz. There's a half-dozen ways I could think of that I could die just because I'm drinking this drink."

Peter took another long drink. The alcohol

went down smoothly. He liked the way it made him feel. Warm inside. Cool on the outside. Sexy. His little widow was warming up to him nicely. He began to fantasize about how he would remove her sexy dress.

"How could you do that?" He sipped again.

"Well, suppose we were together and had just made love. Can you imagine that?" She put her drink down and leaned her chin onto the heel of her hand, staring into his eyes.

Peter nearly gulped down the rest of his drink, almost choking. "I'm with you," he said, because he was. He *so* was. The little minx was missing sex. He could provide that for her.

"Right? And you decided to go into the kitchen and get us something to snack on, something like caviar and crackers. Meanwhile, I'm drinking my drink, not paying attention, and slip and fall and hit my head."

His smiled faded. "Who are you?" he demanded. He looked around. Seated across from their table at the bar was a man watching them. He was the scariest man Peter had ever seen. He was dressed in an expensive suit, he was bald, very muscular, and Peter could see tattoos swimming up his neck.

"Another way would be my husband, who I believed loves me, takes my head and slams it against the side of the hot tub and then drowns me. That could happen just as easily." She leaned even closer. "Or, someone who knows what you did might bring justice for that woman by slipping a very fast-acting poison into your drink. That would work just as well." Alena picked up her clutch, smiled at him and stood.

Peter stood as well, nearly knocking over the table so that the drinks rattled, and heads turned.

Alena picked up her drink and threw it in his face. "Leave me alone. And stop following me everywhere. I've asked you repeatedly to leave me alone." She marched toward the door, her head high.

Peter took a step after her. Then another. The door to the club swung closed after her. He did his best to hurry but his heart beat so hard and his vision blurred. How did she know? He made it to the door, pushed it open and fell at the bouncer's feet.

What had she said? Poison in his drink? She'd put poison in his drink. He grabbed the bouncer as the man leaned over him, trying to tell him, but no sound emerged. He looked up to see the scary man from the bar looking down at him dispassionately.

"Looks like a heart attack to me. You'd better call an ambulance." He watched the man walk away as everything around him began to fade.

Ben Thurston and Darrin Johnson had gone to school together, worked together and done just about everything else, especially hunting and fishing. They'd even shared women. Neither was interested in having their own woman, since there were far too many to tie themselves to one. On Fridays they often went to their go-to fishing place, Lake Merced. By car it wasn't much of a distance, and they often stayed until very late, drinking beer and just enjoying the quiet.

Fishing hadn't been the best, neither was lucky, but they didn't care. They ate the dinner they'd brought with them and sat watching a storm brew out over the lake, threatening to come in on a building wind.

Two men came toward them, walking briskly. Neither carried a fishing pole and they walked with great authority, as if they knew exactly what they were doing and it was all business. They seemed to be headed straight for them.

Darrin exchanged a quick look with Ben. Something about the two men made him uneasy. He started to stand up as they drew near. They didn't pause or slow down, they just kept up that same brisk walk. Both wore trench coats, both wore gloves. One had a gun in his hand. *Gun.* Darrin thought he shouted it, but no sound emerged. He felt the bullet hit, pain blossoming through his chest. He looked at Ben. Half of Ben's head seemed to be a bloody mess. He looked down at his chest. It was the same. He went to his knees and then folded forward, his face hitting dirt and rocks.

The two men never missed a step. They kept walking.

"Hi, Winston," Ice greeted as the man came into his apartment. "I've been waiting for you." He gestured around the apartment. "Do you like the new look? I was very careful to make certain there was no mess. I hope you appreciate that."

Winston had stopped at the door, shocked to see someone in his apartment. Behind him, someone crowded close, all but pushing him inside. The door closed behind him and he found himself in his own apartment with four strange men. The one in front of him, smiling that irritating smirk, had a tattoo of three teardrops dripping from his eye.

"What are you doing in here? What is all

of this? Who are you?"

"You're supposed to be so smart, Winston," Ice said. "You can see I'm wearing my club colors. I'm the husband. Soleil's husband. Soleil. The woman you were setting up to be killed. She's my wife and you still came after her. I just want you to understand that you doing that pisses me off."

He kept smiling, but his eyes were glacier cold. So cold Winston shivered and looked over his shoulder toward the door. A big man stood in front of it. There was no escape that way. His mind raced with possibilities. His best bet was to try to call the cops, get attention.

He noticed the cord running through Ice's gloved hands. "What is all this?" He recognized the materials for explosives. They were neatly set up on his kitchen table, as if he'd been making bombs.

"Well, this is the evidence that is going to convince the cops that you had a very big grudge against a lot of people. The poker-playing bunch, you know, the judge, cops, lawyer, even the medical examiner. Didn't you hear the news? They all died tonight. Most of them at Conner's house, where poker took place. Someone blew them up. The judge was shot. So were Darrin and

Ben, two very good friends of yours. Unfortunately, you were heard arguing with them. That's always bad. The gun's over there on the table as well."

Ice casually walked over to it and picked it up, looked at it and then handed it to Winston. Winston took it without thinking and turned it to point it at Ice.

Ice raised his eyebrow. "Did you think I'd hand you a loaded gun?"

Reality hit. Winston sighed and shook his head. "What do you want?"

"Go ahead and fire it. I could have left one in the chamber," Ice encouraged. "Of course if you hit me, my friend right behind you is going to put a bullet in your head."

"It isn't loaded," Winston said and pulled the trigger.

To his shock, there was a bullet, and he'd fired it into the wall. Ice whistled and went to look at the wall. He dug out the bullet. "You could have shot your way out of here, Winston. That was careless of me. You'd better give that to me."

Winston tried firing it straight at Ice, but the gun was empty. He flung the weapon from him. Nothing made sense.

"They're all dead, you know." Ice indicated the beam above his head. "Every one of your friends is dead, and you're implicated in just about every murder. Even the poison used to kill Peter is in your cupboard. You feel really bad about it, don't you?"

Winston was so busy watching Ice push the cable through his fingers, he'd all but forgotten those behind him. Something bit into his neck and then choked him. It happened so fast there was no way to determine what was happening. Then he was hanging, his feet off the ground, a chair knocked over right under him. He kicked with his feet and reached with his hands to try to free the cord choking him, but it was already too late. The world was going black.

Ice looked him directly in the eye. "You tried to kill my wife, you son of a bitch."

That was the last thing Winston heard before he choked to death.

Soleil rolled over and looked up at Ice. He thought she was the most beautiful woman in the world. When she was like this, drowsy, her eyes half-closed but that soft, welcoming smile on her lips, his heart always stuttered, and his stomach did that slow roll. He loved her. That was the bottom line. He didn't even care anymore that he was so far gone over her.

"Hey, honey," she said softly. Her voice was an invitation, even though he'd woken her from a sound sleep. "Did you finish the floor? What time is it?"

"Yes, we finished it, but it took a little longer than we thought it would. Ran into a problem, but the apartment is ready to rent. Bannister is going to move into that one, and we'll start working on the next one. It's around three."

"You sound tired."

She pushed her fingers through his hair and his scalp tingled. She made him feel good. Welcome. She made him feel as if he belonged there — with her.

"Come get into bed, Ice."

"I don't know if I'm cut out for carpentry work," he said.

"No, you're not cut out to be a carpenter. You're a jeweler. Your pieces are beautiful."

"We all pull our shift," he said. "I don't really mind." He tugged back the covers. She was naked, the way he liked her to be. He slid in next to her and wrapped his arm around her, needing her close. "I love you, princess." He whispered it to her, uncaring that he was giving so much away.

She put her arm around his chest and snuggled close. "I love you too. Go to sleep."

Thank fuck she hadn't looked at the clock.

EIGHTEEN

"Thank you for seeing Soleil here, rather than at your office," Absinthe said. "She's been through a lot what with losing her lawyer, and now all this coming out about her former fiancé."

Jonas Harrington, the local sheriff, and his deputy, Jackson Deveau, both smiled down at Soleil as she stood close to Ice, unknowingly seeking his protection while they greeted the two law enforcement officers at the door.

"Ice," Jonas said. "Absinthe."

"Harrington, Deveau," Absinthe returned while Ice just nodded.

Ice stepped back and gestured toward the great room. "We can go through here to the smaller sitting room. Soleil prefers that." He took her hand and brought her knuckles to his mouth, smiling at her over their joined hands. She gave him that faint smile that told him she was nervous as hell and didn't know what to expect.

"Ice, you don't mind if we speak to Soleil alone for a few minutes?" Harrington said smoothly. "That was part of the deal."

Ice didn't need the bullshit reminder. They weren't kidding anyone. The two men wanted to make certain the club wasn't holding her hostage or in any way putting influence on her that would make her feel she had no choice but to stay with them.

"I have no problem with that," he said. "I'll get coffee. Would either of you like some?"

"Sounds good," Jonas said. "I take mine black."

Deveau, a man of few words, just nodded. "Same."

Ice opened the glass sitting-room door, stopped Soleil just inside and tipped her face up to his. "I'll only be a few minutes, princess. Absinthe will be right outside the room if you need him. You okay with this?"

She nodded. "Yes, of course."

Ice didn't like leaving her when she looked so vulnerable. He hesitated beside Harrington, who was a very perceptive man, and lingered to wait to hear what he had to say. He detested giving anything away to a cop, but he would if it helped Soleil. "Treat her gently," he advised Jonas.

Harrington studied his face, seeing too much. "You really love her, don't you?"

"I married her," Ice said, and turned and walked out. He had to. He needed to be certain he was under control.

Czar had warned him from the beginning that there were too many leads back to Soleil and that, although they'd tied up everything in a neat package for the detectives, they would want to make certain Soleil was where she was because she wanted to be, and that Winston, who appeared to have killed a lot of people, had really done so.

Soleil had a lot of money. More than he'd first realized. He hadn't cared, so when Code had whistled and pointed to the amount, he'd barely flicked a glance toward the screen. He had plenty of money. They didn't need hers. He didn't even want hers. But her money could have paid for some very experienced hit men. He supposed he couldn't blame the cops for having that question in their minds. They could look at her financials and see she hadn't touched her money.

Absinthe had gone over and over with Soleil the questions she was allowed to answer without him sitting beside her. The moment the police were satisfied that she wasn't being coerced, she was to call him into the room.

Soleil had been trained in the best boarding schools both in the country and abroad. She carried herself perfectly, shoulders and back straight, hands folded neatly in her lap, her head up and no fidgeting. That had been drilled into her and came in handy on so many occasions. She could look haughty and annoyed, or vulnerable and sad, depending on what the situation called for. She had confidence in herself, but she was concerned about Ice.

No one believed someone like Soleil, an heiress to a fortune, could possibly have fallen in love with a man like Ice. Law enforcement actually believed the club had kidnapped her or coerced her into staying with them. They believed the club — and Ice — was after her money. She found it insulting on Ice's behalf.

She waited for either to open the conversation, betting it would be Harrington. He reminded her a little of Czar, where Deveau was more like Maestro or Keys.

"Thank you for seeing us, Soleil. There's a lot of people who are very surprised that you married Ice," Harrington said.

"Because he's in a club? I love the club and being on his motorcycle with him.

Given my past history of adrenaline sports, I wouldn't call it that surprising."

"Do you know his real name?" Deveau broke in.

They were going to play good cop, bad cop. She'd heard of that routine. "Of course I know his real name. We're married. When one gets married, you normally share names."

Deveau didn't wither as he should have under her haughtiest, very perfect dry-up-and-die look. He didn't seem the least affected.

"It is?" he challenged.

She didn't even stumble. "His name is Isaak, his brother's name is Dmitry and his sister's name is Alena, just in case you were going to ask their names as well. My last name is now Koval. Is that what you need to know?"

Jonas sent Jackson a quelling look. "Yes, we did need to know those things, Soleil. Winston Trent made some pretty nasty accusations before his death. He claimed you were being held prisoner, that these men were after your money and that you've been ill for some time."

"Ah, yes. The 'mentally ill, I need to take care of her and her money' scam. Do you know how many men actually think that's going to work? Winston inserted himself into my life and I couldn't get him out. Kevin Bennet, my lawyer —" She stopped and swallowed the sudden lump in her throat. She shook her head to clear it. Every time she thought of Kevin, she wanted to cry.

"Kevin was helping me get rid of him. With Winston, no didn't mean no. Even after I made it clear we weren't getting married, he hired an attorney I didn't approve of, or want for one. I had to go behind his back to get rid of the man."

"Why didn't you call law enforcement and file a restraining order?" Deveau demanded. "That seems like the smart thing to do."

"By the time I realized it would come to that, he had already started his campaign to make me look like I needed to go to a hospital."

"How did you meet Ice?" Harrington asked.

"In a bar. Winston had gotten very violent. I ran. I'd met Lana in a restroom of all places, and she'd given me her number just in case I got into trouble. They were all in Vegas because Steele and Breezy were getting married."

"Winston got violent?" Harrington echoed.

She nodded. "I made it *very* clear I wasn't going to marry him. He got angry and punched me several times. I was scared and I ran. I ran the opposite way of where I thought Winston would look for me. That way took me away from the strip and down toward the bars."

"Why didn't you go to the police then?" Deveau persisted.

"He had a lot of cop friends. I didn't know who to trust. I saw the bikes and someone outside wearing the Torpedo Ink colors like Lana had shown me and I went inside. I was too distraught to think it was a dumb idea to go into a biker bar. Fortunately, I met Ice right away, and he took care of me."

"Did he know you were an heiress?" Deveau asked.

"Not then. Probably later, when we talked marriage and I said he had to sign the prenup Kevin had drawn up. He signed it without hesitation."

"Ice signed a prenup drawn up by your previous lawyer," Harrington echoed, exchanging a long look with Deveau.

"Yes," she reiterated. "Without hesitation. If you're thinking he coerced me into this marriage in any way, he didn't. I wanted him almost from the first moment I set eyes on him. He was so sweet to me. He hated that Winston had put bruises on me. I tried to get him drunk and I deliberately tried to seduce him."

Both men exchanged grins. She ignored them. No one ever seemed to believe the truth, that she was the one at fault, not Ice. He always had to take the blame in everyone's eyes. It hadn't been that way, but everyone seemed determined to make him take the blame.

"I will admit I'd been drinking and so had he. When we woke up, the first thought was to dissolve the marriage, although I didn't want to. I liked him. I liked everything about him. I knew it was wrong to trap him into marriage and eventually I thought he'd be really upset about it. Then I saw Winston in the parking lot with a bunch of cops and I panicked. I got on Ice's bike and came here to Caspar. To this house."

Soleil looked around her. "It's so beautiful. He was offering me so much. A home. A family. And him. He's amazing. Caring. Very loving all the time. We don't have fights. We don't even argue. When I'm in the kitchen experimenting, he's right there with me."

"I'm sure you've been kept apprised of the investigation into Winston's death," Harrington said, abruptly switching subjects.

She smiled at him and sat back in the chair. "I think I'd like my lawyer with me now. I'd feel a lot more comfortable."

Before either of them could object, she waved at Absinthe, who was watching carefully. Ice had told her that he was able to lip-read and they'd determined ahead of time which chair for her to sit in so it would force the two law enforcement officers to sit in the ones that would give Absinthe the advantage of reading their lips. He came in immediately and took the chair beside hers.

"Gentlemen," he greeted.

Soleil was a little shocked at how different Absinthe looked when he dressed in a suit. Like the others, he was tatted and had defined muscles. He was blond with strange, crystallized eyes. They were so light blue they looked almost cloudy at times. He had one scar that curved along the left side of his jaw. Incredibly handsome, whether he was in blue jeans or a suit, he was intimidating. He was quiet, and spoke softly, but when he did speak, his voice was so compelling, she noticed the room would go silent.

"Are you all right, Soleil?" he asked, his voice incredibly gentle.

She could tell he was genuinely concerned for her, and that warmed her. She did have a family. She'd been accepted into Torpedo

Ink's circle and they were there, making certain she wasn't alone. Ice had given her that. Her Ice.

"Yes. We're just getting into the investigation into Winston and those horrible people. If I'd stayed with him, he would have murdered me." She rubbed her arms with her hands. The chills were real. She'd had no idea that there were so many people involved.

"As you know, Winston was involved in a con artist ring targeting wealthy women. These men would meet women at fundraising events and then insert themselves into their lives." Jonas Harrington leaned forward. "How much did you know about it?"

"Nothing at all." She could answer that honestly. "Winston would give me a list of names, both men and women, he wanted me to befriend. He claimed he was going into politics and it was important to know the right people. He would need money and donations and wanted me friends with very wealthy men and women. He also introduced me to several of the men that were involved with him in this horrible business." She gave a delicate little shudder.

Ice came in with a tray, putting it down on the coffee table and handing mugs to both Jonas and Jackson.

"Look at you, all domestic," Jonas teased.

Ice flipped him off and then settled himself on the arm of Soleil's chair. She loved it when he did that. She felt surrounded by the two members of Torpedo Ink, and safe. Treasured even. She reached up and took Ice's hand. He threaded his fingers through hers.

Watching Ice carefully, Jonas Harrington smiled at Soleil. She noticed Deveau never took his gaze off her. He was like a hawk, waiting for his prey to make a mistake so he could pounce.

"Where was Ice the night Winston hung himself?"

She blinked, everything in her going still. She looked up at Ice.

"Don't look at him. Look at me," Harrington said. "Where was he?"

Ice remained exactly the same beside her. Relaxed. Not in the least bit tense. Stomach churning, she wished she could be equally as calm. It made her angry, though.

"What are you accusing him of?" she demanded.

"Answer the question," Harrington persisted.

"Watch how you talk to her," Ice said. "I know you have a job to do, but you can be polite about it."

"My husband has been in bed with me every night since we've been married. In case you want to know, we have a very active sex life. I don't think I'd forget if he missed a night with me." She glared at Harrington.

He lifted his coffee cup to his mouth, but she caught the smile before he took a sip. That little smile made her relax again.

"So, he was with you that night?" Deveau persisted.

"Most of the night, yes. He worked with a crew putting in a floor at the apartments over the bar. Bannister was working as well. There were quite a few of the club members working that night. You can ask around."

By their expressions, it was clear they had already done that. She detested that. If they already knew, why ask? They had expected to catch her in a lie. She leaned her head against Ice. "I don't know what else I can tell you other than I'm happy with my husband and grateful I escaped when so many other women didn't."

"I'm happy as well," Jonas said. "Did Winston ever talk to you about being angry with any of these men he supposedly killed?"

"Winston was angry at the world. He believed himself superior to everyone, and if anybody crossed him, he believed in taking retaliatory action immediately. I thought it was proven he killed those men."

"They did trace all the bomb-making supplies back to him. He used his credit card. I suppose he didn't care enough to hide his purchases since he was going to kill himself."

"Honestly, I can see him killing all of them if he was angry. Maybe because he didn't get to me, they were kicking him out, although I didn't think he was the type to kill himself."

Her statement seemed to satisfy the two men when before she wasn't certain what they were looking for. They asked her a few more questions and then seemed to just chat with Ice and Absinthe about local business and Alena's restaurant. Just before they left, they asked her a few more questions about her marriage, and this time, they asked Ice as well.

In the end, they just got up and left. She let out her breath, not realizing she'd been holding it on and off, afraid, but of what, she didn't know.

Absinthe brushed his lips across her cheek. "You did great. I was proud of you." He followed the two men out, leaving her alone with her husband.

Ice pulled her out of the chair and put his arms around her.

"Stop shaking, princess, it's over. They'll leave you alone."

"What was he trying to imply? That you had something to do with those murders all the way in San Francisco? I didn't understand what he was getting at."

"We're MC. Law enforcement thinks all of us are criminals and we're always up to no good." He nuzzled her neck.

"They might be right. Come on, baby. Let's get to the club.

We're celebrating, remember?"

"I've forgotten what we're celebrating."

"We closed the deal with Inez. She owns the grocery store in Sea Haven, and she's promised to help us open ours. We're going into partnership with her so we can use the name. That was important to get the locals to use our store. She'll run it for a couple of months to make certain it's smooth sailing before she hands it over completely to us."

Soleil hadn't expected so many people. The party had gone on for hours. The alcohol buzzed pleasantly through her veins. She'd never laughed so hard or danced so much as she did that night. The locals attending had gone home, leaving only the clubs there, and that was when the real party started.

She sat outside by the firepit while all around them, the party took off. She enjoyed watching others. She'd been introduced to so many newcomers she couldn't remember any of their names, only that some were from another chapter of Torpedo Ink and others were from a club that wanted to patch over to Torpedo Ink.

Ice told her that every man there had attended one of the schools in Russia. She was somewhat surprised, as they all spoke perfect English without a trace of an accent. She was part of all this. Ice had given that to her. She looked up at him with absolute love. He happened to be watching her face in the firelight, and he smiled down at her. The look on his face was breathtaking.

"Come on, baby."

Her heart jumped and then began to pound. She'd been waiting for what seemed forever. She recognized that voice. She knew what was coming and all night, with the pounding beat of the music in her veins and her body, she'd been waiting. Sometimes she loved him so much she could barely breathe. She took his hand and let him pull her up.

She'd been surprised at his restraint. Usually, Ice didn't go very long without wanting to have sex with her. At home, when they were alone, he made love to her at least twice a day. Sometimes more often. He had been gentle with her that morning, so sweet and loving, she'd cried. He could do that, go from wild to tender, and she craved both from him.

He walked her over to a bench set out in the field of wildflowers Lana and Alena had originally encouraged to grow by throwing seed everywhere and hoping it worked. It had. The field had all sorts of colorful flowers blooming in the daylight hours. They seemed to close their petals at night, but it was still beautiful.

They could look out and see the ocean, the way the surf came and went, white foam spraying high into the air as the waves crashed against the rocks. It was a very clear night, and the stars were out in abundance. The moon was nearly full, spilling its silvery light overhead, turning the sea a mesmerizing blue and the field of flowers various shades of green.

Ice sank down on the bench, pulling her down beside him. The moment she sat, his arms went around her and he was kissing her. Transporting her. No matter how many times he kissed her, each time was that fiery slide into another world. She gave herself up to it, to him. He tasted hot, masculine, everything she wanted or needed.

"I want your cock," she whispered into his mouth. "I've wanted it all evening."

"Gotta earn it, baby," he whispered back, his teeth nipping her chin and following the line of her throat to the edging of lace around her tank.

Excitement welled up. "Tell me what I have to do," she said, throwing her head back, pushing her breasts out for him to have better access. "I'll do anything you ask."

"You know I like you naked. I want to see your tits and ass, princess." He sprawled out on the bench, legs in front of him, leaning against the backrest, eyes half closed. Watching her. Making her shiver with that look on his face.

She loved it when he talked like that. She knew the sex was going to be explosive. She didn't hesitate. There was no reason to. They were a good distance from the others, out in the middle of the field. She could hear the laughter and the music. Several women were naked, dancing or fucking. No one paid that much attention. If they did, it was only to get off themselves, and she never had a problem with anyone seeing her worshipping her man. It was hot. Exciting. And she knew it aroused him just as unbelievably as it did her.

She took her tank off and faced him as she removed her bra, spilling her breasts out into the open. Instantly, the cold air had her nipples stiff and hard. He beckoned her closer and she stepped between his spread thighs and leaned down, her hands cupping her breasts to offer them to him.

Ice loved how she looked, bent over, her tits soft and round and so inviting. He waited a few heartbeats so that image would forever stay in his mind and then he leaned forward to take her left nipple into his mouth, his hand playing with the other one. He wasn't gentle. He used his teeth and tongue ruthlessly, sucking hard and then switching to the other tit. He marked them both as he reached for the waistband of her jeans, opening the front.

"Take them off." He settled back in his seat to watch her shimmy the denim over her hips and down her legs.

She'd kicked off her pull-on boots, the ones she wore often just in case he suddenly had the mad desire to bend her over his bike and wanted her naked just like this. Several times, when they were riding in the woods with only a couple of the others, he would feel like he was going to explode, and he'd stop. She never said no. Not one time. He loved that about her.

When she was naked, he beckoned her to him again. Soleil came close and he lifted his boot. She immediately crouched down and removed it for him. He held up the other one, and she did the same. Then he stood. He pulled his shirt off and tossed it on the bench. When she got his jeans off, he sank back down and then patted his lap. "Lie over me, facedown."

For the first time she looked a little nervous, and he fucking loved that look, he loved that she still did what he said. He rubbed her beautiful, firm cheeks. "I love your ass." He kept rubbing. "Do you remember the other morning when you started in on the money thing again and I had to shut you up by shoving my cock down your throat?"

"Yes."

He was very pleased that she sounded excited. "You thought you were going to get away with it because a couple of the brothers were over for breakfast, didn't you?"

There was the briefest of hesitations. He knew she didn't like the fact that they never used her money. If she wanted anything, they used his. He liked it that way. He didn't want her ever to think that he was using her for her money, like everyone else in her life had done. Their marriage had never been about that. He gave her a little experimental swat. "Answer me, Soleil."

"Yes."

Now she was squirming. He kept rubbing more heat into her rosy cheeks. He had his jeans right next to his hand. He pulled out the little items he'd prepared. "I told you to crawl under the table and suck me off, didn't I, baby? I think you liked that just a little too much and maybe you didn't learn your lesson. In fact, I think you bring up money now, just so you can have my cock down your throat."

She didn't respond. He stopped all movement. "Princess? Is that true? Do you do that?"

She squirmed. "Yes." The admission was low. "I love waking you up in the morning, but sometimes that's just not enough for me, especially if you wake me up first."

"You really are a bad girl, aren't you? Especially bringing it up when someone's around. You like showing off, letting them see how good you are at taking care of me. Blowing me is supposed to be about me, not you showing off your skills." He smacked her hard.

She jumped and turned her head to glare at him. "It's always about you. I can't have your cock in my mouth without only thinking about making you feel good."

He rubbed his handprint, spreading the heat, hearing the truth in her voice, and then pushed his hand against her slick entrance, collecting the liquid. He painted it between her cheeks, over and over, and then began to push into the little star there. She gasped and wiggled but he was relentless, burying his finger to the knuckle and then deeper.

"I decided a very hard spanking might be in order, but you like them too much, don't you? You like anything I do to you."

"Yes." She hissed it as he pushed his finger in and out of her as if he were fucking her.

"I know you do. You like it hot, don't you? You're going to love this. You're going to be so hot for me you'll want to do anything at all. This one's new for you, princess, but I know you're going to love it."

"What did you do?" There was suspicion in her voice, but excitement too.

He held the glass penis in front of her. "It's nicely coated in chilled ginger. When I spank your little ass and you clench, you're going to burn so good, honey. I'm going to paint your little clit with this juice, and you're going to be so fuckin' horny you'll be begging for my cock."

He began to slowly insert the glass plug between her cheeks. She gasped and squirmed more. Just the sight of it disappearing all the way to the flared end sent his cock into overdrive. He wanted to fuck her with that erotic image in front of him.

"Tell me what that feels like," he instructed, going back to rubbing her cheeks.

"Warm. It's getting warmer." There was a little hitch in her voice.

"Good." Without warning his hand came down on her left cheek hard.

She yelped and clenched her ass, just as he knew she would. She gasped and blew out, forcing her body to relax.

"I got the juice nice and cold, baby. You aren't ready for the real thing, but do you like your surprise?" He didn't wait for an answer. Instead, he went to work, smacking her cheeks, leaving his handprints, loving the way her soft skin went red for him.

He looked up and across from them: several of the partyers were watching, drinking from bottles and enjoying watching her body undulate and squirm, trying to get rid of the plug. He knew he'd chosen the perfect position, with the moonlight spotlighting her curves and skin. He fantasized that they could see his handprints on her ass. The plug he'd inserted. He knew they couldn't fail to hear her moaning pleas.

He was finding it difficult to concentrate on spanking her hard. His cock ached. Needed attention. He wanted her mouth on him. Around him, the world began shifting just a little, shadows creeping in.

"Ice, you have to fuck me. I'm so hot right now, burning up. You have to help me."

The juice, combined with the spanking, was doing its work, just the way it always did, making her so desperate she'd do anything for him. "You want my cock, don't you, baby?"

"Please, Ice. Yes. Please."

He brought her up slowly and pointed to the ground in front of him. "You keep that plug in. Hold it in place," he cautioned. "Or we start all over again and you aren't going to get what you want."

She immediately did as he instructed and came up on her knees, cupping his balls, fingers massaging gently. She didn't need him to tell her what to do, she had spent time perfecting the art of pleasing him. Giving him everything. She did now. Just the way he knew she would. He caught her hair in his fist and lifted it up and out of the way so he could see her as she licked and kissed at his heavy balls. He knew he wasn't the only one watching.

She licked up his shaft and over the broad, flared head. It felt so fucking good he thought his head might explode. She became frantic as the ginger reached its hottest point, doing its job, making her desperate for him. She began to roll her hips as if she were riding him, making little noises that vibrated around his cock as she took him deeper. He let her do the work, watching her through half-closed eyes, enjoying the erotic sight as she fought her own body while she worked to please him.

"Does it feel good, baby?" he asked.

Her eyes went wide, but she didn't let go of his cock. Not even for a moment, sucking ferociously, her mouth moving up and down on him. He didn't want to give in to the firestorm welling up in him — not yet. He pulled on her hair, forcing her to give up what she loved.

"Ice." She wailed his name.

He pointed to the bench, the side facing the clubhouse. "Crawl up here and lean back. I want one leg up on the back of the bench and the other up, thighs spread wide. I want to see that sweet little pussy begging for my cock." In that position, her cheeks would be clenched again, once more activating the juice if the heat had simmered.

Shadows crowded closer, and he couldn't quite push them back. His cock throbbed and burned. She was also on display for him in all her wanton need. For all of them. Needy. Desperate. Nearly ready for anything demanded of her.

Soleil did what he said, leaning back, one leg hooked over the bench back, her knees spread wide. He just sat there enjoying his fierce arousal, loving that his woman was so beautifully displayed, so desperately in need of his cock. He dipped his finger in the honey spilling from her and began coating his cock. Her gaze stayed fixed on his heavy erection.

"You put this here, princess. Look at you. Everyone loves to look at you, desperate for my cock. Not sure I'm going to give it to you."

He began to pump his hand up and down, mesmerizing her. He'd done this a thousand times. He knew how the need grew and grew to the point he could make a woman so desperate for his cock that she'd do anything he asked. Anything. She would be out of her mind, frantic to quench that fire burning through her ass to her pussy.

He reached out casually and began to

pump two fingers in and out of her, feeling her body clamp down hard on him. Euphoria had him floating in arousal. His cock thickened. He felt his balls tighten. He threw back his head, letting the pleasure take him. He could smell her arousal, the scent carried on the cool breeze.

"You ready for a cock in your sweet little pussy? In your ass? Crawl down from there, baby, come here and suck my cock if you're scared." He kept his fingers pumping in and out of her, while his thumb flicked her flaming clit.

She cried out over and over, riding his fingers, her mouth wide open, her body straining with the need to climax.

"I'll be right here to make it good for you. You need that, don't you? You need them all watching you. Look at them watching you. Crawl to him, baby, suck his dick. Make him feel good the way you make me feel. He wants to fuck your ass. You know how hard that makes you come when the others watch. They all need you." He murmured it softly, all the while staring through half-closed eyes, holding her gaze captive, as his fingers moved in and out of her until she appeared nearly insane with need.

At first, just the sound, that velvet, hypnotizing voice Ice had, added to the ferocity of

Soleil's need. Her body was on fire and she was frantic for him to put it out. Her head tossed back and forth, her body undulated, hips thrusting toward the cock he was stroking just out of her reach. He looked so sexy, his eyes half-closed, gaze locked on her with laser focus. She was so close and knew if he just touched her anywhere, she would explode.

He didn't. He kept murmuring something to her, and the roaring in her ears didn't let the words penetrate at first. She didn't care. She just wanted. Yes, she would do anything he asked of her. Anything at all. She wanted the men to look at her, to see what a sexual being she was. She liked knowing she was making them hot. She liked knowing Ice was watching out for her, putting her on display for his own pleasure.

"Crawl to him, baby. Slide down and crawl to him on your hands and knees. Beg him to fuck you. Tell him how much you need that dick. How big it is. How perfect. You want all of them. Ask for it. Be polite. You know you need it."

The hand on his cock fisted tighter. Soleil could see him swelling. He was as close as she was, but . . . Her breath left her lungs and abruptly her vision cleared. He wasn't with her. He was somewhere else, far away, locked into something that didn't include her. She tried to hear him, to remember the things he'd said.

Not crawl to him. Not beg him. What was he repeating so gently in that velvety mesmerizing voice? Her stomach lurched. She slowly pulled her leg from the back of the seat and sat up. Immediately the glass plug moved, sending a wave of heat through her. She grasped the flared end and removed it. Watching Ice, she stuffed the thing in the ziplock bag. His head was still thrown back, his hand working his cock.

It was all she could do not to lean forward and take him in her mouth, but she wasn't going to let the erotic sight throw her back into whatever scene he had created and then got lost in. She knew about childhood trauma. She'd gone to enough psychologists to pack a room. She reached for her jeans and drew them on slowly, trying to think what to do.

"That's right, honey. I know you're scared. It's all right. I'm here with you."

He suddenly looked directly at Soleil, staring into her eyes with his beautiful blue ones. There was so much pain there she couldn't stand it. His hand curled around the back of her head and slowly began to force her face toward his cock.

"It's all right. You want him to fuck your little pussy. You need it. You're on fire. Let him in. Let the other one have your ass." He stroked the top of her head as if soothing her. "You can suck my cock if you need to. I'll always let you. It will distract you." He rubbed the head of his cock around her lips, back and forth. "We talked about this. The others are watching you. Seeing you. You're so beautiful to them. They need you."

He exerted so much strength, Soleil had no choice but to open her mouth and let him push her onto his cock. He began to wipe her face with his thumb, over and over. "Don't cry. It only hurts for a few minutes and then you'll feel so good. I'll make it good for you."

She couldn't take her eyes from his face. It was twisted with pain. With sorrow. Even with self-loathing. She found herself wanting to soothe *him.* She didn't take control, because he was already moving in her mouth, surging deep and then much more gently, alternating the strokes with various rhythms.

"See, so much better. Suck, honey. Don't cry. You have to stop crying. Feel that now? So much better. He's so happy, you should see his face. Look at the others watching."

When he said that, to look at the others,

his cock swelled, pushing at the soft tissue of her mouth, growing heavier and hotter on her tongue. She realized he did need that sometimes. Someone had conditioned him to need it. He didn't recognize himself as a victim; he saw himself as the criminal. She wanted it over. She wanted to bring him out from the place he was in. She put effort in getting him off, unable to think of any other way to end the flashback.

It wasn't that hard. He was so close. Then his hands were fisting on either side of her head and he nearly jerked her off of him. His blue eyes moved over her face and, if it was possible, he went gray under his tan. She sat back on her heels and reached for her tank, pulling it over her head, ignoring the bra. She never took her eyes from his face.

Ice rubbed his hand over his eyes and jaw and then looked at her again. Twice he opened his mouth to say something, then he just shook his head and looked down at his hands. "I'm sorry, Soleil. There's nothing to say. Nothing. Now you know what kind of man I am."

She handed him his shirt. "I know I love you, honey. I know you did everything you could to help those girls."

He shook his head. "I traded them for

Alena and Storm. If I didn't cooperate, they would take her — take them. I had to get the girls ready for them. Convince them to cooperate and convince them they loved what was being done to them. No tears, because tears meant they weren't into it."

She rubbed her finger over the teardrops dripping from his eye. "For them. For those girls. You did this for all of them."

"If they couldn't cry, I couldn't cry. I didn't want them to have to like what was being done to them if I didn't like it. It was so wrong, Soleil. They would arouse me when I was just a little boy, making me feel so good when they would get these girls to cooperate. They taught me how to do it. *Fuck.*" He spat the word and pulled his shirt over his head. "I need to show you off. I can't stop myself. It makes me hard, but then . . ." He looked at her helplessly. "What does that make me? What did they make me into? I'm like them. Just the fuck like them."

She put her arms around him, bringing his head to her chest. He might not be able to cry, but the tears were burning deep. She felt them. He choked on them. "You're not anything like them. You were a child."

"I grew up. Year after year. I grew and they kept up their demands because I was so fucking good at it." He pushed into her, tightening his arms until she was afraid she would die from lack of air, but she didn't move, just held him, wishing she could take his pain.

"You were still a child trying to save your sister. Your brother. Trying to save those girls. Ice, you think you had a choice, but you really didn't. If you didn't do what they said, they would have gone after Alena and Storm and they still would have taken those girls. You know they would have. You couldn't do anything to stop them. They were sadistic pedophiles, and they murdered your family and took away your home. You had no power." She found herself rocking back and forth with him.

Ice sat back, shaking his head. "I try not to think about it too much because I can't change it. Every one of those girls is dead. After that group used them, they passed them on to others. The others were much more brutal. When each one died, I felt as if I had been the one to kill them. It became harder to cooperate, and when I would resist, they would beat Storm or Alena in front of me. Sometimes they'd rape them. Over and over, in front of me. They would use Alena so brutally and I couldn't stand it . . ."

He lifted his head, looking straight into her eyes. His heart was breaking. Hers was as well. "I couldn't stand it. I couldn't. I went back to doing what they demanded. When I got strong enough, I killed them, Soleil. One by one. It was the only way to stop them. I was just shy of seventeen when I got the last one."

He expected her to condemn him. She saw that on his face. He didn't feel remorse for killing them, only for his part in helping get the cooperation of the girls.

"I'm glad you did, Ice. They wouldn't have stopped. Even if you and the others escaped, they would have found other girls to use." She was careful of her words. "Honey, you're shivering, and you don't even realize it. Get your jeans on and let's just go home."

"You want to stay with me? After hearing the truth? Knowing at every party I'm going to want to show you off and that could happen?"

"I like when you show me off," she admitted. "And if it happens, we'll deal with it, just like we did this time."

He caught her face in his hands and stared into her eyes, searching for the truth. "I don't want to share you with another man. Not ever. I don't want another man touching you. I realized when we went on that run that I could only do this when my brothers surrounded us, not strangers. They help me protect you, and I need to know you're safe. I wouldn't share you with anyone, Soleil. I don't have that urge. I swear to God, I don't have that urge."

She was very relieved to hear him say that, because for a moment she'd been afraid, and that wasn't going to happen. She was adventurous, but not that adventurous. Having more than one man, or adding another woman, had never been her fantasy. Being seen, having men look at her with lust, had been.

"Let's go home, honey," she reiterated.

He looked like he'd fought a battle. "It's going to happen again," he said. "What happened tonight. I don't even know what triggers it. One minute I'm completely into what's happening and the next I'm gone. I wake up and I'm in the middle of a couple of women and they're crawling all over me, all over Storm, and I don't even know what I've said to them."

"You'll be safe with me, honey. Now that I know what happens sometimes, I can find ways to get you out of it." She framed his face and leaned in to kiss him. Her heart ached, was so heavy she could barely stand it, but she knew it wasn't nearly as heavy as his.

She was never going to convince him that he wasn't to blame for the things that had been forced on him. They'd both have to live with it. She kissed him again and then pushed his jeans into his hands while she found his motorcycle boots.

NINETEEN

Spread out, cover the entire area. We can't let him get away. Czar spoke telepathically, the way he'd done all those years ago in the school in Russia. His team was on the move, running lightly over rooftops and through alleys.

He'd been a very young child, no more than five or so, when his father told him stories of wolf packs hunting prey through the winter in the deep snow. How every member of the pack was needed and could be counted on. He'd learned how the older ones would sacrifice their lives in order for the younger ones to live. He had been greatly influenced by his father's stories.

His father had always said wolves were intelligent. They used their brains, and the brain was the most valuable weapon they — or people — had. He'd talked about teamwork and applied it to their family. Co-operation, and how, when they all worked together, they came out ahead. Coordination, utilizing one another's strengths, how even the youngest could contribute meaningfully.

Czar never forgot his father's advice, or the many stories he'd told. After he'd been taken to the school, where he'd quickly realized he was going to die along with all the other children, he'd decided to find a way to fight back. Wolves were in it for the hunt, for the long haul. They were endurance hunters. Patient. His father had made him aware of his brain as a great tool. He'd known the wolves used their brains, and he'd begun to teach the other children he trusted, the ones he could see would fight no matter how badly used they were, to utilize the way of the pack.

He had assigned the children specific tasks based on their age, gender and ability they were required to work on. It hadn't been difficult to get cooperation. They'd been naked, in a freezing basement that had been turned into a dungeon, and they'd all needed to believe there was a way to survive. Each had specific intuitions, and Czar had given them drills to do, over and over, to work on the skills they would need to survive.

In the beginning, he had only shared with

a couple of the children that they would have to kill their tormenters in order to escape. They would have to do so without ever having suspicion cast on them, which meant stealthy, patient work.

He's running, heading down the hall toward the master bedroom. Ice, are you in position to round him up? Reaper asked.

Reaper had been so young, just a little boy, when he'd become Czar's trusted weapon. He never hesitated to stalk and kill, and that was the kind of right hand he needed. Reaper had been only five, but he'd been able to move through the vents without detection, and he'd never hesitated when he'd had to finish off one of the worst.

Then there was Reaper's younger brother, Savage. He had been so traumatized when their older sisters had been murdered trying to stop the brutal pedophiles from taking the two boys. The boys had returned, bloody and in bad shape, only to find their sisters dead on the floor of the basement. Savage had become . . . something else. Worse, he'd been taken by some of the cruelest of the pedophiles running the school, and they'd begun his training. They'd worked at shaping him into a being who craved seeing the marks of pain on flesh. Who needed that just to survive and even more to be aroused and enjoy a woman.

Czar knew, from experience, that when a very young toddler was subjected to training from that early age, and it continued until they were in their early twenties, there was no going back. It was always there. Instincts. First reactions. Need. Savage was damaged beyond repair, but he was a weapon always to be counted on.

In position, Ice replied. *He's going to run right into the room with me. I see him now, but he doesn't see me. He's pulling out his phone, thinking it's safe to relax now and call for help. He isn't certain if anything is real or not.*

Let him make the call, Czar advised. *Whoever he calls is part of this ring.*

Then there was Ice and Storm and Alena. Czar sighed. The three had been brought to the school because they were unusually beautiful children. The boys were twins. Sorbacov, the man behind the murders of those opposing his candidate, had been a sick, sadistic fuck who, for political reasons, had to keep his proclivities a secret. He'd married, had children, but he had gathered the cruelest like-minded pedophiles around him, those with criminal histories, and had given them a banquet. No one had expected any of the children to survive. The moment

Sorbacov had laid eyes on those three little ice-blond toddlers, he was never going to pass on them.

That had been one of Czar's darkest moments. He had almost given up, knowing what was in store for those three babies. Knowing it would be worse than bad, the way it had been for Reaper and Savage. Sorbacov would fixate on them, as would the most brutal and depraved of the vile criminals running the school. The more the criminals had been given free rein, the more they'd thought up to subject the children to. Czar hadn't been much older, and like the others, he'd been powerless to stop the adults — until he thought of his father and his wolf-pack stories.

Even as very young toddlers, Ice and Storm had fought hard to protect each other and their baby sister, Alena. Czar had known then that they had what it took to join his pack. As small children, they'd been helpless against the predators running the school, but once he'd taught them to become predators, like he had Savage and Reaper, they'd become very good at what they did. Too good.

David Swey, the hot dog vendor, had been tailed after he left his home in Graton and traveled toward Occidental. He had gone straight to the mansion that had been previously owned by Walter Sandlin, where Czar's adopted son Kenny had been held since he was a young boy. Swey had waited for someone, peering at his watch over and over, clearly spooked by the creak of the branches against the windows.

It was the perfect environment for Ice and Storm to create an atmosphere of fear. Czar never understood how they did it, but they had some kind of psychic ability to utilize the weather. The wind, the clouds, even lightning and thunder. Right now, the wind was moaning and crying, dashing those branches against windows so that they scraped and shrieked against the glass.

Swey looked around the room nervously. The pictures of Walter and Kenny had been taken down and in their place were photographs of Avery Charles with several little girls. Apparently, he had bought the mansion. The estate, built like a castle, complete with gargoyles crouched overhead, was set well back from the road, and there were few neighbors. The closest ones were several miles away, enabling the mansion to be used in whatever way the occupants saw fit.

Swey held the phone to his ear. "Where the hell are you? I thought we were supposed to meet here at nine. Avery's not here, and let me tell you, this place is creepy."

He listened for a couple of minutes and glanced at his watch again. "I don't have all night. By the time the two of you get here, we'll have ten minutes for the meeting. I have to know what I'm looking for if he has a specific kid in mind. I've got a couple of runaways I've been friendly with. Hopefully one of them will suit him, and it will be easy."

There was silence again as he listened. Again, he glanced at his watch, shook his head and then sighed. "Fine. But just get here, Harold. I'm telling you this place is haunted." He shoved his phone in his back pocket and looked around the room again.

He went over to the fireplace, picked up the remote and turned it on, so the flames danced and added more light. At the same time, the flickering fire threw more shadows, so they crept up the walls, reaching out with dark tentacles toward the ceiling. Swey sank onto the bed, staring into the fire.

Take him anytime. We don't need him, Ice. He's low level. Doesn't know shit about the top dogs. Czar gave the order.

Consider it done.

That was Ice. A glacier. Czar and the others could watch through the camera as Ice came out of the shadows right behind Swey just as the man jumped up and started to pace. Ice matched his strides exactly. Three steps in, Swey glanced at the wall to see his shadow cast against it. Right behind him was a second shadow, and in the hand reaching toward him was a very wicked-looking knife.

Swey gasped and started to turn. Ice locked the man against him and jabbed the knife deep into his jugular. "For all those kids whose lives you destroyed, you sick fuck." He whispered it into the man's ear and then stepped back, letting him fall.

Swey writhed on the floor, blood pouring onto the thick, luxurious and very white carpet. Ice stood watching with a cold, detached expression.

Incoming, Absinthe reported. *Sheriff SUV coming up the drive. Can't identify the driver or if he's alone in the vehicle.*

Lightning forked across the sky, lighting up the darkness, throwing the night into stark relief. Storm's work, Czar was certain.

Harold McDonald, Absinthe acknowledged. *He's alone.*

There was Absinthe. Like Ice, Storm and Alena, he'd been exceptionally beautiful. Sorbacov had seemed to find the children that suited him most. Absinthe had had an older brother, one he'd adored and looked up to. Absinthe was a beautiful soul. All of them could see that. Sweet, compassionate, not at all suited to live like a wolf, planning out kills meticulously and carrying them out. He was brilliant beyond measure. And so very talented.

Sometimes the planning to kill each individual pedophile had taken weeks, or even months, depending on how difficult it had been to acquire the information needed to be successful. Czar hadn't taken chances. They had been little kids and they could never have been seen or heard. Suspicion couldn't have fallen on them or they'd have all been killed outright. That had been where Absinthe came in. His gifts were extraordinary, and he'd practiced all the time.

Absinthe could remember conversations. He could read lips. He could influence with his voice. He could read others when touching them. That was both a gift and a curse. Somehow, he'd learned how to crawl inside minds, and when he did, he could wreak havoc. He was a human lie detector. Over the years those gifts had become even stronger. He'd grown quieter. Czar, like all of Torpedo Ink, worried about Savage the most, but Absinthe was a close second. He was too quiet. Too apart from them.

Czar sighed and shook his head. He had a lot to answer for. He'd turned those children into killers in order for them to survive. That was their only way out, but one didn't come back from that or the things done to them.

There were two teams. Steele, the vice president of Torpedo Ink, ran the second. They always held one team back if possible, in order to have a full team to get one another out of trouble if it was necessary. Czar didn't leave anything to chance. Each team had nine members. They were so used to working together, just like that wolf pack, each of them had a specific role, and they carried it out with the ease of practice.

Together, they were a well-oiled machine, working off a careful master plan that was always fluid, but they never deviated from the safety rules put in place. It was better to walk away before they had completed their task than to die. They were patient, impassive, never bringing their emotions into play if it could be helped. They didn't make mistakes. They had learned from the experience of losing other children that even a small error meant death.

Harold McDonald, still in his sheriff's uniform, parked his SUV in the covered parking spaces just to the left of the front door. The roof ran straight from the parking area to the porch, so no one would ever get a drop of rain on them if they didn't want to. Harold didn't want to.

He strode straight to the door and pulled out his phone. "Yeah, I'm here. I'll keep David here. He's such a coward whenever there's a storm." There was a bit of a sneer in his voice. "You want to tell me what's going on?"

He listened for a moment, his hand on the knob of the front door. "Yeah, okay, but Avery, get here."

He yanked open the door as he shoved his cell phone into his jacket. He stepped inside and closed the door. "David." Moving quickly, he hurried through the great room to the wide hall. "Where are you?"

The house remained eerily silent. A slight breeze ran down the hallway, bringing a chill with it. The wind outside picked up. Howled for a moment. When it did, it brought the sound of a child crying with it. Harold halted abruptly and looked around. He put his hand on the wall.

The crying continued. It sounded soft and pitiful. Hopeless. Harold's breath came out in an angry rush. "David. Shut that kid up." He looked in every direction, trying to figure out where the sound originated.

The wind came down the hall again, that same slight breeze, but the temperature seemed to have dropped. This time a second child joined the first. Harold's face turned slightly red.

"Avery's going to kill you for bringing those kids here without permission. What's wrong with you, David?" He started down the hall again with long, angry strides.

Now a third child could be heard. The voices had that same tone, soft, pitiful, weeping endlessly, without hope.

Harold yanked open the door to the den. He took two steps inside the room and the door swung shut behind him with a loud bang. He visibly jumped. He looked around. The crying was louder, as if he were closer to the children, but there was no one in the room. Cursing, he strode back to the door and grasped the knob. Instantly a jolt of electricity ran up his arm and spread through his body. He almost seized. He yanked his hand back and staggered, rubbing his chest.

That was Mechanic, Transporter's younger brother, delivering the electricity to Harold. Mechanic had some kind of energy field in his body and could use it to disrupt electricity or send the charge outward. He could understand just about any electronics and absorbed information and technology easily. Both brothers, like Absinthe, could read at an astonishing rate, comprehend and retain what they read. Transporter had amazing hand-eye coordination. It was easy for him to drive at high rates of speed with his reflexes and keen sight.

Reaper and Savage had to be the ones throwing the sound of children crying. They could mimic any sound, reproduce any voice. They were doing so now in perfect coordination. With Mechanic and Transporter, they were "herding" the sheriff where they wanted him, just as the wolf pack would do. Terrain could tip the favor to either predator or prey, so the pack would always know exactly the best place to take down their selected victim and how to get him there.

Harold did exactly what they were certain he would. He avoided the door leading back to the hallway, not wanting to have anything to do with the doorknob that had inexplicably delivered jolting volts of electricity to his body. He went to the door leading to the sunroom. Very gingerly, he touched the doorknob. When nothing happened, he grabbed it, turned it and let go instantly.

The door creaked open a couple of inches. The sound of the children crying grew louder. Frustrated, Harold yelled very loudly, "Shut those kids the hell up, David! I swear I'm going to shoot you if they don't stop."

The wails increased, and it sounded as if there were a dozen children crying. Harold put his hands over his ears as if that would drown out the sound. He nudged open the door with the toe of his boot. It was dark in the room. Through the glass of the sun-room, he could see the brewing storm. The wind had picked up and the trees were swaying, bending toward the house, branches whipping around as if in a frenzy.

"Harold. How lovely of you to join me." Alena's voice came out of the darkness. She had the voice of an angel. Soft and musical. "David said you'd be here soon. Make them stop crying. They're so sad. So many of them. They told me it was you. You helped those men and women hurt them. You like to hurt them."

Alena. Czar closed his eyes for a moment. She was one of the two females they'd managed to save. Like Ice and Storm, she had that natural platinum hair, so blond the thick mass looked like mixtures of silver, gold and white. Her eyes were the same ice blue as her brothers'. She was a beautiful woman, but like the men, she had scars. Too many. Terrible things had been done to her as a child. Even more as a young girl and then even more as a teen. There had been no saving her from their pack. If she wanted to live, she had to become what they were — killers. Like Ice and Storm, there was determination in Alena. She had learned, and Czar had taken on another responsibility and another sorrow.

Harold drew his weapon and pointed it into the shadows of the dark room, first in one direction and then in another, turning in a circle in an effort to locate her. "Who are you? What do you want?"

"You don't know who I am?" There was amusement in her voice. "I'm your conscience. I'm the one you should have listened to when you were hurting those little boys. You heard me, but you kept ignoring me."

Harold squeezed the trigger, firing in rapid succession, all along the wall where the voice seemed to be coming from. Each bullet leaving the chamber seemed to turn up the temperature of both the room and his weapon. Sweat broke out. Maybe it was the children and their incessant crying.

"David! Shut them the hell up!" He screamed it and wiped at the sweat dripping from his forehead with his arm. He had a holdout gun in his boot, and for some reason it felt like a brand pressed against his ankle.

"David can't make them stop," Alena said. "Only you can do that. David is dead. You wanted him dead. I heard your thoughts. You wanted to slice his throat so many times to shut him up. You thought he was a weak link, and you didn't like him knowing Avery or you."

Harold let off another round of bullets, nearly emptying his weapon into the wall. "How do you know these things?" he screamed. "David was a weasel. He would have given us up in a heartbeat if anyone caught him. Yeah, I wanted him dead. I talked to Avery a million times about it. So what? Come out where I can see you."

Alena's soft laughter could barely be heard above the crying children. They wailed constantly now, so many of them. "How can a conscience come out where you can see it? You barely hear me when I protest the things you're doing."

Harold whirled around and rushed to the door leading back to the sitting room. Before he grasped the doorknob, he hesitated and then tried to yank. The door refused to budge. The doorknob delivered another very hard jolt, the electricity running through his body, burning through him. He yelled and dragged his hand back. The other one, the hand with the gun, was burning now. So was his ankle where his holdout was.

Cursing, Harold hurried through the room to the other side. He put his hand near the door and immediately felt the electrical energy. He didn't grab it. Instead, he whirled around and screamed at the voice. "What do you want from me?"

"I want you to pay. *They* want you to pay. Can't you hear them crying out for justice? You want that for them, don't you, Harold?"

Her voice sounded so angelic. So pure. So reasonable. Harold found his gun hand coming up toward his head. Gasping, he shook his head and forced it toward the large plates of glass that made up the outside wall. The sunroom looked like a massive porch walled in with glass on three sides. To get out of it, he determined he would simply shoot out the panels. He began squeezing the trigger, shattering the glass.

Each bullet fired raised the temperature of the metal on his gun. His hand burned. He glanced down at the weapon and it glowed red orange in the dark. Startled, he yelped and let go. Inside his boot, he could see the same orange-red glow. His calf burned like a mother. He didn't want to take the time to pull the gun from his boot. He just wanted away from those bawling, sniveling children and that voice that seemed to consume him.

Harold ran toward the glass panels, raised his arms to cover his face and leapt. He felt the glass shatter around him, go into him, dozens of pieces as he passed through. He hit the ground, rolled and stood up, looking back into the room and giving it the finger. He had gotten out. He reached for his cell phone to warn Avery. As he did so, he turned. Something jerked at his chest. He stared into the iciest blue eyes he'd ever seen. They looked like two twin crystals.

"Who are . . ." He staggered and looked down at his chest.

Frowning, he saw a handle sticking out of it. He went to his knees. "What is this?"

"The children you hurt send their regards, Harold," Alena said. Her voice was detached, composed, serene even. She stepped back and walked away.

The main man has arrived. He's driving right up to the front entrance now, Absinthe warned.

Ice and Storm immediately reacted, increasing the rain, dropping the temperature so every drop was icy and uncomfortable. That would ensure Avery would go straight through the front door and not go around back where Harold's body could be discovered. Avery was dressed in a long black trench coat. He slammed the driver's side door closed, took two running steps toward the front door, still under the canopy so he wasn't getting wet, but he turned back.

Avery isn't alone. He has a companion with him. Repeat. Avery isn't alone. Second man is tall, maybe six foot two or three. Looks to be in excellent shape. Sending picture to Code to get ID right now.

Czar rubbed his chin on the back of his hand as he studied the situation. If they aborted now, Avery would know he was under a death sentence and would scurry into the woodwork. The others waited for his decision.

We'll stick to the plan. Reaper, the second man, you and Storm deal with. Ice, Savage, you're still on Avery. Czar hated giving those orders.

He had promised himself that when they found a home, he would find a way to ease his Torpedo Ink family out of what they'd been doing for most of their lives — what he'd gotten them into doing. They had been shaped into killers by him in order to survive. They'd been taught how to seduce and kill by their instructors, so they were "useful" to their government — and Sorbacov — as assassins. They had been fucked up sexually by their childhood training. They had joined an MC club to take down the Swords international president. Now they hunted pedophiles. It was never-ending.

On it, Reaper said.

With Reaper, Storm acknowledged.

Ice and Savage were up, and they needed to get a single name from Avery. It would be nice if they could get more than one. Czar wanted to know the name of the Russian. He was certain he was one of the few pedophile instructors they'd left alive. He was someone who traveled back and forth from Russia, and he was highly intelligent. Czar had every confidence that they'd track him down. Their first priority had to be the collector. He was murdering families and taking innocent children to fulfill orders from his sick clients. He had to be stopped.

Czar rubbed his aching head and watched the rest of the drama unfold. The moment Savage and Ice had Avery in their custody, and Reaper and Storm indicated the stranger was taken care of, the others would go through the house looking for anything they could find that would help them find others in the large ring.

Avery flung open his front door and stepped back to wave the newcomer through.

Code says the man with Avery is named Jay Gordon. He's affiliated with the human trafficking ring both Yeger and Kushnir were involved with. Looks to me like he wants to climb the ladder. They were slightly turned away from me, so I was only partially able to catch what they were saying. Gordon believes with a little backing from Avery he can take the lead. Absinthe delivered the information to all of them.

Czar quickly analyzed the information and added to the pool of general knowledge. *Avery works for the San Francisco PD. He runs their tech department. That gives him access to where all the cops are and what kinds of operations the cops are running. He must be helping the human trafficking ring as well.*

Avery walked with complete confidence through the foyer into the great room without turning on a light. The house had gone quiet. There was only the sound of the wind outside and the occasional creak of an old house settling. Jay followed close behind him, taking a moment to look around and then hurrying to catch up.

"You must love the privacy out here, man," Jay said admiringly. "Must be nice. We could use a place like this. Set the girls up and have the men come to them."

"Too much traffic on a road like this, sooner or later you'd be noticed. Harold can only do so much." Avery turned into the hall. No lights were on other than one shining under the door of the room straight ahead — the master bedroom. "That's weird. I thought they were going to meet me in the den, but it looks like they're in the master bedroom."

He didn't miss a step but continued on down the hall toward his bedroom. "I only use this house on weekends. Or if I have sick days coming, or a vacation. Then it's perfect. I can have a nice leisurely time, and no one can hear the screaming but me, just the way I like it."

"I prefer to hear them moaning around my cock."

Avery shook his head. "You know those teenagers you like aren't into it, right? They're strung out on drugs and do whatever you say because if they don't, someone's going to hurt them. Seriously hurt them. That's the way it works, right?" He stopped at his bedroom door and looked at his guest over his shoulder. "Better to be honest than a hypocrite. Just own what your preference is and to hell with everyone else."

Jay grinned at him. "You do it your way and I'll do it mine."

Avery laughed and opened the door, pushing through. He was halfway into the room when he smelled blood. The room was very warm with the fireplace going and the door closed. Light spilled from a fixture overhead, pouring down on the white carpet, which was inexplicably red. He took two more steps around the bed and saw David Swey lying facedown in a thick pool of his own blood.

"What the hell?"

Even as Avery turned, pulling his weapon, he knew he was too late. The barrel of a gun was pressed tight against the back of his neck. He couldn't see Jay, or anyone else for that matter. A hand reached around him and took the gun from his hand.

From out of his sight, Jay yelled once, the sound low and agonized.

"Take him to another room and have your fun there," Savage said. "We've got work to do in here."

Avery tried to turn, and the barrel pressed tighter against his skin. His heart began to pound. "Just tell me what you want."

"Take off your clothes. All of them."

Avery's hands shook, but his mind was racing. He had another gun. He just had to get to it. It was under his coat and tucked into his waistband at the small of his back. It would be unseen by his attacker even when he took his coat off. He could reach . . . He began to put his plan in motion, shrugging out of his trench coat and allowing it to fall to the floor.

He wished the attacker would say something, but he didn't. The barrel of the gun was very steady. His own hands were shaking. Had the gun not have been pressed so tightly against his neck, he wouldn't have known his assailant was there. He couldn't even hear him breathe.

Unbuttoning his shirt, he went over his movements, acting them out in his mind before he began to shrug off his suit jacket. As his arms went down, lightning fast, he put his hand on the gun — but it wasn't there. It was gone. He came up empty. His jacket fell to the floor.

"Tell me what you want."

"I don't like repeating myself. Get it done or I'll do it for you, and you won't like the results." The voice was implacable.

Avery stripped, feeling more vulnerable than he ever had in his life. He found himself shaking. He went to work every single day in the middle of cops, surrounded by them, and felt superior. He got a secret thrill out of outsmarting them all. He brought his victims here to this mansion out in the middle of nowhere and did whatever he felt like. He was master here. He could force those little brats to do anything he wanted, and there was no one to stop him. No one could shake their finger at him and tell him how wrong he was.

"Get on the bed, right in the middle. You like that mirror so you can admire yourself. Go ahead and look your fill."

Avery stretched out on the bed, getting his first glimpse of his captor. To his shock, there were two of them. By the door there was a smear of blood, but Jay was gone, as if he'd never been there in the first place.

"No, kneel up facing the headboard," the scariest-looking of the two instructed him. He had a pair of handcuffs and he snapped them tight around Avery's wrists and then attached them to the headboard of the bed, just as Avery had done to numerous children. Then the man put something around his wrist, right over his pulse.

His attacker was a big man with plenty of muscle and the deadest pair of eyes he'd ever seen. Avery had been considering taunting his attackers, but he changed his mind. The other one, the blond, was studying the pictures Avery had blown up and put on the walls of his room. He liked to see himself, and he liked to force the little kiddies to see what was coming to them.

"I'm really good at what I do, Avery," Savage said. "Just so you know, I was taught in a school in Russia. The Russian likes to tell you about that school, doesn't he? There were four schools, but he was involved with the school the instructors all liked to call the 'experiment.' "

The tone was casual. Not a hint of emotion. His captor walked into his sight, tall, all muscle, bald head. In his hand he held a short three-foot whip.

"Most people don't realize the pain inflicted by a whip has nothing whatsoever to do with how long that whip is, but you know, don't you, Avery?"

Savage walked over to the wall to study a photograph of a young girl, no more than eight, her back torn and bleeding with whip marks crisscrossing her skin. "They call me Savage, but I can see you just might rival me for that name."

The other one came into his view, and in his hands he held up a rubber plug; it was thick and long, with beads climbing up to the place where the flared end was.

"Savage, we forgot something. He likes this one in particular."

"Thanks for reminding me, Ice," Savage said. "I wouldn't want to miss any of his favorite parts."

Avery opened his mouth to protest, but the one called Ice shoved the terrible thick string of beads halfway down his throat so that he was gagging and choking.

"That's right, you want it nice and wet," Savage said. "Look at that picture you have right in front of you. We're going out of our way to re-create it for you. In the meantime, you be thinking about names. Russian names. And addresses. Think about them as well. And don't forget the collector. He's very, very important to us. That would be a very good name for you to remember. That, and Terrance Marshal's latest address."

Avery tried to shake his head, but Savage pulled the beads from his mouth, and he coughed and spit to try to clear his injured throat. Savage caught him in a powerful grip and thrust his head toward the bed. It jerked his arms horribly.

"Allow me, Ice. You know I don't give a fuck, don't feel a thing when they scream or bleed. Well, that's not true." Without preamble he slammed the rubberized point deep and kept pushing, uncaring that he was tearing through the man's insides. "I've got this right, don't I, Avery? I'm following the series of pictures you took and put on your wall to enjoy. This is the kind of shit you like, right?"

Avery's voice gave out after the steady scream, and he could only put his forehead on the headboard and pant. He was already dripping in sweat and then he heard the whistle of the whip before it cut into him. Savage hadn't been lying when he said he knew how to wield a whip, and he did so, going for maximum pain. He was a very strong man and clearly an expert with the tool. Every time Avery thought he might black out, Savage stopped to give him a rest and then would start again.

"You might want to come up with a name or two, Avery," Ice said, all friendly like. He perched on the edge of the bed. "He can keep this up all night. The thing is, the skin on your back, butt and thighs is pretty much gone. He's going to want to turn you over soon. I'm thinking that thing in your ass is going to hurt like hell when you grind it against the mattress, and that whip on your dick is going to send you someplace you don't want to go."

Savage stopped swinging the whip and

moved to stand in front of Avery so he could lift his gaze and look at him. Savage hadn't so much as broken a sweat.

"Yeah, I think you need to turn over, Avery."

Avery shuddered with pain and fear. All he could do was whimper and shake his head.

Ice nudged him. "Don't piss him off. Seriously, it's never a good thing to get him angry. Just do what he says. Turn the fuck over and start talking."

Avery tried to comply, too scared to do anything but obey, but his arms were not cooperating. There was terror in his eyes. They could stay there for weeks and no one would come. What about Harold? Where was he? But he'd already been waiting at the mansion. That meant he was dead as well and there was no one. He'd created this space for himself so he could be alone with his young victims when he chose.

Savage unlocked the cuffs from the headboard and Avery forced his painful body to turn. Savage gripped one ankle and yanked him down, stretching him across the bed. It hurt beyond comprehension. Savage never changed expression. He simply secured him back to the bed, his legs spread wide.

"You got the name of the collector for us?"

"I don't know him. I don't know him. I swear I don't." Avery's head tossed side to side. "Only Terrance knows. Terrance Marshal. He got his brother Richie a job with us. And the Russian. The Russian knows." He gave the information eagerly.

"Where's Terrance now?" Ice asked.

"He's in the wind. He does that the moment something goes wrong. His brother was killed. He took that as a warning, and he disappeared."

He's telling the truth, Absinthe said. His voice was abnormally distant. They'd tried to protect him by using a pulse monitor Mechanic had created for them.

"You tell everyone you know the collector," Savage said.

"I lied! I lied so they'd respect me more!" Avery screamed, his face so red and puffy his eyes bulged out. He couldn't take his gaze off the whip in Savage's hands.

"How would I know if you're telling the truth, Avery?" Savage asked. "You're an admitted liar." He swung the whip with expert precision and again, using maximum strength.

Avery screamed until he couldn't scream anymore, until he was choking and gasping for breath. Savage stopped. "Again, Avery, who is the collector?"

Avery was sobbing, the sounds of numerous children rising from his memories to join with him. He couldn't stop them. He couldn't get them out of his mind. He'd enjoyed wrecking them. Wrecking their bodies. It had been such delicious fun. Now . . . he just wanted everything to stop.

"I swear I don't know. I've never seen him. I don't know him at all." He was babbling, but he couldn't stop. He begged Savage to stop. He'd do anything if Savage would stop.

He's telling the truth, Absinthe said.

Czar swore. They needed the name. If Terrance Marshal was the only one who knew the man for certain, they were in trouble. They wouldn't find him soon. He had to know by now someone was coming for him. He'd be in hiding. They'd get him, because they'd never give up, but this wasn't going to end in the way they'd hoped.

Savage and Ice spent another hour with Avery Charles. He didn't know the name of the Russian. He didn't know much of anything worthwhile. They got two more names of men in the pedophile ring, but that was it.

Kill him, Czar said. *We can't take a chance this time. We came in as clean as we could, but there might be sweat or something else left behind. We'll burn this place down. Re-*

move everything from any safe you've found, and don't forget the one in the basement. Take the pictures off the wall and leave them out where they can be found. We don't want anyone thinking Avery, Harold, Jay or David were good men.

It took another hour to sift through evidence and decide what to leave for the authorities to find. Mechanic and Transporter wired the house to blow, starting in the basement and going room by room so there would be no recovering from the damage. It was a place of horror, and they didn't want it restored so someone else could create evil in it.

The wind blowing in from the ocean felt fresh and clean on their faces and bodies as they rode home. They took the back roads, riding to try to push away the memories of the children they hadn't saved, both in Russia and here, so close to where they had their homes. There was no way for the wind to clear the demons of their childhood from their minds.

TWENTY

Ice turned his head to look for his wife. He didn't like being without her for very long. Standing on their back patio, dealing with the grill that wouldn't seem to get clean, he was already missing her. She was in the house, saying her last good-byes to the others. As always, the women were lingering. Their men stood around watching them, little half smiles on their faces. He knew they'd give them a few minutes and then one of them would get antsy, usually Reaper, and he'd make his move to collect his woman and go.

Ice could see Soleil through the glass talking to Anya. The two were laughing and then Breezy, holding what looked like a photograph album on her lap, put a hand over her mouth and began fanning herself with the other one. Immediately, Soleil looked at the book, gasped and took it from her, closing it quickly. The women burst out laughing.

He fucking loved that. His world came right just watching Soleil enjoying herself. She wanted a family, and he'd provided that for her. Brothers. Sisters. A husband. He wasn't an easy man to live with, but she didn't seem to mind. She laughed a lot now. She seemed happy and confident, nearly all the time.

She looked up suddenly, her eyes meeting his through the glass, and his heart twisted hard in his chest. She could do that to him, cause a physical reaction that sometimes bordered on pain. He never wanted to be without her. If she was unhappy, his world wasn't right, which meant he had to be careful that she didn't realize he would do anything for her. Any damn thing at all. She blew him a kiss and turned her attention back to the women, and he went back to tackling the maintenance on the grill from hell.

He'd put the thing together with a little help from Storm. First time using it and the wheel had come off, nearly dumping all the chicken he'd been grilling — okay, not him. Absinthe had been grilling. He was certain that Storm had worked on that side of the grill until the upper rack had collapsed onto the lower one. That *had* to be Storm's work.

It might have been a disaster, but Soleil had been laughing so hard, nothing else mattered to him, and immediately, Absinthe had saved the dinner for everyone by cooking it over the firepit. Ice didn't mind the ribbing; he was used to it when it came to cooking. Clearly, he was never going to be the best at grilling, but screw the barbecues, he could live without having them at his home. He'd have parties and bring food in.

The evening turned into night and laughter continued, but Ice had reached the point where he wanted to be alone with his woman. She was a little bit tipsy. She never really seemed to get drunk, just like she said, but tipsy sex sounded good to him. More than good. Evidently, he wasn't alone in deciding tipsy sex was a major perk. Reaper caught up his woman, Anya, tossed her over his shoulder, as he often did when he was ready to leave and she wasn't co-operating, and strode off with her.

Reaper was generally the first to go and rapidly, the others followed. Steele and Breezy said their good-byes and made their way to his bike, hand in hand. Ice almost envied Steele in that he could walk out and ride away while he was stuck with the grill that kept having parts fall off of it. He was still working on it, trying to figure out why the bolts didn't line up properly, when the last member of Torpedo Ink was gone, and Soleil wandered out onto the patio.

"This thing is defective, Soleil. Completely, utterly, defective. I should write to the company and complain. Or at least get our money back." He gave the stupid thing a kick. The wheel wobbled. He cursed. She giggled.

She wrapped her arm around his waist and looked up at him, her smile lighting his world. "Just leave it, honey. You haven't seen that second little wedding album. Alena brought it with her tonight. She and Lana had it made up for us."

"We actually have another wedding album?" He liked the first one just fine.

Ice abandoned the grill, leaving it lurched to one side, the top rack lying partially on the bottom one.

Soleil looked back at it and immediately started laughing. "Look, Ice, it's drunk."

He glanced over his shoulder, and the damn grill really did look a little drunk. He couldn't help but laugh, although it was more that she was laughing than how the grill looked that made him want to smile. He wouldn't have minded shoving the grill into the ocean.

"I think you're a little drunk yourself,

baby," he teased. She nodded. "A little. Just enough for a buzz."

His hand dropped to her ass. He cupped her left cheek and gently began a slow massage. "Just enough for me to get down and dirty with you?"

Her eyes shone bright. "How dirty?"

"Baby, you know me. I go for it. I'd have to say very dirty. I've got plans."

She shivered and leaned her body into his. "I can't wait."

He held the door open so she could get inside. Warmth instantly enveloped them. He loved this room. The fire was on in the fireplace, and the entire room was very warm. He pulled her down onto the couch, where they could look out at the sea or into the dancing flames. Soleil did what she always did.She kicked off her sandals and curled up close to him.

He liked her close and felt very lucky that she liked to be touched as much as he enjoyed touching. Truthfully, it was a need. He needed to touch her. Sometimes all he did was drift his fingers over her breast or take one finger and rub the underside. She never protested or slapped his hand away. She just smiled at him.

"They made us another album?" He reached for it. It was far thicker than he'd thought possible.

"Yes." She ran her finger over the first page. The way she did that caught at him — as if the album really meant something to her. He was grateful for his sister and Lana thinking of it. He wouldn't have. He was trying to learn the things that meant the most to Soleil to anticipate her needs — or wants.

The first few pictures were taken inside the boutique where they'd bought her wedding dress. There was a variety of pictures of the two of them standing in front of the various items of clothing she had needed. Some of them kissing. All of the pictures were shadowy, and very artsy. He could only guess that Maestro had taken the photographs. He was good behind a camera, and he could make almost any shot look special.

Ice turned the page and his heart nearly stopped. There were a series of photographs of Soleil on her knees, her back to the wedding gown, which was on a mannequin, Ice in front of her, his cock in her mouth. Each photograph was different, taken from an assortment of angles, some so the ecstasy was plain on his face, and others captured that sweet adoration she often got on hers when she went to work on his cock.

"Maestro has talent." Ice turned his head

and looked at his woman. "So do you, princess. I had no idea he was doing this. You managed to distract me, and that just doesn't happen."

There was even one photograph that captured a passerby in the background, peering through the window at them.

"I'm not certain we can show anyone this album."

He laughed. "I want to show the world."

"You would."

He turned the pages, seeing her dressing, having her hair styled, putting on jewelry. There were close-ups of his ring, the one he'd meticulously drawn out, cut out and then had laminated. He had since made her wedding ring and his, and both wore them. She'd kept the laminated one. He'd seen it in her drawer, wrapped carefully in a silk scarf. He planned to find her something fancy to keep it in.

There were more pictures of her getting onto his bike in her wedding gown. The chapel with the little grimy man who was all about the money. Ice didn't care, he'd pronounced them man and wife. Kissing his bride. The bar. Walking in, his hand on her tit.

His cock stirred just looking at the faces of the men in the bar as they came in. She looked regal. His princess. Gorgeous. His mouth feeding on her breast, leaving those beautiful marks that told the world she was his.

Their party. The cake. The toasts. So many of his brothers raising their glasses to wish him well. He turned more pages and then he stopped abruptly when her hand came down to prevent him from turning to the next page. He was deliberately slow when he turned his head to look at her. Inside he was laughing, but he did his best to look innocent.

She narrowed her eyes at him. "I believe Maestro is now back taking the pictures."

He pretended to study the series of photographs. "I think you're right."

"You know I'm right." There was pure accusation in her tone.

"You really didn't mind at all."

She hadn't protested, not when he'd undone the lacy halter of her wedding dress to leave nothing between his mouth and her tits.

"You have amazing tits." He touched one reverently. "They photograph so well I'm wondering if you could make a good living just having shots taken of them."

She laughed, just like he knew she would. He turned the page and she was lying on the pool table, spread out for him like a feast and he was eating cake off her. Smearing her tits and bare pussy lips with frosting to lick it off.

Then there was a series of Ice devouring her. He loved the ones Maestro got of her face as an orgasm rushed over her. He'd fucked her with his fingers, right there on the pool table, with his brothers cheering him on. She was beautiful. Glowing. Her skin was flushed and marked by his mouth and hands. Maestro had captured every image. She had reciprocated, using her mouth to get him off, swallowing him down. He remembered every single moment and was very happy they had a pool table so he could re-create that scene, but not tonight.

"I think you're the most amazing man that has ever been born," she said, and touched the photograph of him devouring her, his face between her legs.

"It's my favorite place to be, especially when I wake up," he said. "You're so beautiful, babe, and so —" He broke off and turned back one page. "Look at you, Soleil. The way you look when you stroked my cock. When you crawled in a circle around that pool table top, following me around, your gaze on me. You look so —" He broke off again.

"In love with your cock?" She laughed softly. Her fingers stroked him through his jeans.

"Yeah, but more than that. As if I counted. As if I mattered and what I needed or wanted, you would give me."

The smile faded from her face, to be replaced by so much tenderness he almost had to look away. "I love you so much, Ice. I want to find every way I can to make you happy."

He closed the album reluctantly. There were more pages, but he'd look at them later. Right now, he needed to get his woman upstairs into bed.

"So, babe, gotta ask you." He took his time, using the remote to turn off the fire as they stood to head upstairs. "This morning . . ."

Soleil looked up at him quickly, her long lashes veiling her eyes so she looked innocent. He knew that look. That meant just the opposite.

"Boys were over. We're talking and laughing and having a good time at breakfast, which was fabulous, by the way. You're an amazing cook."

He put his hand on the small of her back as they went up the stairs. He loved the shape of her. The way she felt under his hand. So feminine. That little sway in her hips.

"Thank you, honey. I love my lessons. I've learned so much from Alena."

She had thrown herself into making their house a home. One by one, she was working on each room in the house, slowly redesigning the interior. All the while, she worked at learning to cook. She seemed to really enjoy it. When they went out, which wasn't that often, they went to Alena's restaurant. Usually, she would go into the kitchen to talk to Alena about a specific recipe or Alena would come out to sit and talk with them if she wasn't too busy — which was almost never.

Their bedroom door was always kept closed. Every other door was open in the house, welcoming, but she kept the door to the master bedroom closed. For some reason that gave him the feeling of intimacy. It was theirs alone. Their secret haven where no one else was welcome.

"This morning, you brought up money again. You never do that."

She pressed her lips together and then pulled off her T-shirt and bra, probably in the hopes of distracting him. Ordinarily, that was all it would take, but this time, he wasn't going to get sidetracked. She was always honest with him, and if he asked the right questions, he'd get his answer because she'd done that deliberately, knowing what his response would be.

"Yes, I'm sorry." Her hands dropped to her jeans and she unzipped them and shimmied out of them.

"What did I tell you to do?"

A small little smile of satisfaction curved her mouth. "What you always tell me. Crawl under the table and suck you off."

His cock jumped at the memory. Sitting at breakfast, his plate full, his coffee perfect, and his brothers filling him in on the progress Code had made in looking up each man in the club wanting to patch over to Torpedo Ink. They'd done it for one small club, only because Gavriil had vouched for them, and after meeting them and getting to know them, they'd voted to bring them in. It didn't necessarily follow that a second club made up of Russian assassins, men like them that had gone to one of the other three schools, was a right fit. They had to take their time, get to really know those other men in order to call them brothers.

The sun shone through the windows and he was feeling great when she'd suddenly brought up that she wanted to purchase a new rug for one of the smaller guestrooms, but no worries, she was using her own money. He'd caught her hair in his fist and assisted her to the floor, barking the order to suck him off. Soleil hadn't hesitated. She hadn't fumbled at his belt or when slipping his jeans down when he'd lifted himself off the seat. She'd gone straight to work, making it difficult to hear or think. She'd swallowed every single drop and then meticulously cleaned him, taking her time and doing it right. He'd had a hell of an ache the rest of the day, but he'd felt like a million dollars.

"Why did you bring up money?"

"Well . . ." She hesitated.

Red flags went up fast. She wouldn't lie to him, he knew that, but something was a little off-kilter.

"I wanted your cock in my mouth and I thought you might be upset enough with me that you'd want to teach me a lesson the way you did the last time. It was amazing." She made the confession in a rush, her face flushing.

He lifted her chin with two fingers, forcing her to look at him. "I don't want you ever embarrassed to talk about sex with me. You should be comfortable enough to ask for anything in bed that you want. Anything, Soleil. You don't like something, you tell me. I want to know fast, up front. That's important. You understand me?" They'd had the discussion before, but he wanted to reiterate to her how it important it was.

She nodded and walked across the room to the glass wall, staring out at the crashing waves. Ice shook his head as he removed his boots and socks and then his shirt. He padded across the room barefoot to stand behind her.

"That wasn't the real reason, princess. It crossed your mind, but that's not why. I want you to tell me why." He wrapped his arms around her and covered her breasts with his hands. Her tits felt soft and sexy in his palms. He dropped his chin on top of her head as he stared out into the night.

They hadn't turned on a light in their room. They really didn't need to. The ocean always seemed to give off light, even on stormier nights. The dimmer lighting always made the ambience in their bedroom sexier.

"You've been a little edgy lately. I noticed since the last big party, you've been careful. I realized you were afraid of having a flashback and somehow hurting or upsetting me. It doesn't. You aren't violent."

"But I lose myself and us." That really bothered him.

"For a moment, Ice. You came back to me

right away. You know my touch. My mouth. My body. You know my voice. There's power in that for me. I get to be the one who comes to your aid for a change. You always take care of me. I know I can do this for you and I'm not afraid."

"How about disgusted? The things I did . . ."

"Honey, you were a child. You keep thinking you had power to change it, but you didn't. When we have children and you see how young they are, you'll realize it, but for now, you have me when things get rough, and I swear to you, I'll always be there for you." She turned her head to look up at him so lovingly, his heart melted.

He could see she meant it. His woman would take his back no matter how bad things got, but he wanted to warn her. "It's going to happen again and again. And I have nightmares. They never go away, Soleil."

She nodded. "I'm aware. I spent a lot of time with psychologists. Kevin thought I needed counseling. I think they all needed it after being my counselor." She rubbed his arms and leaned back into him. "I love taking care of you."

"That means crawling under a table to suck my cock?"

"The point was, your brothers were there,

and you didn't flinch, Ice. You feel safe around them. At the party, there were others."

"From other schools, men who suffered other kinds of torture."

She shook her head. "Not pedophiles. Not criminals. They have no idea what you've been through. I don't know and you told me part of it. A small part, but enough that I know only your seventeen brothers and sisters know the entire truth, and maybe not even them. But you feel safe with them. You know they'll protect you."

"No," he clarified, "I know they'll protect you. That's what is important to me. I like exhibition, but not all the time and not when it isn't safe. That's what I've been learning lately. I put you in a dangerous position on that run. It isn't ever happening again. If my brothers are close and we can control a situation, that's one thing, but not when things could go to hell fast. When I can learn to trust the others in other chapters to keep you safe, maybe I'll be able to be okay with showing you off, but I don't want to take chances with you. If I offered you to another man, or group of men, Soleil, I'd probably kill myself."

"I wouldn't let that happen."

He was silent for a moment, rubbing his

chin back and forth on the top of her head. "You're a little wild, and you like it when we have sex like that, out in the open, but I don't want to take chances, not unless my brothers and sisters are close."

"I'm okay with that, honey."

Her voice reassured him. She meant it. The relief was tremendous. "Before I'm so preoccupied with the more important things in life, I need to tell you, I'd like you to do some drawings for me." He nuzzled the top of her head again, liking the way her hair caught in his bristles. "For my jewelry. You were talking about ideas you had, and I got to thinking about them. What I've been do-ing is a piece here and there that calls to me. I see it clearly, and I take a long time to make it because it has to feel a certain way to me."

"Your work is beautiful."

"You haven't painted since we've been together. I made you that little art studio and you haven't gone in once. Sketch in there and then start painting again. You're good, and there's a local gallery in Sea Haven."

Her eyes were so bright they were nearly glowing. "I can do that. I would love it, but Ice, you're very good, and I was only talk-ing silliness. Nothing I come up with is going to equal —" She broke off when his hand came up to cover her mouth briefly.

"I want you to sketch out those ideas. They were inspiring. A few of the jewelry stores I work with have asked for a line they can have in their stores, and it occurred to me that I could do an exclusive line for a couple of stores, the jewelry won't be anywhere but in their store. That way, my work is still very limited, and I can do my one-of-a-kind pieces, but we can pull in a little more money."

She opened her mouth, and he knew immediately she was going to remind him she had money. He found himself smirking.

"Ice. You don't actually have to work if you don't want to. I've got money. You never even looked into my finances."

"What did I tell you to do with your money? Save it for our kids. Give it to any charity you want to give it to. Sponsor a million children in another country. Set up a battered women's shelter or, better yet, apartments with low rent, so once they're on their feet the women will be able to make it on their own. Any damn thing you want, baby, as long as I'm the one taking care of you."

She threw her hands into the air. "You're so insane. I don't have a clue what I'm going to do with you."

"I know exactly what I'm going to do with you. First, instead of fucking your brains out, my beautiful little princess, I'm going to make love to my wife. I'm going to take my time and kiss every single inch of her. I want her to know that she's the most important person in my life."

She turned her head and looked up at him in that way she had, as if he were her sun, the moon and the stars all rolled into one.

"When I'm absolutely certain that she understands that and feels loved, then, because you just keep bringing up your money, and you know the consequences, I'm getting my cock sucked and I'm not going to let you touch it. I'm in control the entire time. Then, you're going to lie across my lap with a very hot little plug in you and I'm going to give you another lesson in remembering that one little rule, the only one I've laid down. Then I'm going to fuck your brains out."

She turned so her naked body was pressed tightly against his chest and slid her slender arms around his neck. "That sounds absolutely perfect to me."

That was Soleil. His woman. Perfect.

TERMS ASSOCIATED WITH
BIKER CLUBS

1-percenters: This is a term often used in association with outlaw bikers, as in "99% of clubs are law abiding, but the other 1% are not." Sometimes the symbol is worn inside a diamond-shaped patch.

3-piece patch or 3-piece: This term is used for the configuration of a club's patch: the top piece, or rocker, with club name; a center patch that is the club's logo; and a bottom patch, or rocker, with the club's location, such as Sea Haven.

Biker: someone who rides a motorcycle

Biker friendly: a business that welcomes bikers

Boneyard: refers to a salvage yard

Cage: often refers to a car, van or truck (basically any vehicle that's not a motorcycle)

Chapter: the local unit of a larger club

Chase vehicle: a vehicle following riders on a run just in case of a breakdown

Chopper: customized bike

Church: club meeting

Citizen: someone who's not a biker

Club: could be any group of riders banding together (most friendly)

Colors: patches, logo, something worth fighting for because it represents who you are

Cut: vest or denim jacket with sleeves cut off and club colors on it; almost always worn, even over leather jackets

Dome: helmet

Getting patched: Moving up from prospect to full club member (you would receive the logo patch to wear with rockers). This must be earned, and is the only way to get respect from brothers.

Hang-around: anyone hanging around the club who might want to join

Hog: nickname for motorcycle, mostly associated with Harley-Davidson

Independent: a biker with no club affiliation

Ink: tattoo

Ink slinger: a tattoo artist

Nomad: club member who travels between chapters; goes where he's needed in his club

Old lady: Wife or woman who has been with a man for a long time. It is not considered disrespectful nor does it have anything to do with how old one is.

Patch holder: member of a motorcycle club

Patches: Sewn on vests or jackets, these can be many things with meanings or just for fun, even gotten from runs made.

Poser: pretend biker

Property of: a patch displayed on a jacket, vest or sometimes a tattoo, meaning the woman (usually old lady or longtime girlfriend) is with the man and his club

Prospect: someone working toward becoming a fully patched club member

ABOUT THE AUTHOR

Christine Feehan is the #1 *New York Times* bestselling author of the Carpathian series, the GhostWalker series, the Leopard series, the Shadow Riders series, and the Sea Haven novels, including the Drake Sisters series and the Sisters of the Heart series. She lives in the beautiful mountains of Lake County, California. Please visit her website at www.christinefeehan.com.